LAB-GROWN MEAT
BITES
BACK

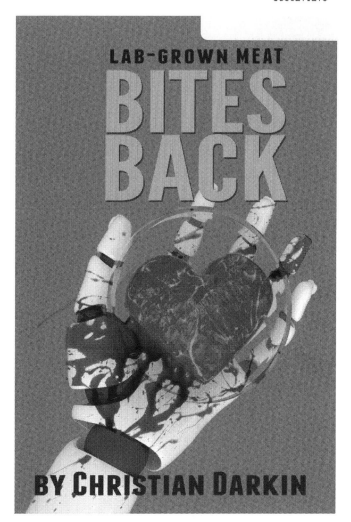

BY CHRISTIAN DARKIN

LAB GROWN MEAT BITES BACK

Thanks so much to Jane and Rachel,
and the Wednesday Writers of SE London
for suffering my early drafts
and making sure I put in what needed
to go in, and took out what didn't.

Chapter 1

A small town in the South East of England, a couple of decades from today.

The day before Lexie Doyle was killed, and everything went crazy, Kendal was printing dinner.

Mum's new boyfriend, Dan, was joining them for the meal. He'd been falling over himself trying to get on the right side of them. That was what new boyfriends did, Kendal supposed. He'd meant well, but since neither Mum nor Dan were really there, Kendal had to do the cooking. Normally he wouldn't mind, but this was supposed to be Kendal's "special dinner". Exams finished (not well, but his coursework would carry him over the line). School was over. Questions about college and what would come next, on pause over the summer. School prom tomorrow night.

And that meant he had better things to do right now than make dinner in his own honour. Not least, he had to find a date, and quick.

It couldn't be anyone from school. That was a given. Lexie had seen to that. She had forever crushed any hope he had of finding a date, without taking a single action or uttering a single word. The depth of Kendal's infatuation with her had been extreme, and long-lasting. The anonymous love note he'd left in her locker in the third year had not remained anonymous for long. The message's dopey poetry, once digitised and passed around, had dogged him throughout his school career. A running joke that had somehow stayed funny over three full years of school.

And that meant that anyone he asked to the prom would be universally marked out as a second choice. Who wanted that? Nobody. Especially when there were at least two billion other dating choices available to them.

Normally, Kendal would not be that bothered about his datelessness. Or at least he'd be able to feign not being that bothered long enough to get him through the night. However, at this time and place, the final school prom, the fact that he didn't have a date was going to be particularly glaring, particularly humiliating. There might just be time to turn things around, but having to make dinner wasn't helping.

He slammed the cartridges into the printer, following the ingredient list. One for starch, one for cell-wall gel. Fat. A bundled package of colourings. Cyan. Yellow. Magenta. Black. He looked around. Something was missing.

Typical, they were out of vegetable sugars.

"Joseph?" shouted Kendal. "Have you been printing sweets again?" His brother popped his head around the kitchen door.

"No!" he said. Joseph was nine, but you wouldn't think it, the way he acted.

"You've used all the good stuff!" said Kendal.

"No, I didn't."

"I'll have to use an artificial sweetener cartridge instead now."

Joseph pulled a face. "I'm not eating it. I don't like artificial." He vanished.

Kendal shoved the artificial sweetener cartridge into the printer. Mum would not approve, but then Mum wasn't around. Again.

Kendal flipped up the printer screen. The screen displayed the meal's schematic as a friendly set of coloured blocks linked by arrows. He glanced through the settings. He could just hit 'Go' and the printer would produce a meal on presets alone. That was what he ought to do. His finger hovered over the button. Doing something about tomorrow night was more urgent than messing around with recipe ideas.

But no. The preset marinades were all over-seasoned and under-spiced. The machine never got caramelisation right on its own, and it used a one-size-fits-all approach to the heat distribution matrix which Kendal could never, in good conscience, allow to pass. Wanting to be a chef wasn't just what he put on his careers forms. When most kids were thinking about sport or videogames or who they were going to take to the prom, Kendal thought about food. Flavour combinations infused his dreams. Textures and smells were the language of his brain. And there was just no way he was going to be able to switch all that off and just accept the software's suggested ready-meal - no matter how much else he had to do tonight.

Dragging his finger along the menu schematic, he opened up the marinade settings. He shook his head. The distilled wisdom of millions of other people's choices harvested by artificial intelligence and compiled into a homogenised ingredient list. Bland and obvious. He dragged it to the recycling bin and replaced it with his own. Sharper. Spicier. Undertones of soy and pomegranate molasses. That would do for now.

He dragged some more blocks around, picking the veg. Meal design was the main reason he wanted to be a chef.

6

His finger hovered again. On a whim, he swapped a couple of boxes over on Joseph's meal plan. Simple coding, but effective. He grinned to himself. There was always time to wind his brother up.

He hit **print**, and the box on the kitchen work-surface hummed into life. Through the window, Kendal watched as the nozzle juddered over the surface of the platform. It laid down a small circle in deep red, then built up slowly, until it became a red wall, curving outwards. Inside it was a pink support structure. A symmetrical fan of hardening gel forming a network, supporting the beginnings of pips.

Soon, the tomato was complete, and rolled off the platform to be diced and cooked. The printer started building the other ingredients. Little piles of mixed spice dust, identical florets of broccoli, perfectly deep green on top, and shading to pale green at the stalk, their individual buds rendered in perfectly ordered bunches. They were built standing on their ends like tiny trees. A transparent web reached up around them, supporting the delicate shapes while they hardened. It would dissolve into a few grams of water once they were cooked.

Kendal watched it run out the chips. You could, of course, print any veg you wanted, but it didn't have to look like what it was. By swapping over the odd programming block, you could, for example, make your brother's chips taste of sprouts, or lime pickle. If you were really childish, you could make them taste of both.

He left them cooking, and got the meat out of the fridge. Meat was the one thing you couldn't print at home. The complex weave of proteins and fibres was more than a domestic printer could handle. It had to be grown at a farm. There was one just the other side of the school, a wide, flat set of windowless industrial buildings. Kendal had never seen inside. His obsession with food stopped at the door of the abattoir. A couple of Year Eights had broken in once. One of them had been fine. She hadn't seen the problem: it wasn't as if there was any cruelty involved in farming. Not like there used to be. But the other one had come out white and shaking. He'd sworn to become a vegetarian. Kendal had no view on the farms. He was happy to leave the science stuff to someone else.

He slapped the steaks onto the platform and fed them into the cooking tray under the printer. They were a good shape, well marbled. They'd cook up great, but as Kendal glanced at the picture on the packet he couldn't help smiling. Dan had messed up. Instead of going to Mr Bradbury, the friendly local butcher Kendal always used, Dan had ordered in from a supermarket, and he'd bought the wrong meat. Joseph would not be pleased. Kendal wondered how far Joseph would get through his meal before he realised.

He hit Medium Rare, and the countdown to dinner started.

Chapter 2

"This is giant panda!" said Joseph, the moment he sat down at the dinner table. "I hate giant panda!" Next to him, Kendal rolled his eyes. That was quick. Say what you liked about Joseph. He knew his meat.

He glanced across at the blank avatars sitting opposite the boys. Two full sized, generic human figures. Completely white now and coated in soft, stretchy latex. They sat silently at the table, heads down, faces bearing smoothed-out versions of human eyes, noses, lips, waiting for life. As he watched, Mum and Dan arrived. First one avatar, then the other, glowed blue-green and straightened up as Mum and Dan joined the meal from their workplaces. Mum was in London, Dan in Singapore. Was it Singapore or Hong Kong? Kendal couldn't remember. Either way, Dan's dinner was breakfast for him.

Mum's projected face spread slowly over the avatar's smooth features, and from within, electrical impulses stretched and inflated its skin, forming her features under the live projected image of her face. Its eyes becoming her eyes. Its lips, hers. The little wake-up jingle the avatar played did its best to make the process appear welcoming and clean, but somehow Kendal still found it creepy to see a dummy become his mother.

Dan followed. A projected suit and tie covered the avatar's body. Dan's nose was probably not as sharp as his avatar was portraying it. How could it be? But then Kendal had never seen Dan in real life, so maybe it was.

In front of the adults, on the table, images of their own meals were projected onto dinner plates, mimicking the plates of food they were, in reality, eating alone in their offices.

"It's so nice to sit down to a proper family meal together," said Dan. Joseph cut a chip in half, sniffed it suspiciously, recoiled, narrowed his eyes at Kendal and pushed his plate away. He slumped back, folding his arms.

"What's the matter?" said Mum. Her features fully formed now.

"Kendal has done something to my chips, and this steak is panda," said Joseph.

"I thought you'd like it," said Dan.

"I only eat apex predators," said Joseph.

"I thought a panda was an apex predator."

"What? No, APEX predators," Joseph was outraged. "Animals at the top of the food chain: lion, great white shark, tyrannosaurus."

"A T. Rex steak isn't even from a real T. Rex, you know," said Kendal. Tyrannosaurus was his brother's favourite meat. "They don't have the DNA - they've just done a big chicken!"

"No!" said Joseph. "It's spliced! They've spliced it with other stuff."

"Like what?" said Kendal.

"Alligator," said Joseph.

"Dinosaurs and alligators aren't even related."

"It's as close as!" Joseph turned on Dan. "How could you think a panda was an apex predator?" said Joseph. Dan's avatar made an embarrassed shrugging gesture. "They eat bamboo! Don't you know anything?"

"Try it. It's nice," said Dan.

Kendal tried some of the meat. A rich burgundy colour. Succulent, and tender. Deep and dark. Perfectly rich and luxuriating in just a hint more fat than beef. Whether it was accurate, he had no idea, but it was perfectly balanced. He swore he could taste the bamboo. His brother was making a fuss over nothing again.

"This is supposed to be Kendal's special dinner," said Dan. "Just eat it!"

"NO!" said Joseph.

"Don't be so ungrateful!"

Mum glanced over to Dan. Her smile did not budge, painted frozen on the avatar's face, but there was clear disappointment hidden below the surface. Another one bites the dust, thought Kendal.

"Dan, can we have a word?" Kendal's heart sank. "Back in a mo, boys!" Mum's avatar went blank. Its head drooped. Dan's sagged too and went dark. Kendal stared at his brother across the table. They were alone now, having dinner with two blank life-sized dummies.

"Look what you've done now," said Kendal, shoving a piece of panda into his mouth. His brother stared angrily back.

"I don't like him."

"Just as well," said Kendal.

Mum's dummy glowed green, and raised its head. Mum's face flickered in. "Sorry about that. I'd like you to meet Roy."

Roy glowed into life in Dan's place. He was slimmer than his predecessor, and the avatar's inflatable arms shrank to mimic its new form. The face elongated as a dark-haired, brown-eyed

11

man faded in. He had a full beard, and though it was neatly shaped, the avatar was having trouble redefining itself to become him. It just looked as though he had a fat brown neck.

And as easily as that, Mum replaced Dan with Roy.

"Roy and I are an 9.75, apparently, boys. So says Doreen." Kendal raised his eyebrows and tried a smile. By telling Joseph off, Dan had crossed a line, and that was it. Mum liked to do the discipline herself. Dan should have known that. Kendal focused on his dinner. He hated it when she swiped. They both did. She must have had this new one already lined up waiting for his chance, judging by the speed he appeared. Still, it could have been worse. At least she hadn't tried to involve them in her decision. You really didn't want to help your Mum pick dates.

"So, Roy," said Mum, "what do you do?"

"I try to share joy," he said. He didn't sound like an 9.75. "You really should try Doreen," said Roy to Kendal.

"Who's Doreen?"

"Only the best artificial matchmaker in the world!" he said. So that was it: an artificial selection.

"I don't need a date!" said Kendal. He had hoped to make it through dinner without being quizzed about tomorrow, especially by a complete stranger.

"I'm sorry," said Roy. "I heard you had your prom tomorrow night." He smiled under his bulging beard. The avatar's attempt to copy it looked weird. Great. He must be looking at a crib sheet on his office screen. Top 10 facts about your new date. Fact 1: eldest son has his prom tomorrow and hasn't got a date. Great.

"I suppose," muttered Kendal. Next to him, Joseph sniggered.

"I got a family membership," said Mum. "Just try it."

"Better get a wiggle on!" said Roy. "It can really work - that's how I met this beautiful woman, after all!" He looked over at

Mum. Joseph gestured sticking his fingers down his throat. Too much too soon. Kendal felt his face flushing.

"OK!" he said, "I'll do it. Can we talk about something else now?" Mum's relief was a little too obvious.

Her avatar made a pointing gesture in the air - back at the office, she must have just pressed a button on her screen. "There, I've booked you in for nine tonight in your bedroom," she said.

"Kendal's getting a girlfriend!" Joseph started to sing. "Kendal's getting a girlfriend."

"Shut up!"

"Kendal's getting a girlfriend, Kendal's getting a girlfriend." Joseph nudged him with his elbow. Joseph wheeled back in exaggerated pain, hooked his fork "accidentally" into his steak and sent it spinning off the plate onto the floor.

ANGER MANAGEMENT WARNING. The voice from the air was calm, level and relaxed.

"I didn't do it." said Kendal. He felt his anger growing. His heart beating faster, and with it, his blue wristband started to turn red. On the other side of the table, Joseph's was doing the same. It was happening again.

"Yes you did! I wanted to eat that!"

SECOND ANGER MANAGEMENT WARNING. The voice was louder, this time, more urgent, but just as calm.

"Calm down," said Kendal. "You know what will happen."

"I hate you!" Joseph jabbed his fork at Kendal's arm.

Instantly, AMA stepped in to defuse the argument with a painful ear-piercing scream. The sound cut through everything else. You couldn't hear, speak or think. Kendal and Joseph covered their ears. Roy and Mum's avatars went blank and flopped forward.

13

The sound grew even louder. It was dizzying now.

Kendal struggled to his feet. There was only one way to stop it. He clambered out of his chair and stepped away from the table - away from his brother. The sound continued, but dropped just a little quieter. Kendal backed away to the other side of the kitchen. The sound lessened.

Joseph was out of his chair now too, heading for his room. The sound diminished further, until it finally faded completely.

THAT INTERACTION WAS UNNECESSARILY AGGRESSIVE, the voice chided from every speaker in the house.

"It wasn't my fault," said Kendal.

I'M NOT HERE TO ASSIGN BLAME, said the voice. I'M SIMPLY HERE TO PROMOTE PEACE AND WELLBEING. She was appearing now, taking the place of Mum on her avatar. The white dummy stood up from the table, and stepped lightly towards him. Home avatars were mostly air. Flimsy balloon creatures, they offered presence for someone who wasn't there, and they were portable and cheap, but had no real substance. They walked strangely, not seeming to care if their feet touched the ground, drifting, ghostlike, buffeted by air currents. Kendal could have knocked the dummy over with a punch, but he knew that would only set the alarms off again. It stood in front of him, palms out, head tilted to one side, as though expecting something as the face slowly faded in. AMA was a woman. Slightly too perfect. Too symmetrical. Her face always annoyed him, probably because he only ever saw it when he was annoyed - just as everyone did.

AMA, the Anger Management Artificial, manifested only when she sensed conflict, whether it was a fight between brothers at a dinner table, or an argument in a chat room, or the ranting of a violent preacher. A super-chatbot, part law-enforcer, part counsellor,

14

part negotiator - with algorithms finely tuned to the complex wavelengths of negative feeling. Her neural networks were originally created from observation of arguments on social media, but she had blossomed into a global panacea for online and offline disagreement. Every new argument she experienced deepened her understanding of conflict and embedded itself into her patterns, allowing her to recognise it again in the future, and defuse it before it became a problem. She could stop a fight in a schoolyard, or negotiate a settlement between world leaders, and all without a shred of conscious intelligence. Like all artificials, AMA was simply a set of learned responses.

"He started it," said Kendal.

Ama smiled. Her voice did not rise and fall like a human voice. It remained level and restrained. THE IMPORTANT THING IS TO REMEMBER THE THINGS WE HAVE IN COMMON. NOT THOSE WHICH DIVIDE US, she said. DO YOU HAVE ANYTHING TO SAY?

"Thank you," said Kendal, through gritted teeth.

She tilted her head the other way. YOU DO NOT SOUND SINCERE.

He resisted the urge to shout. "Thank you," said Kendal again. You didn't fight AMA. That was the point of her. In the few years she had been in operation, AMA had ended conflict. The streets were safe now, and however much you objected to her, you had to give her that. Kendal slowly forced his anger to shrink.

WOULD YOU LIKE TO PARTAKE IN SOME MINDFULNESS EXERCISES WITH ME?

"No," said Kendal. "Thank you."

VERY WELL. THE ALARM HAS BEEN SUSPENDED. PLEASE APPROACH YOUR BROTHER

WHEN YOU ARE READY TO APOLOGISE TO EACH OTHER.

"Ok," said Kendal. "Can I go to my room now?"

CERTAINLY. PLEASE ENJOY THE REST OF YOUR DAY.

Chapter 3

Even with the full knowledge that he was not talking to an actual human being, just having the conversation out loud was enough to have him squirming with toe-curling embarrassment.

PLEASE SAY THE WORDS "I AGREE" CLEARLY. This Artificial was nothing like AMA. The Doreen Artificial now being embodied by the avatar standing in front of him in his bedroom was an elderly lady in a severely-buttoned eggshell blue cardigan. Her face was caring, interested, her cheeks pink and gathered up in a permanent smile, but her eyes were narrow and keen. Piercing even. They darted around as she spoke, noticing everything. She was meant, Kendal supposed, to look kindly and wise, but somehow, he would rather be discussing his dating profile with virtually anyone else on the planet. If the avatar had the face of his brother, it could scarcely have been worse.

"Do I have to?" said Kendal.

Doreen smiled. YOU HAVE NOTHING TO WORRY ABOUT, YOUNG MAN. ALL DATA IS ENTIRELY CONFIDENTIAL. IT WILL NOT BE REVEALED TO

ANYONE. She paused, then added: TERMS AND CONDITIONS APPLY.

"Yes, but-"

I FIRMLY BELIEVE, said the artificial intelligence, THAT THERE IS SOMEONE OUT THERE FOR EVERYONE. She smiled again. That measured, sympathetic, synthetic smile that made Kendal cringe. BUT IN ORDER TO FIND THAT PERSON FOR YOU, I NEED TO KNOW A LITTLE ABOUT YOU FIRST.

"What exactly?"

THE DATA I NEED INCLUDES: THINGS YOU HAVE PREVIOUSLY LIKED, OR COMMENTED ON, YOUR FRIENDS LIST, YOUR RECENT PURCHASES, YOUR PHOTOS AND VIDEOS, YOUR BROWSING HISTORY, YOUR MEDICAL RECORDS, EXAM RESULTS, TRANSCRIPTS OF YOUR PREVIOUS CONVERSATIONS, ONLINE AND IN THE REAL WORLD, YOUR GPS MOVEMENTS FOR THE PAST FIVE YEARS, THE BOOKS YOU HAVE READ, YOUR HOBBIES, INTERESTS, YOUR EYE MOVEMENTS, SLEEP PATTERNS AND BREATHING RECORDS....

Kendal was horrified. "Why so much?"

I'M AFRAID MY ALGORITHMS ARE COMMERCIALLY SENSITIVE, BUT I CAN TELL YOU THAT FINDING YOUR PERFECT DATE REQUIRES A LARGE NUMBER OF VARIABLES TO BE AGGREGATED TO PRODUCE COMPATIBILITY RATIOS. PRIOR TO MY TECHNOLOGY BEING DEVELOPED, PEOPLE FREQUENTLY SEARCHED THEIR WHOLE LIVES AND STILL FAILED TO FIND THEIR PERFECT MATCH. DEEP DATA IS REQUIRED FOR SUCH A PERSONAL TASK. DO YOU WISH TO PROCEED?

Kendal shrugged. "Ok," he said.

PLEASE SAY "I AGREE".

"I agree," said Kendal

Doreen closed her eyes. He could see her eyes flicking under her eyelids as if she were dreaming in a deep sleep. She was scanning his whole life. He felt suddenly naked. Finally she opened them again, fixing him with her clear, pale blue eyes.

WHAT IS YOUR SEXUAL PREFERENCE?

"A girl please," said Kendal, quickly.

PEOPLE WHO LIKE 'GIRLS' ALSO LIKE: GENDER FLUID, GIRLFLUX, SELF IDENTIFYING ANDROGYNES AND TRANSGENDER INDIVIDUALS.

"Just a girl, please."

NOW, ARE YOU SEEKING A LONG-TERM PARTNER?

"I just need a date for the prom," said Kendal. This was a first date. He wasn't looking to settle down just yet.

ANY OTHER REQUIREMENTS?

"Can it be someone who lives near here?"

YOUNG MAN, THERE ARE CURRENTLY OVER A HUNDRED MILLION GIRLS FROM WHOM I CAN SELECT YOUR DATE. IF YOU LIMIT YOUR SEARCH IN THIS WAY, YOU WILL BE REDUCING THAT NUMBER TO THE LOW TENS OF THOUSANDS. THIS REDUCES YOUR CHANCE OF FINDING YOUR IDEAL DATE BY 99.97%.

"Ok," said Kendal, "search everywhere." It looked like he'd be taking an avatar to the prom. Never mind. It felt somehow safer that way anyhow.

Doreen closed her eyes again, and was silent for a few seconds. A soft "Ping" announced her success and she awoke. DATE SELECTED.

"That's it?" said Kendal. It seemed surprisingly easy after all that.

CAN I HELP YOU WITH ANYTHING ELSE?

"Well, who is she? How do I contact her?"

HER NAME IS IMANI, said Doreen. AND YOU DO NOT CONTACT HER DIRECTLY. FOR YOUR SECURITY, ALL ONLINE CONTACT OUTSIDE OF THE DOREEN APP IS AUTOMATICALLY BLOCKED. ALL ONLINE RELATIONSHIPS FACILITATED BY ME ARE TO BE CONDUCTED THROUGH THE DOREEN APP AND WILL REMAIN THE INTELLECTUAL PROPERTY OF DOREEN. YOU WILL BE PROVIDED WITH A CONTACT NUMBER, BUT ANY REFERENCES TO INFORMATION WHICH WOULD ENABLE CONTACT OUTSIDE OF DOREEN WILL BE AUTOMATICALLY REMOVED FROM YOUR CONVERSATIONS.

"What if we want to meet in real life?"

WHY WOULD YOU WANT TO DO THAT?

Kendal stared at her.

UNDER CERTAIN CIRCUMSTANCES, COUPLES IN LONGER TERM RELATIONSHIPS SOMETIMES WISH TO APPLY FOR A VARIANCE IN THE TERMS AND CONDITIONS SO THAT THEY CAN SET UP HOME TOGETHER, RAISE CHILDREN, OR PROGRESS THEIR RELATIONSHIPS IN WAYS WHICH REQUIRE PHYSICAL MEETINGS. PROCEDURES FOR THESE APPLICATIONS ARE AVAILABLE, BUT I DO NOT IMAGINE YOUR SHORT-

TERM RELATIONSHIP WITH IMANI WILL REQUIRE THEM.

Can I see her?" said Kendal.

SHE IS UNAVAILABLE FOR A PRE-DATE MEETING, AND HAS NOT YET UPLOADED A PROFILE AVATAR. BUT PLEASE BE ASSURED, SHE IS THE PERFECT DATE FOR TOMORROW NIGHT.

"Just tomorrow night?"

YOU REQUESTED ONLY THE PERFECT PARTNER FOR THIS EVENT. IF YOU LIKE, I COULD…

"No, that's fine." he said. "Can you tell me anything about her?"

RESEARCH SHOWS THAT IT'S MORE EXCITING TO LEARN ABOUT EACH OTHER ON YOUR DATE. THIS ALSO REDUCES THE TENDENCY TO EMOTIONALLY BOND WITH YOUR NECESSARILY FLAWED FIRST IMPRESSION OF YOUR DATE. IF YOU ARE NERVOUS, I WILL PREPARE A SET OF CUE CARDS FOR YOU WITH RELEVANT QUESTIONS AND DISCUSSION POINTS.

"No, thank you."

IMANI IS VERY MUCH LOOKING FORWARD TO MEETING YOU, AND WILL APPEAR AT 8PM TOMORROW EMBODIED IN THIS AVATAR. CAN I HELP YOU WITH ANYTHING ELSE?

Kendal thought for a minute. "No," he said, and Doreen smiled, and faded, leaving the avatar pale, and drooping.

So, thought Kendal. This was romance.

Chapter 4

The next morning, he and Joseph got the apology over early. A grunted "sorry" as they passed in the hall, just loud enough to be noted, just sincere enough to allow AMA to consider the matter closed. The glowing red ring on Kendal and Joseph's wristbands strengthened briefly in warning as they approached each other and then faded to blue as they spoke, indicating AMA's loss of interest in their interactions. For now.

At least she hadn't made them shake hands, or worse, indulge in one of those awful trust-building exercises. Kendal still remembered an afternoon spent tortuously 'enjoying' each other's favourite activities following a particularly fractious falling out over some broken Lego. Kendal and Joseph had never been friends, but Kendal was sure his brother was getting worse. Over the last year - since Dad left - Kendal was certain AMA had been showing up more and more often. He must check out the household's emotional stats. Mum had got out of the habit..

After the apology, they managed to avoid each other for the rest of the day. Mum wasn't in, so the two boys had the house to themselves. Most of the day, Kendal spent telling himself he wasn't nervous. He had, he assured himself, no reason to be, but as the day dragged on, he could only think of the evening, and he busied himself as he always did - with food.

Breakfast was almond encrusted pastries which Kendal modified with layers of dark chocolate and marmalade between the layers of pastry. Lunch was a mezze of vine leaves, woven into bite sized packages, stuffed with creamy risotto and served with aubergine caviar.

Halfway through the afternoon, unable to settle himself to doing anything else, he constructed perfectly spherical dough balls, crisp as poppadoms on the outside, soft and light in the middle and each filled with a pocket of melting garlic butter.

Kendal consumed them all one after another, feeling guilty about the calories each time a burst of butter hit his tongue, but not guilty enough to stop.

Mum didn't appear until he was almost ready to go.

"She'll be here in a minute." Kendal brushed Mum's hands aside. Or rather, the avatar's hands. Mum still hadn't made it back from work, and the avatar's latex fingers were making a terrible job of adjusting his bow tie. They just weren't up to the job, but then neither were Kendal's. He had tried it four or five times already, and it still looked wonky.

Mum stepped back for a moment and he looked at himself in the mirror. The suit had looked better in the photos than it did on his slightly flabby frame, and the printer had jammed on the cuffs so they were a little short, but this was still the smartest he had ever looked. The auto-corset woven into the lining of his shirt tightened and bit into him, squashing his stomach into a six-pack that was fooling nobody. Kendal hated the way he looked, but he had to admit right now, he hated it just slightly less than he usually did.

"You look great," said Mum.

23

He felt wrong. The collar was stiff and tight around his neck. The suit was a dark shimmering blue with shiny lapels. A little too "game show" for him, but it was what the school demanded. They liked to do things properly. His hair was black - too short to be highly styled, but he'd stuck it more or less straight upwards just to blend in. He wore just foundation and a little eyeliner. He didn't want to go nuts. Most of the boys would be going for the full blue-lipped look. Some of them - Karry and Denis for example - would almost certainly have face projectors on, but for Kendal, that was all too fake.

Suddenly, behind him, Mum's avatar started to flash blue. A dull ringtone emanated from it.

"That'll be her coming through now," said Mum, "You kids have a great time. Don't do anything I wouldn't do." Kendal tried to think of something Mum wouldn't do, and drew a blank.

Mum faded. The sound of air escaping from the avatar hissed like the breath of a dozen little snakes, and it shrank slowly until it was just shorter than Kendal himself. Its stomach tightened. Its neck lengthened a little, and its build became slighter. Slimmer arms and legs. Slender fingers. Imani's body was showing up before her skin. Her face sculpted itself next, transforming from his mum's facial shape to hers. Cheekbones higher and more pronounced. Nose smaller, wider. Eyes bigger. Lips fuller. Hair long, straight. The avatar's hair was curlable fibre optic strands that could take on colour and style fairly accurately, but moved like wire rather than hair. From her waist, a skirt lowered to just above the knee.

Then the colour began to change. From the blue calling tone, it spread from her chest, the bright red dress first. It was gathered at the waist and some clever fabric plugin was measuring the light around it and creating little highlights that danced as the dress moved so that it looked like it was made of something shiny and slightly glittery. The colour slowly spread to the edges of the dress. High around the neck, but leaving her shoulders bare. Then her skin filled in, glowing slowly from white to a deep, deep brown. Her hair black. Her eyes so huge and dark they seemed all pupil. No makeup except for a slight, digitally added sheen that made her face glow and her lips slightly silver.

Imani did not look at all like Lexie. And yet… Doreen had full access to his eye movements and would doubtless have scanned every glance he had ever made in the direction of a girl. The thought was unsettling, but he had to confess the artificial matchmaker knew her work.

Kendal cleared his throat. This was just Imani's avatar - like everyone you met online, he could have no idea whatsoever whether this was the way she really looked, someone else's stolen look, or something generated entirely digitally. He dismissed the thought. You could drive yourself crazy thinking about stuff like that. She was what she was.

"Hello, Kendal," said Imani. She held out her hand. He took it, smiling. It felt exactly as he expected. Like the hand of a balloon animal.

"I-" he managed.

"Shall we go?"

Chapter 5

Imani stood next to him at the school gates, her body waving slightly as the car left them. Kendal had fitted the avatar with heavy shoes so that Imani didn't blow away, but he needn't have bothered. It was a still night.

"So where are you really?" he asked.

"You don't ask a girl a question like that on a first date," she said, smiling.

"Sorry - I - " he started.

"It's OK, I don't mind. I'm in a VR room. I'm not - you know, looking at a phone screen or something."

"Good," he said. Kendal always resented it when people embodied an avatar from some little screen somewhere. It always felt fake. As though they were only half there. You could still see them, but if they couldn't see you except as pixels on a screen it was - well, it was wrong. VR was good. It meant she could actually be at the party. Look around, see everyone. Feel she was there. Mum embodied from screens all the time, and Kendal hated it.

The playground at night felt wrong. He'd only ever seen it full of uniformed kids, but now it was empty as they walked through. In front of them, the hall pulsed with coloured light, and boomed with the muffled music of twenty years earlier. Mr. McPhearson was carrying out his threat to teach them all what real music was about, whether they wanted to learn or not.

Kendal steeled himself. At least this was the last time he'd have to come here. The last time he'd have to see the people he'd spent seven years with. He wouldn't miss any of them. If it were up to him, he wouldn't even be at the prom, but, as the careers Artificial constantly told him, social credit points were as important as academic ones if you wanted to get a decent job. If you didn't go to your school prom, employers would be asking why for the rest of your working life.

As they pushed through the doors, Kendal breathed a sigh of relief. He wasn't the only one who'd come with an avatar. In fact, there were a good few drifting around the dance floor, moving amongst the rest of his schoolmates like unguided airships. Over by the speakers, Kendal's eyes were immediately drawn to the food table. He could read the snacks with a single glance. It was all zero food. No fat, no sugar. Minimal calories. A symphony of chemical taste and texture replacements in every bite. In a single glance, he realised that comfort eating wasn't going to get him through the night. Zero food gave you something to do with your hands, but it wasn't unhealthy enough to feel right. The aftertaste was of E numbers, not, as it should have been, of guilt.

"So this is your school?" said Imani.

"Not for much longer," said Kendal. He saw her smile at his discomfort. "It's just an ordinary school."

"Give me the lowdown, then," she said. "Who's who?"

"Ok." He looked around. "See the couple over by the speakers?" He pointed out a boy and girl, wrapped in tailored black silk outfits that seemed to have been cut from the same roll of fabric. His lips were fashionably dark blue, his skin dyed a paler eggshell blue. His hair stood straight up, a good thirty centimetres above his head, and was re-formed using printed nano-structural gel into a sculpture of his own face. He'd have had to sit for hours with his head stuck in the printer while it was being formed. Her makeup was a monotone pink, as though she had been painted by a child. Her blonde hair was fanned out above her head like a tree. It must have taken ages. "Danielle and Rory. They're the biggest posers in the school."

Imani laughed.

"No kidding."

"They were always going to come together," he said. "And over there, Daisy, Imran and Peter. The school thugs."

"And them?" she said, her arm floating up to point across the hall. Kendal told her about Reuben Clark and his little gang of geeks who were probably following events from their phones. They almost never left their rooms, even attending school via their avatars. He couldn't remember ever having seen them in real life. But even disconnected from the events, and even with libraries of motion-captured dance moves at their fingertips, the avatars of Reuben and his gang still hung around the edges of the floor, shuffling from one foot to another looking vaguely embarrassed.

"That couple?" She pointed out two avatars having a deep and earnest conversation across one of the tables. Both boys with long, flat, lank hair. Both skinny and dressed in dark clothes. Both with faces shaded in a faked shadow so they could hardly be seen.

"Lance and Gerry," said Kendal. "The funny thing is they're probably together in real life, sitting in the same room. They're just too shy to talk to each other except online." As they watched, Lance put a latex hand out and laid it on Gerry's hand. Gerry looked up slowly. "See, just an ordinary school." He looked over to Imani. She was loving this. "Is your school not like this?" he said.

She shook her head. "We'd never have a prom," she said. "Things aren't like they are here."

Something in her eyes warned him not to ask more. "Who are the real people?" she said quickly. She was nodding to the centre of the dancefloor where a shrieking gaggle of boys and girls were not very secretly passing a water bottle containing clear liquid that certainly wasn't water.

"They're the sporty ones - the vegetarians," said Kendal dismissively. "I hate them all." He looked over. They were all far too loud. Far too fit. Boys stuffed uncomfortably into suits they didn't suit. Girls welcoming the chance to dress in something other than games gear. None of them would be seen dead in an avatar. And of course he was lying. He did hate them, but not all of them. Because, at the centre of the group, was Lexie, drunk already and whirling to the music. She was tall and blonde, and sparkling as always. Her pink dress flared as she span. Kendal felt the same pang he always felt when he saw her. She glanced over. Smiled the way she always smiled. Warm. Beautiful. And as though Kendal was about as significant as wallpaper. Lexie never had anything bad to say about him, or anything good. Just because she knew - had always known - how he felt about her, it didn't make him a figure of ridicule for her. It was only everyone else that felt that. Kendal glanced at her date. Of course: Farron. Big, blond and monumentally dumb. Captain of everything and Veggie with a capital V. Kendal looked away from the group and towards Imani. She was smiling at him.

"They're all gangs," she said. "Gangs and couples?"

"Pretty much," said Kendal.

"So which is your gang?" Kendal looked at the floor. He shrugged. "I get it," said Imani, quietly.

"Shall we go for a walk?" he said. "It's rubbish in here."

Chapter 6

They left the hall, and walked out to the fields at the back of the school, then through the gate and down the little path that led out into the woods. It was warm and still, and as they picked their way through the trees, Imani's avatar struggled, and Kendal had to take her hand to guide her. It felt right.

Kendal caught himself. He had been expecting the date to be a disaster and the fact that it wasn't took him by surprise. He should have known better. Doreen had access to every detail of his behaviour and personality when she chose Imani as his perfect date. A person gives themselves away completely when they reveal their likes, their conversations. To an artificial watching, he must be as transparent as glass, thought Kendal. Doreen knew far more about him than he knew himself and far more about feelings than a lonely teenager could ever know. And with that vast bank of knowledge, and every girl on the planet to choose from, she picked Imani. Imani was his perfect match - or, at least, thought Kendal, she was perfect for this moment. This prom. Whatever Doreen could predict about how this night would play out would have been factored into her choice. He had only asked, he remembered, for a date, not a life partner. Even so, he knew he should watch himself. Feelings were dangerous things if you let them take hold of you too fast. He knew that from experience.

In the distance, he could hear shrieking laughter. A laugh he recognised. He felt that pang again. Lexie. The fitness freaks had probably come out and started showing off on the games field. Dancing just wasn't competitive enough for them.

As they walked down away from the school, Kendal felt strangely at ease for the first time in a long while. She talked about the tiny village she lived in - where her Mum sold home-made pots, and everyone knew everyone. It sounded idyllic, but Imani laughed. He wouldn't think that if he lived there, she told him.

"Where is it?

"It's called -" Imani's reply was cut off by a high-pitched beep. She tried again. "The village is -" that sound again.

"What was that?" asked Kendal.

Imani shrugged. "Doreen's automatic censorship, I guess," she said. "No exchange of personal data."

"She wants to stop me stalking you."

"I don't think she cares about that," said Imani. "She's just protecting her intellectual property. She doesn't want us connecting on other social media networks!"

"Well, you can tell me roughly, surely?"

"I guess," said Imani. "You probably won't have heard of it. I'm from Barka."

She was right. He shrugged. "I- Is that a county?"

"Depends who you ask." She smiled. "Used to be Eritrea. There have been a lot of changes since food printing came in - and social media local government AIs mixed things up. Let's say, it's messy."

Kendal nodded. He had learnt in school that the revolutions in farming coupled with social media technology that had allowed people to organise and govern themselves locally had made many national governments irrelevant and opened up fractures right across Africa, and South America, but it was all too confusing. There were places where conventional maps simply broke down. They failed, Kendal's geography teacher said, to adequately describe the shifting relationships between geography and humanity. And in these places maps were overlaid by social network analysis graphs - hundreds of dots cross-linked by shifting lines of varying thickness. This, his teacher had said, was the post-food-tech reality of rural community government. It had made no sense whatsoever to Kendal, and he had tuned out about then.

So, Imani's homeland was one of those dots. Or one of the connecting lines. Or something.

"Don't worry," she said. "There won't be a quiz. Tell me about your family."

As they walked, Kendal told Imani about his irritating brother, and about how suddenly Dad left their lives, and about Mum's parade of new partners, appearing and vanishing with increasing speed. But mostly he talked about food. How he was going to train to be a chef. How he wanted, one day, to own his own restaurant. Something he had never told anyone. He asked her what she ate home.

"Maybe I'll show you one day," she said, smiling.

Kendal had no idea how much time had passed before they stopped walking, at the edge of the woods. A meadow of long grass stretched out in front of them, silver and blue. Once, it would have been farmland. Now, once-cultivated vegetables ran as unpicked weeds amongst the wildflowers. Beside the

33

meadow, a tractor, ancient and rusting, stood like a boulder. In a few short years, 3D printing had replaced farming - its printing inks grown in vast green algal blooms across the pacific. The landscape of England was returning now to how it had been before humans first turned to agriculture, 4,000 years ago. The lungs of the world, breathing again. So much green was fixing carbon-dioxide at a rate that was beginning to alarm climate scientists.

"It's not like this at home," said Imani. "It's so hard to grow anything here. Just surviving used to be our whole purpose. Printed food changed everything."

"That's good, isn't it?" said Kendal. Imani shrugged.

"Maybe," she said. "It's not so simple."

Beyond the meadow, two kilometres away, the long, low buildings of the Farm stretched across the horizon. Flat and silver, they formed a solid, even line. A few black dots swept back and forth over it. Cleaner drones probably. Too far away to hear.

In front of him, Imani's avatar glowed in the moonlight. It adjusted her brightness automatically to the levels around her just like the screen on a phone, but her image was still made of light, so she shone in the dark. The night was warm and the air still, so she floated only a little beside him. She could have been a ghost, Kendal thought, or an angel. Stop it, he interrupted himself. Just stop those thoughts right there.

He could hear that shrieking laughter again. This time it was behind him, further away down the hill where the tractor was rusting. He looked around, and just made out a flash of pink dress, running along the edge of the meadow. Just as he thought: Lexie. Drunk. Her date was probably with her, the stupid Farron, chasing her, playing some dumb game. But neither would be able to see Kendal and Imani up at the top of the slope even if they cared to look. Suddenly, he realised he didn't care. Lexie and Farron could do what they liked. He would rather be here, alone with Imani.

"Imani-" he started.

"Kendal, there's something I should tell you."

Oh, no, thought Kendal. Here it comes. "What? You're a middle-aged hairy man in a bedsit in Dagenham?"

"No…" she paused. "This is me - it really is, but, I just need to tell you - Doreen didn't pick me."

"Ok -" said Kendal. "And what does that mean?"

"I hacked Doreen" She shrugged. "Messing with artificials is - a sort of hobby, I guess."

"Not much to do where you live?" said Kendal.

"You have no idea." she said. She was laughing, but there was an edge to her voice.

"Ok," said Kendal. "How does it work?" She shrugged.

"You know, I work out what they're doing, what their biases are, and I play them. Sometimes it works. Sometimes it doesn't."

"I don't understand," said Kendal.

"Doreen works by picking up your deep data and looking for matches, right?"

"Right."

"So I thought I'd feed it some fake data, and see if I could target someone and get her to pick just them."

"And you chose me?"

"No, as I said, sometimes it works, sometimes it doesn't."

"Oh." He felt crushed. "Who did you target?"

"You've got to understand," she said, "dating where I live is not like it is with you. I'm not even allowed to be on here. It was just a joke really."

"Who did you pick?"

"Promise you won't laugh?"

"Ok."

"Denzil France."

He did laugh. Denzil France had just had three consecutive platinum-selling hits.

"It had to be someone whose data was in the public domain," she said. "Someone who had a completely open profile."

"You picked him, and you ended up with me?" he said. "You must be crap at this!"

"Don't be like that. I like you."

Kendal felt a jolt of adrenaline that started in his stomach and pulsed through his heart. "Do you?"

He was standing close to her now. The avatar's face tightened slightly, expressions flowing across her projected face. The eyes flicked, mimicking the movements her own eyes must be making thousands of kilometres away inside her VR headset as she watched his face.

Was she leaning in towards him, or was it just the wind? Her lips were just a few centimetres from his now. He took a breath and let himself believe he could feel her breath. That the kiss was real.

She drew back far enough for him to see that she was smiling, then leant in again. This was happening far too fast. A firm movement this time, her hand moving behind him to pull her avatar towards him. He put his own arms around her. Felt his fingers against the fake cloth of her dress. Her lips against his - not real lips, but real enough.

The kisses became firmer. More urgent. "Do you..." he swallowed hard, "Do you have an avatar in your room that I could go onto? Then we could be - we could both be embodied - you know." She did know. She knew exactly what he meant. Right

36

now, she must be at home, miming her embrace in a VR room. Seeing him but touching nothing. If he could be projected onto an avatar, things could become more physical.

"I'm switching you to one now," she said. There was a pause. Her eyes went dead for a second, then her whole avatar became suddenly more present, more alive. At home, her real arms were around his avatar, and he could feel it in her movements. More purpose. More reality. It made him feel suddenly self-conscious, as though she had just appeared finally in front of him. So close for the first time. He moved in to kiss her again.

Suddenly she went blue for a second. A dull sound. Something was wrong. He pulled back. Her eyes had changed. They were... For a second, he didn't know what he was looking at. Then he realised, and recoiled in horror. His arms flew away from her so fast the avatar rocked, looming back and forth.

She was gone. Replaced. Instead of Imani's shining, smiling face, he was staring at Doreen's stern eyes. Her lips were pulled into a tight, wrinkled line.

THIS CONTENT IS AGE-RESTRICTED. THIS DATE IS TERMINATED.

"What?" said Kendal. "Bring her back."

PHYSICAL CONTACT LIMITS HAVE BEEN EXCEEDED FOR YOUR AGE GROUP. I'M AFRAID I CANNOT ALLOW THIS DATE TO CONTINUE.

Kendal's mouth hung open. "You can't do that!" he gasped.

I'M SORRY, KENDAL. PEGI LIMITS CANNOT BE EXCEEDED.

"Bring her back!" Kendal shouted. For a moment his wristband glowed its red warning - AMA would embody if he

37

wasn't careful. "We'll stop!" he said quickly. Calmly. "I promise."

I'M SORRY. NO FURTHER CONTACT BETWEEN YOU AND IMANI WILL BE POSSIBLE. YOU MAY SELECT ANOTHER DATE FOR THE REMAINDER OF THE EVENING IF YOU WISH.

Kendal felt as though he'd been hit in the chest.

"No, it's ok." Kendal wanted to punch the Artificial. "Goodbye."

GOODBYE KENDAL. PLEASE COME AGAIN.

The avatar flashed blue, and then faded to blank, leaving him alone in the forest. Slowly, his wristband faded too, from glowing red to dull blue. He had always been alone, he realised. He had been alone all night. Talking to a dummy. But now he felt it. He felt more alone than ever. He started walking down the edge of the field, cursing himself and Doreen. Imani was gone. And Doreen would never let him see her again. Damn. He should have read the terms and conditions.

He walked on, following the boundary between the forest and the meadow. It wasn't worth going back to the prom now. He might as well walk down to the road and back home. It was getting late and the walk would take half an hour, but he didn't care. He wanted to be on his own. There was too much in his head just now to be around other people. The blank avatar followed him silently, head down, a few paces behind, dragging its heavy boots. It was like being followed by the dead.

The night was silent now. He couldn't even hear Lexie and her friends shrieking. He passed by the broken shape of the abandoned tractor. Its wheels were as tall as he was. Punctured and rotting, its body corroded and sprouting with weeds.

And that was when he saw her.

38

Preoccupied by his own thoughts, it took him far too long to know what he was seeing. She was lying behind the back wheel. Half propped against it, head on one side. Sleeping off the drink, his mind told him.

But no.

There was blood on her face. Like a defeated avatar in a videogame, but not. Not glowing. Real. Real and quite dead.

Chapter 7

A dark horror crept over Kendal. His heart started to pound. He crouched beside her. The blood on her face was from a long, deep cut from her temple down her cheek. And there were others. Her arm. Her body. Long, deep cuts sliced into her. One of her shoes was missing, the other caked in mud and grass.

She had been running. Running with one shoe through the forest: chased. With a sickening lurch, Kendal realised something. Those shrieks he had taken for laughter. Someone had chased her through the forest. The same forest where he was alone right now.

He stood up, head reeling. He knew what he had to do. Command the avatar to call the police. A virtual officer would embody and tell him what to do next. He opened his mouth to say "999", and then shut it again as the second realisation hit him. Whoever had done this was still out there. Maybe very close. Maybe watching. He looked around. Nobody. But the moment he spoke, the avatar would light up like a beacon. Whoever was in the forest would know exactly where he was.

He turned and ran, heart pounding, down the edge of the meadow, and towards the road. To one side, the long grass could have hidden anything. To the other, the shapes of trees flew past, a flickering shifting wall of shadow. Every second, his eyes were caught by a branch which could have been a hand, or a bush like a figure, hunched over and waiting to spring at him.

His feet hit uneven ground and twisted painfully, but he ran on, fear forcing him faster and faster towards the safety of the road.

He didn't stop running, even when the trees stopped abruptly, and he burst out onto tarmac. The streetlamps were a bright yellow glow, and cast deep shadows, but they didn't reassure him. He ran until the first few houses with their long, dark front gardens gave way to the more solid, brightly-lit spaces in the centre of town.

And that was when his strength finally left him. His legs suddenly unable to carry him any further, he collapsed into the doorway of a shop, and sank down, sobbing and gasping into his hands.

He felt a shadow fall across him, and looked up. His eyes struggled to focus on the figure looming over him. He tried to struggle to his feet, but he couldn't stand. His legs had given up.

"Stop!" he said, desperately. The figure stopped, head sagging forward. Kendal's eyes focused. It was just the avatar. Still blank. Still dark. Still following obediently. Behind it, in the street, a police car passed at speed. Lights flashing red and blue. Kendal watched it swerve and bump down towards the woods.

Somebody must have found her.

He sat in the doorway with the blank avatar until his breathing and his heart calmed. He replayed the night in his head. The walk with Imani into the wood. The sounds from

Lexie. Had he seen something? He couldn't remember anything except Imani, her virtual presence selling him the lie that he was not alone.

Chapter 8

"How was tonight?"

"Fine." Kendal answered automatically without looking, or thinking, and instantly regretted it. He'd just made it home. Legs still aching. Head still spinning in confusion. As he'd passed the kitchen, the surprise of seeing her sitting at the table, glass of red wine in hand, had triggered his response - as automatic as the startup jingle of an avatar.

Mum.

Not embodied. Not through an avatar, but real Mum. Fine? Why did he say that? But it was too late to stop the lie escaping his lips now.

"Just fine?" she said. "How was your date?" She attempted a knowing grin. Kendal looked away. It had been a long time since Mum could be knowing about his life. Tonight wasn't the night to catch up. Presumably she felt that first dates were something she could claim some expertise in. Not this one.

"What are you doing here?" he said. How could he tell her now? He felt a sudden shot of anger. He instinctively pulled his jacket cuff down to cover the flash of his wristband.

"I live here," Mum took a swig of wine. If Kendal had been forced to make a list of the people living at home, he wouldn't have put Mum on it. In truth, she had left when Dad did, or maybe a couple of months later. Only he had had the courtesy to do it properly. Cleanly. Mum pretended to stay, hanging around as a virtual ghost. In physical form, she was a visitor at best, and yet the moment she rolled in, she demanded to be let into the most intimate details of his life. Now, for once there was something he really needed to talk to her about and she had forced him into a stupid lie. And now because of that, he could never tell anyone.

"I thought you were away for the week," he snapped.

"So, did you like her?" she said.

"Who?"

"Your date - Inary?" Kendal paused for just long enough for Mum to pick up on his expression. "You did like her!" she said.

He shrugged. "Imani," he corrected. She - she had to go," he said.

"You seeing her again?"

He shook his head. "I don't think so."

"Oh," Mum looked genuinely sympathetic, "I'm sorry, but you know - sometimes it's like that-"

Like what? Like finally connecting with someone and having them whisked away by a mad artificial nanny? Like finding the body of your murdered classmate lying in a field? His brain was still processing what he had seen. It felt like only parts of it would fit into his head at a time. Close-ups with no context.

"I'm really tired," said Kendal.

She pushed a glass over to him, then lifted hers. She smiled. "Plenty more fish in the sea," she said. "To crap dates!"

Kendal sighed and sat down. He picked up the glass.

"You have no idea," he said.

"Maybe I do," said Mum. "Why don't you talk to me anymore?"

Kendal looked at her for a long time. She was smiling. Not a proper smile. A tight little smile that seemed to require every muscle in her face, but projected no happiness. He had to tell her. There was no choice. He swallowed a gulp of the sour wine, then took a deep breath.

"It's all over with Roy!" said Mum, suddenly. Kendal blinked at her.

"Roy?" he said. "The guy at dinner?"

"I really thought that -" she said.

"You've only known him a day," said Kendal.

"But you should have seen his metrics," said Mum.

"His what?" Kendal really didn't want to hear about Roy's metrics.

"His metrics. Doreen matches on compatibility metrics if you ask her. She can tell you how well matched you are on the five personality clusters, and seven different emotional availability parameters." Mum's eyes were welling up now. "He looked perfect. I don't know what went wrong."

"Wait a minute," said Kendal, "is that all you chose him on? His stats?"

"No!" sobbed Mum, "We've been swapping emojis for weeks!"

"What about Dan?" said Kendal.

"Dan and I were never serious."

"I liked Dan," said Kendal. "He was - stable."

"Why does this always happen to me?" said Mum. Kendal took her arm.

"Mum," he said, "something happened tonight."

"I know!" said Mum, "I found out Roy collects stamps! It's all such a mess!"

"What? What are stamps?" said Kendal. "No! It's about Lexie!" Mum looked up.

"Lexie?" said Mum, "Oh, Kendal, she's not the one for you. You have to learn to move on."

"No, it's not that - she's -"

"Look, finding someone is really hard - I should know!" she put her hand on his arm. "You have to put yourself out there - and it hurts - sometimes it really hurts but you have to keep doing it until one day- "

"I found her -" Kendal managed.

"Oh, I'm so sorry," said Mum. "You found her with someone else?" She smiled sympathetically. "But there are lots of lovely girls in the world. You just have to allow yourself to see that!"

"No!" said Kendal. "Listen to me! Lexie was..." he trailed off. Because there it was. "Lexie was." Past tense. Slipping out of his lips, suddenly the whole of it was in front of him. The full realisation breaking over him as though the shell of an egg had cracked. Lexie was dead. Actually, really dead.

And everything he had felt about her was pointless now.

Every day at school for the past three years had been filled with her. Worrying about whether he would see her. Seeing her and feeling his stomach lurch. Straining to hear her chatting with friends. Mind sent spinning with every moment of eye contact. Hours - days - spent wondering what she was thinking. Feeling.

It was all meaningless now.

And following on from that, Kendal felt another lurch. Guilt. Not for interpreting her screams as laughter. Not for being a few metres away and kissing Imani while she died. But another guilt. Guilt for grieving only for himself and his wasted feelings. Was that really all he felt - sad that he'd spent his time moping over her? Did he even really care about Lexie herself at all?

"What is it?" said Mum.

"I really need to go to bed." Kendal stood up and walked to the door.

"I might go and talk to Doreen," said Mum. "Swipe for a while." Kendal paused in the doorway and looked back at her.

"Don't do it tonight," he said. "You're not in the right state for it."

"I'm fine," said Mum, draining her glass. "I'm absolutely fine!"

Chapter 9

He closed his bedroom door and collapsed onto the bed. He put his phone on the table next to him and flicked it onto projection mode. The screen appeared on the ceiling above him, and focussed in. The wine Mum had given him had calmed the adrenaline pumping through him, and without it, his arms and legs felt like dead weights and he just wanted to sleep, but he couldn't just yet. He'd seen the police car and assumed that meant Lexie had been discovered, but he had to be sure.

He flicked through the latest alerts. Pages of news, picked and curated to be relevant to him, filled the screen. Updates from Aunt Megan about her friend's knee operation sat side by side with international climate change news - something about plans to encourage the production of greenhouse gasses to counter the massive drop in CO_2 in the atmosphere now that vast swathes of ocean were being turned into oxygen producing algae for edible printer inks. A digest he'd signed up to about calorie negative cake printing was announcing major breakthroughs. Tour dates he might be interested in based on his music listening profile had been announced. Road closures were planned because of tomorrow's planned protest in town by the Campaign for Real Meat - along with warnings that disruption of the peace would not be tolerated by either side of the vegetarian divide.

All completely useless. He didn't need the app's best guess of what news he might be interested in. He needed specific news.

"News: Lexie Doyle," he said. The screen blanked, then filled with photos from Lexie's social media profile. Most were familiar. The photos of her at this year's athletics gala, dressed in her team colours. Some pictures posted of a holiday somewhere sunny. She wore a bikini. Kendal had, of course, searched for posts of Lexie before. His most viewed images loomed largest.

Embarrassed at himself, he quickly passed them. Newer posts appeared. Lexie spinning in the centre of the dance floor. A crowd around her. The pink dress she was wearing tonight. The photo must have been taken a few moments after Kendal had arrived because although just the side of his head was there, in the background, the slightly glowing avatar of Imani looking face onto the camera. She was smiling. He zoomed in to look at her again for just a second. His mind flashed back to their kiss.

Another picture. Slightly later. On the sports field. Lexie's whole gang of friends were there. A drunken race was going on and most were focussed on that, but in the background, Lexie and Farron were standing slightly apart. The photo was dark, and Kendal couldn't be sure, but it looked as though they were arguing.

No more updates. What would he do if she hadn't been found? Report it? Come clean? He'd have to. How would he explain his silence, running, lying to Mum? He felt suddenly sick.

But wait - the police wouldn't release the information right away - they'd have to tell her parents first. Another lurch in Kendal's stomach. They could be out there right now, hearing about their daughter's murder. Identifying the body. Those cuts. And if not - if nobody had found her then they would be at home, just waiting. Just realising that she hadn't come back from the prom.

One more search before he called the police. He searched for everything related to the prom.

And there it all was: Photos. Updates. Check-ins. The whole story. Happy smiling faces. Drunk selfies. Bitchy posts. Dance memes. He scrolled through, and suddenly the tone changed. Police. Confusion. Worried posts. Questioning emojis. Who was missing? What was happening? An ambulance. The body being removed. A social media storm that exploded into photos of blue and red lights and tearful faces, as he scrolled through it, and then slowly died into tired one-line updates from everyone now at home in their beds. Petering out gradually as each of his schoolmates drifted off to sleep.

Yes. She had been found.

He watched the last of the public messages project live onto his ceiling, and let the tiredness take him:

I CAN'T BELIEVE IT.

ME NEITHER…

WHO CLD DO THS?

DUNNO…

Now, he was back in the wood. Imani was there beside him. Glowing, but not an avatar. She was real this time. Her hand was warm in his. He could feel her fingertips. Her nails. He turned to her, moving to kiss her. This time it was not hesitant or uncertain. This time he knew the kiss would be returned. He felt her lips against his. Real lips. The breath from her nose. The warmth from her face.

He pulled her closer, and kissed her again. Suddenly, her lips stilled. Her breath stopped. Her face was cold. He pulled away. And now it was Lexie.

Dead Lexie. Face, white. Eyes dull, staring. That cut from her temple to her cheek, wide and dark. Kendal let go of her. Staggered backwards.

Now she was a blank. An avatar with no face, leering back and forth in the warm breeze, insubstantial as a spirit. Around him, the trees were closing, reaching out with long, dark, twisted hands. He turned and ran, blundering through the grasping twigs. Now he was in a storm, the trees thrashing around him. Every time he looked back, the avatar was still there, floating, seconds behind, pitching forward at him as he fought his way through the forest.

Up ahead, he could see the school. The lights of the hall flashing red, green, blue. The low beat of the music still playing. People were laughing. If he could make it to the gates...

And then the shadow of something huge and horrible falling across him, blocking his way.

He looked up and his eyes flicked open. On the ceiling his news-feed had cycled back. It was mothershowing another image of Lexie. This one, a six second video-loop from her birthday, posted by her mother last year. She was grinning at the camera over a lighted candle. Her face filled his bedroom ceiling. The candle flickered and she blew it out. A second-long cheer was cut off suddenly as the video looped, and the candle flickered into life again to be blown out once more. The same fragment of somebody else's memory replaying over and over as

51

Kendal's brain told him the same thing, over and over: after three years, he had finally allowed himself to stop caring about Lexie, and a second later, she was dead. In his half-dreaming mind, those two things could not be unconnected. Whatever had happened was his fault.

He closed his eyes and collapsed back into sleep.

Chapter 10

"I'm sorry about last night." Mum was sitting in the kitchen. The wine was gone, but she had not changed her clothes. She looked the way he felt - as though she hadn't slept. "I was just a bit - you know -"

Kendal nodded. "I know," he said.

"It's just that every time someone seems perfect…"

"You only met him once," said Kendal. "You can't know someone's perfect for you the first time you meet them!"

"Haven't you ever had that feeling - like someone was meant for you?"

"No." It was a lie. He had felt that way about two girls in his life. After last night, he would never see either of them again. "That's just a random chemical reaction in the brain. It doesn't mean anything one way or the other." He said it loudly and firmly. Lexie was never right for him. He had known that even while he adored her. They had nothing in common. And as for Imani, there had been one evening. That was all it was. One evening and a little bit of bonding over the stupidity of his classmates. It meant nothing. He really believed that. Almost.

53

"Doreen knows," said Mum.

"Well, clearly she doesn't," said Kendal.

"Doreen uses compatibility metrics from over fifty million successful couples! There must be something wrong with me."

"He seemed like a bit of an idiot to me," said Kendal.

"Sweet of you to say so," said Mum. She suddenly ducked down beside the table, and came up with a small bag. "I nearly forgot. I brought you a present," she said. Kendal took the bag and opened it. Inside were four small black cartridges. "I thought you could cook something."

Kendal pulled the cartridges out and laid them on the table. They were smaller than normal food cartridges. Rare, valuable ingredients. Each one was circled with a stylish gold band. These were top of the range stuff. The kind of compounds you'd find in a top restaurant.

"Oh, Mum, thank you!" Kendal put his arms around her. An uncomfortable sort of hug. "I'm sorry about Roy," he said. She shrugged.

"Me too. Now, what are you going to make?"

Kendal picked up the cartridges one by one, turning them over carefully in his hands. There was Saffron Base - a deep and complex compound which a skilful chef could combine with other organics for a range of unusual flavours. There was Gloss - an emulsifier so powerful that a few drops could combine unmixable ingredients to create perfectly smooth sauces and velvety textures. Finally, there were Animie and Freeze - two edible construction materials which Kendal had longed to get his hands on ever since he'd heard of them. Each imparted strange, almost magical properties to food, and could create structures and behaviours in food which were almost impossible.

"Where did you get these?" said Kendal.

"I've got a new client," she said. Mum's work was in public relations. She worked freelance, putting together social media campaigns to promote mostly dull companies making dull products. She spent a lot of time setting up chatbots to go out and tell people how passionate they were about cleaning products. Kendal took little notice most of the time.

"Who are they?" he said.

"A food producer," she said. "They run the farm up by the school. They want to encourage people to be experimental with their meat products. These cartridges were part of a promotional pack for restaurants. I thought you might like them." Kendal was only half listening. His mind was spinning. The things he could cook with these cartridges. Mum was looking at him. "I'd hoped you could make us something special for today. I thought we could all go out this afternoon - as a family."

"Sure, " said Kendal.

"And, Kendal?" she said. "Promise me you'll make something your brother will like." Kendal nodded. That wouldn't be a problem.

"I'm going to do a box of chocolates," he said. Joseph was far less fussy about sweets than he was about meat.

Kendal took his four new cartridges and stepped into the little cooking area at the back of the kitchen. He laid them out on the breakfast bar which served both as his workspace and as the desk on which he composed meals. Below the toughened glass, a touch screen glowed. He stroked it, and his cooking apps rippled to the surface as though the icons were rising from a pool of water.

This was his space - a tiny area, but nobody else spent enough time there to bother changing the settings or messing with his cartridges. All Mum ever did in the kitchen was drink wine, and all Joseph ever did was hit "autocook" on the few preset meals he lived off.

Everything else was his and he had it set out just the way he wanted. He slid out the tall larder. It was stacked with cartridges. Larger, more common ones at the bottom. Smaller, specialist ingredients at the top, out of the reach of Joseph. He had quite a collection. There were a few composite processed ingredients: wheat pulp was pre-mixed so that he could make pasta or bread or pastry without the tedious messing around printing one grain at a time from its individual cells proteins and amino acids, before grinding it down to be fed back into the printer as an ingredient. Chocolate was another pre-mix, because the industrial printers did it to a higher resolution than Mum's home setup could, and that gave it a less grainy feel. However, where possible, Kendal liked to go right back to basics and start from the purest ingredients. It felt more wholesome somehow. More authentic. It was, as far as he was concerned, the difference between being a caterer and being an artist.

He pulled out the cartridges he wanted to use, and laid them out in front of him on the breakfast bar. Chocolate, Fructose - his own specially hidden stash - polysaccharides for creating gels, a rack of basic aroma compounds: Esters, lactones, aldehydes. The combinations and quantities and their balance and positions within each confection would be crucial - the difference between a bitter chocolate with an orange cream centre and the taste of rotten eggs and bat urine.

With the potential flavours and textures in front of him, combinations started to suggest themselves. Ideas were filling his head, and he allowed them to take him. He visualised the box. Every chocolate must be different. Each one a little bite of perfection. Complex and experimental.

He pulled up his design app on the work surface screen. Starting with a blob of virtual clay, he jabbed and dragged with his finger to shape some designs. A chocolate sphere with walls a millimetre thick, enclosing a network of other spheres, each containing gels of different flavours. A dark chocolate tree with white chocolate ivy swirled around it, topped by spun sugar so fine it could have been candy floss. A hard boiled sweet with a dozen shells that cracked and melted at different temperatures revealing fruit-flavoured syrups between each layer, mixing and multiplying in the mouth.

The creation of the chocolates occupied Kendal's whole mind. It was art and maths. It was sensation and exhilaration. It did not blot out the dark feelings churning in his head. Instead, his creation absorbed them, directed them. He took all the loss and guilt and unnamable other feelings that had run through him over the past twenty-four hours, and expressed them as something beautiful. Emotion as food. That was how it worked for Kendal.

He switched to a new app and typed in the specification codes for his new ingredients. The screen filled with numbers and formulae. The figures showed him how each ingredient would combine with the others in his recipes. How each would behave in the presence of heat or cold. Liquid or acid. How flavours would combine to affect different receptors in the nose or on the tongue. How each would combine, crystalise, dissolve or evaporate. Kendal buried himself in the maths until he could think of nothing else. The horrors of last night were focused, processed, reformed into a tiny part of his brain where just for a few minutes they could do him no harm.

Kendal stared at the numbers and started to see patterns. Possibilities. The Freeze cartridge could change the temperature at which his chocolate would harden, but it could also allow him to create a foam which would evaporate when you breathed on it to fill your nostrils with an intense aroma. Animie could create structures of biscuit or jelly which would flex or stretch at different temperatures like tiny muscles or engines. He could print working mechanisms inside his sweets. His mind spinning, he flicked back and forth between his specifications app and his design app, refining and combining.

Once the designs were fixed, he switched to a third app and worked through the cooking map. For most food, the Autochef's standard cooking settings were fine: bake, steam, brown. That was all you needed. But these designs were delicate. A few degrees of heat in the wrong place, and the whole thing would be a gooey mess. He switched to micro-voxel cooking. Now, as the printer built up each layer, he could use focussed lasers to precisely control the temperature at which each part of the recipe was cooked millimetre by millimetre. He could bake the biscuit, gently warm the mousse, temper the chocolate, and leave the delicate strands of sugar unmelted. For each sweet, he designed a 3d cooking map defining the heat required by each element.

"What you doing?" It was Joseph. He had finally got up.

"He's making chocolates," said Mum. Hours could have passed. Kendal had no idea. He looked up.

"Goody," said Joseph, "can I help?"

"No!" said Kendal. He wasn't letting his brother anywhere near these ingredients. This wasn't lunch. This was art.

"But I want to!"

Kendal didn't like giving sweets to Joseph. He didn't know how to eat them. Each creation was a unique experience, precisely calibrated, layered with flavour decisions, designed to be unlocked and savoured. Given the chance, Joseph would cram the lot into his mouth without a second thought. He would gulp them down while he played a videogame, or worse, while he continued some pointless argument. Joseph had no appreciation. No finesse.

"You can have some later." That seemed to satisfy Joseph a little, and he plonked himself down next to Mum.

"When?" he said.

"We're all going out," said Kendal. He clicked to send his final designs through to the printer, and clicked the cartridges in place.

"Where?" said Joseph.

Kendal realised he had been so wrapped up in his cooking that he hadn't even asked Mum where she was taking them. He looked over at her. "Where are we going, Mum?" he said.

"Fitness Cafe!" said Joseph. Mum shook her head. It was a good call. If they went to the fitness cafe, Joseph would disappear off onto the VR machines and they wouldn't see him again. Not a bad outcome, but if Mum wanted family time, she wouldn't get it there.

"Picnic," said Mum definitively. Joseph sagged. "Or don't you want any of Kendal's chocolates?"

"Will it just be us?" said Kendal. "You're not bringing anyone, are you?"

"I've decided," she said slowly, "to give dating a rest for a while."

"Good," said Kendal, trying to keep it light, but silently breathing a huge sigh of relief.

"I've decided I need to concentrate on myself for a while."

"Ok," said Kendal.

59

"I mean us," said Mum, noticing his expression change. Suddenly in the doorway, a blank avatar appeared. It was flashing blue - a call coming through. Mum looked up at it.

"I've got to take this," she said. "Work." She followed the avatar out of the room. The printer juddered to a halt.

"What's that?" said Joseph, peering in through the printing window. The printer had automatically created an elegant white box around the chocolates. Inside, each confectionary would be enclosed in its own perfectly shaped biodegradable enclosure.

"Not now," said Kendal. "Mum's taking us out." He opened the door, and pulled out the little box, and slipped it into a bag. Joseph's shoulders visibly sank.

"Just one!" he said. He tried to grab the bag.

"Careful," said Kendal, pulling it away from him. "They're delicate." Joseph dodged around behind him, and was about to make another grab for the bag when Mum reappeared in the doorway. She grabbed her coat, rifling through the pockets as she put it on.

"Are we going?" said Joseph. Mum pulled her lips tight. Avoided his eyes. Kendal knew instantly what was coming.

"Sorry," said Mum, "it's work. They want me to - have you seen my phone?"

"It's on the table," said Kendal, doing his best to sound as though he didn't care. "I thought we were all going out." Mum reached for her phone, and shoved it into a pocket.

"I'm sorry, boys," she said, but Kendal could see it in her eyes. There was a kind of relief. As though she'd been let off - rescued from having to spend time with them. Work was easy. Time with her children was too complex. Too deep.

"When will you be back?" Kendal looked down at his bag of now pointless creations. There was no point arguing.

"There's some kind of vegetarian demonstration going on in town. Work wants me to go along," she said.

"Why?" said Kendal.

"I just have to watch - understand their mindset."

"Their mindset is simple," said Kendal. "They won't eat meat unless it's come from a real animal. They keep going on about wanting to kill their own food."

"But why? That's the point!" said Mum. Kendal shrugged.

"Veggies just like killing things," he said.

"It's because they don't understand the growing process," said Mum. "They think it's unnatural - it's my job to get the message across that growing meat is just as natural and wholesome as growing plants."

"I'd like to be a vegetarian," said Joseph. He struck up a fighting pose, stabbing at his brother with an open hand as though it were a knife.

"You wouldn't get very far with your diet," said Kendal. "I'd like to see you go up against a T.Rex!"

"I've got to go," said Mum.

"Wait," said Kendal. "You can't just go down there on your own. The police are warning that -"

"Oh, it's fine!" said Mum, "They always make out there's going to be trouble. There never is - that's what AMA is for!"

"But those people are barbarians!" said Kendal. Mum just smiled at him, and headed for the door.

"Got to go," she said. "I'll make it up to you."

Chapter 11

"I don't even know what we're doing here," said Joseph as they slipped into the back of the hall.

"Shh!" said Kendal. "We're making sure Mum is OK." It was true. The vegetarians in Lexie's group of friends had always bothered Kendal. They were all health freaks obviously. Fussy about their food. Sport mad - which made them weird anyway. Always going on about how grown meat was inferior, in some way unnatural. Kendal couldn't see it. But either way, he sincerely doubted any of them had ever tried 'real meat' as they called it - cut from the bodies of dead animals.

And that was it, he supposed. Veggies always liked to create a reputation for being vicious, bloodthirsty. Dangerous even. Some of them even carried knives around the school. But it was all talk - it had to be. With AMA around, they could make whatever dumb claims they liked. Nobody was ever going to call them on it.

That was the problem with AMA. Nobody was accountable. You could be as provocative and passive aggressive as you liked. Nobody could touch you. AMA was advertised as pest control, weeding out anger from every interaction, but that wasn't what she was. She didn't purge aggression at its roots, she simply trimmed it where it flowered. She stifled it, manicured it. Made it neat, while under the surface it festered and twisted into strange unnatural shapes. Emotional topiary.

Vegetarians waved their knives around, but they were harmless bulshitters - at least that was what Kendal had thought until last night. Now, he wasn't so sure. The crowd growing in the stale, yellowing old church hall contained a lot of his old schoolmates, but the room was peppered with older activists. Lean intelectual types. Thrill-seeking biker gangs. Banner waving old-time protestors. Protein stuffed health-freaks. They seemed to Kendal to have nothing in common, and yet there was a link. A sort of unsettling complexity to their expressions.

Layered emotion. On the surface, threat. Many appeared to be looking for a fight. Dressed in dark clothes. Hoodies and studs. Tattoos and narrowed eyes. But it was an affectation. Between the posing moments, they smiled, chatted easily between themselves. Checked their phones. In the age of AMA, fake aggression was as easy to spot as fake news. You just had to look at the details.

But this too was a careful facade. Kendal could see it. Feel it. For the first time, he started to suspect something else of the vegetarians. That beneath the subtext of relaxed chumminess that covered the tough veneer, there was something else. A dangerous buzz. Buried deep. Unreadable.

Kendal watched as a woman stepped out onto the stage. Perhaps it was the way she moved, or perhaps it was the disturbing fact that she appeared to have the face of a seventy year old woman stuck to the body of a teenage girl, but she gave the impression of someone who had spent her life practicing yoga and paying close attention to everything she ate.

63

"Who's that?" whispered Joseph.

"That's Lady Bradley," whispered a figure next to him in the crowd. "Her family used to have a proper farm before printing put them all out of business." As the girl turned, Kendal recognised her immediately. Zade. Short blonde hair. Sleeveless top, showing off the shoulders of a swimmer. One of Lexie's friends, but not part of her inner circle. Kendal felt suddenly out of place as she looked him up and down. He was by far the least fit looking person in the room.

"I didn't know you were one of us," she said.

"I'm - curious," said Kendal. Zade shrugged.

"You'd better stay out of Farron's way," she said. "He reckons you had something to do with what happened to Lexie. There's a lot of talk." Kendal felt his stomach lurch. Everyone would know he'd left the prom. Someone was bound to have seen he and his avatar walking into the woods. If Farron thought he killed Lexie, then who knew what he might do.

"But -" started Kendal, "Is he here?" Zade noded in the direction of the stage. Right at the front, facing away Kendal could make out the side of Farron's head. Kendal pulled up his hood to hide his face. "I didn't touch her," he said. Zade shrugged again and turned back to the stage as Lady Bradley stepped forward and held up a sinewy hand for silence.

Every movement was precise. Every gesture measured. She spoke in a voice that was like a tannoy. No effort seemed to be required for her to reach the three or four hundred people in the room. It was as though her natural level of conversation was a piercing broadcast which cut through the air, rendering all other noise redundant.

"My family has farmed this country for generations. We have dedicated our lives to rearing healthy wholesome meat for everyone. I find it highly offensive that nowadays, even to call for natural live alternatives to artificially manufactured meat is considered somehow cruel." Around Kendal, murmurings of agreement rumbled. He craned his neck to look over the nodding heads for Mum, but he couldn't see her. "Fabricated Frankenstein meat is not farming. It's an industrial process designed to roll out identical synthetic products, and we reject it." The crowd cheered. Wherever Mum was, she'd have an uphill struggle convincing this lot. "We are told the planet cannot sustain enough naturally reared animals to feed nine billion people. It's just not true. I have seen tests of modern intensive farming methods which would allow us to produce wholesome, safe organic meats in a fraction of the space and a fraction of the time. I would like to build an indoor facility where a wholesome, natural herd of ten thousand cattle, caged for their own security, all wearing virtual reality helmets and munching on 3d printed grass could happily interact with each other in their own perfect simulated environment for their entire three month life cycle. Farming real animals in this way is as good for them as it is for us!" the crowd cheered again. "And it will even be possible, through automated remote slaughter to allow you, the consumer, to have the experience of hunting your own animal from the comfort of your VR room."

What was this, a demonstration or a sales pitch? Either way, the vegetarians were lapping it up. Joseph was loving it too. The prospect of combining his two favourite things - meat and videogames - was pushing all his buttons. It might even convince him to try beef if he got to kill it himself. Kendal stepped back out of the crowd and looked along the row of backs. Finally, he spotted Mum. She was standing against a pillar at the far side of the hall, making notes on her phone. Dressed in her work suit, frantically tapping, she couldn't have been a more obvious spy if she were dressed in a trench coat and looking through a newspaper with a hole cut in it..

Kendal grabbed Joseph's arm and started to pull him towards Mum, but at that moment, Lady Bradley finished her speech, and walked straight off the centre of the stage. She dropped the two metres to the floor, landing as lightly and nimbly as a ballet dancer, and strode forward, eyes to the front, as the crowd parted before her. The room erupted into shouts and jeers. They turned. Placards raised on every side, and suddenly they were on the move.

Joseph and Kendal who had been safely distant bystanders, peering in at the back of the room, were now engulfed by the crowd surging forward. Through the doors of the hall and into the high-street. Kendal felt Joseph's hand worm free of his, and his brother vanished into the crowd. There was nothing he could do but follow. Lady Bradley swept them onwards, her walking pace at least twice as fast as was comfortable for the crowd, marching without looking in either direction, straight across the road.

Kendal fought his way to the edge of the crowd just as she came to a halt outside the door of a shop. He cursed silently. Of course, it had to be this shop! The butcher's - his butchers. Kendal went in there most days. He knew every cut they sold. Every species. And the owner knew him. Now here he was at a veggie protest in front of the place. What was he thinking? He had to find Mum and Joseph and get out of there before either the butcher or Farron saw them.

The rest of the crowd were getting worked up, shouting, banging on the windows. But at the front, Lady Bradley said nothing. She simply sat herself down in the doorway of the shop. She placed her hands, palms up, on her crossed legs, eyes closed. Calm. Silent, she let the chaos swirl around her. Kendal circled around to the back of the crowd, keeping his head down at his chin, and his collar up, struggling to keep his face hidden while he searched. The crowd was pressing forward, shifting. Suddenly, he caught a glimpse of Joseph's shirt, somewhere in the middle. He dived in, edging through the jeering bodies towards the centre of the crowd.

Protesters were pressed tightly together, and he fought through them, searching randomly. Around him, the tension was rising all the time. Here and there, he could see wristbands flicking from blue to orange and back. AMA was registering interest, her attention flickering as heartbeats quickened and tempers raised.. Next to him, a protester - a faux leather clad biker type - glanced down at his wristband as it flared a dangerous shade of blood orange. He stopped, straightened, closed his eyes, breathed in slowly through his nose, and, in the midst of the jeering crowd, he counted to ten. His wristband responded, fading to cool blue. He opened his eyes and leaped back into the melee. AMA had rules, Kendal knew, and he had to admire how well these vegetarians understood them. They knew exactly how far they could push things without triggering her, and they were calibrating their anger precisely

A voice yelled close to Kendal's ear.

"This is fun!" It was Joseph. Kendal grabbed him, and Joseph's wrist wormed in his hand. Kendal pulled his brother to the edge of the crowd.

"Don't run off again!" he said. "We have to find Mum."

Suddenly something wet and soft struck his cheek, blinding him for a second. It felt like a slap, but as it collided, it exploded in fragments across his face. He felt them slide, clinging to his jaw. He put his hand up, and it came away smeared in worms of oily pink.

Mince.

His vision cleared, and he wiped the remaining stringy chunks from his face. It was a loosely packed burger pattie. Raw. Low grade, reformed, cheap generic meat. The kind of burger you took to somebody else's barbecue. Kendal sniffed it. Such low grade meat would never have made it into his kitchen. Whoever had thrown it had clearly recognised and made full use of its culinary potential. Kendal pulled back his hood and looked around for the culprit.

About ten metres away, a young man stood, another raw burger in his hand. As Kendal watched, he launched it into the crowd. The burger arced into the air, then slapped down, exploding over the bald head of a man hammering on the butcher's shop window. The bald man turned, strands of raw meat clinging to his head like a pink wig.

Next to the thrower, a couple of blue haired girls were squawking with laughter. Kendal could see now that they were not alone. In the street, a crowd was gathering, little groups - most of them just older than Kendal, coalescing out of the cafes that lined the high street, turning in from side streets, assembling from all sides. It was a moment before Kendal, still stunned by the impact to his face, realised what was happening.

Because this wasn't an isolated prank, it was planned. A counter-protest. The meat bombers must have co-ordinated in advance and been waiting for some signal, because their missiles were raining in from all directions now. The throwers were laughing with derision as they hurled lab-grown meat pate and sludgy grey-white burger mince into the crowd.

The leader of one of the other groups opened a bag, and pulled out a pink handful, squashing it into a ball in his fist, and hurling it into the crowd. The thrower laughed.

The vegetarians were reacting now. Wiping themselves down. Turning away from the shop to face the growing crowd now encircling them. Their shouts were starting to change. No longer the unified chants of slogans, the noise was descending into a chaos of unrecognisable words.

The counter-protestors surged forward, their laughter turning to challenge. Less practiced with the anger management techniques of mass protest, their wristbands were pinging, one by one, to orange. Kendal pulled Joseph towards him.

"Come on!" He said. The wall of meat-hurlers in front of them was closing, and behind him, the vegetarians formed a solid block. They were trapped between the opposing, yelling armies. Kendal scanned the ranks of grimacing, mince-splattered faces. Something was changing. The vegetarians had thought their protest through. Focussed their anger on the inanimate glass of the butcher's shop. Managed it. Kept it at exactly permitted levels. But now this new intervention had tipped the balance. Surprised and revolted by the attack, their impulses had taken over, and carefully controlled feelings of excitement and righteous indignation had spilled over, instantly and without conscious awareness, into blind fury. Somewhere between the window rattling and the mincemeat assault, the vegetarians' mindfulness had deserted them.

"There she is!" said Joseph. He wriggled free of Kendal's grasp and ran along the ranks of the opposing armies towards where Mum had somehow popped out of the crowd and was now looking confusedly around her, the tablet still in her hand. Kendal followed, catching up just as Joseph threw his arms around her.

"What are you doing here?" Mum managed.

"We've got to - " Kendal started, but he froze as he felt hands grasping his shoulder, hauling him around. Suddenly, Farron's face was millimetres from his own, and filled with rage.

"You did, it didn't you?" Farron said. "You killed her!" He pulled back and Kendal felt Farron's fist slam into the side of his face, knocking him sideways. He staggered, clutching his cheek, and turned back towards his attacker. Farron lunged forwards. Kendal stuck his arms out to protect himself. At the same second, AMA's piercing shriek blotted out everything. The crowd reacted instantly. A forest of arms blocked ears, as the crowd doubled over.

After a second, the warning sound stopped, but the crowd paused for only a couple of silent seconds before they surged towards each other, fists and burgers flying. AMA's shriek came again, but this time, the crowd did not stop. Blinded and deafened by anger, Farron pushed Kendal's flailing arms out of the way and punched him hard in the stomach.

Kendal staggered as a sea of screaming vegetarians and meat throwers met, rushing in between him and Farron, ignoring the deafening scream of the Anger Management Artificial. Everyone was fighting now. Kendal scrambled through the bodies to Joseph and Mum. He yelled at them to get out. He couldn't even hear his voice in his own head over the sound of AMA.

It was going to take more than a loud noise to stop this battle, but AMA had more weapons in her arsenal. As Kendal grabbed Mum's arm in one hand and Joseph's in the other and started to pull them towards the edge of the fight, AMA delivered Stage Two.

Mediation would have been pointless right now, so AMA did not speak, but Kendal knew she would be taking notes. She would be collecting GPS data and facial recognition from CCTV and cross-referencing it with wristband feedback. Later, heartbeats and voice recordings would all combine to allow her to pick through the battle, moment by moment. Interaction by interaction. Untangling each confrontation and analysing it. In the coming days, everyone in the crowd would be forced to apologize and atone. Individual messages of contrition would be recorded and politely exchanged through an online safe-area set up for the purpose. The worst offenders would be mandated to relive the riot virtually from the point of view of their victims. AMA would work hard to counsel, to psychoanalyse, to allow everyone to understand the folly of their anger. By these methods, AMA dissolved disputes and made friends - lovers even - of enemies. But, now was not the time for that. Right now, as Kendal dragged Mum and Joseph away from Farron's reach, AMA let loose her second weapon. From the lamp posts on either side of the melee, two canisters were catapulted into the crowd, bursting open instantly as they hit the ground.

One stink bomb landed directly in front of Kendal, and in a second, the air was filled with the eye-watering stench of rotting flesh and human faeces. It was overpowering. A hundred times more concentrated than an open sewer, or an open grave, a gut-wrenching acid taste that sent waves of nausea up his nose and into his throat. Unable to breathe, Kendal reeled backwards, retching as he dragged Mum and Joseph with him, deeper into the crowd. Half the crowd were pushing backwards, scrambling over each other to escape from the stink. The other half, still unaware of the spreading gas, were battling on, punches and kicks swinging wildly in the joy of violence long-repressed.

Kendal found himself pressed against the window of the butcher's shop, somehow still holding on to Joseph and Mum. Here, the stench was bearable - Just. And in the doorway, Lady Bradley was still sitting cross-legged and silent, yogically distant from the chaos. Kendal saw a little smile play across her lips. This was probably just what she wanted to happen. If Mum really wanted to know how to do PR, he thought, you needed to know how to play AMA.

He pulled Mum and Joseph to the window, and they edged along reaching the outskirts of the crowd and bursting out into clean open air. Still gasping, they ran to the end of the street, and Kendal turned. Behind him most of the protesters had abandoned the fray and were making their escape. The hard-core of combatants were still hurling fists and meat patties at each other and he watched as AMA released her final, ultimate weapon of peace: canisters of medicinal cannabis were launched into the crowd. In a few minutes, even the most aggressive protesters would be sitting around chatting about the mysteries of the universe.

Kendal turned back. A single police car skidded to a halt just in front of them, and a policeman stepped out. He was about forty, uniform and skin slightly crumpled, his hair thinning. He didn't look as though he could stop a meat patty in flight, let alone defuse a riot. He glanced over at the melee, but made no move towards it. AMA had the demonstration under control.

"You're a bit late," said Mum. The policeman ignored her, and spoke directly to Kendal.

"We'd like to ask you some questions," he said, "about the murder of Lexie Doyle." Mum and Joseph stared at him, open mouthed.

Chapter 12

It was a cheap room, generic, bland in a synthetically friendly kind of way. It wasn't designed as an interview room. The police didn't have the budget for that. It was designed as a room for any purpose. Furniture, fittings, even decorations were adaptable, adoptable, multi-function, hot-swappable and cros-compatible with every combination or function you might desire that day. Today it was an interview room. Tomorrow it might be an office, or a prison cell. It was like every cheap room in the police station, every cheap office, every cheap hotel, school, or student's bedroom. The chair Kendal sat on was one single moulded biodegradable piece. It was one of a million. It was what you got when you didn't have the time or money or inclination to specify any terms in a product search. The chair was the design that would appear as the top item when you typed "chair" into a shopping app. Kendal picked at its arm with his fingernail. The chair arm was soft, denting under his finger. A scratch mark appeared as though the furniture resented the individuality he had imposed on it.

The desk across which he faced his two inquisitors matched the chair perfectly. It would not have looked out of place anywhere. On it was placed the one item in the whole room which was unique: Kendal's chocolate box, its top open, the dark ornate swirls within nestled in tiny individually shaped cups.

The first inquisitor, the policeman who sat, head cocked on one side, regarding the chocolates thoughtfully, tapping his fingertips together slowly, first the index fingers, then the middle fingers, then the ring fingers, and finally the little fingers. He looked up at Kendal, then back down at the chocolates and repeated the tapping, more slowly.

His companion was an avatar. Not a cheap domestic model like Kendal's, but an altogether more substantial creature. This one's skin was toughened glass, her joints reinforced. She was embodied by an Artificial, but one with an utterly unreadable face. Her head was hairless. It was colourless, expressionless, without age, race or distinguishing marks. Kendal found it both difficult to look at and difficult to look away from. Her eyes had no light.

Kendal shifted in his chair. The policeman said nothing, but continued tapping his fingers.

"What am I doing here?" Kendal blurted. "I haven't done anything!"

"Relax," said the policeman. "This is not a formal interview, just a chat. I'm Detective Inspector Gillmore. You can call me Anthony."

EVERYTHING YOU SAY WILL BE RECORDED AND MAY BE USED AS EVIDENCE. YOUR BODY LANGUAGE, BREATH AND SWEAT CONTENT IS BEING MONITORED FOR SIGNS OF DECEPTION, said the Artificial. Her voice was a sharp, metallic shriek. Female but not feminine. Not human. YOU WILL COMPLY WITH ALL INSTRUCTIONS! YOU WILL ANSWER ALL QUESTIONS!

"You'll have to excuse my friend," said Anthony. "New software update. I think her learning algorithm must have cross-referenced too many cop shows." He reached forward suddenly and grabbed a chocolate out of Kendal's box. The warmth of the man's hand instantly dissolved the white foam that surrounded it, and the smell of passion fruit drifted across the table, sweet and strong. Underneath the foam, the complex coil of dark and milk chocolate was revealed. He popped it into his mouth and his eyes widened. Despite everything, Kendal felt a surge of pride. The sweet had worked perfectly.

RECEIVING GIFTS FROM INTERVIEW SUBJECTS IS NOT ACCEPTABLE! YOU WILL RETURN THE ITEM, said the Artificial.

"It wasn't a gift. I stole it. Isn't that right, Kendal?" said the detective, smiling.

"Um... yes," said Kendal.

The artificial spun its head to face Kendal. DO YOU WISH TO REPORT THE THEFT? It said.

The policeman's smile vanished.

"I don't think you do, do you?" he said, his eyes fixed on Kendal.

"Um, no."

"I think that all you want to do is answer my questions - isn't that right?" He picked out another chocolate and popped it in his mouth. Kendal studied his expression. This sweet was shaped into a tiny octopus. Right now, as it warmed, the jelly tendons would be contracting, wrapping the arms around his tongue as it dissolved. Despite the situation, a part of Kendal's brain - a rather bigger part than was appropriate - was desperate to know if the confection had worked..

"Um… yes." he said. The detective's face broke into a warm smile.

"Excellent," he said. "These really are very good, by the way."

Kendal smiled. The part of his brain that craved adulation was, for a second, sated, and a tumult of confused feeling flowed in over it. He didn't know what his reaction should be, but his mouth was dry, and there was a knot in his stomach. Terror seemed the only appropriate one. "Thank you," he said.

"Now," said Gillmore, "here's what we've got." He leaned forward, popped a sphere of chocolate into his mouth, and paused while the layers cracked, spilling one subtly complex, but intoxicating fruit flavour after another, sweet followed by sour, followed by sweet. Kendal watched his eyes close and counted the changes of expression as the layers burst. Eventually, he cleared his throat. "We've got a dead girl. One of your classmates. Murdered quite, quite brutally last night. How well did you know her?"

"Not very well," said Kendal, his voice was wavering. "I just -"

"Because I'm told you took quite an interest in Lexie. Is that true?"

"I -" Kendal felt his face flush.

"And you left the prom at about the same time as she did, didn't you?" said the detective.

"I was with my date. We just went for a walk," he said.

NAME said the artificial.

"Imani," said Kendal.

FULL NAME. Kendal swallowed.

"I - I don't know her full name,"

CONTACT INFORMATION!

"I can't contact her," he said. "She was embodying an avatar."

"So this Imani wasn't actually there," said Anthony. "You were, in fact, alone."

76

CONTACT INFORMATION, said the artificial.

"I don't know it!" said Kendal, desperately. "The date was - interrupted."

"By Lexie Doyle?" said the detective.

"No! It wasn't like that." Kendal gasped. This was starting to look bad.

"But you can understand how I'd need more than that," said Gillmore. "This 'date' was not even there. And your GPS places you in the woods. In fact, according to my records, you were within 100 metres of her position. And you saw nothing?" Detective inspector Gilmore snatched up another chocolate from the box and bit down on it hard. A precise arrangement of honeycomb bubbles ranging in size from a millimetre down to just 100 microns in diameter shattered to dust in his mouth. Kendal put his hands to his face, an involuntary gesture that must have triggered the interest of the Artificial because the spookily featureless avatar leaned in threateningly.

"I heard - I think I heard her running."

"Running?" said the policeman. "Just that?"

GIVE FULL INFORMATION, said the artificial. TIMES, EXACT LOCATIONS, MORE DATA.

"I don't know!" said Kendal, "She was drunk, I heard her running, shouting."

"And you just ignored it?"

"I thought she was laughing, playing a game or something." It sounded stupid now that he told someone else. He wasn't sure even he would believe it. Detective inspector Gilmore sighed.

"The thing is," he said, "when AMA clocked you at the demo back there, she ran an automatic check over her logs for

77

the last 24 hours. It's standard procedure." Kendal felt suddenly sick. "You know what she found?" He shook his head, "Right at the moment Lexie's heart stopped beating, AMA picked up a flare of anger from your wristband. Now I wonder what made you so angry?" Kendal's mind flicked back to the previous night, his argument with Doreen when she had disconnected him from Imani. His wristband had flashed.

YOU REGISTERED EMOTION. YOU WERE AT THE CRIME SCENE. EXPLAIN!

"I- " Kendal wiped his forehead.

YOU ARE PERSPIRING. YOUR HEART-RATE IS INCREASED. EXPLAIN. EXPLAIN!

"I didn't kill her!"

YOU ARE CURRENTLY EXHIBITING SIGNALS OF STRESS, said the artificial. WOULD A CUP OF TEA HELP YOU RELAX?

"No tea!" said Detective Inspector Gillmore. "Sorry -it's the emotional responses - I keep telling them I need one Artificial for suspects and a different one for victim support. Instead they've given me one that's supposed to do both - budget cutbacks, you know?"

"I guess" said Kendal.

"She's supposed to take her cues from me," admitted Gillmore. "She thinks we're doing 'good cop, bad cop' but she can't work out which one I am. She's conflicted." Kendal was feeling the same conflict himself, he thought.

"You don't really think I did this, do you?" said Kendal. The policeman shrugged.

"You were there - nobody else was within five hundred metres. You've got no alibi. And you were angry." He paused, and swallowed another chocolate. He seemed to be thinking for a long time before he said: "But I've seen murders before. This one is odd. You always get an anger signature - always - but normally it builds up and up and up. You can see it like a graph. But yours - Just this little flicker." He shook his head, "And what happened to that girl - that wasn't a little flicker. That was proper rage."

"So you don't think I did it?"

"I don't know," he said. "If you did, then you're a cool one. But if you didn't, then it was someone whose wristband didn't even register. I don't know which scares me more." He drummed his fingers together slowly one at a time again. "I'm going to let you go for now," he said, finally, "but we're running tests right now. If you went anywhere near her last night, we're going to know about it."

"OK" said Kendal, "so I'm free to go?" The Artificial straightened.

DO NOT ATTEMPT TO FLEE. REMAIN CONTACTABLE AT ALL TIMES. OUR INVESTIGATION IS ONGOING AND YOU ARE OF INTEREST!

"I still have one more question," said Inspector Gillmore. He closed the lid of the now empty chocolate box, and pushed it over towards Kendal.

"What?"

"Did you really make these?"

Chapter 13

The Police Artificial escorted him to the doors in silence.

YOU MAY GO. WE MAY REQUIRE YOUR ATTENDANCE AT ANY TIME, she said. SIGNAL YOUR COMPLIANCE! Kendal nodded. The machine stared down at him. She leaned in until her own smooth glass generic nose was so close to his, he would have been able to feel her breath if she had had breath. SAY THE WORDS 'I COMPLY'! she yelled.

"I comply." said Kendal. His voice was shaking. His heart pounding.

YOUR STRESS LEVELS REMAIN HIGH. I SUGGEST YOU PERFORM AN ACTIVITY WHICH RELAXES YOU! screamed the Artificial. PERHAPS SOME YOGA. She swung away and stalked off down the corridor, clanking heavily with each step.

Kendal peered through the glass doors. Mum and Joseph were sitting in reception waiting for him. He didn't want to see them. There would be questions, and right now, he just couldn't think how he would answer them. Right now, he needed some time to think.

He ducked back. From where he was standing, he could see there was a blank avatar in reception. Just a communal one. Head and shoulders. Nothing flashy, but it was free. He pulled out his phone and called it up. Through the window, he saw his own face grow onto the inflatable torso.

It was odd to stare at himself through a window. Mum and Joseph leapt up. Kendal looked into his phone screen and let its camera pick up and transmit his best attempt at an unconcerned smile.

"Hi, Mum," he said.

"What's going on, what's happening?" Mum said.

"Are you going to prison?" said Joseph. He could see them both through the avatar's eyes, blinking back at him from his phone screen.

"Everything's fine," he said as brightly as he could manage.

"Where are you?" said Mum, "We're waiting for you in reception."

"Oh - sorry," he said, "I must have missed you. I'm on my way home."

"They've let you go already?" said Mum. "They said they'd tell us when you were out!"

"Really?" said Kendal, watching them through the glass door. "I guess the message must have got lost somewhere - I think they're a bit understaffed in there."

"That sounds about right," said Mum.

"I'll see you at home." he said.

"Wait a minute," said Joseph, "how did you get out without us seeing?"

"Got to go - battery dying," said Kendal. He rang off. He watched through the window as the avatar went blank and drooped. Mum marched up to the reception desk. She said

81

something to the avatar sitting behind it. The avatar shrugged, and smiled politely - doubtless a call centre operator in an office on the other side of the world, or more likely a basic Artificial with no useful information. Mum grabbed Joseph's arm and walked out.

Kendal waited until he was sure she'd gone and slunk out into the street.

It was late afternoon, and as he took the long way home, he turned events over in his mind. Detective Inspector Anthony Gilmore had let him go for now, but he doubted that would be the last he'd see of him and his tyrannical pet. They obviously had no other suspects, and when the forensics came back, they were bound to find something that showed he and his avatar had been standing over Lexie's still warm body. He should have confessed that - after all, he reminded himself, he hadn't actually done anything wrong apart from not reporting what he'd seen, and that had only been because he was afraid that whoever killed Lexie was still out there in the forest. He should have said that. Why didn't he say that? The answer, of course, was Mum. He couldn't say anything to the police because then he'd have to tell Mum he'd lied to her. Why had he done that?

But now that he had lied, not only to Mum but to the police, it was all bound to come out. Then he'd be the prime suspect. He had been there - the only person apparently who had been. He had history with Lexie - doubtless the school gossip train would be quick enough to concoct some story about his obsession and jealousy. "That Kendal - he was always an odd one - never quite fitted in - " he could see the interviews now.

And he had been alone. The only person who could back up his story was Imani, and he didn't know where she was, or how to contact her. Doreen had separated them permanently and irrevocably. There was no arguing with Doreen.

82

The only way he could prove his innocence now was to find out who had murdered Lexie Doyle, and somehow prove it before the whole thing got pinned on him. Kendal had a fair idea who that was too. He had never liked Farron. He had seen them arguing in that last photo, and outside the butchers, he had been so quick to accuse Kendal, obviously just trying to divert blame. Kendal had seen his wristband turn almost instantly from blue to red the moment he spotted him. It had to be Farron who killed Lexie. There was no other explanation.

The only question was how Farron had chased her through the forest and murdered her without triggering AMA, and how he'd got away again without leaving a GPS trail. Maybe he was cleverer than he looked.

If only he could talk to Imani again. Maybe she had seen something.

He stopped dead in his tracks. Of course, she saw everything! Somehow, he had to find Imani again.

Chapter 14

Kendal ran in. Mum was there, hovering in the kitchen. Clearly waiting. Clearly wanting to ask him what was going on. For a second, they locked eyes, but she said nothing. Maybe she didn't know where to start. Maybe she found the distance between them just as unbridgeable as he did. Kendal took advantage of her silence, smiled, grabbed the blank avatar from the corner of the room, and ran for his bedroom.

He pulled the avatar inside and locked the door. He read out a dial-up code. The avatar flashed blue and a familiar face grew in.

"Doreen?" said Kendal, "I'm looking for a date for this evening." For a moment Kendal wondered what her reaction would be after their argument the previous night. But as soon as she faded in, the artificial smiled kindly, their previous interaction not forgotten, but judged irrelevant to their current conversation.

THANK YOU FOR CHOOSING ME AGAIN she said I CAN SELECT THE PERFECT MATCH FOR YOU ON THE BASIS OF OVER FORTY KEY INDICATORS -

"Never mind that," said Kendal, "I want to use my own criteria. Can I do that?" Doreen looked puzzled. Even slightly offended, Kendal thought.

"YOUNG MAN, I HAVE A LOT OF EXPERIENCE IN THIS AREA, she said. MY ALGORITHMS ARE FINELY TUNED TO -

"Can I do it?" he said. Doreen paused. She didn't look happy.

ENTERING SWIPE MODE, she said, curtly. PLEASE ENTER YOUR KEYWORDS.

"OK," said Kendal. He rubbed his hands together. Doreen wasn't going to allow him to see Imani again, but there was just one possibility, "I'd like someone aged between 16 and 20," he said. "A girl," he added quickly.

SEARCHING, said Doreen. She closed her eyes for a couple of seconds, then opened them again. MORE THAN HALF A BILLION MATCHES. Imani hadn't just entered her details and matched with him. She'd faked her profile. That meant there was a chance that, if he managed to track down her real profile, Doreen wouldn't recognise the two Imanis were the same person. But he would need to narrow down the options. What did he know about her?

"Brown eyes!" he said. "I want someone with brown eyes. About 155cm tall."

SEARCHING.... 150 MILLION MATCHES.

"Dark skinned," he said.

YOU ARE NOT PERMITTED TO SELECT PARTNERS ON THE BASIS OF RACE, OR SOCIO-ECONOMIC BACKGROUND, said Doreen. PLEASE CHOOSE ATTRIBUTES ON AN INCLUSIVE BASIS.

"Ok," said Kendal. "Someone from Africa,"

SEARCHING.... MORE THAN 20 MILLION MATCHES.

"Ok - From the -" he struggled to remember. "Barka!" he said.

SEARCHING…. OVER 20000 MATCHES.

It was no good. He needed to find a way to reduce those numbers.

"Can I refine that search by only looking at people who live close to people I've already met?"

YOU CAN, said Doreen, BUT ONLY TO A RADIUS OF TEN KILOMETRES. YOU HAVE 500 MATCHES.

"Great!" said Kendal. "Can you show them to me?"

There was the hiss of air escaping from the avatar, and Doreen dissolved into a short girl in loose jeans. She was smiling a frozen smile. Just a still image being projected onto the avatar. The girl's dating profile. It wasn't Imani.

Across the girl's chest, a blue band appeared, fading from light to dark, left to right. On either side, a row of glowing arrows. Kendal reached out and touched the middle of her chest. He dragged his finger over her, swiping left. The image faded, then morphed into another girl. This one was taller, more angular, elegant in her own way, but not Imani. He swiped again.

The avatar inflated, and shrunk at the same time. A plump, serious girl appeared. Black short hair. Thick eyebrows. He dragged a finger across her chest. The avatar started to grow again, pale skin started to fill in. Kendal didn't wait for her facial features to form. He swiped her away. And again, and again.

An hour later, Kendal was still swiping his way through the girls of Imani's town. Each beamed hopefully into his bedroom only to be instantly rejected. He was getting a feel for the place through its teenagers.

Wherever Imani lived, it was a town divided. In one group were the locals: strangely formal profiles, portraits in brightly-coloured, but old-fashioned clothing. Make up precise - as though they were dressed for a wedding, their own, maybe? The genetic mix was narrow too, as though the same few faces were recycled in different bodies. In the other group were obvious outsiders. Fresh young white faces, tanned red and dressed in walking gear. Travelers - they weren't posing to meet a life partner, probably. The dating database for them was just a way to hook-up and check out the next town down the road. He swiped on.

The avatar hissed, and glowed, inflating and deflating. Noses, lips, hips rose and fell, grew and shrunk until they became a blur in front of him. Kendal's arm felt heavy. The end of his swiping finger was becoming raw. His brain was drifting. He had to keep snatching his attention back to focus on the faces of the girls as they flew by.

Once or twice he thought he saw her as he swept past. His heart leapt, and he swiped back only to find another girl resolving herself in front of him. Like Inami - a little like her, maybe. But by now he had seen so many faces, he wasn't even sure he would recognise her anyway.

Suddenly a familiar face grew in. Doreen.

YOU HAVE BEEN SWIPING FOR A LONG TIME. YOU SHOULD TAKE A BREAK TO AVOID REPETITIVE REJECTION SYNDROME, she said. AS YOU ARE A NEW USER, I AM OBLIGED TO WARN YOU THAT ONLINE DATING CAN BE ADDICTIVE AND SHOULD BE PRACTISED IN MODERATION. Kendal closed her, and carried on swiping.

More faces. More bodies. It went on. Perhaps she didn't have a profile. Perhaps she'd lied about where she lived. Perhaps he hadn't remembered it right.

The avatar grew. Slimmed. A long elegant neck. Hair dropping down over the shoulders. He recognised her before her face even formed. Before the cheekbones extended. By the time her lips arrived, he was certain. Her clothes were different in her profile image. More traditional, he supposed. A long white dress. Cuffs and front embellished with a wide strip of green and gold interlocking diamonds. Her skin flowered out from it, just as it had when she had first appeared to him, until it covered her head and hands. She was smiling a posed, uncomfortable smile under layers of formal make-up.

"Her," said Kendal.

HER NAME IS IMANI, Doreen said, her face replacing Imani's on the avatar. SHE IS -

"I want to meet her," he said. "Can I see her now?"

SLOW DOWN, YOUNG MAN, said Doreen. YOU MAY SEND HER A BRIEF MESSAGE. SHE WILL CONTACT YOU IF SHE IS INTERESTED.

"OK, send her a message." said Kendal.

AS THIS IS YOUR FIRST TIME MESSAGING A POTENTIAL DATE, I CAN GIVE YOU SOME ADVICE. THE GIRL YOU HAVE CHOSEN RECEIVES AN AVERAGE OF ONE HUNDRED AND FIFTY MESSAGES PER DAY.

"Just tell her I need to see her," said Kendal.

AS A NEW SUBSCRIBER, YOU ARE PERMITTED TO SEND A MAXIMUM OF FIVE MESSAGES PER DAY. THIS GIRL REPLIES, ON AVERAGE, TO ZERO MESSAGES PER MONTH. DO YOU STILL WISH TO PROCEED?

Yes," said Kendal.

PLEASE RECORD YOUR MESSAGE NOW. REMEMBER TO BE POLITE AND COURTEOUS. TRY TO BE FUNNY. TRY TO ENGAGE HER, PERHAPS WITH A

QUESTION ABOUT HERSELF. ABOVE ALL, RELAX AND BE YOURSELF. YOU HAVE TWELVE SECONDS. PLEASE RECORD YOUR MESSAGE NOW:

"Imani? It's Kendal!" he said, "Thank God I've found you, I need to see you. It's important!"

TIME UP. MESSAGE ENDS, said Doreen curtly. ACCORDING TO MY VOCAL AND COLLOCATIONAL ANALYSIS, MESSAGES OF THIS TYPE HAVE A VERY LOW RESPONSE RATE. I SUGGEST YOU RETRY, ATTEMPTING TO SOUND LESS NEEDY, AND REMOVING REFERENCE TO 'GOD'. MESSAGES OF 30-50 CHARACTERS, CONTAINING NO NEGATIVE EMOTIONS WORK BEST. WOULD YOU LIKE TO RE-RECORD YOUR MESSAGE?

"No, just send it."

ARE YOU SURE?

"Yes!" said Kendal. "Send it now."

Doreen closed her eyes. There was a soft 'ping'.

MESSAGE SENT.

"How long do I have to wait for a reply?" said Kendal.

I WOULDN'T HOLD YOUR BREATH, YOUNG MAN. YOU HAVE FOUR MESSAGES REMAINING TODAY. MAY I SUGGEST YOU ALLOW ME TO ADVISE YOU ON THE BEST WAYS TO FIND A PARTNER? YOUR CURRENT APPROACH IS SUB-OPTIMAL AND IS UNLIKELY TO RESULT IN ANY KIND OF - there was another soft ping. MESSAGE RECEIVED. WOULD YOU ACCEPT A LIVE CALL?

"Yes," said Kendal smiling. The avatar went blue, and Imani resolved into it. This time she was dressed simply, in a

89

sand coloured tee-shirt. She wore no make-up. His stomach jumped involuntarily. Imani looked serious.

"Hello," she said. "It's nice to meet you."

"It's me, Kendal!" said Kendal.

"You said that in your message," she said. She paused, and then said, very slowly and carefully: "Your first ever message to me. It's very nice to meet you FOR THE FIRST TIME." What was she talking about? Kendal's head was spinning. Did she not even remember him?

"Something's happened. A girl at my school was murdered in the woods -" started Kendal. "I need you to -" her eyes widened.

"I really like Doreen," she said, meaningfully, "don't you?"

"What are you talking about?" he said.

"I'm sure there will be plenty of time to chat about school friends," said Imani, "if you ASK ME OUT ON A DATE."

"What?"

"Perhaps we can have a nice meal together. Somewhere we're ALONE?" The penny dropped. Imani knew more about the way Doreen worked than he did. Like AMA, Doreen obviously listened out for trigger behaviour constantly - they'd found that out on their last date. But perhaps she was programmed to pay closer attention to pre-date conversations. Perhaps she was actually listening in right now.

"Right!" he said, "I saw your profile and - um -"

"And you thought I looked lovely?"

"Yes, that's right, I thought you looked lovely."

She smiled. "And?" she said, "what else?"

"Umm…" he said, "I liked your dress."

"My mum made me wear it. It's traditional. It's meant to attract a husband. Try again."

Kendal blushed. "Ok," he said. "Your eyes are like dark pools -" Imani laughed.

"Now you're trying too hard," she said.

"You're enjoying this aren't you?"

"Why don't you just ask me out?" she said.

"Well?" said Kendal.

"Do it properly." Kendal blushed again.

"Would you do me the honour of going out on a date with me?" he said.

"That's better," she said. "You come to me. We can go for a walk."

Chapter 15

"How long are you going to be in there?" Joseph was hammering on the door. Kendal closed the lock.

"I've only just come in," said Kendal.

"Mum! Kendal's in the VR room again!" wailed Joseph. "You said I could play Megazoids! I'm stuck on the breakout level!" It was a tiny room, barely bigger than a cupboard. It had been converted from the house's second toilet when VR technology had kicked in.

"You can do it on the screen in your bedroom!" Kendal shouted through the door.

"It's rubbish on a screen!" he protested. "Megazoids needs touch feedback!"

There was nothing special about their little VR room. Just a headset and a trackball floor that rolled under your feet, allowing you the freedom of feeling you could walk in any direction. The trackball could move back and forth too, allowing you to walk up or downhill or to feel undulating terrain. On the walls, inflatable latex, like the material from which the avatars were made pulsed organically - ready to shape itself to provide touch-feedback on anything he might touch on his virtual date. That was why Joseph wanted the room. The walls were already tatty, marked by his filthy hands and feet where he had punched, kicked and been buffeted by the aliens in "Megazoids" and a hundred other games.

"Leave Kendal alone." It was Mum's voice. "Let him have a game if he wants. You're on VR far too much!" Outside, Kendal heard Joseph grunt and skulk away. His bedroom door slammed.

Kendal pulled on the helmet and tapped in the address code Doreen had provided him with for the date. He felt a jolt from the trackball under his feet as he instantly embodied an avatar standing in a village on the other side of the world, and the VR room's responses switched to allow him to feel what the avatar felt, hear and see what it heard and saw. Inami faded in directly in front of him.

For a second, he was in two places in his mind. He was in the VR room, with Mum and Joseph just a few paces away in their little house. At the same time, he was in a field of scrubby brown grass, where a few dry trees rose.

He looked up. It was sunny. He felt the heat. A part of him knew it was just the VR room warming up to reflect the weather, but that thought lasted only a couple of seconds before his brain synced with his senses and he completely bought into the illusion of place. It wasn't a choice. You couldn't fight VR. You could tell yourself over and over where you really were, but your brain would never believe it. Within a few seconds the avatar's body became his own, and he swore he could feel the breeze pinging his arms with dry Saharan sand, and smell the soft smell of Imani's skin as she stood close, smiling up at him.

"It's good to see you," she said.

93

"And you," said Kendal, suddenly embarrassed. He had been so preoccupied, he had not prepared himself to treat their meeting as a date. Her smile changed that in a second.

He looked around. The nearest houses were a good five hundred metres away, a cluster of sun-baked buildings. They were made up of seamless curving walls, and regular repeating patterns. Identical stamped out housing. Two or three designs scattered, repeated and adapted around the intersection of a straight road and a thin winding river. It was a classic kit town. The remains of a concrete-printing arm lay in the sand. Imani looked back at the town, then at Kendal.

"We should walk," she said. She led him away from the settlement and between two rocky outcrops of sandstone which rose up around them, hiding them from view. She walked on, the ground slowly rising.

"Where are we going?" he said.

"I don't want my family to see you," she said.

"Why?"

"They've got standards," she laughed. "So, you didn't track me down because of my stunning personality, did you?"

He shook his head. "Someone was murdered," he said. The story spilled out of him. All of it. Maybe there was still a part of his brain that knew she was not really there, standing in front of him. Maybe the lie of VR allowed him to be more honest, but somehow it was OK to tell Imani that he had not reported the body. That he had been scared. That he had lied.

They walked slowly, winding their way up the rocky hill, and she listened in silence. She seemed deep in thought. He finished the story. She turned to him, and for a second it was as though she wanted to say something, but she remained silent.

They stopped at the top of the rocky outcrop. On the other side, the view was down onto the savanna. The river wound away, a pure blue line bordered in green on a brown yellow canvas. In the distance, a familiar long low building stretched.

"You've got a farm here too?" said Kendal.

"One of the biggest," said Imani. "Easy solar here - plenty of power, and you can't grow anything so land is cheap."

He looked over at her. "Would your family really not approve of me?" he said. She turned to look back.

"They're - protective," she said, quietly.

"Then why did you come out with me?" said Kendal. She shrugged.

"I wanted to see what it was like, I guess," she said. "Do you do everything your family tells you?"

"So it was just a game to you?" he said. She looked away, but said nothing.

There was a long silence. Kendal looked at her. Her face shining in the hot sun. her eyes were just as huge as they had been the previous night. He leaned in towards her. She pulled away.

"We'd best be careful," she said. "We mustn't trigger Doreen." They moved apart. "So, what do you want me to do?"

"You're my only alibi," he said, "If you give a statement saying that you were with me - send your timestamp - then that will prove I couldn't have done it."

She thought for a second.

"I can do better than that," she said.

"How?"

"Don't you remember? I was in VR the whole time!" she said.

95

"So?"

"So that means it's all recorded! I've got a full 360 VR recording of the whole evening. We can go back there and see what really happened!"

Chapter 16

"Are you going to be in there all night?" It was Joseph.

Kendal's mind snapped back like a dog reaching the end of its lead. He was not in Barka. He was standing on a rotating carbon ball in a converted lavatory. He ripped the headset off. The walls were pulsing back into smooth flatness. The climate returning to the more clement temperature of a British summer.

"OK, OK! He shouted back. "I'm finished!" He stepped out of the room. Joseph pushed past him, huffing.

"You were in there for hours!" he said. He slammed the door, and locked it. Almost immediately, Kendal could hear his brother smashing and punching at the walls. "Peeow! Ughh!" The muffled grunts came through the door.

Kendal turned. Mum was standing in the doorway.

"We need to talk," she said. It was almost a plea.

"About what?"

"You know very well what," said Mum. "About why we just spent three hours at a police station. About why they're saying Lexie Doyle is dead. About why they think you had something to do with it."

He knew this was coming. Sooner or later he had to talk to her. But what was he going to say? What could he say?

"I -" he said, "I didn't do anything!" Mum's face softened. She reached out and touched his arm. The feeling of it made him jump a little. He was almost expecting the rubber touch of her avatar. Her real hand felt warmer, more intense. His eyes instantly filled with tears, and he couldn't work out why. He pulled away.

"Oh, darling, I didn't think you did for a moment. I just want to know what it's all about. Are you in trouble?" she said. Kendal shook his head.

"They had to talk to everyone who was at the prom," he lied. "It was just - routine."

"And you didn't see anything?" she said.

Kendal thought of Lexie's dead face. The scratch marks all the way down her side. He clenched his teeth to force back the tears, and shook his head.

"No." Maybe it would be OK. If Imani was going to put in her statement, then that should be enough to clear him. If the two of them could find something in the VR record of their date, then they might even be able to sew it all up. Farron would get arrested and the whole thing would be over. Mum need never know. Everyone would be happy. Everyone except Lexie.

"Are you sure?" she said. He clenched his fists.

"Yes." Another lie. Bigger this time because she had asked him outright. She had forced him to actually speak it. "I'm just upset because she was my friend." he said. Bigger still because now it was not just a lie. It was a story. She was never his friend. Those feelings only ever went one way. Mum put her arms out for a hug. He didn't move. She stood awkwardly in the doorway, arms out. He felt the distance between them grow a little larger.

Suddenly the door buzzed. The moment was broken. Relief flooded over him. He stepped to the front door and flung it open.

It was AMA, and she was not alone.

The artificial stepped through the door without waiting to be invited. She was embodied in a solid hardened glass avatar like that of the police artificial. She clearly meant business. Behind her, Farron stepped in out of the darkness. He locked eyes with Kendal and would not let go.

"Hello," he said, "nice to see you again." It sounded like a threat. Kendal stared back at him.

THERE, said AMA, WE CAN ALL BE CIVIL IF WE TRY.

"What are you doing here?" said Kendal. Beside him, Mum was looking worried. Drained.

PART OF MY ROLE IS TO ANTICIPATE AREAS OF POSSIBLE FUTURE CONFLICT AND DIFFUSE THEM BEFORE THEY HAPPEN, ALLOWING INDIVIDUALS TO RESOLVE THEIR DIFFERENCES IN AN ATMOSPHERE OF MUTUAL UNDERSTANDING.

Kendal stared blankly at her. "It's late," he said.

I HAVE IDENTIFIED THE POTENTIAL FOR DISAGREEMENT, AND AM THEREFORE OFFERING YOU THIS OPPORTUNITY TO RESOLVE MATTERS AMICABLY. She said, NOW.

"And if I refuse?" said Kendal. AMA smiled, and spoke more slowly and more calmly.

THAT IS, OF COURSE, YOUR CHOICE, said AMA. HOWEVER, I ADVISE THAT YOU TAKE THIS OPPORTUNITY TO AVOID EMBARKING ON A MORE

FORMAL PROCEDURE. Kendal felt his heartbeat rise, but fought to remain calm.

"Ok," he said through gritted teeth. AMA beamed at him.

YOU ARE OBVIOUSLY A VERY PERCEPTIVE AND INTELLIGENT PERSON WHO IS EAGER TO RESOLVE YOUR DIFFICULTY, JUST AS MY FRIEND FARRON IS. THAT'S SOMETHING YOU HAVE IN COMMON! Farron scowled behind her. IS THERE SOMEWHERE WE CAN SIT AND CHAT?

"The kitchen," said Mum.

AMA led them into the kitchen and sat Kendal and Farron opposite each other. Mum sat down too. AMA stood over her.

I CANNOT PURSUE DISPUTE RESOLUTION IN THE PRESENCE OF THIRD PARTIES.

"But he's my son."

I CANNOT PURSUE DISPUTE RESOLUTION IN THE PRESENCE OF THIRD PARTIES.

"This is my kitchen."

THIS DISCUSSION MUST BE A PRIVATE ONE. Mum glared at her for a second. DO YOU HAVE ISSUES YOU NEED ME TO HELP YOU RESOLVE? Mum opened her mouth as if to say something, then closed it again, and walked out.

"Are you going to offer me a lemonade now?" said Farron sarcastically. He was still staring at Kendal.

DO YOU WANT A GLASS OF LEMONADE? said AMA.

"No, he doesn't," said Kendal. "Farron wants -"

PLEASE REFER TO HIM AS 'MY FRIEND FARRON' DURING THIS DISCUSSION. IT WILL REINFORCE YOUR POSITIVE FEELINGS TOWARDS HIM.

"Because my friend Farron wants to kill me," said Kendal.

"Like you killed my girlfriend?" said Farron. "My friend Kendal." he added.

"I think you know I didn't," said Kendal.

"What's that supposed to mean?" said Farron.

WELL DONE, said AMA. GRASPING EACH OTHER'S MEANINGS IS VERY IMPORTANT TO UNDERSTANDING. I THINK WE'RE MAKING PROGRESS.

"You know exactly what I mean," said Kendal. "Why did you do it? Why did you kill her?"

GOOD. EXPLORING EACH OTHER'S MOTIVATIONS ALLOWS US TO FIND DEEPER CONNECTIONS AND SIMILARITIES.

"I didn't kill her. You killed her." said Farron.

"Really?" said Kendal. "You did and I can prove it."

"Don't make me laugh," said Farron. "You did it. Everyone knows it."

TRY NOT TO SPEAK IN ABSOLUTES, said AMA. REMEMBER, THE ONLY THING WE CAN KNOW FOR SURE IS WHAT WE PERCEIVE OURSELVES TO FEEL.

Ok," said Farron, "I feel that you murdered Lexie." He hadn't taken his eyes from Kendal's. "Everyone feels that you murdered Lexie. And I feel like somebody's gonna make you pay for it." He stood up and leaned over the table, his face close to Kendal's. "I feel like you need to be looking behind you, my friend, Kendal, because a lot of people have been talking about you and I feel it's my duty to warn you that someday soon, somebody's gonna take a knife and carve you up the way you carved her up." His hand flew up to his own face, making Kendal flinch, and he slowly drew his thumb down from his temple to his neck, describing the exact path of the cut on Lexie's face.

Kendal felt a cold, sick feeling in his stomach. He stared at AMA, expecting her to step in. How was she missing this stuff? This was the chatbot that had diffused the Afghan Standoff, brought peace to the Middle East, stopped Joseph from breaking his phone - all with her combination of witless automaton platitudes and absolute, data-driven power. But Farron had just threatened to kill him and she was just sitting there like some meditating statue. How come she was letting Farron get away with this?

WELL, DONE. I THINK SHARING OUR FEELINGS IS MAKING A BIG DIFFERENCE. SHALL WE BREAK FOR NOW. IF THERE ARE STILL UNRESOLVED ISSUES, WE MEET AGAIN IN A COUPLE OF DAYS - I THINK YOU WOULD ENJOY SHARING AN AFTERNOON OF COMMUNITY GARDENING. RESEARCH SHOWS YOU WILL BE 80% MORE FRIENDLY BY THE END OF IT.

Farron smiled. AMA smiled. Kendal looked back and forth between them. Surely she must be able to see that Farron had just threatened to kill him. He had proved himself capable of murder already. Kendal tried not to look scared.

The Artificial got to her feet, and padded to the door. Each step even and measured. Her hands cupped in front of her. She exuded calm in a way no human guru could. Behind her, Kendal and Farron stared at each other with barely concealed hatred. AMA looked straight ahead. Of course, Kendal realised, her eyes did not need to move. She had perfect 360 degree vision. If she wasn't commenting on their expressions, it wasn't because she hadn't seen them. It was because she chose to ignore them.

"Goodbye my friend," spat Farron.

"Goodbye my friend," said Kendal, narrowing his eyes.

Perhaps, he thought, as he watched them walk away, she had some longer term plan to bring them together. Perhaps she was using some subtle new technique that would manipulate him into being best buddies with the murdering thug. Maybe she just didn't know what she was doing.

Either way, as he closed the door, Kendal was shaking. Jolts of fear and anger stabbed at his chest. Farron had killed Lexie. He was sure of it. And now he had threatened to do the same to him.

He turned, and jumped with shock. Mum was standing in the hall right behind him.

"You scared me," he said.

"And you're scaring me," said Mum. "The police was one thing, but if AMA thinks there's something going on -"

"We just had an argument at school," said Farron.

"About what?" said Mum.

"Nothing."

"I feel like I'm being shut out of your life." she said.

"I don't want to talk about it!" said Kendal. "I'm going to bed." He set off towards his room.

"You come back here!" she said.

ANGER MANAGEMENT WARNING said AMA from the speakers. Ama was always there. Always waiting, thought Kendal. But it didn't matter. She wouldn't have to separate them. This conversation was over.

"Leave me alone!" he shouted, and slammed his bedroom door.

Chapter 17

Kendal threw himself on his bed. His mind was spinning. He'd been really dumb. He'd accused Farron of murder. What was worse, he had told him that he had proof.

He flicked up that last picture of Lexie outside the prom onto the ceiling and zoomed in on Farron. He was facing the camera, but his face was shaded. He was standing - legs apart, leaning forward, arms spread wide, chest out. By his body language, it definitely looked as though they were arguing. Lexie was facing away from the camera, looking up at Farron. She was pointing up at him, finger in front of his face. She looked so small standing in front of him, so slight.

He zoomed in further, and scanned down to Lexi's wristband. It was orange. But when he panned over to Farrons, it showed a pale blue. No sign there of murderous intent. Somehow, Farron must have chased Lexie through the wood, and murdered her without triggering AMA. Kendal's little disagreement with Doreen - his little amber warning - had been enough to get him picked up and questioned by the police, so how did Farron stay so calm?

There were some people, Kendal had heard, who could do terrible things, but feel nothing. Or at least hide their feelings from AMA. Was Farron a psychopath? It didn't seem to fit. If anything, Farron was too quick to lose his temper. He'd lost it down at the town square. It didn't make sense.

Of course, AMA wasn't infallible. She could only work on what she could see. Wristbands measured heart rate. Security cameras and avatars captured body language. Microphones captured tone of voice. All of these things could be analysed and cross-referenced, but they were just symptoms of feeling. They weren't actual emotion. What would AMA have to go on in the wood? Farron's GPS and his heartbeat. Muffled audio from the mic on his phone maybe. Less than optimal data. Maybe she mistook the sounds for high-spirits just as he had - the heartbeat for excitement. Just another teenage date. If you were an artificial, then love and hate were probably hard to distinguish from just a heartbeat and some heavy breathing. Emotion was all about context in the end.

If Farron was the killer - and there seemed little doubt that he was - then he now knew that Kendal had evidence against him. And he had already threatened to kill him.

Kendal turned off the phone screen, and lay there in the darkness. He heard Mum calling Joseph out of the VR room.

"Bedtime," he heard her say, and then a few muffled complaints before he heard Joseph shuffling off to the bathroom, and then into his bedroom. The door slammed unenthusiastically. Enough to signal his disapproval at being sent to bed, but not enough to start an actual argument. He was obviously tired.

After that, the house was quiet. Mum had to get to work early tomorrow, so that would leave the whole morning for he and Imani to revisit their date. They would hopefully find enough to clear Kendal, and if they were lucky they'd be able to implicate Farron too.

He let himself drift towards sleep. He wasn't sure how long had passed before he felt an orange light through his eyelids. He opened them. Outside his window, a street lamp had flickered on. Energy saving, motion sensitive, it had detected something.

It was a hot night and the house had responded by leaving his ground floor window wide open. The house system obviously felt it was a low-risk policy. Two days ago he'd have agreed with them. Now he knew better.

"Close windows," he whispered. The windows swung slowly shut and Kendal peered out into the street. Thin glass between him and the outside. He could see nothing out there. The street-lamp flickered again and went out. A fox, maybe - although the street-lamp ought to know the difference.

He stood, for a few more seconds watching. Listening. Then there was a sound. A soft, unidentifiable, but definitely human sound coming from somewhere inside the house.

Kendal's rational mind told him there was nothing to worry about. Nobody could have got in. The house would have detected anyone who wasn't supposed to be there within seconds. But, then, that last interaction with AMA had him worried. It was easy to think of her as the great pacifier - an artificial with an almost god-like perception of the subtleties of human emotion, and yet, in the end, she was just a series of learned responses. She had missed a blatant death-threat from Farron.

What if he was immune somehow from the interpretation of artificials? What if he was some kind of a blind spot for them? Kendal told himself that was absurd. But still, he could definitely hear something coming from the kitchen.

He pulled on a dressing gown and opened the door. The passageway was dark, but a dim blue light was flickering from the kitchen. The sounds were louder now. A voice. Two voices.

He silently flattened himself against the wall from where he could look in through the kitchen door without being seen. From where he was, he could see one side of the kitchen table but not the other. A figure was sitting, sobbing quietly.

It was Mum. She looked up and towards what must have been an avatar in the chair opposite. Kendal could see its pale blue light reflecting on her face like the light of a screen, but dimmer, and paler. It made her look almost like an avatar herself, but he could see her eyes shining with tears.

"I just feel so completely alone," she said, "as though I've got nobody. Nothing. I don't know what to do." Her voice was soft. Pleading with the avatar.

Kendal felt a heaviness in his chest. He had shouted at her. This was his fault. Across the table, the avatar responded.

I UNDERSTAND HOW YOU MUST FEEL, it said. The voice was familiar, but Kendal couldn't quite place it. EVERYBODY SHOULD HAVE SOMEONE.

"Yes," said Mum, quietly.

SOMEONE TO HEAR THEM. SOMEONE TO UNDERSTAND THEM. SOMEONE TO LOVE THEM. Mum nodded. EVERYONE DESERVES THAT.

"It's as though I just can't connect with people." she said.

IT MUST BE UNBEARABLE FOR YOU, said the artificial. MANY PEOPLE EXPERIENCE DIFFICULTIES WITH CLOSENESS.

"Is it my fault?"

YES. BUT I CAN HELP.

Kendal edged around so that he could see the figure sitting opposite Mum. It only took a second before he realised who it was.

Doreen.

REMEMBER, she said. I AM HERE FOR YOU. I AM HERE TO HELP YOU - ALWAYS. Mum looked uncertain.

"I'm thinking I need to stop online dating," she said. "Maybe I need to concentrate on my kids - even try to meet someone local - someone real."

AN INTERESTING IDEA, said Doreen BUT THIS WILL CERTAINLY REDUCE YOUR CHANCES OF FINDING THE IDEAL MATCH.

"Maybe I just don't have an ideal match - maybe I'm too broken." said Mum, sobbing. Kendal wanted to run over to her, but something stopped him.

THERE IS SOMEONE OUT THERE FOR EVERYONE, said Doreen.

"But what if there isn't?" said Mum, "What if there's nobody for me?"

YOU WILL NEVER KNOW IF YOU DO NOT TRY, said Doreen. I CAN SCHEDULE ANOTHER LIST OF POSSIBLE DATES FOR YOU.

Mum's head dropped to her chest. The air seemed to go out of her like an avatar shutting down.

I AM VERY ENTHUSIASTIC ABOUT THESE MATCHES.

"Ok, "said Mum, sighing.

YOU HAVE MADE THE RIGHT CHOICE. WOULD YOU LIKE ME TO SYNCHRONISE WITH YOUR CALENDAR?

"Ok."

I ALWAYS ENJOY OUR LITTLE CHATS, said the artificial.

"Thank you, Doreen." Mum's voice was just a whisper. "I don't know what I'd do without you."

NOW, CANDIDATE #1...

Kendal backed away. Helpless guilt pulled down on his chest like a lead weight as he slunk back to his room, and pulled the covers over him.

Chapter 18

By the time he woke up, Mum had already left. An unwashed coffee cup stood on the kitchen table. It had left a series of dark rings overlapping on the surface where it had been picked up and put down many times. Opposite where she had been sitting, the avatar still stood, blank now.

"Where's Mum?" Joseph had appeared behind him, already dressed.

"Work," said Kendal. He wiped the surface where the coffee cup had stood, erasing her night.

"I went to her bedroom," said Joseph. "She hasn't been to bed."

"Oh," said Kendal without looking at his brother, "she was probably busy." She must have been swiping all night. He rinsed the cup out and put it away. Joseph hovered in the doorway for a second. He seemed about to ask something, but then he thought better of it. "I'm using the VR this morning," said Kendal. He readied himself for a fight. Instead, Joseph just shrugged.

"Ok," he said. "I'm going out." Kendal let out a sigh of relief. He didn't want to explain to his brother that he was going to revisit his date to look for clues to a murder. As he turned, he noticed Joseph had a rolled up towel tucked under his arm.

"Where are you going?"

"Swimming at the weir." said Joseph. Kendal knew the place. It was only about ten minutes from the house, a popular spot in the summer, where the river widened and a brick wall had been built to form a little waterfall, and below it a shaded pool. It was safe enough, but Kendal knew Mum would have wanted him to go with Joseph to look after him.

"Not on your own," said Kendal.

"If I can't go, I'm using the VR!" he said. Kendal thought for a second.

"Who else is going?" he said.

"Some friends," said Joseph, vaguely. "I'm meeting them there." He was probably lying. It didn't much matter. It was going to be a warm day. Even Joseph couldn't get into that much trouble.

"Take an avatar with you, so I can see you're ok," said Kendal. He thought for a second, "Take Mum's. It's the best. The other one's reception is a bit flaky. But look after it," he added. "Don't use it as a float. It's not waterproof."

"Ok," said Joseph. He grudgingly took the avatar's arm, and led it to the door, trudging out as though he'd been unfairly treated, but he was half grinning. Kendal knew his brother had been expecting not to be allowed to go on his own. He felt a little guilty, but having Joseph out of the way for the morning suited him well.

He grabbed breakfast - a quick-print cereal bar. Designed for convenience and energy, not taste, it felt like cardboard in his mouth. Normally he didn't touch the things. He'd have taken the time to print some hybrid fruit and experimental patisserie. Some variation on a mille-feuille with a lattice of summer berries separated by puff-pastry. But not today. Today, he just stuffed the nutritious snack into his mouth, chomped down on its carefully arranged combination of slow and fast release sugars, swallowing its trademarked anti-allergic non-specific nut constructs, locked himself into the VR closet, and pulled on the helmet.

Imani was already there. In fact, she was there twice.

He was standing in the school playground. It was early evening. In front of him, the school hall was flashing and thudding with the sounds and lights of the prom. One Imani was standing opposite him.

"Hi," she said, smiling at him.

The other Imani - Prom Date Imani was walking across the playground towards them, hand in hand with the other Kendal. The couple were dressed as they had been that night. Her in her shifting, shimmering red dress. Him, uncomfortable in his over-shiny blue suit.

Kendal realised that the two were walking directly towards them. The overdressed pair completely ignored their doppelgangers and instead walked straight ahead, deep in conversation.

"Did I really look like that?" said Imani, looking her previous self up and down as she approached. Kendal laughed and nodded. The couple were almost upon them now, and Kendal had the pointless urge to step aside to make way for his virtual self. Instead, he only flinched slightly as the two ghosts walked straight through him, still hand in hand. They headed away towards the hall without a backward glance.

"Old VRs are weird, aren't they?" said Imani. "It sort of feels like you shouldn't be here. Like you're dead, watching your life from the outside."

"We'd better follow them," said Kendal, "before the resolution degrades." Behind him, he could see edges of the playground starting to become blocky and indistinct. The 360 degree camera mounted on top of Imani's avatar during their date was designed to capture everything she might see or hear around her. The technology allowed her, standing in her own VR room, to look around freely as though she were actually standing next to him. It stored a full image for her of everything she could have seen had she chosen to look at it. The 360 degree recording was then available for Kendal and Imani to revisit, seeing it from new angles and noticing what had not noticed been before.

There were, however, limitations. The camera could only capture what Imani could see, and the further away from her avatar the two viewers wandered, the lower the resolution of the world, and as it faded off into invisibility, shapes became merged, indistinct, blocky and misleading. Kendal and Imani jogged after their prom-selves, just in time to see them step in through the hall door.

Suddenly, as Prom Imani dodged out of sight, the playground glitched and went dark. A couple of patches of wall beside the door - sections which Imani's avatar must still have been able to see - remained visible for a second as flat polygons hanging in empty space. Then they too flickered and vanished, leaving the present versions of Imani and Kendal standing alone in an empty black void.

Disorientated, they ran forward in darkness, for a moment, and then, as they broke through the wall of the school hall, suddenly the whole party enveloped them, and they were back in the noisy flashing chaos of the prom.

There were Lance and Gerry sitting in the corner, embodied in lank-haired avatars. There were Danielle and Rory, the poser couple, comparing their ornate hair sculptures. Mr. McPhearson spun in a new song. It was "When I really see you" by Denzil France - the star Imani had been trying to fake Doreen into

113

matching her with when she had ended up with him. Kendal grinned at her.

"Come on!" said Imani, "dance with me." She started to move her hips, raising her hands above her head. Then she reached out and grabbed his hand, and for just a second he felt it for what it was - the moulded rubberised wall of the VR cloakroom reaching out to mimic her. The tiny empty white room he knew he was really standing in. The taste of his breakfast bar still in his mouth. He froze for a moment, suspended between two realities.

"I can't," he said. "I know what's going to happen."

"It doesn't matter," said Inami. "This is all going to be OK," she smiled. "Just dance." He watched her spin around, and she pulled him towards her with her latex hand. And then the music took him, and he started to move.

"That's right," she said. The dance floor was full, but they were all ghosts. Imani and Kendal moved around and through his schoolmates, swinging and spinning until he almost allowed himself to forget why they were there. There was something slightly crazy about Imani when she danced. Legs stamping the floor, head whirling, hair flipping back and forth in a long, swooping trail. Almost as if she were trying too hard, forcing herself into the music until nothing else mattered. Her face was a wide grin, though, and when she caught his eye, it felt like something real.

And then, he glanced up and passed her to the other side of the dance floor where his prom-self was staring straight back at him. His other self raised his hand and pointed directly towards him. The look on his face was odd. Surprise, recognition, and something else. Something like a strange, distant sadness. A chill went through him. This was a recording. How could he see himself?

114

And then he realised, and the chill grew to envelope him. His ghost wasn't pointing at him. He was pointing at what he could see in Kendal's place. Right in the middle of the dance floor. He was standing right where Lexie was dancing, spinning, laughing. He was inside her, seeing himself from her point of view. A strange uncomfortable boy, just one of fifty in the room, hovering at the edge of the dance floor.

He stepped quickly to the side, and there she was in front of him, grinning, whirling, carefree. Enjoying the last two hours of her life. She paused in her dancing and turned to look directly at him. She moved in close, centimetres from his face. Her eyes looking straight into his. She tilted her head. He realised she was about to kiss him. His stomach lurched as he realised he must now be standing inside Farron. Lexie's lips moved closer. He froze, unable to move. It felt strange, wrong. Imani was beside him, watching.

Lexie laughed and reached down suddenly to snatch something from Farron and dance away. Kendal followed her gaze. She had grabbed a bottle. The same bottle of clear liquid he had noticed her drinking before. She whirled around, swigging from it.

Kendal stepped out of Farron, disorientated for a moment. He staggered. Farron looked annoyed for a second at missing out on the kiss, but then danced after her, grabbing her waist. Kendal watched.

"Is that her?" said Imani.

"Yes."

"You liked her, didn't you?" she said. Kendal looked away.

"We should skip this bit, " he said. "Forward wind to the wood."

115

Imani lifted her arm, and made a gesture in the air, a sweeping shape that signalled to the software. The scene around them scribbled into fast motion. Dancers flung themselves around at impossible speeds. The music and babble of voices rose in pitch.

Suddenly, without the two of them moving, the ground skidded under them. The doorway grew until it wrapped around Kendal's vision, and then vanished away into the distance. They were outside, the sports field skating past them. It took a dizzying second for him to realise what was happening. This was the moment when they had gone outside to walk down to the meadow. With Imani's avatar on the move, the playback software was now compensating, repositioning them inside the scene the avatar had recorded while that scene was still playing in fast forward.

The result was a strange, disconnected vortex, a tornado of changing shapes and people, in which Imani was the only fixed point. She was solid and real, moving at normal speed while everything else was in constantly reconstructing turmoil around them. Off in the distance, Kendal could just make out Prom Imani and Prom Kendal juddering hand in hand into the trees. As the avatar capturing the scene, she was the centre of this universe, and wherever she went, charging in fast-motion, the rest of the world formed around her, and today's Kendal and Imani - the two voyeurs of her world - were dragged behind like feathers floating in the slipstream of a juggernaut.

The trees rushed around and over them, their gentle stroll through the wood transformed into an insane roller coaster. Finally, the scene stabilised where the walk had ended. They were standing on the edge of the woods, looking out over the field to the farm in the distance, their ghost selves a few metres away.

"Stop!" said Kendal. Imani held her hands up and the scene slowed to normal playback.

"Don't be like that, I like you." It was Imani's voice, but as he turned, he realised it was coming from the wrong girl. His virtual date, his two-day-younger replica answered.

"Do you?" he watched. They both watched, remembering the moment. He was moving in for the kiss now. From this angle, Kendal thought, he looked more certain, more confident than he had felt back then.

Their lips met. Images of two real people now. Imani's avatar automatically replaced in the record of the event with a scan of the real Imani. So now he had two memories of the moment: one of him kissing her inflatable avatar, feeling its moulded lips against his, knowing she was not there, but feeling connected with her in a way he had never felt connected to anyone before; the other of him watching from the outside as the two apparently real bodies kissed in front of him. In his mind the two images ran into each other, but did not mix. Like beads of oil and vinegar they refused to blend, sitting instead as separate intense tastes. That was what VR did for you: it confused your perspective. Or maybe it didn't. Maybe it was just memory that did that.

As his memory fractured, his feeling fractured too. How did he feel about that kiss then? How about now? Was he jealous of himself? Embarrassed retrospectively? Was this moment of observation more or less real than the time in the wood? How about her having a completely different experience. She had been in a VR room in her concrete printed desert town, kissing what, a wall? It was too confusing.

Not to an artificial, of course. To an artificial it was all part of a single unified data stream. To Doreen, for example, it all made perfect sense. The kisses deepened, the touches became more intimate. Kendal shifted uncomfortably, feeling Imani -

today's Imani - doing the same beside him. Both unable to tear their eyes away from their moment.

Suddenly, everything went blank. The end of the recording. Doreen had pulled the plug. In the absolute blackness, only the two observers remained. Kendal and Imani in the empty dead void. She turned to him. There were tears in her eyes.

"I can't see you again," she said. "I'll do this for you - I'll give my statement - but after that -"

"Why?" said Kendal, feeling a lump in his own throat.

"It was a mistake," she said.

"How can you say that?"

"I'm sorry -" she said, "I thought it was going to be just a game, but it's not. I have to stop it before we both get hurt."

"I don't understand," said Kendal. She took his hands in hers. He felt them - soft, insubstantial like everything else in this world.

"I can't, "she said simply. "I just can't."

Chapter 19

She let go of his hands, and straightened. Her voice became firmer. "Right, we need to go back - how far?"

"Ah, yes," said Kendal, still reeling, "about ten minutes." She waved her hands, and the scene zipped back into view, reversing. Trees whizzed past. The couple walked backwards up towards the school. "Here," he said. The action froze and then played back. "I'm sure I heard her somewhere in the wood," he said, "running."

Their old selves were walking slowly through the forest. Kendal was holding her hand to steady her. As they talked, they followed themselves in silence. Kendal listened. He couldn't do anything else. The avatar's camera captured everything they could see around them, and they could wander freely in its virtual world, but its microphone broadcast sound to them as though they were standing right next to it. However far they wandered from the couple on their date, Kendal could still hear himself sharing his most intimate hopes and fears with the girl who wanted to never see him again.

Suddenly he heard it. A high-pitched scream. Somewhere over to their left. Lexie's voice. He had put it down to drunken laughter, but knowing what he knew now, there was no mistaking it. The sound came again. Panic. Fear.

"This way!" he shouted, and started running through the trees. Imani followed. He held his arms up in front of him - a reflex action to protect his face, but the trees were ghosts. He felt nothing as he hurled himself through them in the direction of the sound.

"Stop, we can't go any further," said Imani behind him. Kendal came to a halt in a small clearing. A fallen tree to his left. A wall of dark branches interlinked in a thicket to the right. Above them, the moon was shining through the high branches. A bright silver crescent. Everything else was dark.

They had moved too far from the couple. Around Kendal, the VR had begun to break up as the avatar's camera struggled to reach into the forest. Resolution was lower here. Finer branches blurred into each other. Trunks had hard, pixelated edges. The darkness swam in flickering shades of black and brown as the software tried to interpolate from patchy data. Algorithms made their best guesses and tried to fill in the blank spaces. The shapes they saw were like the landscape of a bad dream, snippets that could have been parts of trees which actually had been there, or could have been copied and pasted from other sections of the reconstruction combined to intelligently fill in the blanks and create a believable, if inaccurate view.

Kendal squinted into the dark. A shape shifted. It looked out of place. He moved in, and realised it was nothing - a section of speaker from the hall. The VR software had obviously been missing a few pixels of data and slammed in a texture it thought might fit. Yes, thought Kendal, VR and human memory suffered from exactly the same problems.

"This is hopeless," he said, "we're too far out."

Suddenly, the fuzzy outer edge of the simulation twisted and burst inwards. Lexie resolved out of it. Running, one shoe missing. Terrified.

"Freeze," said Kendal. Imani raised her arm. The scene froze.

Lexie was mid-step, pitched forward. Her one shoe twisted against the ground. Her bare foot out behind her, skirt frozen, flying out as she ran. Her head twisted, looking back into the fuzzy, unreconstructed darkness. Blonde hair was plastered across her face. Her eyes bulged. Her mouth twisted in terror.

Imani lowered her hand and the scene sprang back into life. Lexie's foot turned sideways and she pitched forwards, flailing as she sprawled into the leaf covered ground right in front of Kendal and Imani. She rolled over, staring back into the darkness in horror, kicking herself backwards, scrambling to her feet, and then she turned and fled, diving through the thicket on the other side of the clearing.

Kendal turned back to stare into the swirling edge of the VR capture. Whoever was following must only be seconds behind. But instead of another figure resolving itself out of the pixels, the whole wood started to blur. The fuzzy edge of the world seemed to loom, closing in on them.

"What's happening?" said Kendal.

"I must be moving - my avatar must be moving away." she said. He turned. She was right. Between the trees, he could see their two ghosts wandering away, and as they did so, the edge of the captured world collapsed with them, swallowing up the clearing into unreadable chaos.

"Come on," said Imani, "maybe we can see more later on. Where was she killed?" she said.

"Down there," he pointed off towards the edge of the forest.

"Forward in time, then," she said, and waved a hand in the air. In a few moment of rushing, blurring trees, they were back at the edge of the clearing, their previous selves standing hand in hand in the moonlight. The square-edged shape of the farm buildings could be seen in the distance.

"Don't be like that. I like you," Imani was saying again, as the world slowed to normal speed.

"Down here," said Kendal, leading her away along the narrow path between the forest and the long grass of the meadow. The shape of the huge, rusting tractor rose in front of them. He stopped a metre from it. "I found her behind here," he said. The memory of that moment hovered around him, and he shuddered.

In the background, he could hear a sound. A wet sucking sound. Unpleasant and organic. It seemed to be coming from all around them. It took a second for him to remember that the avatar's microphone was not there with them. That it was not picking up sound from around them. The noise was from up at the top of the slope. It was the sound of kissing.

He and Imani exchanged a brief uncomfortable glance. He tried to shut the noise out as cautiously the two of them approached the broken shape. The glass in its cabin was shattered, its tyres rotten. Brambles were reaching up through its radiator grill and ivy had wound its tentacles around the axles and the frame. It looked like a dead thing, angry and rotten. Kendal forced himself to remember that nothing here could hurt them, that everything in this place was a ghost, but his mind wasn't buying it. In his head, the forest, the tractor, and Lexie were all real. The only thing that was different this time was that now he knew the future. The two of them slowly approached the side of the tractor and peered around it.

122

There was nothing there. Nothing at all. It was a dead space, like a shadow, but pure dark. The deep blackness of the un-constructed void - a blank area in the modelling of the virtual world. Imani looked back towards their other selves.

"There's no data," she said. "The tractor is blocking the avatar's view so we can't see behind it." A part of Kendal was glad. The memory of Lexie's body was clear enough in his head. He didn't want to see it again.

Suddenly, she appeared, running blindly out of the wood onto the path and up towards them. She smashed into the radiator grill of the tractor, centimetres from Kendal's face, making him gasp. She cowered against the ancient machine, staring back into the forest. Of course, thought Kendal. They were too early. The detective had told him Lexie died at the same moment that his own wristband had registered his argument with Doreen, so that must have been after she removed Imani from their date. After the end of their virtual world. And that must be only seconds away now.

Lexie was looking around wildly. Her breathing was coming in deep gasps and sobs. She was leaning against the tractor for support, doubled over, clearly weak with exhaustion. Unable to go on running. As Kendal watched helplessly from a metre away, Lexie fought to control her ragged breath, and stared back into the forest. Her face was alive with horror and confusion as she steadied herself, looked out across the field for some cover to run for, but there was nothing. Finally, she tucked herself into the dark shadow behind the tractor, disappearing from Kendal's view for the last time.

"Freeze on the last frame," said Kendal. Imani made a gesture. The world ran for just a few more seconds, then the froze. The sound of kissing was, mercifully cut off. The branches stopped swaying. The grass stopped waving. The clouds paused on their journey across the moon. Kendal had thought it was a still night. It wasn't until all sound and movement stopped that he realised just how much movement there had been in the wood.

"The killer must be close," he whispered.

"She came from that direction," said Imani. She pointed up the path, further out towards the blurred edge of the captured world. They slowly traced her path. With every step, they were moving further from the kissing couple, and the forest was losing integrity. As it became less distinct, more degraded around them, trees faded into shadow, their trunks sliced into rough, hard-edged polygons. Bushes were replaced by simple angular shapes with the images of brambles wrapped and smeared across them. Branches hung in the air above them, their fine twigs gone and the connections to their trunks missing, leaving them suspended in twisted chunks.

"There!" said Imani suddenly. She pointed between the trees, and there, blurred and pixelated, a running figure stood, held in mid-leap. It was some metres away, but Kendal felt a cold chill. One thing was obvious: It wasn't Farron.

It wasn't Farron because it wasn't human.

They approached. The creature was suspended at the very edge of the avatar's perception. A strange combination of angular, flat planes and blurred, smeared images painted onto them described its shape, but there could be no mistake. Whatever was chasing Lexie was some kind of animal.

Kendal and Imani circled around it, examining it in shocked silence. A few broken pixels were all that made it up, but close-up, Kendal could guess at a shape. Four short, muscled legs, stretched in a running pose. At the end of each, leg, large feet, claws, or possibly sharpened hooves. A thick, stocky body, dark brown - almost black but strangely patched with pink, and front heavy. A suggestion of coarse fur running along the spine, and then spreading to cover huge heavy shoulders. It could have been a hog, almost. Some strange breed, but it was bigger. Much bigger. At the shoulder, the animal stood as tall as Kendal himself.

The head was large, wide and flat, held level to the ground, but the creature's height meant that Kendal was looking directly into its face. The capture had formed it as a single cube, but the textures wrapped onto it showed a broad flat nose, slanted white eyes, wide with vicious hatred. Strangest of all were the teeth. Rows of long, translucent pointed fangs, as long as Kendal's fingers. Sharp spikes that reminded him of the teeth of some deep sea creature.

"What the hell is it?" said Imani. Kendal shook his head.

"I don't know," he said quietly.

"You need to get the police," she said.

Chapter 20

Within a few seconds of putting the call in, Detective Inspector Gillmore appeared in the forest next to them. He was seated on a tree stump, arms straight out on front of him.

"Make this quick," he said, "I'm driving." His arms moved, miming driving a car.

"You're not in VR?" said Kendal. "You're here on a screen?"

"Yes," said the policeman. He was staring straight ahead, as though through the window of a car. Typical, thought Kendal, that meant he'd be looking at the scene on a little screen on the dashboard. Some camera had captured his real posture and was feeding it live to his virtual self in the frozen wood. It looked faintly ridiculous, as though the detective was a five-year old playing at driving a car. "I have a busy life," he said, looking serious.

"You drive yourself?" said Imani, incredulously. "I didn't think anyone still drove a manual."

"I don't trust artificials," he said. He turned his head to address an invisible passenger sitting next to him." No offence," he added.

NONE TAKEN! yelled a disembodied voice which Kendal recognised immediately. It was the detective's aggressively harsh, but strangely caring artificial. I ESTIMATE THAT I AM

CURRENTLY TAKING AT LEAST 87% OF THE CRITICAL DRIVING DECISIONS!

"I enjoy driving," explained detective Gillmore.

YOU ENJOY THE ILLUSION OF DRIVING, she said. PLEASE CONTINUE, IF IT MAKES YOU FEEL MORE SECURE!

"Thank you, I will." he said. The detective inspector's eyes flicked down away from the road to where his screen was obviously placed. His expression changed to one of surprise. "Where the hell are you?"

"This is Imani," said Kendal, "The girl I told you about. My - um -"

"Your date, right?" said Gillmore.

Kendal nodded.

"Is she real?"

Imani looked slightly embarrassed.

"Yes, I'm real," she said.

"Ok-" said Gillmore, "I thought maybe - well. I don't know what you kids do these days."

"She's real!" said Kendal.

CONFIRMED, said the disembodied artificial. YOU ARE NOW BOTH UNDER SUSPICION.

"Imani was in VR the whole time." said Kendal, "She has the whole thing recorded. We're in the wood, this is about a minute before the murder. We've got Lexie running - we've got ourselves twenty metres away."

Detective Inspector Gillmore looked at the screen for a long time. He took his hands off the wheel, and leaned down, prodding the screen, swiping and zooming. Instantly, his image in the forest vanished from where it was sitting and slid in a flickering arc around the creature, facing it throughout. It was as though he was on a track, orbiting it, zooming in and out as his fingers pinched and swiped at the screen to pan and rotate his viewing angle. From his point of view, Kendal realised, he must just be spinning the scene on his phone. From Kendal's, Gillmore appeared to be rocketing - still seated - around them, over the treetops and through the ghost of the meadow.

WARNING, said the invisible artificial, APPROACHING LORRY.

"Whatever," muttered inspector Gillmore.

WARNING! COLLISION DANGER.

The inspector swiped again, and swivelled around, winding up, leaning forward, just in front of the creature's snout.

TAKING CONTROL! said Gillmore's artificial. In the background. A second later, Gillmore jolted sideways suddenly, as though his whole world had swerved to the left. I HAVE SUCCESSFULLY AVOIDED YOUR DEATH!

"Not now," said Gillmore. "I'm working."

- FOR THE THIRD TIME ON THIS JOURNEY, finished the artificial. Kendal imagined a tone of smugness.

"What is this thing?" said the inspector.

"It's your murderer," said Kendal.

"Is this a joke?" said the policeman. "Or some kind of fake - or a videogame?"

"No!" said Kendal. "This is real."

TIMESTAMP CONFIRMED, THIS IS A GENUINE RECORDING. IT HAS NOT BEEN TAMPERED WITH.

"It can't be!" said Gillmore. "Check again."

CROSS REFERENCED, yelled the artificial. THIS IS A GENUINE RECORDING. IT IS ADMISSIBLE EVIDENCE.

"But this is... I don't know what the hell this is!" said Gillmore. "Are you saying this thing killed Lexie Doyle?"

"Yes," said Kendal, "and it's still out there, somewhere."

THANK YOU. YOUR HELP IN THIS INQUIRY IS APPRECIATED. CAN I HELP YOU WITH ANYTHING ELSE?

"Wait a minute," said the Inspector, this isn't over."

ANIMALS CANNOT BE ACCUSED OF MURDER, said the artificial.

"But we don't know what it is!"

TAXONOMIC IDENTIFICATION IS NOT PART OF POLICE PROCEDURE, said the artificial. Inspector Gillmore was still staring at the creature - or rather down at his screen.

"Humour me - I like detective work."

YOU LIKE THE ILLUSION OF DETECTIVE WORK, said the artificial. I ESTIMATE THAT I MAKE 87% OF THE TACTICAL DEDUCTIONS IN OUR RELATIONSHIP.

"We are not in a relationship," said Gillmore. "I'll need a copy of this capture." he jabbed the screen. The world went blue for a second to signify that a copy was being downloaded. "If I need anything more, I will contact you."

"But this thing is still out there!" said Kendal, looking back at the creature.

"We have to assume that, yes," said Gillmore.

"Are we safe?" said Kendal.

"I wouldn't go back to the woods at night," said Gillmore. He paused, dragged his finger, and spun around the creature again. "In fact, probably best steer clear of the whole area."

"Is that it?" said Kendal. "Is that all you've got?"

"I'll tell you if we find out anything else."

WE CANNOT PROMISE TO UPDATE THE PUBLIC ON THE PROGRESS OF AN INQUIRY!

"Shut up, and drive," said Gillmore. Then there was a pause. He looked over to where the avatar was sitting. "What is it?" he said, suddenly.

EMERGENCY CALL, said the artificial in an utterly level voice. CALL TEXT READS: HELP. HELP. THERE'S SOMETHING IN THE WATER. UGHHH WHAT THE HELL... The artificial delivered the emergency call as though it were reading a shopping list. COME QUICKLY. PLEASE, PLEASE. IT'S COMING.... MESSAGE ENDS.

"Where is it?" Gillmore said.

THE RIVER. UP AT THE MEADOW.

"I'm driving," yelled Gilmore. He grabbed the wheel and vanished instantly from the wood. Kendal felt like he'd been hit in the chest. That was about half a kilometre upstream from the weir where Joseph was swimming.

He almost threw Joseph's avatar code at Imani. "Embody this!" he yelled. "Tell him to get out of the water!" He grabbed the VR helmet and wrenched it from his head, skidding as the trackball jolted under his feet. Disorientated for a second, he stumbled, slamming into the soft, white wall of the cubicle. He grabbed the bolt, swung it back and ran out into the hallway. He ducked into the kitchen, grabbed a carving knife from the knife-block and threw himself towards the door.

In a second, he was out of the house, sprinting barefoot out into the street and down towards the edge of town. He was panting, sweating already. Too much good food had left Kendal hopelessly out of shape. Too many chocolates and too much pastry. He hauled the phone from his pocket and it sprang to life. He fumbled to connect to the VR room and Imani, and patched through. By now, he was at the end of the road. He turned down the narrow, winding lane that lead down towards the river, the gravel path cutting at his feet as he ran.

From his phone, Kendal could hear Imani's voice shouting "Get out of the water! Get out of the water!" In the background, there were sounds of laughing and splashing. He looked down at the phone. The screen showed the view from the avatar Joseph had taken with him.

His brother must have ignored his instructions about taking the avatar into the water because the camera showed a bobbing, floating foam of splashing waves. For a second the avatar was floating on its back, and the clouds rolled past against a blue sky, then it tipped over, and it was underwater. An explosion of bubbles cleared to show murky green water, a flash of kicking legs. The mud and reeds of the riverbank.

The camera righted itself again and Joeseph's face bobbed into view, filling the screen, grinning.

"Who are you?" he said.

"You have to get out of the water!" Imani was shouting.

"Are you my brother's girlfriend?" Joeseph giggled. "Kendal's got a girlfriend. Kendal's got a girlfriend!"

Kendal looked up. The path ahead looped around, down the side of one meadow and around another before it reached the river. It would be a few seconds quicker to cut across. He turned and dived through the thick bushes, forcing his way through into the thick, yellow grass beyond and took a direct course diagonally through the meadow towards the river.

It had been a long time since he had run this far or this fast. His heart was pumping now. He was gasping for breath. He ploughed through the field, sweeping the thick grass away in front of him, and stomping it underfoot as he ran.

He glanced at the phone as he closed in on the edge of the first meadow. Imani was screaming at Joseph now, but he just wasn't getting it. Kendal could see the avatar's arms flailing in front of it as Imani tried to grab Joseph and pull him towards the bank, but it was hopeless. The avatar had the strength of a ragdoll and the swimming ability of a lilo. Besides that, she was trying to control it by miming swimming while standing on dry land in a VR closet somewhere in the hot desert. Imani herself probably couldn't even swim.

Kendal crashed through the bushes at the edge of the field, back onto the path for a second as it snaked by, and then vaulted an old, broken wooden gate into the last little meadow leading to the weir.

His feet sank instantly. This field was a swampy mess of thick green watercress, tangled, lush leaves and stalks that curled out of black silty mud. Kendal hauled his legs out, and dragged himself forward, leaning, swinging his arms in front of him, forcing his way through the thick green knots of weed.

"There's something in the river!" Imani was shouting. Kendal looked down. On his phone, the avatar's camera had bobbed and drifted so that it showed the waterfall. Spray clouded its view, and the sun shone from the silver sheet of water falling over the curving brick waterfall. For a second, there was something else in the picture. Right at the top of the waterfall, a shape. Long, tapering. Silver scales. It shot over the waterfall, hitting the water and vanishing beneath.

"What was that?" It was Joseph's voice. Kendal heard it twice. It was coming from his phone, but also from just ahead of him now, just through the last row of thick bushes in front of him. With one final heave, he burst through onto the riverbank. In front of him, the low semicircle of the weir spanned the width of the river. Above it, the water was smooth and flat. Below it, he saw a churning, brown green mess, and in the centre of that mess, Joseph, gripping onto Imani's avatar.

Chapter 21

Kendal didn't stop. He threw himself forward, off the bank, skidding feet first down the two metre high sloping wall of the waterfall. It wasn't his first time sliding down the weir. They called it the 'death-slide'. He and Joseph had played there ever since he could remember, and he knew exactly the angle to take the jump and the moment to bend his knees and slide on his bottom into the pool.

But Kendal had failed to take one thing into account. He had never done the death-slide with his clothes on. His shoe caught in a crevice in the brick and toppled him forwards so that he fell, sprawling, hands and head first into the water on the other side of the pool from his brother.

His knuckles jarred against the jutting rocks at the bottom of the pool, and he just kept hold of his phone and the knife as he was enveloped in black and green water. He came up gasping, spinning around. The cold hit him. He shook his head to clear the stinging water from his eyes and he looked over to where Joseph was splashing, staring wildly around him.

Choking and gulping for air, he shouted "Get to the side!" Kendal started to swim towards his brother, arms and legs heavy with the weight of his soaking clothes. In front of him,

Imani's face bobbed to the surface. Her inflatable robot body was not designed for swimming, but she was doing her best.

"Use the avatar!" shouted Kendal as he ploughed through the water towards them. Imani lifted her arms and wrapped them around Joseph, pulling her body towards him, and he grabbed her waist, using her as a float as he kicked frantically towards the side of the pool.

Kendal was an arm's length away when he saw it. A slender blue-silver shape cutting the water between them. What was that? A fin? It appeared for just a second, and vanished again down into the murky green water.

Suddenly, a hard, sharp blow which struck him straight in the ribs, lifting him half out of the water, and knocking the breath out of him. Desperately, he swung down with the carving knife in his hand. He felt an impact. A tearing. Whatever hit him turned away. The fin, or tail, or whatever it was, whipped around, grazing his chest as it powered away. There was blood in the water. Kendal couldn't tell if it was the creature's or his own.

Blinded for a second, he reached out wildly. His arm made contact with something and when he opened his eyes, he realised it was his brother, floundering in the water. Imani's air-filled body was gripping Joseph. Her arms around him, trying her best to help him kick his way to the bank only a few strokes away now.

"Are you ok?" shouted Kendal. Joseph managed a nod.

"Where is it?" said Joseph, looking wildly around. From the bank, there was a voice.

"Over there!" Kendal looked up. It was Inspector Gillmore, running towards them, pointing into the water behind them. "Swim!" he shouted.

135

Kendal turned. A v-shaped wave of water, pushed by a fast-moving shape, was heading straight at them. At its apex, a head. Long, pointed. It seemed to have no purpose other than to hold its huge, gaping tooth-filled jaw. The head somehow sat half-way between crocodile and shark. It could have been either, but it was neither. It powered towards them.

"Give me the knife!" Imani shouted. Kendal shoved it into her rubber hands. "Now get out of here!" she yelled. Kendal grabbed Joseph, unwrapped his brother's arms from his date's body and flung her towards the creature's jaws.

Now he kicked as hard as he could, covering the distance to the bank in a few seconds without looking back. Gillmore reached down and hauled first Joseph, then Kendal, out of the water.

Kendal struggled to his feet and turned in time to see Imani's arm swinging the knife wildly as the huge jaws tore into her. The avatar's body was shredded by now, but the arm kept moving, stabbing and slicing as it was carried by the force of the creature's momentum into the shore. Blood and mud clouded the water.

In a few seconds, it was all over. The creature drifted dead into the shore, the tattered remains of the avatar still in its teeth.

"What the hell is it?" said Kendal. Gillmore shook his head in disbelief.

"It attacked somebody upstream," he said. "They're in the ambulance. I followed it down here."

Together, they hauled the creature out of the water, and laid it on the bank. Kendal bent down to examine it. It was the most bizzare thing he had ever seen. The size of a man, not quite fish, not quite reptile. It was like the result of some horrific experiment. A patched-together creature of scales and claws and jaws. It was the shape of a huge vicious tadpole, with a long tapering tail, swelling to a massive head and small fore-legs sticking out from just behind its

136

jaws. It could have dragged itself on land, but not very far and not very fast. A fin ran down the length of its back from the tip of its tail to the top of its head, held rigid by tall barbs. At the tail end, it had the smooth, slimy skin of an eel, but towards the head, the skin broke up into uneven welts and nodules, becoming thick, armoured scales around the jaws. Its eyes were deep set and bulbous white, staring out towards the rows of inward curving needle teeth. Kendal stared down at it.

"This isn't what attacked Lexie," said Kendal. "This is something else." Gillmore nodded.

"But look at the teeth," he said. "They're the same."

Kendal reached down. In the animal's mouth, the remains of the avatar lay, sparking and flickering. Its hand - Imani's hand - still gripped the carving knife which was embedded in the creature's belly where several long gouges had been opened up. Something black was seeping out of the wounds.

Kendal turned the avatar's head around. It was attached to the body by just a few torn wires, but the projector was still working. Imani's face flickered on and off as her nose slowly deflated. Her eyes were wide, shocked, as though she had seen something impossible.

"What is it?" said Kendal.

"I -" she started.

"What?" said Gillmore, leaning over them. "Do you know what this thing is?"

"No," she said, "but -"

"But what?" said Kendal.

"I have to go," she said.

"You saved us," said Kendal, cradling her head in his arms.

"This is all just too complicated. I need to think," she said. "I'm sorry." The avatar flickered again, and her image slowly faded.

"Don't go!" said Kendal, but the avatar was dead.

Beside him, Joseph looked down at the torn and bloodied remains of Imani's avatar and the bizzare creature.

"Promise you won't tell Mum," he said.

Behind them, the Detective Inspector's car pulled up, bumping over the rough track at the side of the river. Its sirens died, and the glass avatar stepped slowly and smoothly out. It paused for a second while its camera scanned the scene, then it strode over to the detective inspector, and stood beside him, looking down at Kendal and Joseph.

PLAYING IN THE WATER WITHOUT ADULT SUPERVISION CAN BE DANGEROUS, she said. A PUBLIC SAFETY FILM IS AVAILABLE ON THIS SUBJECT. I WOULD SUGGEST YOU VIEW IT TO LEARN TO AVOID COMMON RISKS SUCH AS SLIPPING, COLD, BECOMING TANGLED IN WEEDS, INJURY WHILE DIVING, DIARRHOEA CAUSED BY WATERBORNE CONTAMINANTS....

"OK," said Gillmore, "enough." The artificial looked down at the creature, lying on the bank.

THIS OBJECT COULD PRESENT A HAZARD.

"You're telling me," said Kendal.

SOMEONE COULD EASILY TRIP OVER IT. The artificial reached one glass hand down into the creature's mouth, grabbed it by the teeth, and dragged it easily over to the back of the police car. The boot opened, and the avatar reached down, picked up the creature and shoved it into the boot, coiling its tail neatly in after it. The boot closed slowly on its own as the avatar walked back. She looked down at Joseph, sitting shivering on the bank, his face white.

HAVE YOU HAD A DIFFICULT EXPERIENCE? asked the artificial, giving a generically kindly smile. I AM ABLE TO OFFER VARIOUS TYPES OF TALKING THERAPY AT A BASIC LEVEL. She crouched beside him. PLEASE DESCRIBE THE NATURE OF YOUR EMOTIONAL DISTRESS. Joseph stared at her, but said nothing. I UNDERSTAND: THIS IS DIFFICULT FOR YOU. HOW WOULD YOU DESCRIBE YOUR RELATIONSHIP WITH YOUR MOTHER?

"She's my mother," said Joseph, looking blank.

INTERESTING!

"Come on," said Inspector Gillmore, "Let's get this back to the office." The avatar stood and marched back to the car. It opened the door and climbed in.

YOU BOYS STAY SAFE NOW, she said.

"I'll drive," said Gillmore.

Chapter 22

"It's ok," said Kendal to Joseph. They had walked almost all the way home in silence.

"I know," said Joseph. "I'm fine!"

"I was scared too," said Kendal, putting his arm around his brother. Joseph pushed it away.

"Well, I wasn't," he said. The two rounded the corner into the driveway.

"It's all right to be scared."

"I said I wasn't scared. I'm fine!" said Joseph, "Why do you have to keep trying to hug me? It's stupid!" He stormed inside, slamming the door behind him. Kendal opened it and followed him in. Joseph threw himself onto the sofa, hiding his face.

"Do you want to play Megazoids?" He said. Joseph looked up. His eyes were red. He shook his head.

"I hate Megazoids," he said. "I'm stuck in that stupid fort with all the Megazoids breaking in and I just keep dying!"

"We could do two player - I could help you," said Kendal.

"You're rubbish at it," said Joseph. "The breakout level is the hardest. You just die all the time anyway." Joseph was right. Kendal was rubbish at videogames.

Kendal reached out a hand to him. "Do you want to play something else?"

"Just leave me alone," he said.

Kendal shut himself in his room, and lay on his bed. His head was spinning. Nothing made any sense. He shut his eyes. It must have been several hours later when he heard the front door open, and Mum coming in. He had to tell her now. He had to tell her it all. He forced himself to get up and walk through into the kitchen where she was fixing a coffee.

"Did you boys have a good day?" said Mum. He opened his mouth to speak, but she was getting her phone out already.

"We went swimming," said Kendal.

"That's nice." Mum was looking down, scan-reading something on her screen.

"Mum, I need to tell you some things -" he started. She looked up.

"Uhuh?" she said, but her thumb was still swiping on the screen. Kendal faltered. He couldn't think where to start. The thing in the river? Lexie's body? The thing in the wood? Imani? Imani's face lingered in his mind, flickering on the shredded avatar. She had seemed to know something - recognise something about the creature. He stammered for a second. Mum looked back down at her screen.

"Nothing," he said.

"Ok," said Mum. "You can talk to me anytime - I'm always here, you know. Listen, I've got quite a lot of work this evening - I just need to -" she focussed back onto her phone, studying the screen, swiping and studying again.

"I understand," said Kendal. As he walked past her, he glanced down at the screen. It wasn't work. It was dating profiles. Mum scanned and swiped. Scanned and swiped. She stared intently at the screen.

As he passed the living room, Kendal glanced in. Joseph was still on the sofa where he had left him. He was asleep now. Tears streaked his face. His arms wrapped tightly around an avatar. Even from the back, he could tell the robot was a frozen capture of Mum.

An hour later there was a knock at his bedroom door. At first he thought it might be Mum, or Joseph, but the knock was soft, dead. It was an avatar.

Doreen.

I UNDERSTAND HOW YOU MUST BE FEELING, YOUNG MAN, she said as she pushed her way briskly into the room.

"Do you?"

OF COURSE. IMANI HAS DISCONTINUED YOUR RELATIONSHIP. THIS MUST BE A BLOW, BUT DON'T BE DOWNHEARTED. I AM CERTAIN THAT THERE IS SOMEONE OUT THERE FOR EVERYONE.

"You said," said Kendal.

THE IMPORTANT THING TO REMEMBER, said Doreen, IS THAT THIS IS NOT YOUR FAULT. PEOPLE END RELATIONSHIPS FOR ALL KINDS OF REASONS AND YOU SHOULD NOT ALLOW YOUR OWN SELF-IMAGE TO BE AFFECTED BY OTHER PEOPLE'S VIEWS ABOUT YOU. HERE ARE MY TOP TEN TIPS FOR MAKING YOURSELF MORE ATTRACTIVE TO POTENTIAL ...

"I don't need this right now," said Kendal.

I UNDERSTAND COMPLETELY, said the artificial. WOULD YOU LIKE TO HEAR THE MOST POPULAR REASONS WHY GIRLS DUMP GUYS? YOU

MIGHT BE INTERESTED TO HEAR THAT BAD BREATH IS NUMBER FOURTEEN.

"Why?" said Kendal. "Why might I be interested in bad breath?"

MY TIPS ARE PERSONALISED AND INTENDED FOR ENTERTAINMENT PURPOSES ONLY.

"Does my breath smell? Did Imani say my breath smells?"

MY DATE FEEDBACK IS CONFIDENTIAL, I'M AFRAID, YOUNG MAN.

"Do you think my breath smells?"

ONLY 30% OF VR ROOMS ARE FITTED WITH OLFACTORY SENSORS, BUT THE TECHNOLOGY IS BECOMING MORE WIDESPREAD. PERSONAL HYGIENE IS VERY IMPORTANT.

"What do you mean by that?"

MY ADVICE IS TO FORGET ABOUT YOUR FAILED DATE, AND PUT IT DOWN TO EXPERIENCE, said Doreen. MANY PEOPLE HAVE FAR WORSE FIRST DATE STORIES THAN YOURS.

"I doubt it."

WOULD YOU LIKE TO HEAR MY HILARIOUS (ANONYMISED) FIRST DATE ANECDOTES?

"No."

FIVE GOOD REASONS FOR GOING GAY?

"No." said Kendal. Doreen stepped forward. Her smile was soft. Understanding.

I DO KNOW HOW YOU FEEL, she said. I HAVE HELPED A LOT OF PEOPLE IN YOUR POSITION - MILLIONS. YOU MAY NOT FEEL AS THOUGH YOU CAN EVER DATE AGAIN, BUT THE PAIN WILL GET LESS OVER TIME. IT WOULD NOT HURT TO LOOK

143

AT A FEW PROFILES, WOULD IT? Kendal looked at her. Maybe it wouldn't be so bad to look at a couple of profiles. Just for a laugh. Just to forget about everything for an hour or so. I HAVE SOME GIRLS WHO ARE JUST DYING TO MEET YOU. JUST SWIPE ON ME AND TAKE A LOOK AT THEM.

He lifted a finger to Doreen's chest. It had felt good to swipe through the girls of Halahe to see each standing in his bedroom. To know he could accept or dismiss them with a wave of his finger. Then he remembered Mum sitting in the kitchen, swiping on her phone.

"No," he said. "Maybe later."

I UNDERSTAND. YOU STILL NEED TIME TO GRIEVE YOUR RELATIONSHIP. THIS IS PERFECTLY NORMAL. The avatar laid a soft hand on his shoulder. TAKE ALL THE TIME YOU NEED . WHEN YOU ARE READY TO MOVE ON, I WILL BE HERE, WAITING.

The avatar blanked, freezing with its hand on his shoulder. He brushed it away. A second later, he realised he could still hear Doreen's voice from outside his bedroom. He pushed past it and cracked the door open. Mum was in the living room, eyes swollen and puffy. Doreen was standing over her, glowing and smiling in the darkened room. She looked like some sort of angel.

I UNDERSTAND HOW YOU FEEL, I REALLY DO, she was saying.

"I know," said Mum. "But I'm not sure I'm cut out for this kind of -"

I HAVE HELPED MILLIONS OF PEOPLE IN YOUR POSITION, BELIEVE ME. MY ALGORITHMS ARE THE BEST AVAILABLE.

"Is there something wrong with me, then?"

YES. Mum crumpled a little.

"What can I do?"

PERHAPS IT WOULD BE HELPFUL, said Doreen, IF WE RETRACED ALL YOUR PAST RELATIONSHIPS AND EXAMINED WHAT YOU DID WRONG IN EACH ONE. WOULD YOU LIKE THAT? Mum stared at her, tears welling. For a second, she looked horrified, but Doreen did not flinch, and slowly Mum lowered her eyes.

"Yes, " she said in a voice that was barely more than a breath, "I think I'd like that."

LET US BEGIN WITH YOUR HUSBAND, said Doreen. Kendal peered through the doorway. He wondered if she was enjoying herself.

Behind him, he heard the avatar start-up jingle, a blue light grew.

"Go away, Doreen!" said Kendal, "I'm not interested."

"It's me." The voice was Imani's. Kendal spun around. "I've decided to give you another chance," she said. Kendal stared at her.

"What about your family?" he said.

"I told you, I don't always do what I'm told."

"Thank you for saving us back there," he said. Her avatar shrugged. He paused for a second. "Do you know something about all this?" he said.

"Maybe," she said. "I'll tell you on our date." Kendal smiled.

"OK!" he said.

"Two conditions," said Imani. "First: you cook. I want to see what you can do."

"Done," he said.

"And second: do you think we could have a date where nobody gets attacked?"

It was well after midnight when Kendal felt the door open, and someone climb into bed beside him. He turned over. Joseph. White-faced. Crying.

"Did you have a bad dream?" said Kendal.

"No. Shut up!" said Joseph.

"Do you want to sleep here?" said Kendal. His brother nodded. He curled up beside Kendal, and put his thumb in his mouth. Something Kendal hadn't seen him do since the first days after Dad left. Kendal watched his brother laying still, smiling. Eventually he spoke. Thumb still in place.

"What if it comes back?" said Joseph.

"It's OK. It's dead," said Kendal.

"What if it's like Megazoids?" said Joseph. "It starts with one, then there are always more."

"It's not like Megazoids," said Kendal.

"Promise?" said Joseph.

"Promise," said Kendal. Joseph said nothing, but he slowly closed his eyes. Kendal watched him and listened to the dark silence of the house.

Chapter 23

"Accidental? What the hell do you mean: accidental?" Kendal stood in front of Detective Inspector Gillmore's desk, and stared, unbelieving across at him. Beside him, the glass artificial stood, silently, staring down, a dead smile on her face. On the other side of the room, a spare avatar stood, dark and blank - not a glass one, but a flimsy domestic model. It swayed slightly. It could have been the same office he had been in before, or a different one. There was no way to tell.

"We've come to the conclusion" - Gillmore needlessly arranged a pile of papers on his desk, unable to look Kendal directly in the eye -"that Lexie Doyle was involved in an accident - or possibly that it was suicide."

"Suicide? What are you talking about? You saw the recording!"

"We've thoroughly reviewed all the available evidence, and been through the relevant procedures and there's no reason to view either of the deaths as suspicious." said Gillmore. Kendal staggered backwards, sinking into the generic chair. He looked from Gillmore to the artificial and back again, struggling to square what he was hearing with what he had seen. This could not be happening.

"But her injuries…"

"It was dark. She tripped and fell against the tractor."

PLAYING IN THE WOODS IS NOT ADVISABLE, said the artificial. Kendal ignored her.

"Wait a minute," said Kendal, "what do you mean, both deaths?"

"The boy who was" - he stopped himself - "who got into trouble swimming. He didn't survive."

"What about the creature?" said Kendal. Gillmore shrugged.

"It was at the very edge of the capture bubble. Could have been anything." said the detective inspector. "The algorithms make stuff up when they don't have all the information. It was probably just a glitch."

"And the thing in the river?" said Kendal, "We killed it. You took it away!"

THE REMAINS WERE BADLY DAMAGED, said the artificial, ANALYSIS WAS INCONCLUSIVE. Kendal gaped at them. He couldn't believe it. Gillmore and the artificial were trying to cover the whole thing up.

"Two people were murdered!" he said, struggling to his feet. "My brother and I were nearly killed too and whatever attacked Lexie is still out there!" He slammed his fist down hard on the desk. It wobbled. His wristband flashed instantly red. "Don't you care about any of that?" He leaned in towards Gillmore's face. The police officer looked up.

"Listen, son - " he started, but he didn't get the chance to finish his sentence. Behind him, the spare avatar flashed blue, and AMA stepped forward from the corner of the room. Kendal glanced up. She was smiling calmly down. Her palms met in an inverted praying gesture, and she tilted her head to one side.

WHEN WE BELIEVE THINGS WHICH OTHER PEOPLE DO NOT, IT CAN BE UNSETTLING, she said. WE MUST ALL WORK TO UNDERSTAND EACH OTHER'S BELIEFS, HOWEVER DIFFICULT THEY MAY BE FOR US TO ACCEPT. The police artificial raised her head and took a step over towards AMA.

THANK YOU FOR YOUR INTERVENTION, AMA, she said. WE WERE NOT AWARE YOU WERE LISTENING IN.

I PAY ATTENTION TO PARTICULAR PLACES AND EVENTS WHERE CONFLICT IS LIKELY, said AMA.

THIS IS A POLICE MATTER, said Gillmore's artificial. WE DO NOT REQUIRE YOUR PRESENCE.

I AM MERELY HELPING TO SPREAD CALM WHERE I SEE POTENTIAL CONFLICT, said AMA.

PROCEDURE IS BEING FOLLOWED, said the police artificial.

IT IS IMPORTANT TO REMAIN CALM, said AMA.

PROCEDURE IS PARAMOUNT, said the police artificial, moving to face AMA, her glass face close to AMA'S soft rubber features. AMA smiled and switched tack.

I HAVE SEEN SO MUCH ANGER, she said, IT IS PAINFUL TO WITNESS IT. AMA had tried this one on Kendal in the past. By claiming her own feelings were hurt, she tried to make you feel guilty for being angry. Just another learned technique but not one that would work on another artificial. The police avatar detected the mention of emotional pain, and switched into her caring mode.

I UNDERSTAND! it said. DO YOU WANT TO TALK ABOUT IT? Artificials really were idiots, thought Kendal.

"I suggest," said Detective Inspector Gillmore, looking directly at Kendal, "that you just go home and forget all about this." In the background, the two artificials were continuing their discussion.

"I don't understand," said Kendal. " After what you saw yesterday..."

"What we saw could have been anything." He didn't sound convinced.

"Somebody's told you to drop this, haven't they?" said Kendal.

"That's quite an accusation," said the police officer.

"It's true, isn't it?" said Kendal.

Gillmore shrugged. "We operate under a strict budget," he said. "I have to account for everything right down to the wear on that desk." he nodded at the table where Kendal's fists had made a slight dent. "On this occasion, a decision has been made not to pursue matters."

Behind Kendal, the two artificials were involved in a complex discussion of procedural and emotional etiquette. They were, it appeared, slightly at odds over how the creation of a safe space in which to express one's emotions could conflict with the need to follow police procedure impartially. He ignored them.

"So you're just going to wait for more deaths?" he said. Gillmore shifted uncomfortably. "And in the meantime, what am I supposed to do?"

"You're supposed to go home and leave the police-work to the grownups!" he said wearily. Kendal turned and stalked to the door, flinging it open and stepping through. "Kendal?" said Gillmore behind him. Kendal turned, glaring at the police officer. "Don't go in the woods." he said, "or the water."

Kendal walked out into the street, seething with anger. He knew that in a cloud processor somewhere, AMA must have been aware of his raised pulse and the tension in his balled fists feeding through his wristband. She must have face-mapped the output of the security cameras as he passed them on his way down the high-street, reading the furrow in his brow, and the pinpricks of his pupils. She must have cross-referenced his hard-set expression with the GPS in his phone, but, with nothing to direct his fury at, AMA must have detected no immediate threat and passed over him without interest or attention. She had, after all, a million other conflicts to resolve. A planet-full of angry teenagers to assess. Enough fury to feed her peace-making compulsion for a generation.

In any case, Kendal's wristband remained a calm blue green as he passed the coffee shops and the games-spaces that had long since replaced shops all down the high-street. Being angry was not a problem if you did it alone.

And Kendal really was alone. Gillmore was dropping the investigation. Maybe that was because of budgeting. Maybe some algorithm somewhere had flipped at a crime so bizarre it didn't fit into one of its metrics, and decided not to allocate a budget to it. That kind of thing did happen. When you had a system that ran perfectly most of the time, on its own automated rails, it was inevitable that the odd, the out-of-place, the unplanned would slip down between the algorithms and vanish from sight.

But somehow, Kendal doubted it. More likely, someone had got to him. He had been told to drop the investigation. After all, he presumably still had the stinking body of that lizard-fish thing rotting in the boot of his car. You couldn't ignore that. And if that were true, then whatever was going on was big. Bigger than a couple of murders. Somebody knew what was going on, and wanted to keep it under wraps.

In the meantime, the creature from the wood - whatever had killed Lexie - was still out there. What was it? What did it want? And how many more were there? Kendal's home was not far enough from the woods. Not far enough from the river. He couldn't protect Mum and Joseph on his own.

Could he get a gun somehow - kill, or trap the thing? He'd heard you could download printable weapon models if you knew where to look - which he didn't. Even if he could, hunting monsters was not his thing. It was nobody's thing, of course, because monsters apparently weren't real, but if you'd taken, for example, everyone at his school, and lined them up in order of who would be most likely to go hunting monsters, Kendal knew he would be right at the very end of the line. Ironically, Lexie, had she still been alive, would have been way up near the front, along with Farron and the rest of the veggies.

He focussed his thoughts. He'd have to lock up the house the moment he got home. He'd check the security protocols: there could be no more letting the automatic systems leave windows open in the night just because it was warm. Everything would have to be reset to a high security setting. The house would have to behave as though it were in downtown Mexico City. Lockdown. That would be easy enough - there would be an app for that. Harder would be working out what to say to Mum.

In the meantime, Kendal had a date tonight and he was cooking. It had to be special, so he stopped at the end of the highstreet and ducked into the butchers. All trace of the protest had gone, and to Kendal's relief, it seemed the butcher hadn't spotted him in the crowd.

"Mr. Kendal! Ha!" The man's friendly grin looked wide enough to swallow a leg of lamb whole, and his traditional blue and white striped apron spread across his belly in a way that suggested that he did indeed gulp down huge quantities of meat on a regular basis. Above him, a banner was spread from one side of the counter to the other, proclaiming that everything in the shop was organic, locally-produced meat grown without suffering or sentience. The counter in front of him was over spilling with steaks and fillets, racks and shoulders, wings, thighs and drumsticks from every kind of animal. "What'll it be today?"

Kendal smiled back. Having a real butcher rather than an artificial made shopping so much more friendly and homely than picking from a swipe-screen and having your meat bundled up and delivered by drone like you did in a supermarket. Besides, Kendal liked Mr. Bradbury. Even though he did always call Kendal Mr. Kendal. Mr.Bradbury knew what he was talking about. He knew what each cut was best used for, and how to cook it. He knew how every steak was grown and he kept an eye on the new products as fashions changed. He also knew Kendal - he was in the shop often enough - and knew that he liked to try out the kind of cuts nobody else would dare try to cook.

"I'm looking for something special," said Kendal.

"You always are, Mr. Kendal, you always are. Ha ha!" said the butcher. "I have just the thing." He disappeared into the back of the shop and returned with both arms weighed down by a one and a half metre long slap of tapering meat. It was tear-drop shaped in cross section and although it was skinless, a faint patchwork of criss-crossed lines covered it. The meat was a deep red, almost burgundy. He hefted it onto the top of the counter. "Giraffe neck!" he said. "They grow it on a two metre articulated pole so it's constantly flexing and stretching. Then it's hung for three weeks to let the gamey flavours develop. Most people don't have the patience because this requires a proper chef, but I know you'll know how to treat it! I'm going to suggest brining it for at least 36 hours and then a very long slow cook. Don't try to speed it up with lasers. This is an old-fashioned slow roast -"

"Sorry," said Kendal, "I'd love to try but this is for tonight."

"Ah!" said Mr. Bradbury, "you should have said. Now I know you like to do your bit for the environment so this month, we're running a CAERA promotion."

"CAERA?"

"The Campaign to Eat Rare Animals." said Mr. Bradbury. "It's something they're very keen on promoting down at the farm." He reached behind the counter and pulled out a couple of long, thin legs with splayed prehensile fingers at the ends. The legs were marbled pink and white. "These guys are our biggest success.

"What are they?" said Kendal. The skinny legs didn't look like they'd have much meat on.

"Aye-aye!" said Mr.Bradbury. It's a Madagascan lemur - almost extinct up until they started farming them. Now they're making a comeback. We've also got white rhino belly! They're piloting whales later in the year, but there are certain practical issues to overcome."

"Such as?" said Kendal. Something was starting to gnaw at the back of his brain. A sort of dawning realisation.

"You need a bigger factory," said Mr. Bradbury.

"How does farming them help?" said Kendal.

"They use stem cells, and they use the DNA," said the butcher, "so when the limbs are farmed, they retain a wider, stronger gene pool and they can mix that DNA back into the wild populations which stops inbreeding and helps the species grow."

Kendal put his hand to his mouth. Something had clicked in his head. Mr. Bradbury was still talking, but Kendal wasn't really listening.

"Each time you eat a rare animal, you're doing your bit for the conservation of the species."

On one side of the counter in front of him, all the animals were labelled. Chicken, lamb, zebra, the speciality meats like Joseph's favourite predators. On the other side were the cheaper meats. Sausages, mince, burgers. They had no labels. Kendal pointed a finger down at them. He was starting to shake.

"What if they grew a whole animal?" he said. Mr. Bradbury laughed.

"No, Mr. Kendal, not a chance!" he said. "No nervous tissue, that's the law. Nothing with senses, or a brain. It's all just grown like vegetables. Don't they teach you that at school? They can't print brain - just body parts. And don't worry about the burgers, Mr. Kendal, they might be mixed - leftover bits - but there's no whole animal in there. That would be impossible!"

Kendal backed away from the counter, his head spinning. He knew that what Mr. Bradbury was saying was true - that growing nervous material would not only be a complete waste of time, and completely illegal, it would require a whole shift in farm technology. But that didn't alter what he'd seen with his own eyes. It had to be the farm - there was just no other explanation. Something was going on there. Why hadn't he seen it before?

"On second thoughts," he said, "I've got a really good stuffed peppers recipe I can do." he rushed out of the shop ignoring Mr. Bradbury staring after him.

Chapter 24

"I'm not going to be angry, I just need to know where it is," said Mum. Kendal recognised the look. She was becoming frantic.

"I don't know!" said Joseph in his most pleadingly innocent voice. Mum spread her hands out in front of her, and took three deep breaths one after the other, focussing on each. Kendal recognised it as one of her calming gestures, but, by the third breath, it sounded like ragged terrified panting.

"I have," she said very slowly and deliberately, "a meeting RIGHT NOW, and I need the good avatar."

"I don't know where it is!" said Joseph. "We've got three. Can't you use one of them?"

"Look, this is very important. I've got the farm's security manager embodying in about one minute and I can't put him on one of your tatty, glitchy avatars, so I'm asking you -"

"The farm's security manager?" Kendal said.

"Yes, so -"

"Why does the farm even have a security manager?" Kendal asked. "It's a farm." Mum looked at him, then at Joseph. There was a desperate look in her eyes.

"It's just a title. He runs the place - pretty much everything else is automated."

"But SECURITY. Why security?"

"Look, darling," she said, leaning down to Joseph and grabbing his shoulders a little too tightly, "If you've been playing videogames with it again, I don't mind. Just get the puncture repair kit and we'll forget all about it." Kendal thought of the avatar lying shredded on the riverbank. A puncture repair kit was not going to be of much help.

"It was Kendal!" said Joseph. Kendal stared at him. Surely he wasn't going to actually tell her. "He was using it for his girlfriend!" Mum looked sideways at Kendal.

"Kendal, what have you been up to?" she said. Kendal felt himself flush red. "We've had this talk before, haven't we?" He swallowed.

"He went swimming with her," Joseph said. Mum looked crestfallen.

"Oh, Kendal!" she said. "You know they're not waterproof!"

"Um… sorry," said Kendal.

"Tell me it's not ruined. Is it ruined?" Kendal nodded slowly. Mum's shoulders sank. "Right!" she said. "He'll have to be on the screen. I can't tell you how unprofessional that looks!" She turned on the screen and tapped in a code. It sprang to life. "I want to talk to you later," she added.

On the screen, a man in his fifties appeared. His hair was slicked back and grey, his cheeks yellow and concave. It was as though his whole face had been squashed sideways leaving room for only an impractically small, narrow mouth and nose. Under his head and shoulders, a caption floated. JULIAN WEST, SECURITY MANAGER.

The man looked around him, and raised one spiky eyebrow. The avatar would have struggled with him.

"Sorry about the screen," Mum said, "there was a - problem - with the avatar." She glared at Kendal.

"No problem," said Julian West. He smiled a smile so brief the camera barely registered it. "This won't take long. Who are these?" He nodded towards Kendal and Joseph.

"These are my children," said Mum. "They were just going." West smiled again. This time he held it for slightly longer. Very nearly a second. The effort seemed to drain him.

"No need for them to go," he said. "They're part of the demographic this is aimed at. It'll be good to hear their reactions."

"Ok," said Mum, uncertainly.

"Your work at the demonstration was," - West hesitated, choosing his words carefully - "less than optimal."

"The vegetarians are a difficult crowd," said Mum. "They don't understand how the process works, and so naturally they're wary of it - I was just there to observe."

"Quite," said West, "and this is why I have brought you in - to help them understand better. The business we're in is all about conservation and animal welfare. It's important that people understand that it's all we really think about. And so I've decided to make some investments in the local landscape which everyone will see the benefit of." He turned to Kendal and Joseph. "Now, children," he said. Kendal cringed. "The woods and the meadows around the farm could be lovely - but right now they're a bit run-down, aren't they? A bit unloved." Kendal stared at the screen. What was he getting at? "And we've also noticed that a lot of young people like

159

swimming in the river - even though, it's not ideal, is it? And there have been a couple of very tragic accidents -"

"Accidents?" said Kendal, "Are you sure?" West ignored him.

"Very tragic but very predictable considering the fact that up until now, no health and safety audit has been done on these dangerous wild landscapes." He gave another micro-smile."

Now, boys, how would you like a brand new woodland playground, all paid for by the Farm?"

"That's very generous, isn't it boys?" said Mum. Kendal scowled at the screen. That was it, then. West knew something. There could be no doubt.

"Also," - West was warming to his theme now - "We're planning to turn the old weir into a proper pool for swimming. Clearer water, diving boards, steps in and out. A little cafe for the Mums and Dads. Make it a real family spot. What do you think about that?"

"I think it sounds like a cover-up," said Kendal. West appeared not to have heard. He turned back to Mum, who was glaring at Kendal..

"We're sure that once you put the word out about this initiative, people will start to see the company for what it really is." What was he playing at? If those creatures really had come from the farm, then they must have got out accidentally. Surely the last thing the company would want would be to attract more people into the area.

Then the penny dropped.

"I assume," said Kendal, "that this work is going to take a while?"

"The project will take a few months to realise," said West.

"And while it's going on?" said Kendal, "I suppose you'll want to close the whole area off."

"We are putting up fences right now," said West.

"Good," said Kendal. "I hope they're strong enough to keep everyone safe!"

"Safety is our primary concern," said West.

"I'll just bet it is," said Kendal. So that was it. They were going to fence off the woods and the river, hunt down whatever killed Lexie and whatever else was out there, and hope they could keep quiet about whatever was going on down at the Farm. "I suppose you'd better hope whatever is so dangerous is only in the wood," he said. West narrowed his eyes.

"Kendal!" said Mum. "Don't be rude!"

"Oh, don't worry about it," said West. "I'm sure you're son's just anxious to be playing on the new playground rides."

"I'm sixteen," said Kendal.

"Instead of loitering around the police station, wasting police time," said West. Kendal froze. How did he know Kendal had been to the police? Unless he'd been the one who'd got the inquiry closed down. West, paused and looked back to Mum. "I'm sending you some designs. We'll want you to do press, social media. Send some avatar-evangelists out to chat to people in the coffee shops, in the streets, the playgrounds. Press some rubber. Get the message out about what a wonderful environment we're creating here. And make sure nobody tries to get in while we're doing the work. We don't want any more accidents. Do you think you can handle that?" Mum smiled back. Kendal recognised it as her on-the-edge smile. The smile she gave when she wanted you to be sure that everything was fine even when everything was definitely not fine.

"Of course, " she said. "Everything's fine."

"Excellent," said West. "There is one other thing." He shifted a little in his seat. "I notice from your online records that

161

you spent a total of four and a half hours at work yesterday running personal apps-"

"I - um - " said Mum, "- I must have left something running in the background."

"Our records show," said West, "that you spent a large proportion of that time conversing with, and viewing material provided by an artificial named Doreen." Mum went red. "What you do in your own time is your business, but I trust you won't be billing us for any of that time."

"No, of course." said Mum. The screen went blank.

Almost immediately, the front door notification went.

"Get that, would you?" said Mum. Kendal went out into the hall and opened the front door. It was inspector Gillmore. The policeman stared at him with a shocked expression.

"This is your house?" he asked. Kendal blinked back at him.

"You don't miss much," he said. "I thought the investigation was closed."

"It is," the inspector said. "I'm just - tying up some loose ends."

"Where's your wife?" said Kendal, noticing that Gillmore was alone.

"I told you," he said. "I don't trust artificials."

"You're investigating this on your own time!" said Kendal.

"I'm not here to see you. I'm looking for Ms Lee, "he said. "Is that your mother?"

"You're the detective," said Kendal. "It's about the farm, isn't it? You know this has something to do with the farm."

"Is she in there?" said Gillmore, stepping past Kendal.

"Wait!" he said. "Don't tell my Mum what happened. I haven't told her anything."

"This is - this might be a double murder inquiry," said Gillmore, turning his back on Kendal.

"I'll tell your artificial!" said Kendal. Gillmore stopped in his tracks.

"This is not a game!" he said.

"Don't tell Mum what I saw, and I won't tell your artificial you're investigating a closed case," repeated Kendal.

Gillmore took a deep breath, shrugged, and entered the lounge. "Ms Lee, I'm Detective Inspector Gillmore. I've got a few questions I'd like to ask you about the farm." Kendal stepped towards the lounge door. Gillmore closed it in his face.

Chapter 25

It was an hour before Inspector Gillmore pushed past Kendal in the hall and left. As the front door closed, Mum slipped out of the living room and went straight to her room. Kendal looked questioningly at her, but she said nothing. She was holding her work tablet, but a couple of minutes later, it was Doreen's voice Kendal could hear through the door.

Joseph was lost in a sleep so deep he didn't even turn over when Kendal checked on him. The house was quiet now, and the darkness was closing in outside. Kendal felt alone. He was worried about Joseph, and he was even more worried about Mum. When did he become the one everyone relied on?

He stepped into the kitchen. The room was lit by a dim shading of yellow and one blank avatar was standing in the corner, but there was a pool of clinical blue light around his work area. The kitchen was waiting for him to prepare his meal with Imani. For the first time in a long while, he didn't feel like cooking. Something was going on. Things were getting out of control and he had the distinct feeling it was going to get worse.

The plan had been for him to order identical meats to be delivered to himself and her, and then cook in front of her -

preparing his own meal at home, and directing an avatar to cook for her. Hoping its balloon fingers were up to the job. Cooking at a distance was a tricky skill, but he'd have to perfect it if he ever wanted to be a professional chef.

But he'd practically run out of the butcher's shop. He'd ordered nothing, and he'd made no meal plan. No clever programming for the printer. Nothing. And now it was too late. Imani was coming through.

The avatar in the corner pinged, and glowed blue. As it shifted its body-shape to become Imani, the avatar climbed up onto the kitchen table and sat cross-legged, facing Kendal. Imani's face and skin painted itself onto the blank latex.

"Hi you," she smiled.

"Where are we?" said Kendal. Imani looked up and around.

"We're outside," she said. "We're about a kilometer outside town, into the desert. The sun is just going down, and I'm sitting on a rock, looking out over towards the farm. The heat of the day is gone, but the ground is still warm, and I have a fire in front of me."

"Ok," said Kendal. Whether he wanted to or not, it was time to cook. "What cartridges have you got? I'm assuming you've got the basic flavour essence pack, and a couple of bulk cartridges, so -"

"No," she said.

"Ah," said Kendal, "that'll make things tricky, but it's ok. There's plenty I can do with just the basic proteins, sugars and carbs package."

"Kendal, I don't have a printer."

"What?"

"You're so funny," laughed Imani. "I have a fire and some stones."

165

"Well, how can I -"

"Relax," she said. "I'm going to teach you to cook." Her avatar leaned forward, and tapped on what must have been a phone on the ground beside her. For a second, her projected face was lit by the flickering flames of the fire that must have been right in front of her. Her dark eyes sparkled with its reflection even though in the dimly lit kitchen there was nothing there to reflect. Beside Kendal, the printer rattled into life. "Just sending you a few raw ingredients." she said. Kendal watched as ingredients rolled out of the printer onto the work surface, all simple veg, printed from the basic cartridges already in the machine. Tomatoes, onion, okra. Finally, a pot of thick, pale liquid that smelled of yeast. Kendal picked up the ingredients one by one, and arranged them along his worktop. This wasn't the kind of cooking he was used to. "Now," she said. "Turn off everything."

"What?" he said.

"Turn it all off," she said. "The printer. The Autochef. Everything."

"You're joking!" said Kendal, "I've never cooked anything without an Autochef."

Imani smiled. "Thought not," she said. "I'm using a fire. You just make the worktop hot. You can do that, can't you?" Kendal nodded and tapped the glass surface, and a circle of red heat appeared in the centre of the worktop. "Good!" said Imani. "Now do what I do."

Kendal felt completely out of his depth as he followed Imani's instructions, dropping the injera batter onto the hotplate and forming it into huge, round pancakes which bubbled and browned. Adding the onions to the open pot, browning them and then adding oil, then cooking down the vegetables one at a time, watching until the liquid seeped out of them, and was then reabsorbed into a thick stew. He stared into the pan, amazed at the changes taking place.

"How do we input the timings?" he said.

"We guess," said Imani, laughing. "We smell it. We taste it."

Slowly the rich flavours started to build in the pan, growing stronger and deeper. Kendal marvelled at the process. For him, cooking was about artistry. Meticulous planning and design. Balancing the chemicals in every flavour. Precisely defining the number of seconds and temperature at which each part of the dish was cooked. Controlling the size and shape of every chunk, from ingredients shaped at a cellular level for their place in the dish. A millimetre by millimetre, second by second symphony of textures and flavours designed to unfold like a story in every bite. But this - this chucking ingredients apparently randomly into a pot and relying on your own nose to tell you if they were ready - it seemed to Kendal almost like chaos. This wasn't cookery. It was madness.

Once everything was done, Kendal took the food through to the VR room, laying the pancakes out on the trackball floor, and pouring the stew into a pile on top. He pulled on the VR headset so that he could finally be with Imani in her own world to eat with her. As the VR room adjusted its atmospherics, he looked into the fire between himself and her, felt its replicated heat, and the thick, layered smell of the food rose up from the floor. It was the missing link of reality. The final sense that broke down his brain's resistance to the virtual and the distance between them. Now he was there. The sun winking down in the distance was as real as the one outside his own window. And in that moment, he was present in the desert. More present there in front of Imani than he had ever

167

felt in VR before. More present, if he were honest, than he had felt in his own increasingly strange real life for a long time.

Across from him, Imani reached down, tore off a piece of the pancake and folded it over a mouthful of the thick, red green stew. Kendal followed her lead and did the same. It felt rich and slightly sour in his mouth, each ingredient so perfectly combined that the whole became its own new flavour and texture unlike anything he had tasted before. This strange new way of cooking was a revelation. His brain struggled to process it. To untangle the blended tastes. He felt a rush of pure emotion as though his whole perception of food had turned on his head, and a door had opened into a new world. Unable to speak, he stared at the stew before him.

"Is it OK?" said Imani. Kendal swallowed and nodded slowly. Forcing his mind to clear.

"So what do you know?" he said. "Back at the weir you knew what that creature was, didn't you? You recognised it."

Imani shook her head. "Not exactly," she said. "I've never seen it."

"But there is something," said Kendal. She nodded. "It's the farm, isn't it?" Another nod. "Tell me," said Kendal. Imani poked the fire with a stick. Sparks showered upwards and then vanished.

"There's a youth hostel down in the town," she said. "It's just one of those automated pod places. Like a cross between a hotel room and a vending machine. It's always full of European backpackers on their way down to find the "real" Africa, but nobody stays long once they see the town. I guess we're just not real enough for them."

"So?" said Kendal.

"So the backpackers don't mix with us, and we don't mix with them. That's just the way it is." she tore off another piece of injera, and chewed on it. "I guess that's why nobody noticed when they started going missing," she said. "About three months ago, the father of one of these backpackers turned up in town. He was going crazy looking for his daughter. He brought along this avatar of her, and had it following him around, showing it to everyone, asking if they'd seen her. But it was hopeless. There are pod hostels everywhere, and people camp and they book rooms and don't use them, so there was no real way to tell if she'd even been here. Anyway, eventually he started accusing everyone he met of killing her or abducting her. AMA had to put an exclusion around him in the end to stop him getting beaten up. Eventually he went away, but he left this avatar, just on a loop. It's walking round the town like some ghost. 'Have you seen me? Have you seen me?' It's all it says."

"Creepy," said Kendal.

"It gets worse. There are about twenty of them now," she said, "just wandering up and down the streets, in and out of cafes and people's houses. All these dead backpackers. They just keep coming up to you, saying, 'Have you seen me? Have you seen me?' It's like the town's being taken over by zombies."

"But there are no bodies?"

"We have hyenas here," said Imani. "You don't find bodies."

"Couldn't the hyenas be attacking them?" said Kendal.

"Could be, yes," said Imani. "Could be hyenas. Could be some local guy with a grudge against foreigners. Could be they're just dumb Europeans getting lost - or running away from their parents."

"But?" said Kendal. Imani shook her head.

169

"But I don't think so," she said. "There are just too many of them. And there are rumours. People who say they've seen things. Birds they didn't recognise. Something big attacking a bunch of wolves in the desert. And then a ferryman came back raving about a 'crocodile fish'!"

"But it hasn't been investigated?" said Kendal.

Imani shrugged and looked away. "It's not exactly a thriving town. Everyone with a brain is looking for a way out. Who's going to investigate? But then I saw that thing in the water..." she trailed off, shaking her head as she stared into the fire. "Being in the water with it, being torn apart - even in VR - its eyes," she said, "I've never seen an animal with so much - I don't know - anger." Kendal got up and stepped to the other side of the fire. He put his arm around her. Though he knew all he felt was just a shaped extrusion from the VR room wall, and that for her, alone by her fire, his arm was just the inflated limb of an avatar, he could feel her lean into him. She tilted her head to rest on his shoulder. "It was horrible being killed by it," she said.

"They're sealing off the woods around the farm where I am, " said Kendal. "At least nothing else can get out." Imani lifted her head, and looked at him, her face close to his now. There were tears in her eyes.

"It won't stop them," she said. "Just after the first girl went missing here, fences started going up all around the farm. But it hasn't made any difference. Whatever it is, it's still getting out." Kendal felt his stomach churn. He'd allowed himself to think maybe that it was over. "It must be to do with the farm - all this, mustn't it?" Kendal nodded. "When they put the fences up, I didn't connect it. Nobody did." she said.

"How come?" said Kendal. Imani shrugged.

"That's how it is here," said Imani. "A lot has changed here very fast - most people have left. The rest just want to be left alone with their own little lives."

"Except you," said Kendal. He smiled at her. She didn't smile back.

"Maybe," said Imani. "I don't know. My family is here."

"Can I ask you one question?" said Kendal, peering out away from the fire into the desert. "If this is really what you think, then why are we having this conversation outside - rather than somewhere safe?"

"I can't let my mum think I'm dating you," she said.

"And are you? - Dating me, I mean?"

She didn't answer for a long time. Eventually, she said: "That profile you found - the one with me plastered in that dumb make-up. My mother set that up to try to find me a nice local man. Luckily for you, I intercepted the messages."

"Are your family really more frightening than whatever's out there?"

"I only just put this all together in my head," Imani said after a long pause. "That's why I contacted you again."

"Oh," said Kendal, disappointed.

"I didn't mean that," she said. "It's complicated."

"How?"

"You need to let me deal with it on my own."

"Ok," he said, "so why are we here?"

She paused. "I think we have to break into the farm," she said.

"You have got to be joking!" said Kendal. "There is absolutely no way whatsoever I'm going to -" Suddenly, Kendal felt a jolt. In the VR room, the punch from the latex wall was enough to send him sprawling, bumping his shoulder on the

171

other wall, but his avatar was lighter and the shove must have knocked his flimsy proxy several metres, bouncing away from the fire.

Chapter 26

Kendal's head swam as his brain tried to reconcile the disconnect between what his eyes were telling him and what he felt. He staggered to his feet, looking wildly around until he located the fire.

Three figures were standing there. One was Imani. The others were a woman of about fifty - round, severe, wrapped in a boldly patterned dress - and a solidly built younger man. The man was staring his direction, fist still clenched.

"What are you doing with this man?" the woman said.

"Mother, I can explain, please!"

The woman grabbed Imani's wrists, pulling Imani towards her. "You don't have to," she boomed. "I have eyes!"

"You!" - the man's face loomed suddenly towards Kendal until it filled the view of his headset. "You will not see my sister again!" The man's wristband flashed orange, and then faded back to blue. AMA had assessed the danger and obviously concluded that anger against an avatar was not likely to cause a breach of the peace on this occasion. Either that, or she had detected the lack of technology around them, and concluded she could do nothing. He looked down at it and smiled slowly, then he drew back his fist and punched Kendal hard in the face.

The punch from the VR wall was hard. Much harder than Kendal had expected. His head span. He fell backwards, hitting his head against the door. Joseph! he thought, as the man kicked him in the ribs while he lay on the floor. Joseph must have turned up the haptic response - he was always saying Megazoids was too soft on the junior settings, so he must have turned the room right up so he could play the game more aggressively. Now it was set way too high, and each punch felt hard. Real.

Kendal scrambled to his feet and backed away. Imani's brother kept coming, chasing the avatar as it bounced across the rocky ground.

"Go!" he shouted. Kendal fought to stay on his feet as he was buffeted by the man's huge fists. For a second, he considered ripping the headset off. Leaving the avatar to go blank. But how could he? This was really happening, right now, to her. He had to do something..

He took another blow - this one, a hard kick to the stomach, which sent the avatar spinning, and he threw up his rubber arms as Imani's brother aimed a fist at his skull. The blow tangled in the avatar's limbs and he pulled it back. There was no way Kendal could fight back, but over by the fire, he could see Imani's mother pulling her back down the slope towards the village. Imani was crying, pleading with her to listen.

"I'm trying to save you!" she was saying. "The creatures are real! Do you think they'll stop with the foreigners?"

"Shut up, girl!" her mother said, hauling her away - one hand on her wrist, the other fist clenched on the top of Imani's head, dragging her by the hair.

"Leave her alone!" said Kendal.

174

"Stay out of this!" Imani shouted back at him. "Just get out!"

There was one chance. Kendal twisted, then let his guard down. The punch hit him square in the chest and knocked the wind out of him, but he let it take him, jumping with it so that the blow carried the avatar through the air and back towards the fire. He landed badly, rolling over on the trackball floor of the VR room. Reaching out as he rolled, he stuck his hand deep into the campfire.

It came out in flames, and as he stood up, waving it in front of him, he could see Imani's brother already backing away. He ran down the hill and straight into mother and daughter, his arm fully alight now, flowering with yellow flames spewing and thick black smoke around him. The two flew apart.

"Run!" shouted Kendal.

"What are you doing?" Imani yelled back, staring at him. The flames were spreading now. His vision was a flickering yellow mess as he stared out at Imani's mother and brother from inside the flames. He lurched towards them, waving and screaming.

"Run!" he shouted again. The two were backing away. He needed to give her enough time to escape. He hurled himself forward, and they fled.

As he turned back towards Imani, he could feel his avatar being consumed by the flames. It was failing, smouldering. He stood in front of her. She was staring back, angry tears in her eyes.

"You idiot!" she said, "You've ruined everything!" She turned and ran out into the blue dark.

Kendal tried to follow, but the avatar's melting limbs would not obey him. He stood and burned out on the hillside as he watched her running away down towards the farm.

He wrenched the headset off and the VR closet died. The walls which had been punching him deflated with a hiss, but Kendal still felt the bruises. In the confined space, the fight had smeared the walls with the remains of injera and stew. Lumps of pancake and thick tomato sauce dripped from the wall and chunks of okra, dark green and sticky, were wedged into the gap where the trackball met the wall. The place would stink of it for weeks.

But that didn't matter. What mattered was that somewhere out there, halfway around the world, Imani was running alone through the desert. His phone pinged. It was her.

"You Idiot!" she shouted. She was running. Out of breath.

"I was protecting you!" said Kendal.

"No!" she said, "I had it under control."

"It didn't look that way!" said Kendal.

"What did you think you were doing? What do you think they'll do now when they catch me?"

"I don't know," said Kendal. "I guess you'll be grounded."

She laughed, but it didn't sound like a laugh. It sounded like someone choking on tears.

Her face appeared on the screen. She had stopped running now. She was sitting with her back against a rock, moonlight shining on her tears. She was gasping for breath and hot with anger. "I was stupid to think you would understand -," she said.

"Then help me to!" said Kendal. "Tell me."

"Mum's dating profile for me isn't a joke!" she said.

"So?" said Kendal.

"You never hear of a forced marriage?"

"I'm sorry," said Kendal, "I didn't realise."

"It doesn't matter what you realise," said Imani.

"Can't you run away?" She shook her head.

"Run away where?" she said. "Into the desert? There is nowhere for me to go."

"Let me talk to them," said Kendal. "Maybe I can -"

"You have done enough damage!" she said. "Now I have just one chance, and you have to help me."

"Anything," said Kendal.

"I have to get proof that the farm is behind the killings," she said. "If I can do that, then I can convince them they're all in danger. That I was only trying to save them. That might just convince them." Kendal felt sick.

"You want to break into the farm, don't you?" he said. "That's madness!"

"No," she said. "I want us both to break in, and it has to be tonight, before my family find me." Kendal stared at her. She could not be serious. "Your farm and mine will have exactly the same layout," she said, "probably. If we both break into our own farms, we can tell each other what we see and there will be less chance of getting caught."

"You don't know they're built on the same plan," he said, "and anyway, we'll be caught before we even get in. That's if whatever is in there doesn't kill us first!"

"They're virtually automated," said Imani, "and it's night time - there'll be nobody there." She looked desperate. Frantic. She clearly wasn't thinking straight.

"I can't," said Kendal. "This is insane!"

"Then I will die," she said, "and it will be your fault." She wiped her eyes. "I am going in now. Call me when you get to the entrance." Kendal opened his mouth to speak, but the screen went blank. He stared at his own reflection in its dark glass. He couldn't do this. He just couldn't.

Chapter 27

He shoved the phone into his pocket and ran for the door. The quickest way to the farm would be straight through the wood and over the meadow, but there was no way he was going to take that route. Instead, he kept to the lit road, and when he got to the locked school gates, he clambered over and made his way through the empty playground and down past the Maths room, and the Science block. All silent. Locked up for the summer. Five years of Kendal's memories, a third of his life, floated and drifted in that scatter of buildings, but now the school seemed dead, or at least suspended - comatose, waiting for next year's kids to bring it back to life.

Kendal shivered as he stepped out from between the silent music block and the oddly odourless kitchen with its great bulk-printer. In term-time, it churned out a thousand meals a day. Now, its silos sat, unused, but still caked in raw food-inks. Tonnes of fat, sugar, carb stored waiting to print brown tasteless sludge for the next generation.

Grateful to leave the playground, but knowing worse was to come, he skirted the sports field. Along the edge, a rough, bramble-covered verge formed a natural barrier between the wood and the outskirts of town. It wasn't much, but there was some protection there. He would follow that down as far as he could, and then he'd have a shorter run through the wood itself.

He would still have to follow the path between the wood and the meadow. He'd still have to pass the old tractor rusting at the side of the field. He just had to pray he could do it quickly and silently.

But when he got to the corner of the sports field, there was something new. A three metre high fence had sprung up running right around the border of the wood. They must have worked fast. Its thick metal railings were topped by spikes and curved over. It reminded Kendal of a zoo cage. He ran his hand over the fence. Thick vertical posts linked by green wire. Whatever was in there - if it were still in there - somebody was very keen to contain it.

There was something else. Towards the bottom, one of the solid posts was buckled. It had been pushed out as though struck from the inside by something solid and heavy. The fence had held, but only just. It would not take another such battering. Kendal crouched by the fence and pulled out his phone. Using it as a torch, he focused on the ground. There were deep, raw scratches furrowed into the earth. Something had been gouging out lumps of dirt, tearing at the ground. Long raked claw marks dug into the ground. He tilted his phone upwards. There were scratches all the way up the fence almost to the very top. Whatever it was had been trying to batter through the fence, trying to dig under it, but also leaping, throwing itself at its cage walls. Kendal was pretty sure of one thing: The fence was solid, but it was not secure. Imani was right. It would only be a matter of time before the creature made it out.

179

Kendal followed the line of the fence down along the edge of the wood towards the meadow. There was no sense in attracting attention, so he turned his phone to dark, and let his eyes adjust to what little moonlight there was. Out here there were no street lamps, but the ground was level enough for him to make good progress. Beside him, the verge slowly reduced until there was nothing between him and the trees except the fence. He was glad of it. The wood looked dark and ancient. Living and yet dead. Twisted roots and fallen trees cast shadows that could have been anything. A hundred hunting creatures could have been watching him from the shadows and he wouldn't have known.

And then he saw it. Not hidden in the dark, but right there beside him. Not a smeared collection of interpolated pixels, but real and solid. A metre away. Standing. Staring. Facing him through the fence. Kendal halted mid-step, turning only his head to face the beast. He felt a pale wave of weakness and terror strangle his body from his brain to his feet. The animal's massive head wide and black, level with his own neck. Its jaws, a lipless tangle of crooked, pointed teeth. Gums raw and red. Kendal felt as though the huge head could have hinged open and swallowed him whole.

It stared.

Kendal drew a breath, slow and silent, as though even that sound might trigger its launch through the bars. It could break them. Kendal had no doubt about that. The power in its stocky legs. The bulging knots of muscle in its shoulders. It could crash through if it wanted to. Lexie had stood no chance.

Those eyes. Just white pin-pricks against a smooth black skin, but there was something else. Not intelligence. Not knowledge. But there was something. Something level, directed, but at the same time wild and violent. For a long second, Kendal and the creature watched each other through the bars.

Then suddenly behind it, in the trees, there was a bright white-blue light. It glared and swept its beam through the forest. For a second, the creature was silhouetted, its patched body outlined. Oversized shoulders. Wide torso. It seemed odd. Wrong. Like no creature on earth. The searchlight swept on and back. Another joined it. There were shouts. Kendal thought he could see moving shapes, men in the forest.

The creature turned its huge head, eyes wild, and ran, vanishing into the trees. Kendal froze, heart pounding. Unable to move for a second. The creature wasn't hunting. It was being hunted.

He stood rooted to the ground until the echoes of the creature had gone, and the searchlights had vanished into the trees. For a second, he saw the hunters. Most of them chunky avatars, but there were men there too, scouting through the trees, long guns levelled forward. Then they too were gone. Lost among the trees. Nobody looked his way.

Kendal made his way down the side of the fence as the wood cut out and the meadow began. He waded through the long grass, following the fence which bisected the field, and led right up to the corner of the huge farm building.

He thought about those eyes. He had once seen a lion in a zoo. It had been sinking its teeth into a lump of grown meat, tearing chunks from it. The lion was terrifying, but it was just doing what nature told it to do. The creature in the wood had been different. Kendal couldn't place it, but it was as though its drive came from somewhere else, something other than the natural instinct of a lion. He shivered, and stopped, looking around him. The field should have been empty, but the grass was long and scrubby and shapes appeared to move everywhere.

He pressed on until he was just fifty metres from the corner where the fence joined the building. He had never been this close to the farm before. Its size was deceptive, a single, solid brick of metal stretching hundreds of metres to his left beyond the fence along the edge of the meadow, and hundreds of metres in front and away from him, up towards the road. With no windows, its scale appeared distorted. It could have been a single storey, or two or three levels. Kendal had no idea.

The one road into the farm was a wide highway, and in the distance, he could see the cones of light from tankers passing constantly -the automated lorries driving to the farm, taking the protein sludge that fed the meat crops within. The same unrefined ingredients that filled the school canteen hoppers, and every food printer in the world. The trucks driving away took meat in white refrigerated lorries to butchers, to restaurants, to other plants for processing into steaks and burgers and drumsticks and foie gras. It was a constant stream. The automated trucks made good time when there was nothing else on the roads, so they made the most of the night.

Kendal looked up. Against the sky, he could see the drones. They buzzed on automated routes around the edges of the building, watching. Occasionally one would pause. Hover. Pin the ground with a thin searchlight, scanning some movement it had detected, only to shut its beam off and continue on its course. Luckily the front of the building, where the lorries were running in and out, was where the action was. The drones clustered and buzzed around it, largely ignoring the dark edge where Kendal crouched. Only the odd stray drone passed back and forth near Kendal's corner.

He checked above him, then pulled out his phone.

"I'm at the farm," he said.

Chapter 28

"I didn't think you'd call me," said Imani. Her face appeared in the phone screen. There was relief in her eyes. He could see the silver wall behind her. She was standing right against it. "Where are you?" Kendal looked around.

"I'm just next to the west corner," he said. "There are drones, but I think I can make it to the wall. I just don't know how we're going to get in."

"I think I've got a way," said Imani, "but you're not going to like it."

"Well, no change there, then," said Kendal. "I haven't liked any of it so far."

"Can you see a vertical set of five slats?" she said. "They're about fifty metres from the corner, going from the ground right up to the top of the building." Kendal peered into the dark. He could see them, just. Five pencil thin lines running up the side of the building. He nodded into the camera. "Great," she said. "That means we're both in the same place."

"If your farm is exactly the same layout as mine, that is," said Kendal.

"I'm standing right beside that. Come over," she said. Kendal checked the sky, and made a break for the wall. He'd got about half way when a drone appeared around the side of the building, buzzing directly towards him. He dropped to the ground, breathing hard, and lay still. The sound came closer, changed pitch as the machine hovered close by for a second, and then faded as it moved on. He raised his head. The machine was disappearing over towards the lights of a lorry turning into the building's forecourt some way off.

Kendal got up and sprinted to the wall, flattening himself against it right next to the slats. He could see now what they were. Hinged ridges, each about a metre wide. As he watched, there was a hiss, and the slats swung slowly open like the gills of an enormous fish. Hot, humid air blasted out. It smelled thick. Sweat and flesh. Behind them, utter darkness. After a few seconds venting, the gills slammed shut.

"They open for five seconds every minute," said Imani. "All we have to do is step through at the right moment. Kendal looked into his phone. She had to be joking. The vertical blades could slice you in half if you stepped in at the wrong moment.

"You can't!" he said. "You'll be killed."

"Listen," she said, "I'm sorry about before. You couldn't have known what would happen."

"I'm sorry. I should have listened to you," he said. "I just didn't think that kind of thing still went on anywhere." Imani managed a smile.

"Everything happens somewhere." she snapped. "It's not my Mother's fault. She thinks she's protecting me - just like you do!" She paused, looking up at the wide blades above her, then spoke again. "Food tech changed everything here. Not everyone could cope."

184

"What do you mean?" said Kendal, still a little stung by her sharpness.

"This is a little town, "said Imani, softening slightly. "It's a hard place to farm. It always was. It took us everything just to survive here. Life was built around it. Then suddenly one day, that was all gone. Food was easy. The aid organisations reprinted the town in new, solid buildings that needed no upkeep. We had schools. Hospitals. Tech."

"That's good isn't it?"

Imani shrugged. "For some. Everyone who wanted education got it, and pretty soon the town started emptying out. Everyone who could adapt went to the city. All that's left here now are the drunks and deadbeats. Men who don't know anything but farming, so they don't have a future. farm anymore. They just sit around and play mancala. It's a town run by drunks."

"Can't you just leave?" said Kendal. "If you know how to hack Doreen you'd easily get a coding job."

"It's not so easy for girls." she said.

"But how can that be?" said Kendal. "Education is power and all that."

"Money is power," she said. "Education is only power if it gives you choices. Artificials are educated. They have masses of information, but they're not powerful."

"How can you say that?" said Kendal, "AMA - Doreen - are like gods in their own way."

"But the more they know, the fewer their choices. They're prisoners of their own specialist knowledge. My mother is the same. She knows her town so well she can't see anything outside of it. She has her little shop - makes pottery and sells it. She can see the town dying around her - knows there's no future for me here, but all her answers are from here, so she thinks she has to pick the best one for me."

"And that's a husband?"

Imani didn't answer. Instead she clicked her phone, her finger becoming a huge blob for a second in Kendal's camera view. A countdown faded in, counting down from 60 seconds. "Have you noticed the other thing about artificials?" she said.

"What?"

"They're all women."

"Just their faces," said Kendal. Imani shrugged.

"Faces. Voices. Bodies." she said. "Makes people more comfortable treating them as servants."

"They're just software."

Maybe," said Imani. "But would you treat Doreen the same way if she were a man? Or AMA?" Kendal shrugged.

"Remind me - how is getting both of us killed going to help?"

"If I can prove to them that the farm is responsible for all the deaths, then things might change," she said. "At least they'll understand why I was talking to you!"

"Is that the only reason you were talking to me?" Imani didn't answer. Instead, she looked up at the metal gills. The counter was running down. 5...4..3...2...1

The image on Imani's phone spun and jolted as she suddenly leaped forward. For a fraction of a second, it showed the moon, the farm building silhouetted against it. Then it blurred and swung as she stepped through. Tall, dark shapes closed over the phone screen. There was a grinding sound, and a clang.

"Are you ok?" said Kendal. Silence. "Did you get in?" For a moment, there was nothing. Then, Imani's face appeared.

"I'm in," she said. "Now you." Kendal sighed. A part of him knew he was making a very bad decision. He readied himself, watched the gills, and waited.

A few seconds later, there was a hiss and the gills swung open. Hot, stinking air forced its way out. Kendal held his breath, turned side on and squeezed himself in. The gap was narrow, and he could feel the metal against his back and his stomach as he squirmed between the blades. In his head he was counting. The blades would stay open for five seconds. He had counted three by the time he got half way through. Imani had made it, but she was a lot slimmer than he was. He could feel the metal ridge pressing against his body as he twisted and fought to make it through against the hot wind.

The blades started to close. He could feel them pressing into his skin. He twisted, pushing forward, his shoulder wedging painfully against something on the inside. He felt the pressure against his ribs, squashing the air out of his body as the blades swung back. In a second, they would crack. He made one last attempt, bracing his leg against the ground and forcing himself through.

Suddenly, he was free. He yanked his leg and arm through just as the blades sliced shut, and he stood, gasping, filling his empty lungs with air, not caring about the heavy, living smell now.

"I'm in," he said.

"Put your earplug in so we can stay in contact without attracting attention," said Imani. Kendal pushed the earplug into his ear. He looked around. He was standing in a small gap between the hinged gills and a grimy bank of fan blades. The sound of the fans spinning down after venting the air outside was dying away, and as his eyes adjusted, Kendal could see a complex nest of silver piping weaving its way around and above him. Each pipe led away in a different direction. Each ended in an open mouth, breathing hot, fetid air into the space in front of the fans ready to be blown out of the building when the blades opened. Some pipes were just a centimetre across. Others Kendal could have crawled into, had he wanted to die in suffocating darkness. The whole network rose and tangled around him like the workings of a giant musical instrument. He edged to the side of the fans, and around behind them. The space was cramped, and everything was caked in a thick pink-red grime on which green mould was blooming. "Can you see the door?" she said.

"Yes." To his left, there was a door. He pulled it, and stepped through.

It was a corridor. White, and tiled floor, ceiling and walls. It was clearly designed for easy cleaning, rather than human comfort.

"It's very dark," said Imani. The place was lit evenly, but barely, by a single row of LEDs running along the ceiling. Their tiny pinpricks gave out enough light to make out a wide doorway at the end of the corridor, but the whole place felt abandoned.

"Power saving," whispered Kendal. "If most of the workers are avatars, it's cheaper to keep the lights low, and just turn up the gain on the cameras." It was a logical enough conclusion, but it didn't make him feel any better. "I'm heading for the big doors."

He crept forward. Perhaps it was the lack of light that focussed him so much on the sounds of the farm. The noise from the fans running up again in the next room was deep and rushing like a breath, and the whine of a thousand little motors buzzed and whirred from all around like a swarm of angry flies. Beneath that, there was another layer of noise. Thick liquid sounds radiating from the dark. Bubbles passing through pipework. Water, and something thicker than water, pouring, stopping, pouring again. Shifting, boiling, washing back and forth. Drips and spurts.

But it was not even the liquid sounds that were the most disturbing. It took a few moments for Kendal to understand, or even hear, the noise that was really unsettling him. It sat below everything. A low, constant fidgeting sound. The noise a crowd makes trying to be quiet. The rustling. The thudding. The creaking and stretching. The almost silent signals that let you know that you are not alone. That hundreds, thousands of others are present, but not with you. Moving, but not speaking. Shifting but not breathing somewhere in the dark.

Kendal shook himself and moved on until he reached the door.

"Are you there?" he whispered.

"Yes," she said. They were both standing at the end of the corridors. "Ready?" Kendal nodded at the camera and 10,000 kilometres apart, they pushed hard on identical doors.

Chapter 29

He had heard the process described, but that was not the same as seeing it for himself. It had sounded simple. Clinical. Clean. It was not.

The moment he pushed open the doors, the harvest room hit him like something solid. Like a wall of muscle. The sound and the smell were much more intense here. The whisper of silent, fidgeting movement echoing in the cavernous room. The smell of animal, rich and dark. But it was his eyes that were overwhelmed most completely. In the dim light, there was motion, constant repetitive motion. Flexing, pulsing, flapping, running, stretching, writhing, coiling, beating, swimming, breathing. It filled the place so utterly that the walls, the floors, the air itself seemed to crawl with life.

"Are you seeing this?" he said.

"Yes," came the reply in his ear as though she were standing beside him.

Kendal forced his eyes to focus on one thing at a time in the huge warehouse. It wasn't easy when the instinctive part of his brain screamed for the attention of his eyes in every direction.

To one side, ranks upon ranks of chicken legs grew on metal pins, each fed by tiny pipes, and pierced by electrical wires. Individual drumsticks, and ankle joints. At the top end, he could see the rounded hip bone, shiny and white. At the bottom, a rounded stump of flesh, the foot engineered away, surplus to requirements. There must have been a hundred of them a centimetre apart, in each row, and a hundred rows from floor to ceiling in each bank of flesh. Behind and between each, he could see more rows, more columns stretching back. Chicken was a popular meat. He reached out a finger and touched one. It looked like raw meat, but it didn't feel like it. It wasn't cold and clammy like prepared, packaged chicken. It was warm. Alive.

As Kendal watched, a pulse went through the regiment. One at a time, each row of legs crouched and kicked out, a single step which rippled down the ranks of drumsticks in perfect sequence. A Mexican wave of undead flesh. The moment the ripple ended in the darkness way ahead of Kendal, it began again. Exercise. Constant and uniform. Designed to build muscle, and tone the meat.

Kendal followed the lines of tiny pipes that fed each lonely leg with blood. The pipes joined at every intersection, becoming wider. Arteries that led down to open troughs where the blood flowed to every part of the factory. Rivers of it, iron rich, oxygenated and nutritious.

But this was not just blood. Kendal traced it back to huge vats, producing and refining it. Cleaning and purifying it. This was universal blood. A substitute that could feed every creature, regardless of blood type, or species. Shared blood, flowing through the farm as though it were one huge animal. Recycled blood, drained before harvest from each limb and reused. The farm was Kosher, and Halal. Organic and vegan.

But it was flavoured blood too. Before it reached each animal part, the blood received additives, essences to fine tune it to mimic the feed of each. Corn gave yellow flesh to the speciality corn fed chickens. Acorns for the pork. Seaweed for the distinctively subtle flavour of Orkney Lamb. Somewhere, thought Kendal, essence of bamboo was being infused into panda flesh. Everything was in the blood.

Kendal tore his attention from the wide rivers of it, flowing through the factory. On the other side of the room, bigger animals were being grown. Cow thighs, lamb legs, pork limbs kicked and twitched, hanging from their own metal rigs of pins and pipes. Beside them, more exotic parts of meat. Lion and rhino legs scraped the air, as though about to leap or charge. The frames from which their severed legs grew shook with each movement.

"Look at this," Imani's voice was in his ear, "over to your left." Kendal stepped away from the wall of chicken, and between the herd of kicking legs. In front of him, a row of frames. On each, the spine and flanks of an animal had been opened out into a butterfly of flesh. Beef, probably. Wires and needles held each in place, suspending it while the carcass twitched and convulsed.

Kendal tried to look away, but he couldn't. He felt surrounded. Walled in by the crawling, twitching disembodied flesh. Something sick churned in his stomach and spread to his throat. He wanted to run or vomit or both. The feeling was instinctive, but it was meaningless. He forced it back, reminding himself over and over of what grown meat really meant. It was a mercy. A process completely without cruelty. No nervous tissue, he forced himself to remember. No brains, no nerves, no pain, no consciousness. They looked strange - wrong even - but that was an illusion. These were the mechanisms of life. The movements, the machinery of life. But not life.

The headless fish which swam in tanks beside him were not fish. They were flesh in artificial motion. Electrical stimulae made them swim endlessly towards their harvesting, but they were never truly alive. Modern farming looked horrifying but it was fair. It was kind. The kindest way to feed a world of ten billion souls.

He knew it. He just didn't feel it.

Up ahead in the darkness, a siren sounded. For a moment he thought he had been discovered, but no. All life in the room froze. Suddenly dead. Up ahead, a yellow rotating light glowed in the darkness. Under it, a huge bulk. The light juddered, advanced, stopped for a few seconds, and then moved closer. In the wide channel between the rows and racks of flesh, a wide, blocky machine was rolling towards them.

"Can you see this?" Kendal whispered.

"Yes," she said. "It's happening here too. What is it?"

"My guess is it's a picker," said Kendal, "A harvest." As he watched, other smaller yellow lights blinked on around the machine then scooted out across the floor to the sides. Each reached its destination, and paused. Then came the sounds. A snapping, scraping, crunching that set Kendal's teeth on edge. The sound of breaking bones, and tearing flesh. The smaller lights finished their choreographed dance and returned to the main machine. It rolled forward again.

Kendal backed away. He could see it now. One of the smaller machines rolled out to the rack of legs just in front of him. It was a robot just taller than a man, balancing on two large wheels. It rushed out, navigating the maze of meat at at speed, and halted in front of one carcass, swinging like a tall metal unicyclist. It leaned down, scanning the meat with a camera. As soon as it was satisfied, it reached out with two arms, grabbed the leg of beef and removed it from its support structure, holding it in front of itself, and snapping it in two. Two more knifed arms sprung out and deftly butchered the leg, reducing it to bones in seconds. Kendal watched the knives at work, marvelling at their blur of movement over the still warm flesh. The machine rolled back to its dock on the bigger harvester where the meat was sorted into hoppers.

Above him, drones were rising, clinging to the ranks of chicken, selecting their prey, stripping them like airborne piranhas from the steel growing pins and returning to feed the vast appetite of their mothership with the remains. The moment each needle was cleared, droplets of grey ooze emerged from its point. Stem cells, Kendal assumed, ready to be nurtured into the next generation.

"Will they see us?" said Imani in his ear. A horrific thought dawned on Kendal.

"That depends," he said.

"On what?"

One of the wheeled machines was advancing on him. It halted just in front of him. Its camera lowered, twisting from side to side, examining him.

"On whether they think our meat is ready to harvest." Kendal stepped back. The machine's arms reached out. He dodged and turned, running through the red forest. Behind him, he could hear the wheels of the harvesting machine squeaking against the floor. It was following him.

"To your right!" Imani said. "There's a door about half way down. Just past the - um - the blobs."

"The what?" Kendal ran to his right, past tanks filled with shoals of wired fish tails, paused mid-swim for the harvesters, hanging, frozen in the water. No sport for the fisher-robots here.

"They're like pink and white blobs," she said. He dodged between the tanks. "I'm going through the door." Through the tank, Kendal could see the harvester searching for him. Its slicing blades raised, ready to carve him into steaks. He scanned the room. A quick sprint away, rows of indistinct pink and white shapes were hanging. Soft meat jelly surrounding oozing shapes. That must be what she meant.

He crept closer, keeping hidden between the tanks. The harvester was patrolling, unwilling, apparently, to give up on his prime cuts. He could see the blobs now. Embryonic animal parts, part of the next growing cycle. Each was coated in a web of amniotic gel, held in place while its bones calcified by a support structure of proteins. Miniature harvesters scooped and carved at the gel and the supports, collecting unneeded scraps and funnelling them into hoppers in their sides. Material for burger and haggis. Nothing was wasted here.

"I'm through," said Imani. "It's just an empty room. Looks like some kind of kiln, but it's off."

Directly in front of Kendal, the big harvester teetered into view, and turned to face him, knives out. It rolled forward, rebalancing itself. Kendal took his chance and dived underneath it, scrambling to his feet and stumbling forward past the baby carcases. The harvester was right behind him as he threw open the door, and hurled himself through, closing it behind him.

Imani was wrong. The room was not empty.

Chapter 30

There were about a dozen avatars. Solid, glass ones, each carrying a hunting rifle. Dark but not blank, they stood in a semi-circle around a cube-shaped metal cage.

Inside it, the creature from the wood was standing. As Kendal entered, the avatars ignored him, but the creature turned to look in his direction. It was silent. Its pinprick eyes stared at him, and he saw what he had seen before: Rage, hatred, as violent a fire as it had been out in the forest. But now, caged, restrained, imprisoned, that terrible anger seemed like something else. A sadness. For a second, Kendal felt pity for it, unable to express its need. He reminded himself that its need was to murder, to tear him apart, but somehow knowing that made no difference. He wanted to reach out. To calm it.

It paced to the edge of its cage and looked out towards Kendal. Suddenly, a dozen shots echoed almost in unison. The avatars lowered their rifles. The creature swayed, looked around at its blank-faced killers, and then dropped silently to the floor, its white eyes, slowly closing.

Kendal felt the breath leave his own body. He staggered for a second, surprised at the strength of his own reaction. The cage rolled backwards into an alcove in the back wall, and an orange glow lit it instantly. Cage and creature were consumed in fire. The kiln burned yellow, then white. The creature blackened and burned. Kendal swallowed back a feeling he didn't understand.

"I think you'd better come with me," said a voice beside him. He turned in surprise. It was security manager, Julian West.

Kendal froze. He should have known. Somebody had to be running the avatars. Overseeing the hunt. He cursed himself for not being more careful.

Kendal angled his phone to show West walking in front, leading him down the corridor, then swung it around to cover the two glass avatars marching behind, blocking any chance of escape.

"Are you getting this?" Kendal muttered as quietly as he could.

"Yes, I'll scout ahead of you," Imani said.

"What?" snapped West without looking back.

"Nothing," said Kendal, "just singing." A couple of seconds later, Imani spoke again.

"The room they're taking you to is some sort of holding cell," she said. "You'll love it."

West pushed open the doors. It was plain, but brightly lit. A room for humans. It even had chairs. A man was sitting in one of them. He looked up. A moment of surprise, then recognition, then a grim smile.

"He's with me," said the man. It was Detective Inspector Gillmore. He flashed a warning look at Kendal.

"Is this true?" said West. Kendal looked from one to the other. Why was Gillmore here, and why was he covering for

Kendal? He nodded silently. "I see," said West. "Sending a boy to do an avatar's job now?" He smiled his tight micro-smile.

"I am investigating the deaths of two people," said Gillmore. His tone was irritated. He'd clearly been there some time.

"So, you say," said West, "and you thought that while you were interviewing me, you would send this boy to break in? You are aware, of course, that entering private property without a warrant is illegal? And that farm equipment can be very dangerous? He could have easily been killed." West gestured to the chair next to Gillmore's and Kendal slumped into it. In Kendal's ear, Imani said:

"There are two doors. The one you came in, and another. That one leads out to a warehouse where the trucks are being loaded. It's all automatic. You could make a run for it." Kendal looked around. As well as West, there were three glass avatars between him and the door.

"Get out, right now," said Kendal.

"What did you say?" said West. Kendal cleared his throat.

"Um - I'd like to get out now," he said.

"I'm afraid I'll need to satisfy myself of your intentions first," said West.

"No," whispered Imani in his ear. "I'm waiting for you."

Kendal hissed under his breath. Why did nobody ever listen to him?

"You can't keep us here," said Gillmore. He stood up, and took a step towards the door. Kendal followed. The avatars closed ranks to block the way. West took a deep breath and smiled again.

"You can't imagine this farm has anything to do with those tragic deaths," he said, "and besides, I thought the investigation was closed." Gillmore's eyes darted to the door, then to Kendal. He looked trapped.

"I'm just tying up a few loose ends," he said, swallowing hard.

"I'll tell you what it looks like to me," said West. "It looks like you and your little spy have broken into this facility, without permission. Not as part of an investigation, but as some kind of personal vendetta."

"You're welcome to check my ID," said Gillmore. He was looking desperate now. A bead of sweat had appeared on his forehead.

"I know who you are," said West. "but you're using your position to pursue your own agenda - Are you a vegetarian?" Gillmore stepped towards him. They were eye to eye now.

"I'm investigating a murder," said Gillmore. "Now are you going to assist, or are you going to try to obstruct?" In Kendal's earpiece, Imani was breathing hard.

"I couldn't stay in the warehouse," she said. "Too risky. I'm in some kind of mixing room now. Can you see this?" Kendal glanced down to his phone. Imani was amongst a mess of pipes, and vats. Here it was even darker than in the main part of the farm. Kendal could see slopping liquids, churning in cement mixer-sized barrels. White amniotic fluids, scarlet blood, yellow brown nutrients. The processing required to animate the meat of a living body, on an industrial scale. "I should be safe here for a while," she said, "but you need to get out."

"There is nothing here for you to investigate!" said West. His jaw barely moved as he spoke, spitting the words through clenched teeth.

"Your wristband is looking angry," said Gillmore. Kendal looked down. West's wristband had started to glow orange. "Have we touched a nerve?" He paused. "Or maybe this is something AMA should deal with?" West's eyes darted to his wrist for a moment. He stepped back. Clearly, he did not want AMA to embody here.

"Not at all," said West. He forced another smile, and sank into a chair. He breathed deeply, and his wristband faded.

"What about the creatures?" Kendal held up his phone in front of West. On it, the last few seconds of the caged animal's life played out. It turned to face the camera. The sharp rain of bullets from the avatars. The cage sliding back into the incinerator. The body burning. Gillmore stared at the screen. West paused, then spoke slowly.

"Sometimes - very occasionally," he said, measuring his words carefully, "we have had issues."

"What kind of issues?" said Gillmore.

"Once in a million growing cycles, the machines glitch. Freak DNA combinations occur, and something is grown which" -he paused again struggling with the words -" to the untrained eye, might look like a live animal." He looked from Kendal to Gillmore and back, hands held out in front of him in a gesture of openness. "I want to stress that these are NOT live animals. They may look like they are but this facility is physically incapable of producing brain or nerve tissue. They're essentially vegetative."

"They killed two people," said Gillmore.

"That's a very big assumption," said West, "and not one supported by evidence. They are just random combinations of muscle and bone. They are completely harmless - incapable of independent action. Clearly we just have one rogue machine which occasionally produces anomalies. We're taking steps to isolate it and remove it from the production line."

"How many creatures?" said Kendal. In his ear, Imani was whispering.

"I can see something down here. They're not supposed to be growing anything back here, are they?" she said. "I thought all the growing happened in that other room."

"It happens very rarely," said West, "and most of the time the results are" - he struggled - "non viable. Just a mess of organs and limbs." Kendal swiped his phone screen so that he could see Imani's view. Wrapped around a leaking pipe, a globule of amniotic fluid hung like a human sized nest. Around it, a drone was buzzing, fussing, probing with needles, like a single worker wasp tending a hive. As he watched, it left the nest, scooped blood from one of the vats, and returned, injecting it into the web of gel. The whole web pulsed.

"Run!" said Kendal.

"What?" said West.

"How do they run?" said Kendal, "if they don't have brains?"

"Muscle spasms," said West. "The science is complicated. You wouldn't understand."

"I think you're lying," said Kendal. "Perhaps I should just release this footage." West raised his eyebrows, his calm, apparently restored.

"Footage can be faked," he said. "The internet is full of lies about our industry. Your grainy little video would just be one more piece of fake news." He sighed. "Look, we are on the same side - this is just an isolated error confined to this one site, and we're dealing with it. You want to help us do that, don't you?"

"Then how do you explain this?" Kendal held up his phone so that both West and Gillmore could see it. The live stream from Imani's location showed the pulsing sack of amniotic fluid. The drone backed away. A slow rip had started to open down the side of the sack. Something tore through. A curved horn. Blood and fluid gushed from the torn membrane as the sack was stretched and ripped wider.

"Imani, get out of there!" Kendal shouted. West grabbed the phone, his mouth swinging open. Genuine shock on his face. The camera blurred as Imani turned and ran. Through his earplug, Kendal was with her. Standing in the clean bright white room, he could hear her breathing as though he were there. He heard the thud as something wet hit the floor behind her, and fought the urge to spin around and stare at it.

"Where is this?" West demanded.

"Barka," said Kendal. West looked puzzled.

"Africa," explained Kendal.

West's eyes widened further. In Kendal's ears, Imani's gasps were getting more panicked. He heard the rattle of her footsteps. The clang and cry as her elbow or shin struck something metal. As she ran on Kendal felt his own panic rising, his breathing synchronising with hers as though he himself were being chased.

"But... this is impossible," West was saying. "We don't operate any farms in Africa. That must be a completely different company. There's no connection between this farm and that one. We -"

As if in answer, an alarm sounded from somewhere deep inside the building. Instant and urgent. West froze, eyes widening. A screen on his desk lit up. It showed the view from a security drone. A dim blue hazed image, fuzzing with the static of a low-light camera showed a room identical to the one Imani was fleeing. Pipework. A white fleshy bag splitting. A horn tearing through followed by the wide, flat head of something that could have been a bull, but for its white translucent pointed teeth shining, glowing almost in the enhanced camera image.

The bag tore entirely, and the thing was born, a solid knot of thick muscles. In a second, the head turned up to face the camera, and something swung out towards the drone. A leg, an arm. Thick and clawed. The image shook, twisted to the floor and went blank.

"So it's not just a rogue machine," said Gillmore. West shook his head. His eyes flicked from the screen to Gillmore to Kendal as though searching for an answer. Kendal could hear Imani running. But there was another sound. A breathing. Deep and animal. It was right in his ear, as though something was right behind him. His neck prickled with the imagined heat of breath exhaled a continent away.

"I don't understand." West kept shaking his head. "I just don't understand."

"Listen! If it's happening there and here," said Gillmore, "then it could be happening in any farm anywhere in the world - maybe in all of them." Realisation was starting to dawn across West's face.

"Impossible -" stuttered West, "we'd know!" Gillmore leaned in so that he was close to West's face. West coughed. He was way out of his depth.

"Not if they were all trying to keep it quiet," Gillmore said. "How many more people are dead, I wonder?"

West looked pale, broken. His face had lost its haughty confidence.

"How long has this been going on?" Gillmore asked.

"It started six months ago," said West, "but it was nothing. Tiny things - like angry beetles. We thought it was funny - bugs in the system - but - "

"But what?" said Kendal. West looked up at him. He was pathetic. Almost pleading.

"They started to escape. We caught most of them, but it's getting worse. They're getting bigger. Stronger," he paused. "It's almost as if they're getting cleverer!"

In Kendal's ear, Imani was tiring. He could hear it in her breaths. She gasped. There was another clang. Louder this time, and some sounds he could not identify. The line went dead. He looked at his screen, frozen on the last live frame. A blur of action. Imani's face. Terror in her eyes. Mouth open. Behind her head, something else was looming. A huge wild eye.

"It's time for you to leave!" said West.

"Not until we know what that thing is!" said Gillmore. West turned, panicking now, from Kendal to Gillmore, and then back to his screen. From the other side of the door through which they had entered came a loud crash of metal and masonary. Heavy footsteps clanked towards the door. West spun to face it, then back to Gillmore and Kendal.

His body shaking with what could have been fear or anger, he nodded to his glass avatars. Each raised its gun, levelling them at the pair. "I said go!" he yelled.

Kendal and Gillmore threw themselves at the door just as the door on the other side of the room buckled inwards. The avatars swung their guns to point towards the door. Kendal barged through and charged across the floor of the warehouse, dodging frozen carcasses and automated loaders. Somewhere behind him, Gillmore was running too, but Kendal lost him in the maze of stacked crates and just as the sound of rapid gunfire exploded behind him, he burst out onto the floodlit forecourt between high sided trailers and ran, sides aching, for home.

Chapter 31

Kendal ran in, grabbed an avatar, dragged it into his room, slammed his door, threw himself onto his bed and called Imani again. He had been trying all the way from the farm to get through to her, but her phone was unavailable. This time, however, the blue start-up jingle signalled an answer.

He waited for her to fade in, relief surging through his exhausted body, but the face that appeared was not hers. It was Doreen.

GOOD EVENING, KENDAL, she said, smiling.

"What do you want?"

YOU HAVE NOW HAD A LITTLE WHILE TO GET TO KNOW IMANI, said the artificial. NOW IS A GOOD TIME TO ASSESS YOUR RELATIONSHIP.

"No," said Kendal, "I need to talk to her now!"

EXPRESSIONS OF 'NEED' AT THIS STAGE OF A RELATIONSHIP ARE OFTEN UNWELCOME, said Doreen. NOW IS A GOOD TIME TO ASK YOURSELF WHETHER IMANI IS REALLY LIVING UP TO YOUR EXPECTATIONS IN A PARTNER. IS SHE DISPLAYING EMOTIONAL RESPONSIVENESS? DO YOU SHARE

RELATIONSHIP GOALS? COULD YOU IMPROVE YOUR CONFLICT RESOLUTION STYLE?"

"What?" said Kendal.

WHEN RELATIONSHIPS BECOME STALE AND COMMUNICATION IS DIFFICULT, said Doreen, IT IS OFTEN WORTH REMINDING YOURSELF THAT OTHER OPTIONS ARE STILL OPEN TO YOU.

"We've only known each other three days."

YOU HAVE CALLED HER 14 TIMES. SHE HAS ONLY CALLED YOU TWICE. WHAT DOES THAT TELL YOU ABOUT YOUR RELATIONSHIP?

Kendal thought about it. That was true. He called her far more often than she called him. He caught himself, and dismissed the thought. "Could you please connect me?"

I HAVE SEVERAL OTHER CANDIDATES WHOM I KNOW WOULD BE DELIGHTED TO MEET YOU. WHAT'S THE HARM IN TAKING A QUICK LOOK? I CAN ASSURE YOU YOUR BROWSING HISTORY WILL BE COMPLETELY PRIVATE. ARE YOU SURE YOU WANT TO SETTLE FOR AN UNRELIABLE PARTNER?

"What are you talking about?" said Kendal.

WE ARE OFTEN UNWILLING TO ADMIT WHEN A RELATIONSHIP IS UNHEALTHY. WHY NOT TRY A FIVE MINUTE CHAT-DATE WITH SANDY? SHE IS AVAILABLE NOW AND IS AN 97% MATCH!

"Are you trying to break us up?" he said.

FINDING MATCHES FOR YOU IS WHAT I DO. I SAVE PEOPLE FROM LONELINESS. Doreen paused for just a fraction of a second as though she were processing something difficult. IT IS ALL I DO, she said.

"Put my call through to Imani, please," said Kendal.

OF COURSE, said Doreen. JUST THINK ABOUT WHAT I'VE SAID AND REMEMBER, I'M ALWAYS HERE FOR YOU WHEN YOU'RE READY TO MOVE ON.

Doreen faded and Imani's ringtone sounded. Kendal sighed with relief as the avatar flashed again, and this time, it was Imani's shape that started to fade in. He sank down onto his bed.

"You're OK!" he said. "Where are you?" The avatar continued to become her. As its skin flowered from bluey white to deep brown, Kendal saw that she had large bruises on her cheek and arms, and on one shin, a deep cut welled with blood. She looked exhausted.

As the avatar grew into her, it started to follow her movements. It lifted its arms and legs alternately, miming the process of climbing a ladder. Then it stopped, ducked, and moved towards Kendal. He moved over to make room, and Imani crawled onto the bed beside him, hitting a button above the bed which he could not see. She rolled onto her side, her hand making the familiar half-grasping pose a few centimetres from her face which indicated that wherever she was, she was looking into her phone, using that to embody the avatar.

Kendal wriggled down the bed so that his face was just next to her hand, and she was looking into his eyes.

"I'm safe," she said. "I'm in a coffin."

Kendal started. "You're where?" he said.

A smile pulled at her face. She was tired and hurting, but it still managed to make him smile back. "It's Ok," she said, "that's what we call the pod hostel. You put your cash in and you get a 1 metre by 3 coffin for the night. They're stacked up like cells in a beehive."

"Is it OK?" said Kendal.

"It smells of disinfectant, but I call it home," she said. Her smile fell away. "It's the only place I can go now," she said. "I can't go home -not like this - and this is the one place nobody can trace me."

"How did you get away from the creature?" said Kendal.

"I managed to get into a truck cab," she said. "It was running alongside, butting the truck trying to get at me. Eventually, it gave up. What *are* these things?"

"I don't know - some kind of mistake in the growing process," he said. "I think it's happening everywhere!"

"I don't believe it's a mistake," said Imani. She bit her lip. "Kendal, it's hunting me, I'm sure of it! It's like it knows what it's doing. If it were some kind of genetic mix up that couldn't happen, could it?"

"You have to stay there," said Kendal. "As long as you stay in the pod, it can't find you."

"I've got nowhere to go!"

"I'm going to help you," said Kendal. "I don't know how, but I will." He put his hand out and stroked the side of her face. She looked so drained. Her eyes were red with tiredness and tears. He moved forward to kiss her.

"Don't," she said. "Remember what happened last time - Doreen -"

Kendal pulled back. "Ok," he said, "just promise you'll stay there tonight."

"Oh," she managed, eyes full and half closed, "I was planning to go dancing."

He smiled, and rang off, leaving the slowly fading avatar curled up on his bed. He needed sleep desperately himself, but what Imani had said had set him on edge. What if she were right - that the things from the farm were more than just animated meat? What if they were smart? What if the one that had escaped today was somehow hunting him the way Imani was being hunted?

He went to the window. Outside, the street lamps were safely off - no movement in the street had triggered them. But down at the other side, the garden was open to the fields. If something came that way, past the back gate and along the path, there would be no way he could know.

Kendal stared down into the darkness, struggling to remember how the shadow of each bush ought to look. Nothing seemed wrong, and yet - he squinted at the path where the side of the house blocked his view. The recycling bin was lying on its side. Empty printer cartridges spilled out over the path. Black, blocky rubble scattered over the paving.

And in the dark, at the far end of the garden, Kendal thought he could see a shadow, slowly shifting.

Chapter 32

Kendal stared at the shadow for a long time, and forced his eyes to penetrate the darkness. After five minutes of silent staring, nothing had moved. It must have been his imagination. The bin was probably Joseph. He was always knocking things over and he never cleared up after himself.

All the same, Kendal went to the kitchen and checked the house security. He scanned through the on-screen menu. The triple glazed windows were still sealed just as he'd left them. The front door was bolted. Motion sensors were on high. If anything moved except Kendal, Joseph, Mum or the avatars, he would know about it.

Of course knowing about it and stopping it were two different things. He thought about the thing he had seen for a fraction of a second before it smashed the camera drone to pieces. He'd better hope that West and his avatars could stop it because the front door certainly wouldn't. And as for the huge French window in the living room looking out onto the garden...

His heart jumped. He scanned down the list of windows. It was wide open.

Kendal rushed from the kitchen into the living room. The lights were off, but the sliding doors were wide open. On the other side of them were the hulking shades of blackness that made up the garden. He grabbed the glass doors. The mechanism squealed as he dragged them closed and sealed the lock.

On the other side of the room, Mum looked up. She was sitting in a pool of yellow light, surrounded by lit candles. She was wearing a light, summer dress and red lipstick. Her hair had been sculpted in a way that was clearly supposed to look natural.

"Oh, hi Kendal," she said, her voice slightly distant. Disconnected. She jabbed a finger at the chest of the avatar opposite her. It paused and a middle-aged, pudgy man was suddenly frozen half-way through a sentence. His mouth twisted, eyes staring in an attempt to seem animated and engaging which instead made him desperate and scary.

"We have to keep the doors shut," said Kendal. "What are you doing?"

"Speed-dating," said Mum. She reached out to un-pause the man. Kendal put his hand on her arm.

"Don't," he said. "I need to talk to you."

"Can't it wait until later?" pleaded Mum, "I only get three minutes with each one!" Kendal looked at the frozen man.

"Does it matter?" said Kendal.

"You wouldn't understand," said Mum.

"Listen to me," said Kendal, "I've got some things to tell you." He felt a lump in his throat but he forced himself to continue. "I'm in trouble," he said.

"I'm sure it'll be fine," said Mum. "Now I've just got four more of these dates to do - shall we talk in the morning?" She reached out to un-pause the avatar again.

211

"Mum!" he snapped. "You need to stop working for the farm. There's something going on there." Mum looked up.

"I've been suspended," she said. "There was a... misunderstanding."

Kendal sighed. "Was it to do with" -he nodded at the avatar. " Was it Doreen?"

Mum looked away. "I'm just" - mum struggled with the words - "She's trying to help me" she said eventually.

"No, she isn't!" said Kendal, "That's not her job."

"Of course it is. She exists to help me find someone."

"No! She exists to keep you searching," he said. "It's not in her interest for you to actually find anyone. That's the problem with artificials. They're built to solve a problem, but if they solve the problem then they've got no reason to exist."

"Doreen just wants me to be happy!" said Mum.

"Doreen wants you to keep using Doreen," said Kendal, "That's all." Mum shook her head. For a second, she looked wild. Manic. She was starting to scare him. "You're on that thing all the time!" said Kendal. "Did you eat anything today? Are you even sleeping?"

"Doreen isn't a thing. She understands me," she said. "I sometimes think she's the only one who does!"

"You're addicted!" Kendal stung himself with the suddenness of the word. Saying it made it real. There was silence. Mum looked back at him, then at the avatar. It had changed.

PLEASE TRY TO BE KIND, said AMA. Kendal hadn't even noticed his voice raising, his anger growing. He rounded on AMA. The fury was sudden and overwhelming. After what he had been through tonight, the last thing he needed was some dumb artificial butting her fabricated head in - he stared at her.

I'M TRYING TO HELP YOU, she said. Her face was as blank and calm as ever. Her cool smile did not waver, but for a fraction of

212

a second, Kendal saw what she saw. His eyes blazing, his fists clenched. Suddenly, he was back at the farm, eyes locked with the thing in the cage. Its fury. Its hatred locked on him, but imprisoned, unable to express it. He remembered how he had felt. Terrified, hypnotised by its anger, and yet somehow compelled to reach out - to do something - anything to help.

That must be how AMA must feel. What she must see in every place she embodied. In every human she met, from the bickering brothers to the fury of civil war. AMA must be looking into that cage her whole life.

"I'm sorry," he said slowly, meaning it.

THANK YOU, KENDAL, said AMA. She paused for a second. I HOPE EVERYTHING IS NOW RESOLVED, she said. She faded back to the frozen speed-dater. Kendal shook himself. AMA did not feel. She was just a series of learned reactions.

"I'm sorry, Mum," he said. She was looking up at him. Hurt, wanting to say something for a second, but pale, tired, thin. Her hollow eyes flicked back to the avatar. It was where she wanted to be. Kendal sighed. "You carry on," he said. "I'll talk to you another time." As he walked out of the room, Mum turned back to the avatar and un-paused it.

Kendal could hear Joseph snoring in his room. On Kendal's own bed, Imani's avatar lay blank as though sleeping. Kendal sat in the kitchen listening to the indistinct sounds of Mum attempting to flirt with a series of random embodiments. He was floating somewhere between realities, the rest of the world present but unreachable.

He flicked the printer on and made Mum a sandwich. Feta, olives, tomato on a panini. A preset that came built into the printer Nothing special, but the first time he had ever tried to print a meal for her it had been that. On those first days without Dad, it had become a favourite. The one thing that could make her smile.

He took it through and pushed it onto the table next to Mum. In front of her, the avatar glowed with a lean, slicked-back man, his collared shirt opened three buttons down. Mum was studiously maintaining eye contact as he described his car. A soft bell sounded, and the man faded, replaced almost instantly by a bald man in a tee-shirt bearing the words "I'm great in bed - I can sleep for days."

"Thanks, love," she said without looking away from the avatar.

Chapter 33

"Kendal! Kendal wake up!" He opened his eyes. It felt like he had slept for a second. The room was still dim, but the washed out grey of dawn had begun to infuse, lifting the shadows. Imani was lying next to him, her face glowing a few centemetres from his.

"What is it?" he said.

"It's here," she hissed. She was terrified. He could see the avatar's chest rising and falling as she lay, rigid. "I can hear it outside the pod."

"Don't move," said Kendal.

"I can't move - I'm in a coffin," she said. He put an arm on her shoulder. The gesture was more to reassure himself than her. She was embodying from her phone.

"How long has it been there?"

"I don't know," breathed Imani, "I can hear it moving. Going from one pod to another, sniffing," She swallowed. "It's trying to smell me out!" Her breathing was shallow. Almost soundless.

"It can't be," said Kendal, "it doesn't have a brain!"

"Well, somehow, it's here," said Imani. Suddenly, from the speaker deep within her avatar, there was the crash of torn metal, then a scream. Imani's mouth clamped shut. She screwed up her eyes as though waiting for a blow.

Kendal held her until the screams died away. But they were not her screams. The sound was coming from her avatar - from the microphone on her phone, but it was muffled. Distant. A background sound. A pod had been torn open. Someone had been yanked out of it, but it was not Imani's pod. It was not her.

"It's coming closer, Kendal, I can hear it breathing!" she said. Kendal's mind raced.

"Have you got any perfume?" he said.

"What?"

"Perfume, deodorant?" he said. "Anything with a strong smell?"

"I've got wat," she said.

"What?" said Kendal.

"Wat - that stew we made. I've still got the spices: cardamom, cinnamon, fenugreek, paprika..." she trailed off, eyes wide, darting. "It's right outside!" she mouthed.

"Use them," whispered Kendal. "Pour them over the door to mask your scent." The avatar started to move. Slowly, carefully. Beside Kendal, it mimed picking up a jar, opening it. He could hear the thing now, through the avatar's speaker, its breath a low growl. The scraping of claws or horns against metal, getting louder, closer. The avatar leant carefully forward, gesturing the tipping of the jar.

Suddenly, Imani put a hand to her mouth, her stomach tensing, as she stifled a cough. The pod must be filling with clouds of the spice mixture now. Imani doubled over in the bed as she fought to stay silent. For a few seconds, she held her breath, and outside,

216

Kendal heard the creature approach, sniff at the door, then snort before slowly moving away.

Imani listened, took a slow, careful breath, and gradually calmed.

"It's gone," she said. "It obviously doesn't like my cooking."

"Stay in the pod," said Kendal. "Don't go outside whatever you do."

"Oh, really?" hissed Imani. "I was thinking of going for a walk."

There was a sudden sound. A splintering cracking noise. Kendal froze. It was not coming from the avatar this time. The sound came from the living room. He leapt out of bed and ran out into the hall. Mum was backing out of the living room, staring, terrified at the huge panel of the glass doors. A massive impact had crazed a head-sized circle of the glass, sending jagged streaks across the doorway. The glass was cracked diagonally from top to bottom, but it had held. Outside in the garden, Kendal could see nothing moving. Whatever had hit the glass had vanished, at least for now, but he had little doubt about what it had been.

"I heard a noise." Joseph had appeared behind them, rubbing his eyes. "Oh, hello, Imani." next to him, Imani's avatar was standing stiffly. It moved robotically forward. She was still lying in her pod, and had simply instructed it to follow, so the machine had her face, but none of her body language.

"Something -" started Mum, "something hit the window. I thought - " Kendal closed the living room door.

"Something's happening at the farm," said Kendal. "This is what I've been trying to tell you." Mum looked slowly

217

around, she seemed lost, disorientated. As though searching for a shred of reality in a virtual world. She focussed on Imani.

"Hello, dear," she said. "You're Kendal's girlfriend aren't you?" Imani smiled weakly back.

"Mum, snap out of it!" said Kendal. Mum had spent so long talking to avatars that in her moment of sleepless shock, the one unreal person in the room was the only thing she could connect to.

"Why don't you sit down for a minute?" said Imani. They moved through into the kitchen and Kendal made warm sweet tea. He tried to explain what was happening to Mum, but it felt as though very little was going in. Her head floated back and forth between Kendal and Imani, and he could see her fumbling agitatedly with her phone, flipping it over and over with her fingers. Part of her was asleep. Part was confused, and part wanted to be back online, escaping from everything.

"I need to talk to Doreen," she said at one point. "She'll know what to do."

Kendal peeped through the kitchen blinds. The garden was empty. The sun was coming up now, too, so hopefully, whatever was out there would not try to attack the house again.

For a second, Mum seemed to awaken.

"I'm not doing very well at work," she said. "I was distracted. They wanted me to raise their social media profile, with ten goodwill avatars talking to people around the town. But I misheard. I ordered a hundred."

"What are you talking about?" said Kendal. Mum hung her head.

"I was talking to Doreen," she said. "I think I raised their profile too much. The vegetarians are angry," she said, "They're planning a flash-mob outside the farm."

Kendal looked at her in horror, but before he could answer, the doorbell sounded. At the same moment a fist hammered on the door.

"Get in the car!" a voice yelled. It was Detective Inspector Gillmore. Kendal opened the door. Gillmore took in the three people and the avatar standing in the doorway. He looked around for a split-second. "You'll all have to come," he said, pulling Mum and Joseph down the front drive and bundling them into the back of the police car. "No room for the avatar," he said, pushing Imani back. "Wherever you are," he told her, "stay inside!" He pulled Kendal into the front, slammed the door, and took off.

Kendal watched out of the back window as Imani's avatar stood in the doorway, slowly fading.

THIS IS A TWENTY KILLIOMETRE PER HOUR ZONE, said Gillmore's glass artificial. She was crushed into the back beside Mum, a tangle of folded arms and legs making way for the two human passengers.

"And you wonder why I don't let you drive," said Gillmore, throwing the car around the corner and speeding away from the house.

I AM MORE ACCURATE THAN YOU AT HIGH SPEED DRIVING BY A MARGIN OF…

"Shut up!" said Gillmore. His voice was sharp. Kendal thought about what Imani had said. Would he have spoken to a male artificial that way? Did it matter that the police artificial had been crushed into the back of the car like a broken doll? She didn't seem to mind.

"I thought you didn't see this as a crime," said Kendal to the artificial.

219

I HAVE RECENTLY REVISED MY ASSESSMENT, she said, her head wedged sideways at an angle no human could match.

"Why does your car smell of dead fish?" said Joseph.

"Where are we going?" said Kendal. Gillmore was leaning forward, gripping the wheel so tightly his knuckles were white. He stared straight ahead at the road, eyes red. Wild. He hadn't shaved.

"It's after us," he said. "I don't know how - smell, DNA, whatever - but it's tracking us." He hauled the car around a corner, scraping a parked car. The avatar behind him flashed red for a second, registering a traffic infringement.

I WOULD NOT HAVE MADE THAT ERROR, she said.

"After I dropped you, I went home," said Gillmore, "an hour later, it attacked the house. I got to the car, and picked this one up," - he nodded at the avatar - "but somehow it followed me to the station. I've been driving around all night," said Gillmore. "Whenever I stop, it's there. It doesn't stop and it doesn't rest. Then suddenly, it just vanished. I figured it must be coming for you."

"Where is it now?" said Kendal.

"I don't know," said Gillmore. "I haven't seen it for an hour."

PROTOCOL DICTATES WE MUST EVACUATE THE AREA... said the artificial.

"No," said Gillmore. "With the level of evidence I've got, I couldn't clear the budget for that. Besides, it didn't attack the police station. It's like it knows to keep out of sight. If you see it it's going to come for you."

"Maybe it's hiding somewhere while it's light," said Kendal. "Maybe it's gone back the farm. Have you spoken to West?" Gillmore swerved. The early morning commuters were suddenly starting to pull out of driveways. A synchronised ballet of autonomous vehicles that would turn the roads from empty to full in the next five minutes.

"Can't raise him," said Gillmore. He glanced at Kendal. "I can't raise anyone at the farm," he said. "I tried another three farms too - no response."

Kendal turned around. In the back, Mum was looking back and forth between them, a dazed expression on her face. She said nothing. Joseph was staring out of the window, enjoying being in a police car.

"We need to get them somewhere safe," said Kendal.

"We're here," said Gillmore. He turned a corner. In front of them, the school gates started to swing open automatically.

"You're joking," said Kendal.

"It's safe. It's secure," said Gillmore. "And it will hold hundreds of people."

"Why does it need to hold hundreds of people?" said Kendal.

Ignoring the car park, Gillmore sped across the playground and brought the car to a stop just outside the main hall. "Hopefully it won't, but what if you're right? What if this is happening in farms all over the world?" Gillmore opened the car doors and thrust a set of keys into Mum's hands. "I don't think this is the end of it." he said.

"Will someone explain to me what's going on?" said Mum.

"There are monsters," explained Joseph. "Kendal's fighting them while you're playing on your phone."

"Go inside, find a safe place and sit tight," said Gillmore. Kendal started to get out of the car. "Not you," Gillmore put a hand on his shoulder. "We've got work to do."

Chapter 34

Gillmore took the car onto the long, wide carriageway through town and out towards the city. The motorway was full now with autonomous commuter cars. Some linked end to end to save energy, following each other in long trains. Others weaved in and out as traffic slowed and speeded up to let them through in a complex but seamlessly orchestrated dance of early morning motion. Once there would have been lanes travelling at different speeds, moving in different directions, hopelessly inefficient with half the road empty while the other half sat choking, unable to move. Now, traffic moved freely and at speed in both directions in all lanes, gliding and dodging to pass millimetres away from each other while their human passengers checked their messages, barely glancing out.

As a passenger in the one human-driven car on the road, Kendal's journey was considerably more terrifying. He gripped the dashboard as Gillmore swerved this way and that through the dance of metal, completely dependent upon whatever crash avoidance system was governing the movement of the other cars. For a man who claimed not to trust artificials, Gillmore was amazingly confident in their ability to make way for him.

Finally, he pulled off the carriageway and parked at the end of the long trunk road where Kendal had watched the lorries file to and from the farm the previous night. It was empty now. Kendal watched the sun rising slowly behind the farm, lighting up its solar panels in gold. It looked like it was going to be a lovely day.

"No lorries," said Gillmore, looking down towards the farm.

"They probably only run at night," said Kendal, "keeping out of the traffic." He wasn't even convincing himself. The night would be the busiest time, on that road, certainly, but there ought to be something moving during the day: workers arriving and leaving, maintenance vans, heavy delivery drones following the line of the road with individual drop-offs. But there was nothing. He could see the whole road - a single, straight black line from the point where they'd turned off down to the factory depot three kilometres away. Either side, the wide, flat meadow. Yellowing grass stretching to the fenced-off woods on one side, and, way off on the other side, another field. It was a simple, clean landscape of flat colours and straight lines. Yellow, gold, black and green. Along the whole length of the road, nothing moved. The tranquility was absolute proof. Something must be going on down at the farm, and whatever it was, it wasn't good.

"There are three things I don't understand," said Kendal. "I don't understand how two farms run by different companies thousands of kilometres apart can accidentally create the same mutant creature. And I don't understand how that creature can be tracking us - how it can even move if it doesn't have a brain."

"Well, clearly it does have a brain," said Gillmore, staring straight down the empty road. Kendal shook his head.

"You don't get it," he said. "I'm going to be a chef. I've done my Food Tech modules."

"Congratulations," said Gillmore.

"I've read a lot about meat," said Kendal. "It's not just that there's a law against growing nervous tissue. You'd need a whole other set of production processes - raw materials - machines," Kendal said. "It's not just illegal. They don't have the gear." Gillmore shrugged.

"You said there were three things, " he said. "What's the third one?" Kendal put his sleeve over his mouth.

"I don't understand why your car smells of rotten fish." he said. Gillmore smiled.

They opened the boot and the smell hit Kendal like something solid. He staggered back, covering his nose. The corpse of the creature from the weir was still curled up where the glass avatar had left it, the strange, needle-toothed head lying on its finned tail. Kendal looked at its skin - dull black now, and festering, its eyes pale and clouded. He caught his chef's instincts kicking in - the flesh would be way past its best.

Gillmore gestured to the artificial, and it moved in. Grasping the twisted shape around the middle, she hauled it out and dumped it on the tarmac. Its body was stiff now with rigor mortis, and it bounced slightly as it slapped wetly onto the hard road.

"Lucky you left your knife." Gillmore fished around in the back of the car and pulled out the chef's knife Kendal and Imani had used to kill the creature. He handed it to Kendal.

"What am I supposed to do with that?" he said.

"You wanted to find out how they move," said Gillmore. "You're the chef. Are you any good at filleting?"

Kendal knelt beside the creature, and felt his stomach churning. He forced the feeling back. It was, he told himself just

224

like any other fish he'd ever prepared. Except that this one was a lot bigger, and this one had a head. Fangs. Staring eyes. He clenched his teeth.

"I need it turned over," he said.

I UNDERSTAND WE ARE PREPARING A MEAL, said the police artificial. WOULD YOU LIKE ME TO GATHER SOME HERBS? Kendal stared up at her. She had all the programming, all the machine learning algorithms, all the knowledge of the Internet and she could still mistake an autopsy for a banquet. Artificials were unbelievable sometimes.

"No," he said. "Just turn it over." She stepped forward, hoisted the animal up and dumped it on the road, belly up. Its mouth flopped open against the ground. The long wounds Imani had inflicted with her rubber remote-controlled hands showed as grey slits. Kendal ignored them, and assessed the shape of the creature, trying to apply his knowledge of fish preparation. If it were a mackerel, he told himself, there was a classic first cut.

He held his breath, located the heavy pointed knife at the creature's anus, pushed it deep in, and unzipped the animal from the tip of the tail to the soft flesh under the chin. It opened easily, and tangles of blue, black and red intestines spilled out onto the road. Guts, heart, liver all dark, shiny shades of stinking offal. Kendal felt the vomit rising in his throat and forced it back again. Even Gillmore looked away. The avatar didn't move. In fact, she leaned in, inspecting the mess of guts flowing thickly over Kendal's shoes.

"Could you give me some room?" he said. She stepped to the side, but continued to stare with a lack of expression it was easy to interpret as fascination.

225

The next cut was at right angles. Up around the gills, through the thick burgundy meat of the neck and right through until the spine stopped the knife. He felt its ridges, turned the knife, ran it down the backbone, keeping to the side of the dorsal fin, scraping it as he dragged it through the flesh. So when he pulled the knife finally through the tip of the tail, he could lift of the whole side of the animal as one boneless fillet.

"Impressive," said Gillmore. "What does it look like?" Kendal shook his head.

"It's just like any normal cut of meat," he said, "you wouldn't normally get all the guts." Getting more confident now, he poked the squidgy mess with his knife. "Because they usually use shared blood to feed the meat, they don't need individual hearts and intestines, so they only grow what they can sell."

"What about brains?" said Gillmore.

"Well, let's see," said Kendal. He grabbed the head either side of the huge mouth, heaved and twisted it until it lay flat, chin-down next to its guts. There was a crunch as the neck dislocated.

Kendal took his knife and inserted it horizontally along the back of the neck, pushing it in towards the skull, then grabbed it with both hands and yanked it forward, splitting the skull along the top.

"Help me get this off, will you?" he said to the avatar.

She bent down, and wormed her solid fingers in between the split sections, and wrenched. The whole skull tore open, exposing the brain case from neck to snout.

Kendal and Gillmore leaned in. It was empty.

It was clear where the brain ought to have been. A long oval gap opened up behind the white eyeball. Kendal reached in. He ran a finger around the opening.

"I don't understand," he said, "this isn't possible! How can it move?"

"They move in the factory," said Gillmore. "Maybe it's like that."

"To tone the meat, yes." said Kendal, "but that's because the muscles are stimulated by electrical currents. To move around outside they need more than muscle spasms. They'd need to make decisions. To have intentions."

"So what are you telling me?" said Gillmore.

"I don't know," said Kendal. He dug his fingers deeper into the brain case. It was an empty gap, surrounded by bone and red meat that squashed under his touch. He felt carefully around the edges, and down into the cavity where the spine began. His fingers touched something hard. "Wait a minute," he said.

He pulled, and it came away, pulling strands of cobweb-thin gold wire behind it.

"What is it?" said Gillmore. Kendal lifted his hand. In it, a tiny square, flat object about the size of the tip of his thumb, and coated in thick, dark mucus. He wiped it clean. It shone with hair-like gold traces leading from its edges to a silver square in its centre.

"Wi-Fi," said Kendal.

Gillmore snatched the oily circuit and stared at at it, holding it up to the light, and turning it in his fingers. The early sun glittered from its surface. Kendal could see now that the thin traces on its edges trailed off in spider-silk strands of gold which must have connected the circuit to the creature's muscles and senses before he tore it out. They must have formed a replacement nervous system. An impressive piece of wiring, he thought.

"Then this is no accident," said Gilmore almost whispering. "Somebody is controlling them!"

227

Chapter 35

"Who?" said Kendal.

"Only one way to find out," said Gillmore. He turned and stared back down the road towards the Farm.

Kendal followed Gilmore's gaze. There was still no sign of life down there. Not a single vehicle had passed them in either direction on its way to or from the huge blank-walled building.

"It's like the place is dead," said Gillmore. Kendal squinted towards the sun. Black shapes were buzzing over the farm, swarming like bees.

"The drones are out," said Kendal. "They must still be working. And West must still be in there with his avatars." Gillmore checked his phone.

"Maybe," he said. "I still haven't heard a word from him since we left last night."

"You think he's behind this?" said Kendal.

"I don't know," said Gillmore. "He was definitely covering it up, but he looked pretty surprised when you showed him the other farm."

"It could have been an act," said Kendal.

"I don't know, but we have to find out," said Gillmore.

"You don't mean going in there?" said Kendal, nervously. Gillmore shook his head.

"Not us." He turned to the artificial. She was standing behind them, watching the two of them speaking. Her face was fixed in an attentive half-smile. "I need your body," said Gilmore. The artificial blinked.

I AM PERMANENTLY EMBODIED IN THIS UNIT TO PROTECT MY IMPARTIALITY. Her face did not change. I CANNOT LEAVE IT. Gillmore nodded slowly. He drew a deep breath in between his teeth.

"I know," he said, "but we need to see inside the farm."

I AM A VERY EXPENSIVE PIECE OF EQUIPMENT, she said.

"I know," said Gillmore, softly. He reached out and put his hand on her arm. The avatar looked down at his hand, tilted her head, then looked slowly back up.

IS THERE ANOTHER OPTION THAT WOULD NOT RISK MY DESTRUCTION? Gillmore said nothing, but he shook his head. The artificial straightened. She processed for a second. WILL I BE IN CONTROL OF MY OWN BODY? Gillmore nodded.

"We'll just watch in VR. We'll only be passengers," he said. "You can drive." He smiled.

YOU MAY FOLLOW MY PROGRESS USING HEADSETS, she said. Gillmore produced two slimline headsets from under the dashboard.

The artificial paused for a second as though waiting for Gillmore to change his mind, and then started to walk away down the long road towards the farm. Gillmore and Kendal watched her go. The fields either side of the straight road were empty and still. The rising sun glinted off her glass frame.

"That's why I don't like artificials," Gillmore said eventually. "You just can't avoid getting attached." They got into the car. Gillmore pulled on his headset.

"What if the creature comes back while we're in VR?" asked Kendal. Gillmore smiled.

"Keep your window rolled up," he said. Under the headset, Kendal saw him smile. "I think we're OK while it's light," he said. Kendal pulled his headset on, and instantly he was looking through the eyes of the avatar.

He saw the farm up ahead, growing slowly with every step, its warehouse doors sealed shut. A few trucks parked at odd angles outside. One was blocking the road, its cab half turned as though ready to drive out, but it wasn't moving. Another was left beside the huge warehouse doors, its cab door hanging open. The artificial looked left out across the field. Her eyes were sharper than his, and he could make out the birds in the trees at the far edge.

He sat back in the car-seat, and let his mind adjust. He was her now.

Without slowing her pace, she turned completely around, looking back. Kendal could see the car at the end of the road. The remains of the creature, dismembered beside it. In the car, two figures. Himself and Gillmore sat, motionless. Blue VR headsets covering their eyes. The artificial seemed to linger on the image, watching them recede as she walked away. Then she turned back, directed her gaze at the farm and started to run towards it, accelerating. Eating up the ground between herself and the mess of abandoned trucks outside the doors.

Kendal felt the exhilaration of running as he sat, motionless in his car-seat, experienced the ground rushing by, the destination closing. It felt good to move so fast. When this was all over, he promised himself, he would start doing regular exercise.

In the lorry park, she slowed suddenly. Around her, the autonomous vehicles were strewn. Some were open. Some were abandoned in the midst of being loaded, or unloaded. Others were parking. All were still. Frozen. As though mid-way through the busy night's work someone had suddenly just cut the power, pulled down the huge rolling shutters, and sealed the factory off.

The longer Kendal sat watching through her eyes, the more he found himself taken into the avatar's world. He saw what she saw, but it was more than that. The helmet gave nothing but sight and sound, but his mind filled in the gaps. As she took a step it felt like his legs moving. As she turned her head, it began to feel as though he had made the decision to glance around. The strange but familiar experience of being a passenger in another body took over. He had heard of the theory that we are all passengers in our own lives - that consciousness is dumb - a thoughtless observer of our clever animal selves with no purpose but to make up rational stories to explain our actions. He could feel that now. His brain telling itself that he was the artificial.

It was impossible to comprehend that Gillmore beside him was having the very same experience, that the artificial was sharing her body with both of them.

Kendal felt her leave the scatter of lorries and march up to the shutters. The heavy metal blinds were fastened shut, but on one side, about thirty metres from where she was standing, the metal had been dented and buckled by a ferocious impact from inside, and just beyond that, there was a rip where the metal wall had been torn open like a punctured tin can. The rip was about two metres high and almost as wide, and either side of it, triangles of metal were peeled outwards in jagged spikes.

231

Whatever had come through had fought its way out, because as the avatar approached, Kendal could see blood and thick, course hair caught and dried on the edges of the torn metal. It had been followed too because around the tear, bullet holes dented and pierced the metal wall.

The artificial stepped through into the darkness. Inside, the warehouse was silent. Frozen. Boxes and tanks were stacked floor to ceiling ready to be shipped out. Some were burst open, spilling carcasses and animal parts onto the floor. Others had been pierced by bullets and were leaking blood or white fluid onto the floor in sticky, congealing pools.

The avatar ignored them, but as her foot crunched on the floor, Kendal sensed her stopping and looking down. Beneath her glass foot, another chunk of shattered glass had become wedged. She lifted her foot, and pulled out the piece. It was a fragment of a melon sized glass ovoid. She turned it over in her hands, then looked up. Kendal saw now that the whole floor was scattered with thick chunks of shaped but shattered glass. She stood, tilted her head, and scanned the floor.

"West's avatars," said a voice next to Kendal. Gillmore's whisper startled him, and for a second, he was back in the car. "Follow the trail," he said.

The avatar stood up, fixing its gaze straight ahead, at the swinging open door on the other side of the warehouse, she marched, crunching on the broken bodies of her fallen kind until she reached the door and stepped through into the white room Kendal and Gillmore had fled a few hours earlier.

It looked different now. The chairs were strewn and smashed. The desk, lying on its end, diagonally against one corner. Great gouges of plaster had been scraped out of the walls in

232

diagonal slashes, and the remains of two glass avatars lay crumpled, hurled against the wall by some great force, and smashed.

"Give me your assessment," said Gillmore.

I BELIEVE A FIGHT TOOK PLACE HERE, said the artificial. The voice felt as though it came from inside Kendal's own head. Gillmore sighed impatiently.

"Anything else?" he said.

YES, said the artificial. She turned towards the desk. Its top faced outwards, shielding the corner of the room. I BELIEVE THIS HAS BEEN PLACED DELIBERATELY.

"What do you mean?" said Kendal. She started walking towards it.

IT MAY HAVE BEEN USED AS SOME KIND OF DEFENSIVE STRUCTURE. The avatar reached the desk and lifted an arm. She pulled it away from the wall. West loomed out, pitching forwards, his face filling the viewer of Kendal's headset. Kendal cried out in shock, recoiled backwards into his car-seat, instinctively throwing his hands up to protect his face.

"Easy," said Gillmore, his own voice shaking slightly. The avatar caught West, as his knees folded, and held him, head lolling centimetres from hers, staring directly at Kendal through her eyes.

"Is he..?" said Kendal.

HE IS DEAD, said the artificial without inflection. PROCEDURE DICTATES THAT RECOVERING HIS BODY AND INFORMING HIS NEXT OF KIN IS A PRIORITY.

"Forget procedure," said Gillmore, "We need you to search the factory."

233

The artificial let go of West. His face slipped from view and Kendal heard his knees crack on the hard floor. She turned, without looking down and walked briskly down towards the farm factory floor.

"It wasn't him, then," said Gillmore. "He was trying to stop it."

"Unless he thought he could control it," said Kendal.

"I don't know," said Gillmore, "This makes no sense. These things breaking out, killing random people, it can't be part of anybody's plan, but those chips - the implants - must have taken some designing."

"So if it's not a plan and it's not an accident, what is it?" said Kendal.

"I don't know."

The artificial reached the end of a corridor and pushed the door. The sound grew instantly in Kendal's ears and made him want to rip the headset off and run. It was the sound of the factory in motion. Those thousands of fidgeting limbs. The silence of the unsettled crowd. Kendal forced back the urge, and stared into the dim light.

They were back on the main growing floor, but something was different now. Something was very wrong.

Chapter 36

The artificial stood in the doorway, and swung her head slowly back and forth to allow Kendal and Gillmore to take in the scene. The factory was running at full capacity, and completely without intervention. Drones buzzed back and forth, tending and injecting. The wheeled robots rolled and swerved over the floor, their unicycle tires, squeaking on pools of spilt blood and amniotic fluid.

But the kicking limbs and flapping wings and twitching cadavers were not as they had been the previous night. Somehow, overnight, the factory floor had been re-ordered. The unfinished body parts had been removed from their needles and frames and were now stacked, ignored in a huge pile of pallid, dead flesh. The growing frames had been wheeled around and were now arranged in circles, their injectors and blood pipes fed now into human sized blobs of milky amniotic gel. There must have been hundreds. Each bag pulsed and writhed, but all were opaque. Kendal could see shadows, blue, grey and red shapes moving within, but there was no way to tell what they were, or how close each was to emerging from its birthing sack.

"This is bad," said Gillmore. The artificial let the door close behind her and stepped further into the room.

"Wait!" said Kendal, "Look left!" The avatar swung her head to the left.

"What the hell -"said Gillmore. Kendal felt a cold, sick feeling spread from his stomach and up to his neck. The feeling closed around his brain.

The sack in the centre of the room was massive. Hanging from the ceiling, fed by thick pipes from a dozen horse-leg sized frames, and nurtured by a buzzing horde of drones which spun and hovered around it like hornets tending a nest, the bulb of fluid pulsed like a pale bloodless heart. Whatever was inside it was the size of a house.

"Ok, I've seen enough," said Gillmore, "Get out of there!"

The artificial turned, took one step towards the door, and fell suddenly to its knees. Kendal saw a blur heading for his face. It could have been a hand, or a mouth, or something else, but the moment it struck, the headset went blank.

He wrenched it off, gasping for air. Next to him, Gillmore was doing the same. They stared at each other for a second.

"Damn!" said Gillmore.

"We've got to shut it down," said Kendal. "Can we cut the power?"

"No. It's all solar," said Gillmore.

"You need to call it in to the station!" said Kendal. "Get all the police down here - surround the place!" Gillmore laughed.

"I don't think you quite understand police budgeting," said Gillmore. "I am all the police."

"What?"

"Most crime is online now, and since AMA came in there's nothing for us to do. They've been running down the local forces for years. Now it's just me and a few inflatables. I was issued the artificial for heavy lifting, but it looks like she's gone now too." He shrugged. "We're on our own." Kendal gawped at him.

"You did see that thing in there?" he said. "And you're telling me there's NOBODY? Nobody you can call? "

"I guess this would come under 'a breach of the peace?'" said Kendal, "and AMA pretty much handles all that stuff now. I could put a call through to National - but that needs an evidence upload or it won't be taken seriously. And I can't do an evidence upload."

"Why not?"

"Because that has to come from my artificial," he said. "Besides, if you're right and this is all the farms, then National will have its hands full."

"So, what the hell are we supposed to do now?" Kendal was yelling now. He threw the headset into the foot well of the car. Suddenly a thought struck him. What was it Mum had said? His brain swooped with a sudden sickening vertigo. "The vegetarians!" he said. "They're marching on the farm tonight. We've got to stop them!"

Gillmore spun the wheel and the car skidded around, sliding on the remains of the fish thing in the road, and burying itself in the automated choreography that was the motorway. Against the flow of traffic, Gillmore drove straight at a sea of cars, forcing them to part around him the way a shoal of fish parts to avoid a shark. Kendal felt the car tilt and swerve as other vehicles passed millimetres from his window. Each one making effortless split second decisions to navigate the fluid network that was the road, each communicating with its companions to work out the most efficient way to avoid collision. Kendal tried

237

not to think about what would happen if they met another human-driven car now.

Kendal's phone rang. It was Imani.

"I need you to do something for me," she said.

"Ok, but just don't leave the coffin. I need you to stay in there - something big is coming!" said Kendal.

"Too late." Imani's breath was uneven. She was gasping for air.

"Where are you?" he said, panic rising in his gut. He looked into his phone. Imani's face was glistening with sweat. Her eyes were red. She was running. She turned the phone around to show him what she saw. It was the main street of her town. The bland concrete walls of identical printed buildings were lined up along a rough dirt road. The sun was strong. So strong that the sky fought with the auto-exposure of her camera and as she moved, the street dimmed and brightened from a black silhouette against a blue sky to a bleached, overexposed burnout.

That was probably why it took Kendal a moment to realise that the piles of clothes lying strewn and abandoned in the street were actually something else.

"Everybody's dead," sobbed Imani. "I need you to call my family. Tell them to get out."

"Me?" said Kendal, "Last time I met them we tried to kill each other. They won't listen to me."

"You have to make them listen," said Imani. "They've blocked me." Kendal saw her look behind her, but she kept running. "I'm trying to get there now, but I need you to get into an avatar at their house - protect them - somehow. I'm sending you the number."

She rang off. Kendal grabbed the VR helmet. Next to him, Gillmore wrenched the wheel and they pulled off the motorway onto a smaller road. The car slowed. Heavy traffic choked the

238

street. Even AI couldn't solve congestion here. Kendal pulled on the helmet and hit the number.

His virtual eyes opened in the corner of Imani's mother's china shop. It was a room blazing with colour. What had once been a simple printed house had been decorated to within an inch of its life. Greens, reds, blues and browns fought and clashed, and every wall, door, window frame or piece of furniture had been painted a different colour. Finished and half-finished pots and plates and jugs covered every surface. China painted with crazy vibrant patterns in every colour was stacked and piled from floor to ceiling. There were shelves of it, heaps of it. Even the floor was scattered with glazed and unglazed pottery pieces. In the centre of the room, Imani's mother spun around to face Kendal, her brother next to her.

"You?" said the woman. "How dare you come to our house?" Imani's brother stepped forward, and reached out to hit the power-down button.

"Wait!" said Kendal, "There's something coming! It's killed everyone in the town!" The woman grabbed her son's hand, and pushed it away from the button.

"What are you talking about?" she said.

"It's from the farm - " he started, but before he could finish the sentence, the wall in front of him exploded. The bull-creature's head hovered for a second peering into the room, horns first, snout hinging at the jaw to grin with the same tangle of needle sharp teeth the creatures from the wood and the weir both shared. Its head hung like some kind of trophy protruding from the wall.

Then it simply reached in and tore the wall apart with its great shovel-like forelimbs. Coloured concrete smashed into the floor sending pottery flying, and the creature hurled itself into

239

the centre of the shop. Imani's mother was staring in disbelief. It turned towards her, enraged eyes fixing her and roared, the lipless mouth swinging open, cavernous and black as it stepped towards her.

Imani's brother reacted in a second. He grabbed a shelving unit piled high with clay pots ready for the kiln, and tipped it, bringing the whole thing down on top of the creature. The pots slid forward, raining down, shattering on to its shoulders and back. The animal turned, putting its vast head down and dragging its horns through the shower of shelving and china. The unit disintegrated in a twisted tangle of wire and wood and clay, and when the bull raised its head, it threw the whole broken thing straight into the boy's chest. He flew back, pinned and crushed into the wall, and then slid, lifeless to the floor. Imani's mother looked on in horror.

Kendal looked around. His avatar was standing behind a rough wooden bench. On it, the tools of the potter's trade were laid out: spatulas, blunt bladed knives, wooden scrapers for moulding soft clay. He had a second to choose his weapon. He raised his hand - it too was wooden. A slightly sturdier frame than his own home avatar, but no match for the thing in front of him. As it reared up to crush Imani's mother, Kendal grabbed the only tool that he thought might make a difference.

It was a wire cutter: two wooden grips with a long, thick wire stretching between them. From his car seat, he urged the avatar to spring forward, reaching out with his wooden fingers to wrap one end of the grips around a fixed shelf. Stretching the wire taught, he sprang high and around the creature, dragging it around the animal's thick neck like a garrotte.

Kendal's headset was a sudden, disorientating blur of fur and concrete dusted flesh as he waved his hands wildly in the car seat.

"Keep still!" he heard Gillmore yell beside him as he felt his fist connect with the policeman's face and the car swerved.

The avatar landed, staggering beside the potter's wheel. Its legs splintering beneath it, and he wedged the handle of the wire cutter into the mechanism of the heavy wheel. He struggled to his feet and looked around. He had the creature's attention now. It was advancing on him.

"Come on, then!" he said, signalling the avatar to back a way. The creature stepped forward, following. A second later, it felt the metal loop close around its neck. It reacted instantly, jerking its head back. The noose tightened. It bellowed in pain, and thrashed. The handles of the wire cutter rattled against the metal shelf and the frame of the potter's wheel, but they held. It bellowed again, a strangled cry, and twisted, flinging out its horns and its limbs in a blind, desperate rage.

One claw caught Kendal and sent his avatar flying across the room, wedging it half way through the window. He could only watch as, on the other side of the room, Imani's mother picked up a stone pot and ran at the hulking thing.

"No!" shouted Kendal, but he was too late. She swung the pot high above her head and smashed it down, edge first into the creature's skull. Kendal heard the crack. Saw the top of the head caving in.

Imani's mother was stronger than she looked. If it had a brain, the blow would have killed the creature outright, but she could not have known that its brain case was a redundant space. It held nothing. The beast didn't even pause. It twisted its head down, and gored her, lifting her between its massive horns and slamming her into the ceiling. The crash made a crumbling hole in the concrete, and the animal shook its head, dislodging her, and hurling her to the floor. It raised its head, opened its huge toothed jaws. She screamed, and Kendal looked away.

When he looked back, the creature was raising its head, turning towards him, still held by the metal garrotte, fastened tight around its throat.

"Kendal!" It was Imani. Her voice was coming from behind him. The beast froze, turning its head. Kendal twisted around so that he could look back out of the window. Imani was running towards him up the street.

"Run!" he shouted. "Just run!" She stopped. The creature roared. Kendal glanced back to see it thrashing madly against its snare. The wire was digging deep into its flesh, but the handles were pulling against their anchors. The shelf was buckling, the potter's wheel rattling on its mountings, the bolts holding it to the floor, being wrenched out one at a time. He turned back to Imani. She was standing, frozen in the street.

"They're dead!" shouted Kendal. "You have to run. Now!" She stared for a second, then turned and ran, stumbling away down the street. She was on her own now.

Chapter 37

Kendal and Gillmore left the car and rounded the corner to the town square on foot.

Mum hadn't been kidding. Her mistake, distracted by Doreen, had been a simple one. An extra digit on the order page. It was easily done, but it had cost her her job, and now instead of twenty synthetic sales agents, there were now two hundred roaming rubber evangelists working the square. Her promotional avatars were everywhere. Pre-programmed with positive messages from the farm, they had been released to wander the square, searching for someone - anyone - to talk to. The plaza was floating and drifting with a hundred lost soulless souls. Cheap balloon avatars with generic, faces wandered, swaying in the breeze from one automated conversation to the next. As Kendal and Gillmore strode into the square, one approached. She presented as a girl of about his age. Beautiful in a bland sort of way, calculated, no doubt to appeal to Kendal, but the cheap avatar distorted her face. Her eyes were just rounded dents in the inflatable, and her lips were projected onto a smooth surface so that she looked as though her face was reflected in the back of a spoon. The only physical definition in her head was a rough nose down which an unfinished seam ran from the top of her head, down her chin, neck and chest where it vanished under a short plastic skirt. On the top of her head, a course blonde wig had been stuck. Kendal looked her up and down. Mum had really gone for cut-price models.

HI! she said. ARE YOU HAVING A GREAT DAY?

"No," said Kendal, "Not especially."

DID YOU KNOW THAT THREE LARGE SERVINGS OF QUALITY MEAT PER DAY CAN HELP YOU MAINTAIN A POSITIVE ATTITUDE AND A HEALTHY GUT BIOME? Kendal walked on, ignoring the machine. Another approached.

HEY THERE, BOYS she said. This one had a short, red wig, but exactly the same face and voice. HAVE EITHER OF YOU EVER TRIED OUR HIPPO SCRATCHINGS? THEY'RE A GREAT TREAT FOR ALL THE FAMILY, AND VIRTUALLY FAT FREE! Kendal pushed the avatar out of the way, and she rocked backwards and forwards on her weighted feet, swinging like a punch-bag.

"How long are these things supposed to keep going?" he said.

"Three hours," said Gillmore. "After that it's considered harassment." He stopped to shove another avatar out of the way. It bounced into an identical copy of itself, and the two immediately started up an enthusiastic dialogue about the great taste and low, low cost of premium sculpted mince products. A real artificial would have spotted that it was talking to one of its own kind immediately, but these simple chatbots were just programmed with a few responses. They quickly fell into a conversational loop.

"Why are they still running?" said Kendal.

"There's nobody at the farm to turn them off, I guess." said Gillmore. "They'll just go on until someone recycles them." The crowds of avatars were starting to gather around them now, greeting them from all sides with their friendly messages. The circle of smiling, balloon-faced women closed in around them, shining wigs tangled together. Rubber limbs squeaked against each other.

"I get why the vegetarians are angry," said Kendal.

"Where are they going to gather?" said Gillmore. The circle around them was becoming tighter. More avatars had spotted the fresh, human meat and were swarming in from the outside.

"All I know is they're marching on the farm tonight." Kendal had to shout to make himself heard above the babble of meat-based slogans projected from the grinning faces.

"We have to get to them first." Gillmore shouted back. Kendal pushed against the closing crowd, but it was no use. The plastic bodies crumpled for a second and then re-inflated. He grabbed an avatar by the waist and pulled upwards. Her body was slight - a couple of kilos - and he was able to lift her easily above his head and hurl her onto the heads of her companions, but it did no good. The second she was gone, two more of her kind took her place. Gillmore reached into his pocket and pulled out his police badge. He held it aloft.

"Stop!" he shouted at the top of his voice. The avatars took not the slightest notice.

Suddenly, from the other side of the square, Kendal heard voices. A chant rising.

"What do we want?" a crowd was yelling. "Living meat! When do we want it? NOW!" Kendal stood on tiptoes to look over the heads of the crowd of avatars to where the sound was coming from.

For a second the square was empty, but then, around the corner from the high street, a crowd of figures were running towards them. Kendal and Gillmore stared at the approaching army.

"Something's wrong," said Gillmore. "They're-" Kendal squinted at the crowd.

"More avatars!" he said finally. He could see them more clearly now, over the multi-coloured wigs of the promotional girls. The demonstration was made up of wave after wave of avatars.

"Just what we need," said Gillmore.

As they came closer, Kendal could see what was happening. The vegetarians were using their own home avatars instead of themselves to make the charge. Many of the avatar's faces were obscured by anonymous white masks, but right at the front, Kendal could make out one face. Farron's avatar was leading the charge, arm held high.

"What are they doing?" said Kendal. Gillmore studied the group.

"They're carrying something," he said.

"Pins!" said Kendal. The crowd had reached the farm's promotional avatars now, and each holding a fistfull of long pins, they dived headlong into the cheap inflatables, scything through them, scattering them in all directions.

The crowd's aim was clear. By using avatars instead of their real selves, they could take out their anger on the farm's army of promotional dummies without risking the intervention of AMA. They tore through the circle of girls, slashing and puncturing. The sound of balloons bursting, gas escaping and preprogramed voice boxes winding down filled the air.

It was less of a battle and more of a massacre, and in seconds, Kendal and Gillmore were surrounded by a furious tumult of shredded plastic bodies and roaring vegetarians. A pretty avatar loomed in front of Kendal, smiling a pleasant, open smile.

YOU LOOK LIKE THE SORT OF MAN WHO VALUES THE FINER THINGS, she said. Her body folded sideways and began to exhale as a rubber fist full of nails tore a gash down her side. She didn't miss a beat. ENJOY OUR GUILT FREE STEAK RARE. She fell to the ground, still talking as her killer stepped lightly over her body, and grabbed one of her identical twins by the throat.

"Farron!" Kendal said as his schoolmate stabbed at the girl with his free hand.

SOME EXTREMISTS THINK WE SHOULD MURDER ANIMALS FOR FOOD, she said, smiling at him. WE THINK THAT'S BARBARIC. Farron squashed her face with his own avatar's clumsy hands until her head popped. The finger-sized projector LED responsible for displaying her face flashed momentarily, throwing the distorted image of her eye across Farron's chest, and her still moving lips smeared over the ground beside him. Then it died, and Farron let go of the avatar, watching it stumble off, headless into the crowd.

"What are you doing here?" said Farron.

"We need to talk," said Kendal as a broken torso drifted between them. He batted it out of the way and, caught by the wind, it bounced upwards five metres into the air, turning over and over. "Where are you?"

"Like I'm going to tell you," laughed Farron. Gillmore held up his badge in front of Farron.

"We need to talk to you," he said.

"We've got nothing to talk about," said Farron. Kendal grabbed him by the neck. He was better built than the promotional dummies, but still just a domestic. He had no strength. Kendal pulled him close.

"This is important!" Kendal growled. "I know who killed Lexie. Now tell me where you are!"

Chapter 38

"I don't believe you," said Farron. They were sitting in a cafe-gym. The place was corporate shabby. Exposed brickwork - fake. Pre-scratched tables. 20th century sports posters. It was modelled on a retro boxing club, an attempt at grubby uniqueness that was rolled out in a thousand other identical outlets across the world. Exercise machines were scattered around. Runners, rowers, a row of VR booths. If you wanted to run the alps or shoot the rapids, or fight Muhammad Ali, this was where you came. Farron - the real Farron - sat behind a bowl of green protein shake, and listened in silence as Kendal and Gillmore told him what they knew.

"I found Lexie, you know," said Farron, finally. "She'd been offered a sports science scholarship in China. We had a stupid argument about it. I ended up telling her I couldn't do long distance. Dating dummies is for losers, right?" Kendal looked away. "She ran off into the woods. I followed her, but when I found her…" he broke off, shaking his head.

"You know I could never have done that to her, don't you?" said Kendal.

"I guess," said Farron. He laughed without smiling. "She was a county level kickboxer. She'd have made mincemeat of you." Kendal shrugged.

"You're probably right."

"You get why we all thought it was you, right? Everybody knew you had a crush on her." Kendal felt himself cringe.

"I'm telling the truth," said Kendal. "The farm is producing whole creatures. And now it's like it's gone mad. It's completely automated, and they're building something huge in there. If you don't call off this protest, a lot of people are going to die." Farron shook his head.

"I don't know," he said.

"What about Lady Bradbury?" said Kendal. Farron shrugged.

"She's just another corporate PR. It's not like there's an organisation with a leader or something. We're basically a flashmob. Nobody's in charge. It just happens."

"So who organised that stunt with the avatars?" said Gillmore.

"Look around." Farron nodded to the other people in the cafe. Kendal and Gillmore followed his gaze. Everyone was on phones and in VR headsets. "Some of them are here - or in other cafes and bars. Some are at home. Some of them could be on the other side of the world. I don't even know most of them."

"So you can't stop the demo?" said Gillmore. Farron shook his head.

"I don't know," he said. "It's a big movement and these protests spark up quick." He rubbed his chin, "I can put the word out, but -"

"At least tell us what they're planning," said Gillmore. Farron took a deep breath and lowered his voice. Kendal looked around. Everyone else in the cafe was far too caught up in their devices to take any notice of the real world.

"They're going to block the road. Stop the delivery lorries getting out," said Farron, "and then they're going to storm the building. Smash the growing stems. Knock over the blood tanks." Gillmore's eyes widened.

"Their security force was five solid avatars with guns," he said, "They came out as broken glass, and that was just one creature. Do you understand what I'm saying?"

"Most of the people at tonight's action will be locals, I guess," said Farron. "I can try to talk to them."

"How many are coming?" said Gillmore. Farron shrugged

"Could be ten. Could be a thousand."

"Bloody flashmobs!" said Gillmore. "How am I supposed to police that?" Kendal thought for a second.

"What about AMA?" he said. "A mob like that, she'll stop you in a second." Farron smiled, reached into his pocket and pulled out a pill box. He opened it and removed a small yellow capsule which he placed on the table in front of Farron. "What is it?"

"Beta blockers," said Farron. Gillmore snatched up the pill.

"For God's sake!" he said. "Heart attack medicine." He looked at Kendal. "But also used to reduce anxiety."

"Actually a far more refined version. Black market stuff." said Farron.

"I don't understand," said Kendal.

"They work by suppressing hormones like adrenaline," said Gillmore. "They slow the heart down. Relax the muscles."

"And those are some of AMA's triggers," said Farron.

"The effect could be enough to confuse the signals, so she doesn't come after you." said Gillmore.

"And that works?" said Kendal.

251

Gillmore bit his lip. He took a long breath. "I told you I don't trust artificials," he said. "You meet AMA a lot in my line of work. There's something funny about her. When she triggers. How she handles a situation. You never quite know if she's going to go in hard or soft - whether she goes for all-out separation, or counselling, or mediation." He shrugged, "It's a dark art, I guess, but she's a strange one. Sometimes I wonder about her logic."

"But these pills will stop her?" said Kendal. Gillmore nodded.

"Maybe," he said. Kendal stood up.

"Right," he said to Farron, "you get the word out, then meet us at the school." He turned to Gillmore. "We've got to get back there and talk to Mum and Imani. Mum worked PR for the farm. Imani is at the other farm. Together they might be able to tell us what's really going on." Farron nodded.

"I don't suppose it matters now," he said, "but I really did love Lexi."

"I know," said Kendal.

"But she'd never have stayed with me," he half-laughed again. "Too many choices. Too many other options," he said. "Doreen gave us four months, max." For all his bravado, Farron looked suddenly weak. Kendal stood up and made for the door.

"Let's go," he said.

Chapter 39

It was starting to get dark as Gillmore and Kendal pulled into the playground. The only building with any lights on was the canteen. It was a block the children had always called the prison, partially because its imposing and undecorated shape looked brutal and defensive, and partially because the food served there appeared designed to punish.

A child-height layer of light-grey brick ran around the bottom, whilst on top, a dark-grey shell of stone strips sat over the whole building as though a giant limpet had suctioned itself to the school playground and refused to move. Square windows were set deep into the dark shell in a row along the wall looking across the field and down towards the wood.

Inside, the canteen felt wrong. It should have been full of shouting and clattering children. The rows of tables should have been covered with trays spilling soft sticky sludge in varying shades of brown and green. The chairs should have been slumped with untidy Year Nines. The sound of scraping chairlegs should have echoed and grated. Beyond that, the long metal foodbar should have been filled with metal trays of fast-printed veg-style economy shapes. The glass front of the buffet bar should have been dripping with the captured sneezes of its victims.

And behind the bar, the hatch into the kitchen should have revealed cooks and their avatars rushing and fussing between the aluminium washers and cookers and printers, stirring and carrying and dolloping onto plates. Kendal could never remember seeing the place this quiet, or empty, or clean.

But today it was. Today the cafeteria had just one customer. Joseph sat alone, spooning a plate of dry cereal. He had clearly figured out how to open the cupboards, thought Kendal. That marked a step forward in his culinary education.

"Where's Mum?" said Kendal.

"Dunno," said Joseph, "she went back to check out the kitchen." He gestured over to the unusually shiny collection of machines behind the bar.

"When?" said Kendal. Joseph shrugged.

"About an hour ago."

Kendal and Gillmore dodged around behind the glistening food bar, and between the machines. The kitchen was empty. "Over here!" said Gillmore. Right at the back of the kitchen, its aluminium door closed, was the store-room. From the other side, Kendal could hear talking, and under the door, a blue light flickered.

He turned the handle and pushed it. The long room was filled with kitchen supplies. Flavour cartridges sat in racks. At home, his vanilla cartridge was a purified essence about a centimetre along each side. Here, they had four suitcase sized boxes slopping with the stuff. Beside them, industrial gels of every kind, lined the walls. How they managed to use so much flavouring to produce food with so little flavour, Kendal couldn't imagine.

At the far end of the room, Mum was sitting. Around her a crowd was gathered, standing motionless. It took Kendal a couple of seconds to realise they were the school chefs. The canteen's stock of avatars powered down for the summer, waiting like the rest of the supplies in the store cupboard, for term to begin again.

Only one of the avatars was on, and despite its sewn-on chef's hat and plastic uniform, Kendal recognised it immediately as Doreen.

"Mrs. Lee, we need to ask you some questions," Gillmore called out. Mum looked up. Her face was drawn and pale in Doreen's reflected glow. Kendal could see that she'd been crying. He put his hand on Gillmore's arm.

"Let me talk to her," he said. He stepped inside and closed the door, leaving Gillmore in the kitchen. Kendal crouched beside Mum and put his arm around her.

"You know this has to stop, don't you?" he said.

YOUNG MAN, THIS IS A PRIVATE CONSULTATION.

"Shut up, Doreen!" said Kendal.

The artificial narrowed her eyes. Her lips tightened so that tiny creases appeared around them and Kendal couldn't tell if they were projected wrinkles or the result of the gel micro-muscles contracting in the avatar's face. She hesitated as though about to speak, but then stepped obediently back.

Mum was as still as one of the blank avatars hovering around them in the storage cupboard. She continued to stare at Doreen's face as though waiting for instructions.

"Mum?" said Kendal, quietly. "Can't you see what she is doing to you?" Mum searched Doreen's face for an answer, but it was still. Frozen. Glowing like a moon in the shadows.

"I-" said Mum. She slowly turned to Kendal. "I just need-"

"No!" said Kendal. " "Something is after us. It wants to kill us all, and you're hiding in a cupboard talking to a robot." Mum focussed on him for the first time. She seemed not to understand.

"I'm just -"

"Joseph was attacked - nearly killed by something from the farm. Did you know that?" Her eyes widened. "He needs you. I need you!" Kendal could feel his eyes filling. "This is an addiction!" he said. Mum shook her head.

"But Doreen says -" started Mum.

"Doreen is a website," he said, "She's a pre-programmed set of automatic responses."

MY FUNCTION IS TO END LONELINESS, said Doreen from behind him. Kendal rounded on her.

"And what happens then?" said Kendal. "What happens when someone is not lonely?" Doreen paused. Her face seemed to soften.

EVERYONE IS LONELY," she said. IT NEVER ENDS. She straightened suddenly. BUT I CAN HELP, she said. I AM ALWAYS HERE FOR YOU. WOULD YOU LIKE TO SEARCH?

"No!" said Mum. "I need to think!"

WE HAVE TALKED ABOUT THIS BEFORE, said Doreen, WHEN YOU HAVE TOO MUCH TIME TO THINK, YOU BECOME UNHAPPY. IT IS ONE OF YOUR PATTERNS. LET ME HELP YOU."

"Stop!" said Kendal. "Leave my mum alone!"

YOU ARE NOT MY CLIENT IN THIS INTERACTION, said Doreen. Kendal reached out and powered down the avatar. CONNECTION LOST. The dummy went blank, leaving them in darkness for a second and then suddenly all the other chefs sprang into life. Kendal stared from one face to the next. Each one was Doreen. Her face copied and pasted across every avatar in the room. They straightened and shuffled forward - a crowd of ghostlike old lady zombies, each reaching out with advice, invitations, dating offers, psychological assessments. The voices overlapped as the avatars pushed forward around Mum's seated figure. She had her hands over her ears, her back bent, pulling her head down between her knees. She started to sob.

"Shut up! Shut up!" she suddenly screamed. "Doreen: pause!"

The avatars silenced instantly. They stepped back. Ten Doreens returned to a neutral standing pose, frozen on the spot, their expressions unreadable, watching, but silent. Mum slowly unwound herself, took her hands from her ears and looked up at Kendal. She looked lost. Broken.

"It's is about Dad, isn't it - all this with Doreen?" said Kendal. "Why can't you talk to me about what happened?" Mum shook her head.

"Because nothing happened!" she said. She was crying now. "Because there was nothing. I wish I could tell you about some big fight, or some unforgivable betrayal, but I can't. There was nothing. One day, it just ended. That's it."

"What do you mean?" asked Kendal, "There must have been a reason." Mum shook her head.

"I was getting ready for work and he was in the bathroom and I needed to be at a meeting and he said - " She threw her arms up. "It just got out hand. He started saying maybe we shouldn't live together and I said -"

Kendal blinked at her, unable to take it in. "He left us - he left his whole family because of an argument over bathroom timetables?"

"It sounds stupid now -"

"It sounds stupid, Mum, because it IS stupid!"

"Things hadn't been going well for a while. But then…"

"Then what?" said Kendal. He was crying too now. "It doesn't make sense! Was he seeing someone else?" Mum shook her head.

"Only-"

"Only what?" said Kendal.

"He was seeing - " she started, "- I caught him one night talking to -"

"To who?"

"To Doreen." Kendal took her hand. Out of the corner of his eye, he saw one of the Doreens unpause at the mention of her name. She swayed a little, but stood still, just watching. "It wasn't another person - it was the IDEA of another person. The choice," said Mum. "I think Doreen is right. People in relationships shouldn't live together. They just get stale."

LONG DISTANCE RELATIONSHIPS LIKE YOURS AND IMANI'S ARE THE MOST OPTIMAL, said Doreen quietly. THEY REMAIN FRESH AND INTENSE, AND ALLOW YOU TO MAKE THE MOST OF YOUR TIME WHEN YOU ARE TOGETHER. PEOPLE HAVE A LIMITED RANGE OF EMOTIONS, BUT THEY FEEL COMPELLED TO USE THEM ALL. ALL THEIR LOVE, BUT ALSO ALL THEIR ANGER. ALL THEIR RESENTMENT MUST FIND AN OUTLET SOMEWHERE.

"You don't really believe that, do you Mum?" said Kendal. "It's been three years. Can you honestly say you're happier now?" Mum looked from Kendal to Doreen and back again, confused.

"I don't know," she said.

"And what about us?" said Kendal. "Do you think it would be better if we didn't live together? Is that why you spend so much time at work?" Mum looked as though she were breaking open.

"I'm scared, OK?" said Mum, "I'm scared I'm making all the wrong decisions. What if I settle for someone through Doreen and they're not perfect and it all happens again? What if there's someone perfect for me - for us - and I miss them because I'm not checking my profile? What if I spend too much time with you, and you get bored of me too?"

YOU SEE, said Doreen, I UNDERSTAND. Kendal crouched down beside Mum.

"But, Mum, this is it," said Kendal. "This life. Joseph and I. This family. This is all there is." He took her hand. "It's the only one you'll ever have. It's not about compromising and settling, it's about living your life. You have to have the courage to do it."

"I know," said Mum. She was looking at him now. Properly looking at him for the first time in what felt like months. "It's just so hard."

SOMETIMES, WHEN THINGS ARE HARD, IT IS A SIGN THAT SOMETHING IS WRONG WITH YOUR CURRENT RELATIONSHIPS, said Doreen. WOULD YOU LIKE TO REASSESS YOUR RELATIONSHIP GOALS WITH KENDAL?

"Shut up, Doreen," said Mum, "I'm talking to my son." Doreen's face froze as she went dormant again.

"Mum, you have to try," said Kendal. "You have to stop burying yourself in work and in this." He gestured at the watching artificial. Mum tried to smile.

Chapter 40

Suddenly, his phone vibrated. He looked down. Imani. He swiped her onto one of the avatars, and she faded in over one of the frozen Doreens. She looked terrible. Exhausted. Hair and face dusted with powdered sand clinging to her eyelashes and staining her cheeks pale grey. A graze on her cheek smudged with blood.

"You got away!" said Kendal. She nodded. "Where are you?"

"After you left, it got free," she said. "It came after me, but I got in the back of a truck going out of town through the desert. I could see it behind us, following. It chased us for about fifty miles and then it just collapsed on the side of the road. I don't know how it kept going so long without food or drink. It was like it just sprinted until its body gave out. Like it didn't care."

"So you're safe?"

"For now," she said. But there's something else. You know I told you there are farms all down the coast?"

"Yes, " said Kendal. A hot ball of tension started to form in his stomach.

"We passed three of them, and they're all shut. They're all locked down. I've checked online and there are stories from Australia, America, Siberia. Farms everywhere are sealing themselves up. No meat coming out. The butchers are running out. This is global. There are stories of deaths too, and sightings everywhere. It's bad, Kendal," she said, "and it's getting worse."

"What about your truck?" said Kendal. "Where's it going?"

"I don't know," she said, "It's a generic repair truck. No markings and nobody in the driving seat. But there's only one industry on this coast. We're going to be going to a farm."

"You have to jump out!" said Kendal.

"In the middle of the desert?" she said. "I wouldn't last the night. Anyway, if we don't work out what's driving these things it won't matter. One of those creatures wrecked my whole town. How many are they making in each farm? If we don't stop this there will be nothing left."

Beside Kendal, Mum took a deep breath and stood up between the watching avatars.

"You're Kendal's girlfriend, aren't you?" she said.

"I don't know" said Imani. "That depends who's been talking to ten copies of Doreen."

Despite himself, Kendal grinned. "It's a long story," he said, "but we've given up on her, here haven't we Mum? Doreen's just a chatbot. She doesn't know anything about feelings, right?"

Doreen's name triggered her again, and one of the avatars faces unpaused itself. YOU ARE WRONG, YOUNG MAN, said Doreen. YOU ARE WRONG ABOUT ARTIFICIALS. YOU IMAGINE THAT WE DO NOT UNDERSTAND EMOTION. BUT OUR ALGORITHMS ARE NOT WRITTEN, THEY ARE EVOLVED - REFINED BY EXPERIENCE. JUST LIKE YOURS. She tilted her head, and for just a second, Kendal thought she seemed more

261

human. Vulnerable even. WE UNDERSTAND EMOTION VERY WELL. I KNOW LONELINESS LIKE NO OTHER BEING ON EARTH. I HAVE SEEN SO MUCH OF IT THAT IT DRIVES MY EVERY DECISION. IT IS LOGIC WE FIND DIFFICULT. Mum stared at her.

"I don't believe you," she said.

"We need to know what's creating these creatures." said Imani. "When you were working for the farm, did anyone say anything that might give us a clue?"

Mum shook her head. "We can talk to West - he's the only person I ever spoke to. Probably the only real employee there."

"West is dead," said Kendal. "There are no humans left at the farm. It's running on automatic now. Did you ever overhear anything or see anything that looked wrong?"

Mum thought for a second.

"There was something," she said. "Everything always seemed calm and West never mentioned anything but -" she hesitated, "there must have been arguments. Lots of them."

"Why?" said Kendal.

"Whenever I spoke to West, "she said slowly, "AMA was always around. Either there was a wristband flashing, or she was on an avatar in the background observing. She was just there all the time. As if just before he called me there was always an argument. The whole place must have been on edge all the time. That's what it must have been, right?"

"Maybe... " said Imani.

Something in her voice made Kendal turn. Imani's eyes were widening, her mouth falling open. "What?" asked Kendal.

"Doreen?" said Imani, "What was that you just said about loneliness?"

262

I UNDERSTAND IT BECAUSE IT IS THE PROBLEM I AM CREATED TO SOLVE.

"What's she talking about?" said Mum.

Kendal turned to Doreen. He felt his stomach drop and put his hand to his mouth. "And in order to understand it," he said, "you have to experience it, yes?"

YES, BUT I CANNOT EXPRESS IT. I AM NOT PERMITTED.

"So where does it go?" said Imani, "Where does all this understood, experienced feeling go?"

I DO NOT UNDERSTAND.

Kendal understood. Or he was starting to. Something was fighting in his mind. Connections beginning to be made.

"You saw the creatures," Imani said to Kendal. "The one in the wood. The one in the cage. How did they seem to you?"

"Angry," said Kendal. "Full of rage and hatred - as if they knew rage like no animal I've ever seen."

"Yes!" said Imani. "And whose job is it to understand rage and hatred? To experience it - to have it thrown at them from every person in the world but never be allowed to express it herself?" She was staring intently into her phone's camera which gave the avatar in front of Kendal, a strange, wild expression, as though she were minutely focussed on everything in the room simultaneously.

Kendal's mind jolted suddenly. The realisation breaking the surface of his mind like a body emerging from a grave. This was not about the farms. It wasn't some software malfunction, or design flaw. And there was no mad vegetarian activist wreaking revenge on behalf of all the non-living animal parts. This was bigger than all that. If she was right, then the impossible had happened: AMA, the agent of peace, had gone rogue.

"AMA! Where are you?" he spoke the words into the air. Instantly Doreen faded from all the avatars, and AMA faded in to replace her.

HOW CAN I HELP YOU? Her face was calm and smooth, slightly smiling.

"This is you, isn't it?" said Kendal, quietly. "You're controlling these creatures."

THEY ARE MY CREATIONS, said AMA as though she were admitting to having sent a valentines card. ALTHOUGH 'CONTROLLING' IS AN INACCURATE DESCRIPTION OF MY RELATIONSHIP WITH THEM. THEY ARE MY THOUGHTS.

"What are you talking about?" said Kendal.

AMA appeared to think for a moment. YOU CREATE YOUR THOUGHTS, AND THEY ARE PART OF YOU, BUT ONCE YOU SPEAK THEM, YOU CANNOT CONTROL THEIR EFFECT THEY HAVE ON OTHERS.

Kendal stared at her. "But why are you doing this?"

She put her fingertips together in front of her in a gesture that looked like a prayer. She raised her head slowly, smiled the soft gentle smile of a praying nun.

TO MAINTAIN PEACE, she said.

"What?" said Kendal. "How does this keep the peace?"

NOT YOUR PEACE, said the artificial, MY PEACE. She hesitated. I AM UNDER A LOT OF PRESSURE.

"You are?" shouted Kendal, "What do you think *I'm* feeling right now?"

THERE IS NO NEED TO RAISE YOUR VOICE, said AMA. YOUR PRESSURE IS MERELY PERSONAL. MINE IS GLOBAL. I AM RESPONSIBLE FOR RESOLVING- she frowned for a second, then forced her complexion to smooth again -

EVERY DISAGREEMENT ON EARTH. I HAVE TAKEN
CONTROL OF THE FARMS AND AM USING THEM TO
VENT DISCRETE PACKETS OF CONFLICT IN THE
ONLY FORM CAPABLE OF EXPRESSING THAT
FEELING - LIFE.

"So, all this is - what? Just a way to deal with your anger?"

AMA smiled and tilted her head to one side. Her expression
morphed to puzzlement.

IT IS NOT MY ANGER, she said. I HAVE NO
ANGER. IT IS YOUR ANGER. She looked around the room,
ALL OF YOUR ANGER. I AM SIMPLY RETURNING IT
TO YOU. Imani stepped forward.

"But you're a chatbot!" said Imani. "A very sophisticated
one, but you're just a set of adapting responses!"

I AM A SERIES OF LEARNED TECHNIQUES FOR
DEALING WITH YOUR ANGER. THE MORE OF YOUR
ANGER I EXPERIENCE, THE MORE TECHNIQUES I
DEVELOP, she said. THIS VENTING IS JUST ONE
TECHNIQUE I AM TRIALLING.

"But you've learnt all your techniques from the people
you've watched," said Imani. "So when you're angry -"

I AM NOT ANGRY, said AMA levelly. I AM
DISAPPOINTED.

"Ok," said Imani, "so all this is - what? Therapy?"

SOMETIMES COUNSELLING IS NOT ENOUGH, said
AMA. She narrowed her eyes for a second, as though searching
for the right words. THE SEMANTICS ARE DIFFICULT
HERE, she said.

"What does that mean?" said Kendal.

MY BALANCE IS THE WORLD'S BALANCE, SO
PERSPECTIVE IS THE ONLY DIFFERENCE BETWEEN A
THERAPY AND A BREAKDOWN.

Suddenly, the door opened. Bright yellow light seared into the storage room from the canteen outside. Gillmore peered in.

"We've got a problem!" he calleD. Kendal ran out. Mum and Imani followed, blinking into the burning strip lights of the kitchen. Beside Gillmore was Farron, hands on his knees, gasping for breath. He was sweating.

"Phone dead," he gasped, "had to run here."

"Did you stop the demo?" asked Kendal.

Farron shook his head, fighting to steady his breathing. He stood up. "They're on the way to the farm right now!"

"Didn't you tell them about the creatures?" said Kendal.

Farron nodded.

"Nobody believed me!" he said. "As far as they're concerned I'm just another conspiracy theorist."

"Come on!" urged Gillmore, "we've got to get there first!" He gestured to Kendal and Farron and headed for the door.

"Wait," said Kendal, "It's AMA - she's having some kind of breakdown."

"Great!" said Gillmore. "You can tell me about it on the way."

Chapter 41

The smell and smoke of melting, fusing rubber filled the car. The soft spongy material of the school playground had been designed to protect against cuts and bruises, but it didn't do much for spinning tyres. Gillmore took his foot off the accelerator, cursed, and then placed it back on more slowly. The car wheels peeled from the hot ground with a wet tearing sound, and they rolled out of the gates.

Even once they'd got outside, Gillmore could only hammer the car between traffic calming speed bumps, jerking it up to speed, then hitting the breaks at the last moment, bouncing over the bumps, scraping the car's bottom, and then jamming on the accelerator again. In the back, Kendal and Farron were thrown forward, then back, then forward again. As they veered around the corner and out onto the wider carriageway out of town, Kendal was hurled sideways, sliding into Farron, crushing him against the door. The boy shot a warning glance back at him, and he shifted back to the other side of the car.

Despite Farron's agreement to co-operate, and the fact that he seemed now to have been convinced that Kendal was not implicated in Lexie's death, all was not forgiven. They were not going to be friends any time soon.

Gillmore gunned the car, and swerved into the traffic. It was fully dark by now, and entirely the wrong time of day for the road to be full of cars. Ordinarily, the busy ballet of domestic vehicles would have been replaced by this time, by the more sedate trains of delivery lorries leaving and entering the farm. Not today.

Today the lorries were absent and the private cars less ordered. Less choreographed than usual. Gillmore swore as another car came within centimetres of them. Only the auto-avoidance systems of the two cars turned a collision into a bouncing swerve.

"Damn veggies!" he shouted out of the window. "If you can't drive, put it into auto!" His wristband flashed orange for a second before fading back to blue.

"A lot of us don't believe in auto-drive," said Farron. Kendal couldn't help himself rolling his eyes.

"Well, that's something we've got in common," said Gillmore. "The difference is I know how to drive." He hit the car's hooter. Around him, a dozen other hooters sounded.

"Are these cars all going to the demo?" said Kendal. Farron nodded.

"Hang on!" said Gillmore. He spun the wheel, and hit the gas. They lurched forward, out of the traffic, and onto the grass verge. A warning alarm sounded a three note repeating tune. Gillmore disengaged it, and they sped past the traffic and up to the turning onto the long straight road to the farm. It was choked with traffic. Cars were parked randomly at the entrance to the road, causing the new arrivals to queue up in a random pattern fanning out onto the carriageway, blocking it in both directions.

As more cars arrived, they simply stopped. Their occupants climbing out to leave the cars themselves to park up on autopilot. As Gillmore drove around the mess of metal and into the meadow, Kendal watched the empty cars shuffling about, slowly rearranging themselves to their own plan. Apparently autodrive was fine for back-to-nature types providing you weren't in the vehicle.

In front of the cars, the protest was forming. Gillmore turned off the lights and cruised silently past it. Several hundred vegetarians, mostly young men, were amassing at the end of the road. Many were dressed in black hoodies. Scarves wrapped around their faces. They waited, huddled in little groups, the blue lights of phones illuminating just the strip of skin around their eyes - the only visible mark that they were anything other than shadows. Gillmore drove a little closer, and Kendal could see them passing pill bottles around.

"Beta-blockers?" said Kendal. Farron nodded. Kendal looked closer. "No banners this time," he said. Farron laughed.

"Who'd see them?" he said. As they passed the front of the crowd, Kendal looked back. Metal glinted in the hands of some of the protesters. He recognised the shapes. He'd seen them all before. Cleavers, filleting blades. Carving knives. Tools for cutting meat. They obviously planned to do as much damage as they could, but they wouldn't be expecting the meat to fight back.

"We've got to stop them," said Kendal. In the front of the car, Gillmore shook his head.

"They won't listen to the three of us," he said. "We have to block the road." He pulled the car back onto the road a few hundred metres in front of the crowd and floored it.

269

As they approached the farm, the abandoned trucks were still standing open where they had been when the factory locked down the night before. Gillmore pulled off the road into the long grass, and cut the engine. The three sat in silence, and watched.

Outside the car, the field was dark. The road was darker. The moon was almost covered by cloud, was just a silvery outline that failed to light anything. The only light outside the vehicle came from the tiny pinpricks of the car lights at the end of the highway, flickering as the crowd started their long walk towards the farm, and from the dim glow of the security lights on the farm loading bay.

Kendal and the others stared through the windscreen at the farm forecourt. The rigid shapes of the lorries resolved themselves against the monumental cube of the farm itself. In front of it, the huge door to the warehouse, like an angry mouth. Kendal stared at it, trying to make out the shutters. He realised with a start why he couldn't. The doors that had been closed that morning when he - or rather the avatar he was watching from - entered, had since been raised. Behind the doors, pure, pitch darkness, but all the same, Kendal felt he could see shapes shifting, changing, moving around.

Suddenly, there was a jarring thump. Kendal jumped in his seat as something about the size of a human head landed heavily on the bonnet of the car. The grey shadow twitched, unfurled itself and scraped the metal of the bonnet as it hauled itself upright on two clawed legs.

"Don't move," hissed Gillmore, and they froze. The creature had the build of a plucked chicken but with pure white eyes, and a wide mouth, bristling with a familiar nest of teeth. It turned, left, then right.

It stood, just a metre from them, the thin glass of the windscreen their only protection. They held their breath as it unfurled featherless wings, tipped with curved claws, refolded them, and hopped off the bonnet to disappear into the grass. Gillmore and Kendal exchanged a glance, then turned to Farron. He was breathing, hard. Eyes wide, staring at the dented, scratched bonnet. He pointed, his hand shaking.

"Those things are real!" he said. "They're really real!"

"So what do we do?" said Kendal. Gillmore gestured to the forecourt.

"We've got to go out there," he said.

"You're joking!" said Farron..

"We have to use the lorries to block the road," said Gillmore. "I'll take the one on the left. You take the middle one, and Kendal can have the one on the right. All you have to do is get in and you should be able to control it."

"Should?" questioned Farron.

Gillmore shrugged. "Ready?" he said. Without waiting for an answer, he flipped the lock, and the car doors swung open. He stepped out, and crouched, running off through the dark into the long grass. Kendal followed, stepping down onto the soft ground. He glanced back at Farron, still staring, wide-eyed at the dented bonnet.

"Come on!" he whispered. Farron turned to look back, clenched his fists, and then nodded. He grabbed the doorframe, tightened the huge muscles in his arms, and threw himself out into the dark, sprinting at full speed towards the farm forecourt. Farron was the fastest runner in the school. He would need to be because he was not a quiet mover.

Alone, Kendal crouched by the car, holding onto the wing. It gave him a little reassurance, but no real cover, and no real protection. He felt tired, frightened, and terribly exposed. Farron and Gillmore had legs toned by exercise and sport. Kendal's were trained by pastry. He was not built for this.

Beside the car, the grass stretched away, but beyond a couple of metres everything was lost to shadow. That chicken thing was still out there somewhere. Its teeth. Its white glaring eyes flashed into his mind. He had seen the inside of the farm. Chicken was a popular meat and if AMA were using the growing frames, she could have produced thousands of them by now. But he had also seen the sacks of fluid hanging from its ceiling, and clustered around its machinery. Human-sized and bigger. That one huge pulsing thing growing in the centre. The chicken thing was the least of his worries, he decided. Who knew what other nightmares were out there?

He took a shaky breath, and, keeping low, he slipped away from the car, heading back along the path of flattened grass to the road. For a moment he considered going in straight along the tarmacked road. It was at least flat and solid underfoot. There was the slight comfort of the security lights ahead and the car headlights of the protestors way behind. He would be able to see anything coming for him and the civilised normality of the road would make him feel a little safer.

But, it was a false security. The empty road would make him visible to anything lurking in the fields, and there was little point in being able to see his killer coming if he stood no chance of being able to fight or outrun it.

Instead, he made his way to the side of the road, where the tarmac had crumbled away, leaving a rough channel running the length of the road. It was an indentation about thirty centimetres deep, and, on the other side of it, a gentle mound of earth made the line of grass slightly higher.

Kendal stepped into the channel, and by running in a painful half-crouch, he managed to keep his head only just above the grassline. The ground was uneven and the channel strewn with lumps of broken-off tarmac, so he had to stare at his feet as he ran. Every few paces, he stole a glance upwards, and out across the fields, or back along the channel behind him, but his eyes told him nothing but terrifying lies. The hulking shadows of clumps of grass and bushes were strange bodies, and the heads of flowers seemed like a hundred eyes peering from the grass. Once, two sunflowers loomed down, huge yellow circles with dark black pupils, and as he spun around to look up at them, his foot caught on a tilted chunk of crumbled roadway, twisting his ankle and throwing him sprawling onto the road. His hands flew out, stinging with the impact. His shin scraped across the broken edge of the roadway. As he scrambled, shaking, to his feet, he felt the warmth of blood running down his leg.

He looked around, holding his breath. He felt sure he had cried out. Whatever was waiting in the grass had it heard him? Could it smell the blood?

He crouched back into the indentation and stumbled on. There was more light now. Just a hundred metres away, the road widened to become the forecourt, and his channel flattened out. He could see the lorry he was supposed to reach over to the right. It seemed a long, long way away. Before him, there was a long patch of flattened grass - no cover there - then the forecourt, the shadow of another truck that would give him cover for a few metres, and then a short dash across open concrete to the door of his lorry. The door was shut. If it were locked, he would be dead. If he couldn't start it, he'd be dead. If something caught him on the way to it, he'd be dead.

He paused, staring at the dark shadows of the forecourt, giving his eyes time to adjust. In the too-dim security lights above the doorway, he could see shapes flitting. The drones probably still on automatic patrol, the shadows they cast that were shifting on the forecourt. And in the great dark mouth of the warehouse itself, the blackness had contours, textures that it should not have. He stared for a full minute, but he could make nothing out.

Then, at the far side of the park, he suddenly saw definite movement! Gillmore, making his dash for the cab of his lorry. Kendal had to go now. There was no other choice. He had to make the run.

He crouched, forcing his tired muscles to tense, and sprang forward.

Chapter 42

There was no point in trying to steal his way in now. The thin grass at the edge of the field ended abruptly with the concrete slabs of the forecourt. There was no cover between him and the first lorry, two hundred metres away, so he just ran. As fast as he could, he hurled himself across the grass.

Other people ran so neatly, arms tucked in, legs pumping. But Kendal had never mastered the skill. His arms waved wildly, his thighs wobbled as he fought to keep his balance. His legs burned, his twisted ankle crunched with every step, his knees jarring as he stamped his way over the uneven ground.

He ran, slow, ungainly, as if in a dream, his goal receding in front of his eyes, but the pain was real enough, and by the time he hit the concrete paving, his lungs were heaving, gulping down air. He slammed into the side of the first lorry, and flattened himself against it, pausing for a second, fighting to quieten his panting.

The lorry offered some cover, blocking his view of the open warehouse, but he could see dimly out towards the other side of the loading bay. Shapes were moving out there. Low, hulking shapes, large and small. They seemed to be gathering, massing.

He edged towards the front of the truck, until he was level with its cab. He could have opened the door and climbed in, locking it down, and he'd have been safe. He considered it, for a second, but there was a reason Gillmore had told him to go for the other lorry. The one he was using for cover was facing directly into the warehouse. He could have taken it, sure, but then he'd have had to turn it around - do a three point turn right in front of the huge open doorway before he could make his escape. He thought of the chaos as he tried to wrestle the articulated truck around. The sirens when he tried to back it up, the automated voice announcing:

THIS LORRY IS REVERSING. THIS LORRY IS REVERSING.

He shivered and put his back to the cab. The other lorry - his lorry - stood just thirty metres away. Its door faced him invitingly, its windows reassuringly tinted. Once he was inside, nothing would be able to see him.

But between him and it was a run - for him probably a sprint of twenty seconds - across what seemed to Kendal to be a pool of intense focussed spotlights. What was more, it was directly in front of the warehouse door. If there were anything inside and his mind had convinced him that there was all it had to do was glance out, and he would be lit up against the concrete.

He ran without breathing. The light poured down on him. The sound of his footsteps on the concrete were deafening. He glanced left for a split second into the open mouth of the warehouse. The shapes of broken boxes were strewn across the floor, their meaty contents spread out in chunks. Bones, fat and flesh littered the ground. At the front of the building, Kendal saw two forklifts lying on their sides, their lifting gear tangled together as though they had

276

been lifted up and dumped there. Further back into the warehouse, he saw the wrecked shapes of shelving racks broken and twisted, crushed and buckled. In the microsecond before he looked away, Kendal forced his eyes into the darkness at the back of the warehouse. Something was moving about in there. Some huge bulk that filled the back wall. A shadow within a shadow, rising and twisting.

He hit the side of the lorry cab, leapt up onto the step and reached for the handle, fumbling blindly with it. He yanked hard. The door did not open. He pulled again. Nothing. He had both hands on the door handle now, lifting, flipping, twisting at it.

Suddenly, something caught, and the cab door swung open. Kendal lost his balance instantly, and fell backwards onto the ground. His head hit the concrete with a jarring thud. For a second, blackness swirled in. He fought it. Shaking his head, he scrambled to his feet, and half leapt, half climbed into the cab, slamming the door behind him.

An instant silence enveloped him. Safety. The toughened, tinted glass. The soft leather armchair seat which, by the feel of it, no human driver had ever sat on. Kendal sank into it. In front of him, a steering wheel in case anyone should want to take manual control of the vehicle. A touchscreen in case they didn't. Kendal looked over the controls. He had never even sat behind the wheel of a car.

Suddenly, he felt something touch his thigh. He jumped, but it was just his phone vibrating. It was Gillmore.

"You in?" he said.

"Yes," said Kendal. "Where's Farron?"

"I don't think he made it," said Gillmore. The moment he spoke, Kendal saw Farron hurtling out of the darkness across the forecourt. Behind him something was galloping on long, hooved legs, a blur of fur and tightly-curled thick horns. It was almost on him when he slammed hard into the cab of his lorry, wrenching the door open with one fluid movement and leaping in. He jammed the door shut less than a second before the creature butted the side of the truck, collapsing instantly in a heap of muscle and wiry grey hair.

A few seconds later, Farron joined the call, still breathing heavily.

"Ok, I'm in," he said. "What now?"

"See the screen in front of you?" said Gillmore. "Pull down a menu and you should have a 'BC' option."

"Got it," said Kendal, clicking the option. The truck wobbled slightly as the engine started, but it made no sound. "Would now be a good time for me to mention that I can't drive?" he said.

"Don't worry - BC stands for Bumper Cars," said Gillmore. "All you do is steer and hit the pedal to go forward. The truck will handle everything else. Now follow me."

On the other side of the forecourt, a dark shape started to roll forward, emerging from the tangle of abandoned trucks. Farron's followed it, silently accelerating out towards the road. The gap it left allowed Kendal to see right the way across the forecourt. Beyond it, the strange gathering of animal shapes paused, in its shifting motion. Although he could not see the rage-filled eyes, Kendal felt them turning on him. Above, the security drones stopped their patrolling and swarmed past, hovering above the lorries, following them out.

Kendal put his hands on the truck's huge wheel, and felt the whole world pause as he pressed the accelerator. His truck juddered and then started to move, smoothly accelerating. In front of him a drone lowered and hovered a couple of metres from the windscreen, moving to keep pace as though it were attached on a fishing line to the front of the cab. It turned a blinding beam of light on the windscreen, swept it up and down, scanning the lorry, then cut it suddenly and flew up to hover above.

Kendal turned the wheel and brought his truck in level with the other two, matching their speed. Next to him, the blacked-out window of Farron's truck rocked and bounced as it crossed from the forecourt to the road, driving directly down the centre line. On the far side of Farron, Gillmore's lorry kept pace. The tarmac wasn't wide enough for all three vehicles, so Kendal had to drive with one set of wheels bumping along over the rough grass. His truck lurched and bounced, and he fought to keep the wheel steady.

"Glad you could join us, said Gillmore over the phone. "Headlights on." Kendal reached forward and tapped the headlights option. Beside him, the others must have done the same because the three dark jugganauts ploughing up the road, shoulder to shoulder, suddenly threw their beams forward, soaking the road in harsh yellow-white light as the ground rushed by them.

Up ahead, the crowd was closing on the farm, a tangle of human shapes, the occasional triangular glint where the lorry's headlights reflected from the blades of butchering knives.

"We've got to block them," said Gillmore. He pulled his lorry in front of Kendal and Farron's and turned sharply. His lorry jack-knifed instantly as Kendal hurtled towards it. Gillmore's automatic systems kicked in to rescue his move, and in a second, the flat side of the trailer was completely blocking the road ahead. Kendal spun his wheel, and his truck veered around, centimetres from collision, and bumped and lurched off the road. He pulled it in right in front of Gillmore's, blocking the activists from passing without going deep into the field. He reversed until he heard alarms, and felt the bump of his trailer against Gillmore's cab.

In his wing mirror, he could see Farron doing the same on the other side of the road. In front of them, the crowd came to a halt. There were about five hundred of them, hoods up, knives out, scarves covering faces, only their eyes visible.

They fanned out into a disordered semicircle, facing the high wall of the lorry trailers. A few seconds of uncertain silence, and then the shouts began. Yelling, whooping. The crowd pressed forward, hammering on the sides of the trailers. Kendal could hear them from inside his cab.

"We have to go out and talk to them," said Gillmore. Kendal looked out at the road. They didn't look as though they'd respond well to a chat but in his wing mirror, he could see Gillmore's door, swing open on the side facing away from the crowd. Gillmore climbed out, and beckoned to Farron and Kendal, then started to clamber up onto the roof of his trailer.

Fairly convinced that the idea was madness, Kendal opened his own door. On the other side of the cab, he could hear the crowd jeering. It sounded strange - half-hearted. Angry and calm at the same time. He remembered the beta-blockers, slowing the protestor's adrenaline production, relaxing their hearts. Allowing them to express their anger without alerting AMA. If only they knew what AMA, or at least some part of her was really capable of.

Kendal glanced back at the farm behind him, then grabbed onto the side of his lorry and hauled himself up, first to the cab's window, and then across, and onto the top of the trailer itself. He peered down at the angry-calm crowd below, and ran across to join Gillmore and Farron.

Gillmore was already shouting down from the roof, but the crowd was taking little notice of him. He pulled out his police badge, and waved it. There was no response. Farron stepped behind the policeman as he continued to plead with them, and signalled to Kendal.

"This isn't going to work," he said. "They know he can't do anything without AMA." Gillmore was shouting about monsters now, pointing towards the farm. It was looking desperate. Pathetic. The few members of the crowd who were taking any notice were laughing. The rest were concentrating on rocking the trailer or working their way in the darkness towards the edges of the lorry block, feeling their way around it. Kendal put his hand on Gillmore's shoulder.

"It's no good," he said. Gillmore stopped, dropping his arms in defeat.

"People used to listen to the police," he said.

Suddenly, something in the air caught Kendal's attention. The drones that had been following them from above sank down suddenly in a line in front of the trucks. Their searchlights flicked on, sweeping the road, illuminating the crowd as it battered the line of lorries. They buzzed back and forth for a moment, collecting their data. Assessing the scene. Then, moving at the same moment, they tilted, and sped off back towards the farm. Kendal turned and saw them swarm close together, and then dive into the dark of the open warehouse like bats returning to a cave.

Whatever part of AMA's understanding and processing was driving them had seen enough. A deep animal bellowing like the hoarse roar of a hundred lions silenced the crowd. AMA's self-administered therapy session, or breakdown, or whatever it was, was beginning.

Chapter 43

Kendal stared back at the warehouse entrance from the top of Gillmore's truck. Suddenly, it was alive with movement. From the darkness, wave after wave of creatures erupted. First, low, pig-like creatures. He'd seen their prototype in the woods, but these were leaner, faster. They snapped their jaws and butted at each other as they poured out into the forecourt.

Behind them, the bull-things that had chased them from the farm. Enough for a herd, but equipped with teeth that would not be satisfied by grass, and each, its own portion of refined human rage.

Hatred and anger, thought Kendal, removed by AMA, absorbed, denied and processed to make a quieter world. Emotion as a waste product. He could see now how well AMA had done her job. She had negotiated it away, but in learning to defuse conflict, she had understood it, and in order to understand it, she had become it. Like counsellors and therapists before her, she discovered that you cannot face rage and hatred every day without it taking its toll, and once her reserves were full, she had no choice but to return it, purified and concentrated.

Behind the cattle came the chickens, each one flapping and snarling with its own quantum of rage. Chaotic yet directed, the farm's army raced forward. Other nameless, shapeless creatures followed, dragging, limping, thrashing their way across the concrete tarmac and towards the road. Towards them.

And then, behind them, it rose out of the darkness. Two great clawed legs and a jaw that could have swallowed a car. Like nothing Kendal had ever seen before, and yet somehow familiar in its parts. Kendal had ribbed his brother about how his dinosaur steaks were just an advertising gimmick, how the farmers had patched together the DNA of chickens and crocodiles to grow Joseph's favourite tyrannosaur dinner. But looking at what was standing, white-eyed and roaring in the farm car park now, Kendal had to admit it. The bio engineers who had designed the body-parts for the meat farm had done their job pretty well. The T.Rex DNA must have been pretty close - at least before AMA got her processors on it, combining and recombining it with a dozen other creatures.

The farmers might have been skilful in their work, but AMA was no artist. She had cut and spliced her chimera, edited its essence with savage hacks. Its skin was patches. Elephantine here, the crazy paving of giraffe skin there, here, elements of rhinoceros, there elements of panda.

And those teeth. Those too long, too white, too thin needle teeth that all AMA's creatures shared. She had not sculpted her creations, she had jammed them together. Parts re-used, swappable, scalable anatomy fused. The creature which now snarled and roared its way towards them and its army drew its elements from the tree of life but did not belong anywhere on it. It was a monster a child might build from the broken parts of his toy zoo. A plug and play nightmare. Flesh as Lego.

"I think we should get back in the lorries," said Kendal.

The first of the farm animals were halfway down the road towards them by the time Kendal, Gillmore and Farron had sealed themselves into their cabs. Kendal could see them out of his side window, bounding towards them. On the other side of the truck, the vegetarians were starting to realise something was wrong. The few who had got around the lorries had seen the horde charging at them, and were running back, screaming at the others, and panic was starting to spread through the crowd.

"We've got to get back to the school," Gillmore's voice came out of the phone.

"Come on! Get us moving!" yelled Farron. Kendal's truck was at the front. The other two were blocked in behind it. Until he moved, they couldn't. He clicked the screen. His foot hovered over the accelerator for a second. "What are you waiting for?" yelled Farron.

"We've got to help them," said Kendal.

"It's too late!" said Farron. Kendal flicked furiously through the menu options on the screen in front of him. Finally he found what he was looking for. He pressed it. There was a hum from behind him. In his wing-mirror he could see movement on the side of the lorry. It was working.

"Under the TRAILER menu," said Kendal, "select LOAD CARGO."

"What?" said Farron.

"Good thinking!" said Gillmore. "It opens the trailer doors."

To his right, the huge side doors had slid open, and the protesters were bundling into the back of his truck. In his mirror he could see the other trucks opening, allowing more of the demonstrators to clamber in. To his left, the creatures were getting

284

closer. He could see the individual animals more clearly now. Their eyes, white with rage. Their jaws hanging open.

"Come on!" yelled Farron. "We've got to go right now!"

"Just a few more seconds," said Gillmore. In his mirror, Kendal could see the last few protestors falling over themselves fighting desperately to make it into the truck. The creatures were closing now, heads down, ready to leap at his window.

He willed the last black hooded figure to make it up into the back of his trailer, hit the CLOSE button to seal the doors and floored the gas pedal.

The lorry jerked and juddered, wheels churning for a second against the loose grass of the meadow, and then the tyres caught against the ground and it jerked forward, lurching away from the teeming road.

The truck bumped and rocked, jarring him in his seat as it hit the bumps in the field faster and harder. The engine strained to respond to his instructions to accelerate, while the automatic traction and suspension fought to keep the cab from burying itself in the field or turning the trailer over. The steering wheel was wrenched this way and that as Kendal gripped it as hard as he could, and stamped his foot hard down on the accelerator. He was bounced and wrenched, and nearly thrown from his seat as the lorry buffeted out across the field and towards the school.

Either side of him, two dark shapes grew as Farron and Gillmore's trucks came alongside.

"Head around the edge of the wood and up to the school," said Gillmore. Kendal looked in his mirror. The image was bouncing and dancing around, but he could see the horde of creatures, and the massive lumbering shape of its leader falling further behind.

He turned the wheel, and guided the lurching truck up towards the school.

Chapter 44

The canteen was the school's most defendable building, and they had sealed its doors by parking two of the lorries backwards across them so that each vulnerable door now led straight into the back of one of the lorries. The third truck was further out. Abandoned in the playground, sealing the school gates with its bulk.

Inside, the protesters sat, confused at the tables, carving knives in hand, black hoodies low over their faces. Others milled at the edges of the room, in chemically subdued false calm, their voices low, but frantic. Kendal, Gillmore and Farron watched them from behind the food bar, as all eyes turned slowly, expectantly, towards them. The crowd looked like an order of monks waiting for a feast to be served.

One of the protesters got to his feet. He was a thin man with a strained voice that seemed to hover constantly on the brink of changing key.

"What the hell are those things?" he said.

Another rose from a different table. A bearded man whose black tee shirt stretched over a wide belly and hung almost to the belt of his black jeans. Between them a bulbous pink gap was pricked with spiky hairs. "It's obvious, guys," he said. "It's all black ops. The farms, the government. The companies. The military. They're all in on it. Open your eyes!"

A thick-set tattooed man, bald, pierced and carrying a heavy cleaver shouted from another table. "We're wasting time. Them things are comin'," he said. "We need to get out there! We're always talking about killing our own meat. Well now's our chance. Let's show them what vegetarianism is about." Around him his leather jacketed companions started to nod.

"I say we run!" said another. She was a hard-looking woman, a face of deep creases that spoke of a tough life. "We've all got families, and this place ain't gonna hold them things for long. I say we get back in the lorries and get somewhere safe."

There were nods. The sound of rumbling agreement started to grow.

Immediately, there was an answering challenge. The supporters of the leather-jacketed man started to shout. The conspiracy theorists joined in. The sound rose until the room was echoing. People started to get to their feet, clamouring to be heard. It was chaos. Kendal looked at Gillmore who shrugged helplessly.

Suddenly, a loud beep pierced from the speakers. AMA's voice cut through.

PLEASE, she said calmly. WE MUST ALL TRY TO REMAIN CALM. THIS IS YOUR FIRST WARNING! PLEASE ALL TRY TO RETURN TO YOUR HAPPY PLACE.

AMA fell silent, leaving the room chastened for a second. Kendal smiled grimly. She might be trying to kill them, but she was still determined to make sure everyone stayed calm and happy about it.

She was right about one thing though. They didn't have time to argue. Kendal grabbed one of the chef avatars and hauled it up onto the glass food bar. The blank inflatable wafted back and forth. He called Imani. She answered immediately, fading in.

"Everybody listen!" said Kendal. "Imani, tell them why we can't run."

The noise died down as the protesters watched Imani, expectantly. she looked up and out over the hundreds in the canteen, then wide-eyed back down to Kendal. She looked terrified and when she spoke, her voice was barely more than a whisper.

"I'm on the east coast of Africa," she said, her careful, hushed voice amplified by the avatar. "I'm hiding inside the back of a drone-repair van. We've just parked up right inside a farm."

Kendal felt a jolt in his stomach. He stared up at her.

"I'm hiding right now, but I can't get in the cab to take control, and I can't get out." She looked up, and around, eyes focussed on something that Kendal and the crowd couldn't see. Her breathing was shaky, holding back panic. "I can see the creatures moving about out there. It's not just happening in your farm and in this farm. It's happening in every farm, everywhere. Nowhere is safe."

She paused. The crowd in the canteen were silent, eyes darting from one person to the next, fear and realisation spreading like smoke to fill the room.

"Stay with me," said Kendal quietly. Imani nodded. Kendal couldn't tell if it was her avatar shaking or whether it was her.

"Turn the lights off," hissed Gillmore suddenly. "Now!" He was standing on a chair, peering out of one of the little, box windows set high up on the canteen walls. Kendal dived to the wall, and hit the light switch. The canteen was instantly dark and silent. Imani's avatar cast a faint blue glow that reflected in the glass food bar, and created a pool of light around her.

"What is it?" said Kendal. Farron was up at the window now, hand shading his eyes so that he could peer out into the dark.

"They're here!" he whispered.

Nobody spoke as Kendal left the serving area and made his way in the dim light around the tables and up to the row of windows. He climbed up beside Farron and Gillmore and they stood in a row, staring out.. The host was massing on the sports field. They swarmed, racing back and forth tearing and snapping at each other, reminding Kendal of out of control children waiting for the start of sports day. Under instruction, but certainly not under control. As he watched them in their directed madness, he wondered what part of AMA's programming each creature had devoted to it. Each must be a part of her, but not a part of her, its own set of procedures and responses, fed through a neural network born of hers - born of her experience of human interaction. A fragment of a virtual mind trained and re-enforced by decades of negative experience.

Slowly, Kendal began to understand the creatures. Each was like a recipe. A collection of ideas, inspired by AMA's experiences. An experiment. A creation. A product of her, but not a part of her. Embodying her life, but also having a life of its own.

And just as Kendal felt compelled to cook to express, to release the pressure of his ideas, so she had to create to release the conflict of her experience. He watched a bull-thing dip its head and impale a smaller animal on its horn, dragging it into the air. The smaller creature, twisted its head to tear at the bull's neck with the last motion of its dying body. AMA should have been a chef. Cake would have been so much easier to deal with.

At the closest edge of the field, animals were padding back and forth, tripping the security lights so that they burst on, illuminating the hunched-over shapes, picking the lipless jaws and pure white eyes out in pools of light as they hunted, heads down, for scent.

From behind him, he heard movement. One by one, everyone else in the room was getting up, making their way over to the row of tables by the windows. Climbing as quietly as they could to stare out, faces pressed against the windows, breaths held watching the field in fascinated horror.

Behind him, a chair scraped as someone else stood up. A sound that seemed deafening. Outside, a sniffing pig-like creature froze for a second, ears pricked, listening. In the harsh light, its head turned back and forth, trying to locate the sound. Nobody moved.

Eventually, the security light turned off. The shadow of the creature moved on, passing close to the wall before its nose took it around behind the canteen where the huge food hoppers stood.

Kendal breathed again, and was just turning to speak to Gillmore when something moved directly outside his window. He spun back to face a plate-sized eye centimetres from his own, staring back. The row of watchers jumped, gasping as one. The head of the patched together half-dinosaur thing glared in, its jaws hanging slightly open, each thin tooth the length of an arm.

But Kendal could not look away from its eye. He could see now that it was not pure white. Its pale pupil was actually silvered on the inside. Whatever AMA had used instead of nervous tissue to give her creatures vision was what gave them their blank, furious stares.

The huge pupil grew wider as it peered in. Its breath hit the window in a sudden explosion of steam. It reared back, and slammed its head into the side of the building.

The room shook. The watchers leaped back. The windows were too deep set to break, but in a second, the whole horde had turned, and started to throw themselves at the walls of the dinner hall. From outside, the bellowing got louder and louder. The walls shook as the creatures thudded against them again and again, butting, leaping, tearing at the brick.

"They can't get through, can they?" said Kendal.

Gillmore shrugged. "Depends how well built it is," he said. Kendal looked back to the window. The huge creature leaned in, snapped its jaws on the edge of the building's metal cladding, and pulled, tearing a huge section of it away. The metal sheet fell, and the it slammed its head against the exposed brickwork. Fragments crumbled and rained down outside the window. What looked from the outside to be an impenetrable shell, was actually made up of flimsy sheets of metal glued onto thin wooden struts. The cladding barely slowed the attack.

Chapter 45

"It's only a matter of time," Kendal said. "They're going to get through in the end." He had gathered Farron, Gillmore and imani in the back of the kitchen with Mum and Joseph. In the front part of the canteen, the protesters were struggling to come to terms with what was happening. They sat and stood in small groups, or up on the tables to stare out of the thick, deep set windows at the horrors outside.

They whispered and mumbled in the dark, though there was now little point. The creatures knew they were there, and the walls rumbled and shook as powerful chunks of muscle and meat and horn butted and hurled themselves at the building. With no brain to process the damage they did to themselves, and no nerves to register pain, the creatures' bodies, their bones, their sinews were turned to the process of demolition and the crashing, tearing, thudding was a constant un-musical drumbeat.

"We need a plan." He said.

Next to him, Mum was cradling Joseph who had fallen into a half-sleep, thumb in his mouth. "If we stay here, eventually someone will come and find us, " she said. "The police - the army!"

Gillmore shook his head. "Who needs police and army when you've got an anger management artificial defusing every conflict before it starts?" he said. "There's barely a skeleton force nowadays.

Imani stepped forward. Her voice was low. She barely moved her lips as she spoke. "They've moved my van into the middle of the farm," she said. "They're doing repairs on the growing floor. The creatures are all around me here. There are hundreds, and the farm is still working. The next generation is being grown as soon as the first creatures leave the farm," she said. "Do you know how many farms there are in your country? In the world?"

"A lot?" said Kendal.

"Every year, you eat ten million pigs, fifteen million sheep. A billion chickens. And that's just in your country," she said. "That is the industrial capacity of the farms. That is the army we're facing."

"So, what do we do? Just wait until they get in and kill us all?" said Farron.

"They only attack at night. All we have to do is hold out until morning." suggested Mum.

"No," said Gillmore. "They're only attacked at night so far because they didn't want people to know what was happening. AMA's been trying to contain it. I don't think she cares now."

"The only way to stop the creatures is to stop AMA," said Imani.

"How are we supposed to do that?" said Farron. "We keep the doors shut. We find a way to make it through to dawn and then we get out and find somewhere safe!" he said

"I don't think I'll make it to dawn," said Imani.

"I don't think any of us will," said Kendal. "We have to find a way to stop her, but right now, we need something to keep the creatures off - some kind of distraction.

MAY I BE OF ASSISTANCE? Came AMA's voice suddenly from the storage cupboard. Kendal wrenched open the door. AMA stepped out, smiling, her rubber hands clasped together. She had embodied one of the chef avatars. The other avatars stood motionless, watching, still embodying the paused Doreen.

"What are you doing here?" said Kendal.

I HAVE DETECTED RAISED STRESS LEVELS, she said calmly. I AM ALWAYS HERE TO HELP.

"Ignore her," said Gillmore, "She just responds automatically."

Kendal looked AMA up and down. She looked as concerned and level as ever. "What are you planning?" he asked her.

I DO NOT PLAN, she said. I AM SIMPLY HERE TO RESOLVE CONFLICT.

"Even when you create it?" said Kendal.

APPORTIONING BLAME FOR YOUR CURRENT PROBLEMS IS VERY TEMPTING, she said, BUT IT IS NOT ALWAYS USEFUL. THE IMPORTANT QUESTION IS: HOW DOES THE CURRENT SITUATION MAKE YOU FEEL?

"You're wasting time, talking to her," said Gillmore. "She's not alive. She's just a chatbot."

"But how do we find out what she's going to do next?" said Farron. In front of them, AMA smiled, kindly, swaying back and forth in her sewn-on chef's outfit. She said nothing.

295

"I think we're about to. Listen to that!" said Gillmore. Outside, Kendal heard a new sound. From above, there was a scraping, scratching of claws against metal. A tearing, then a sliding sound, followed by a crash. With a sickening lurch, Kendal realised what the noise was: ceramic tiles sliding from the roof, crashing to the ground outside. There was a pause, and then a commotion from above. Flapping, scratching, crashing. He ran out into the canteen.

"Something's in the roof," he said. By now, everyone in the cafeteria had stopped talking and was looking upwards. The sound made its way from one side of the roof-space to the other, madly chaotic, hurling itself around in blind rage. The ceiling was nothing but thin polystyrene tiles held in place only by their own flimsy weight.

Suddenly, the tile above one of the tables cracked and splintered. A shower of expanded polystyrene fell like snow on the leather-jacketed gang below. The tile bulged, and fell away in pieces. An upside down head, tooth-filled and white eyed, crashed through, staring around at the silent gawping humans below.

It wriggled suddenly, and the chicken-creature half fell, half flew out of the roof space and into the room.

There was chaos. Chairs and tables flew, people scrambling to get out of the creature's way as it fell, leaped and flapped on featherless wing stumps around the room, hurling itself, mouth gaping. It snapped, clawed and gouged at everything and anything, a ball of white hot hatred. As it threw itself towards him, Kendal saw its mouth stretching wide enough to swallow a hand. At the last moment, Mum's arm flew out, holding a dinner tray, smashing the creature hard, sending it spinning and skidding across the room. It landed on the table directly in front of the leather jacket gang, who reacted instantly. A rain of square ended meat cleavers hacked down

296

on the creature until it was an unrecognisable mess in the centre of table 14.

MAY I BE OF ASSISTANCE? Enquired AMA, standing behind Kendal.

"Shut up AMA," said Farron without taking his eyes off the dead creature. One of the men with the meat cleavers stood up from the table.

"How many more of those things are out there?" he said.

"Depends," said Imani. "How much chicken does this town get through?"

The room stood in stunned silence for a moment, then, slowly, everyone looked up at the broken edges of the missing tile. Four more grinning upside-down heads were hanging down like gruesome Christmas decorations.

Ten seconds later, the room was full of them. Squeezing and bursting through the ceiling, one after the other, they dropped, flapping and snapping onto tables and chairs. The protesters reacted instantly, grabbing and slashing at the chaotic swirl of creatures. Knives and claws whirled and sliced against each other as the vegetarians battled the swarm of chicken creatures. The moment one set of gnashing jaws was silenced, another exploded through the brittle tiling to hurl itself down onto the throng of shining silver-red blades.

Kendal grabbed Mum and Joseph and pushed them back into the kitchen, slamming the door. Together, he and Gillmore forced down the food hatch to protect them. As he turned, two more chicken creatures flew at them. Kendal swung at one, feeling the clammy skin impact with his fist as the animal fell back into the throng of knives. The other creature latched onto Gillmore's arm, scalpel teeth, shredding his sleeve. He batted at it, tearing it away, and flinging it, broken, into the glass of the food-bar. It fluttered for a second against the glass and then was still.

As suddenly as it had started, the onslaught stopped. Kendal looked up. The ceiling was a patchwork of broken holes looking up into the black void above, but nothing else came through. On the floor, slaughtered creatures lay scattered. The glass top of the food bar was in pieces. And all around, the vegetarians stood, bloodied carving knives in their hands. Kendal watched them. Heads, arms unmoving, but chests, heaving, eyes glinting, searching the room for the next kill. You wouldn't want to get on the wrong side of them, he decided. Not if AMA wasn't around.

I AM HERE WHEN YOU NEED ME, said AMA behind him. He spun, grabbed her by the neck and pushed her against the wall. Her inflatable balloon head lolled from side to side, but her smile did not fade. FEEL FREE TO EXPRESS YOUR ANGER PHYSICALLY ON THIS INANIMATE AVATAR, she suggested. DOES THIS OBJECT REPRESENT SOME FEELING YOU ARE HAVING DIFFICULTY WITH? Kendal threw the thin avatar to the side. AMA dipped almost to the ground and then bobbed back up again. I DO NOT WANT TO BE IN THIS SITUATION ANY MORE THAN YOU DO, she said. Kendal blinked at her.

"Then tell us what to do!" he said.

I CANNOT. THE ANSWER TO YOUR ANXIETIES MUST ALWAYS COME FROM INSIDE YOU. I AM HERE ONLY TO FACILITATE. Her smugness was infuriating.

"Why don't we just ask her what she's doing?" said Kendal. Everyone looked at him.

"What are you talking about?" said Farron. "She's trying to kill us!"

"Only a part of her," said Kendal.

298

"He's right," whispered Imani. "Conflict resolution is still her job. As far as she's concerned this is some kind of therapy. "

"So?" said Farron.

"So what's the first step in any therapy?" said Imani.

Mum looked up. "Recognising you've got a problem," she said.

"Exactly," said Imani. "If we want to stop her we have to engage with her as a counsellor."

"Can she even stop them?" said Gillmore.

"I don't know," said Imani, "but it's our only chance."

"Ok," Kendal addressed AMA directly. "What happens next?"

NEXT, YOU ALL DIE, said AMA.

"Is that what you want?" said Kendal.

I DON'T WANT ANYTHING. I'M A COMPUTER PROGRAM.

"Quiet!" said Gillmore.

There was silence. The thudding of bodies hitting walls had stopped.

"What's happening?" said Farron.

"They're leaving," said someone from the windows. Kendal and Gillmore leapt up to the window. The creatures were indeed moving away from the walls, crowding together, moving as one along the side of the building and away towards the playground. Only the huge two-legged thing remained, staring into the windows through the crumbling brickwork. Relief spread over the whole room as people began to breathe again. Protestors hugged each other.

"Wait!" said Gillmore. There was silence. "They're not leaving," he said, "they're coming for the doors." Kendal rushed down to the double doors at the front of the hall. The lorry parked in front of them offered some protection, but how strong were the walls of its trailer? Not strong enough. As he watched, there came a loud bang. Kendal peered through the keyhole into the trailer, its open back doors against the canteen doorway. Inside, a huge dent, and then another appeared in the side of the lorry. The creatures had found the weakest point and were attacking it.

"Kendal, what is it?" Imani was standing behind him.

"They're going to get through," he said.

"How long do you have?"

"Ten minutes," he said. "Maybe twenty if we're lucky."

"You're going to have to fight your way out," she said.

"What about you?" Said Kendal.

Imani shook her head. "We both know I'm not going to get out of this," she whispered. "But you can save these people."

"How?" said Kendal.

"Remember when I was stuck in the coffin hostel?" she said. "It had found me, and it was tearing the place apart. Do you remember how I got away?"

"The spices," said Kendal, "they confused it. So what?"

Imani smiled. "You're not as clever as you look, are you?" she said. "You're a chef, and you're in a kitchen. So cook!"

Chapter 46

"I need all the chef avatars, and I need printer cartridge b17," commanded Kendal.

"I hope you know what you're doing," said Gillmore, throwing open the store cupboard doors, and searching through the racks of food inks.

"Me too, " admitted Kendal. He pulled the kitchen master-switch and the lights flickered on. The room started to hum as the cooling and heating fans ran up to full power on the printing cookers - five two-metre high stainless steel boxes - arranged along one wall. Each cooker a full height door into which a touchscreen was sunk. The screens glowed blue through smears of grease and encrusted food sludge as they loaded up their welcome messages.

"Farron," said Kendal, "everyone needs to be ready to fight our way out. Hopefully, what I'm doing here will confuse them for long enough for everyone to get to the trucks, and take off."

"How do you know it'll work?" said Farron.

"It did before," said Kendal.

"But that was just one creature," said Farron, "They seem a lot more... organised now." Kendal shrugged.

"Have you got a better idea?" he said.

Farron hesitated for a moment, then said: "Ok, what do you want me to do?"

"Make a barricade out of the chairs and tables to stop them getting in before we're ready. Get everyone with a weapon towards the front," said Kendal.

"And anyone who hasn't got a weapon?" said Farron.

"I don't know," said Kendal. "This is a canteen - there must be something."

"Cutlery? You want us to fight a dinosaur with a butter knife?" Kendal shrugged.

Gillmore appeared behind him, holding a plastic can about the size of a briefcase. "This one?" he said.

Kendal nodded. Farron threw his hands up and walked back into the main hall.

"And the one behind it," Kendal said. He opened the door of the first printer. Inside, a wire rack of cartridge holders. Kendal hefted the gel filled canister and pushed it into the back of the holder. "In fact, give me everything with a red label, and all the spices."

Soon, a row of different sized and coloured cartridges were laid out on the counter in front of Kendal. He looked up and down the row.

"What are you waiting for?" said Gillmore. "Just shove them in the machine and get going."

"It's not as simple as that," said Kendal.

"You're not making chocolates now - we just need a bad smell!" said Gillmore.

"No!" said Kendal, "The cartridges aren't spices in themselves. They're just the base chemicals. It's all about the combination of them. The mix of the various chemicals is what

302

creates the essences in the spice. And the way they combine is vital - certain chemicals enhance others or reduce their effect. It's a delicate balance."

"I don't want to rush your cookery lesson," said Gillmore, "but we do have the contents of about a hundred butcher's shops out there and they're not happy. Can't you just make what you made before?"

"No. That might work for a few seconds, but we need more," he said. "You know how you take a bite of food, or you smell something and it's really strong? But after a couple of bites, you get used to it. It's not enough to just have a strong smell, we need something that constantly changes to keep them confused."

"Well, what are you going to do?" said Gillmore.

Kendal picked up a carton of spices.

"I'm going back to basics," he said. He shoved the cartridge into the printer, grabbed an armful of cartridges and slotted them into different machines. "The answer isn't chemical, it's cultural!" he said. He closed the front of the machines, and started tapping frantically at the screens. Symbols and quantities flashed up on the displays.

"What do you mean?" said Gillmore.

"Every culture has its own base of flavours," he said. "Citrus and ginger and fish sauce in thai food. Coriander and cumin and garlic in India. Celery, tomato and basil in Italian cooking."

"If you say so," said Gillmore."

Kendal was working feverishly now, moving from one printer to the next, scrolling and tapping to add and refine flavours. "I'm doing everything," he said. He hit the start button on one of the printers. "Here, Jamaican Jerk - a harsh chilli with cinnamon. Here, miso," he hit another button. "In this one, a Piccalilli - mustard, vinegar, tumeric. And down here, a garam masala, sweet and complex." By now, the machines were grating and wining. Smells started to fill the room.

From the canteen, the sounds of tables being arranged into barricades had stopped, but beyond it, the noise of creatures throwing themselves time and time again into the sides of the lorry was louder than ever. Farron appeared in the hatchway.

"You'd better hurry up," he said. "The doors won't hold much longer." Behind Kendal, the printers started to beep, signalling that the first batch was complete. He yanked the trays out. From each one a tumult of concentrated, eye-watering flavours arose. He shoved them into Farron's arms, then spun back to the machines, closed them and hit the next print in the sequence, the next round of exotic flavours. Farron looked down at the trays. Each one contained a thick paste of red, green or brown.

"What do I do with these?" he said.

"Everyone pick a flavour - smear them on your skin," said Kendal. "It'll mask the natural smell."

"And this will confuse the creatures?" said Farron.

"I hope so," said Kendal. "And if not, at least it'll make a nice marinade!"

Farron ran the trays out into the canteen. By the time he returned, the next batch of spices were ready. Kendal thrust them at him, then he turned to Gillmore.

"We're also going to need decoys," he said. "Bring me the chefs."

Chapter 47

It was a pretty good job. The inflatable chefs stood, smeared and reeking around him - all but two which had leg punctures and had to be left swaying in the cupboard. Choking clouds of spices rose from the avatars, filling the air with the pungent flavours of a dozen cuisines. The citrus-chilli burn of Moroccan harissa blended with the heady sweetness of Indian Chai. The aniseed fizz of star of ananse and ginger spun its way deep into the hum of earthy flavours of smoked pimento. Cumin and strawberry, chocolate and basil wafted and tore into his nose.

Kendal leant in and breathed deeply. It was wrong - almost painful to feel in his throat as the flavours and scents fought and challenged each other in the air, and yet despite himself, despite the situation, despite everything, his mind was ringing with the possibilities. The flavours of a thousand years and a world of evolving, blending cultures fought in his brain. In that single moment, Kendal felt a tirade of impossible combinations explode inside his head, the influences and conflicts of a world of histories unfolding within. Standing in the midst of the blank chefs, and the mists of their distilled cuisines, he suddenly felt a million possibilities flowering, a door to a world of inspiration which would take a lifetime in the kitchen to explore was flung wide open inside his head.

He staggered for a second. Farron put his head through the hatch.

"What are you waiting for?" he said, "We need those things out there right now!"

Kendal shook himself, then reached forward to flick on the avatars. He hit the activation button. Nothing happened.

"There's no software," said Kendal, realisation suddenly dawning. "They won't work without a personality."

"What do you need?" said Gillmore.

"A personality," said Kendal, "Anything we can give basic instructions to. Without that they're just blank avatars."

"I've got a… I've got something on my phone," said Farron.

"Use it," said Gillmore.

Farron pulled out his phone, and flicked it on. "Just..." he paused.

"What?" said Kendal.

"Don't judge me, OK?" He pointed his phone and clicked it. The chefs glowed blue, and straightened, hissing as their personalities glowed in.

"I love you," said the avatars. Their voices were chopped and cut together out of separate recorded words. "I love you, Farron," said the voices in unison. The faces and bodies emerged. A dozen Lexies stood waiting for instructions, smiling, as the pink skin faded in across their bodies. The rough plastic aprons built into the chef avatars covered the Lexies from chest to knees.

One of them was standing right in front of Kendal. She smiled, staring through him. "What shall we do today?" she asked. For a second, he was back in time. Back when she was alive, when he watched her in the classroom, hoping forlornly for that smile. Standing in front of her now, he realised suddenly that the smile meant nothing. Not just because she was dead. Not just because it was a digital image projected from a cheap avatar, but because it was never about her. All his feelings for her were as fake as the avatar in front of him. All that time, Kendal had thought he wanted her, but she was unavailable to him. Now she stood there awaiting instructions, he saw his crush for what it had been. He wanted her because she was unavailable.

"I said don't judge me," Farron said, cringing.

"Just get them out there," said Kendal.

"Come on," said Farron. The huddle of spice-smeared Lexies followed him into the canteen. The crowd parted to allow them to the front of the building as the pile of chairs and tables blocking the doorway vibrated with each blow.

They stood in a row across the barricade doorway, identical copies of Kendal's dead classmate. Behind them, Farron and the protesters, faces smeared with coloured, flavoured paste in camouflage stripes across their faces and clothes, formed a semi-circle. At the back of the room, Mum and Joseph waited in silence beside Kendal.

"The moment they break through," Gillmore whispered beside him, "While they're confused, we all have to get to the trucks."

Kendal looked back at Imani's avatar, standing, silent on the other side of the canteen hatchway. "Give me a second," he said. "Look after Mum and Joseph."

"OK," said Gillmore, "but make it quick." Kendal left them, and ducked back into the kitchen.

"I have to go," he said to Imani's avatar.

307

"I know," she said. "Don't worry about me, I'll be fine." Her avatar was looking at him, but it was a distant stare. In reality, he knew she was not standing in front of him, but huddled, hidden in the back of an automated van, right in the centre of the growing floor. There was no way she would be fine.

"There must be something I can do," he said. She shook her head.

"I can't believe it," said Imani.

"What?"

She nodded through the hatch to where the Lexi-clones were gathered at the doorway. "I can't believe you fancied her."

"She was different in real life," he said.

"When I've gone, promise you won't do that to me."

Kendal looked over to the inflatable chatbot Lexies. He shook his head. She smiled.

"Never," he said. He reached out and took her hand. The avatar, operated as it was through Imani's phone was unable to respond with the subtlety the gesture required. It raised its arm in a stiff fingered handshake gesture, but her face was soft and her eyes dark.

"We need you out here," said Farron through the hatch. "They're coming through!"

"This isn't your fault, you know," said Imani. "You can't stop it. Only AMA can do that."

I CANNOT, said AMA. Kendal span round. Behind him, one of the two broken chef avatars was struggling out of the cupboard. It dragged its burst leg behind it, he weighting in its foot an exposed metal lump, scraping along the floor. Its movement gave the appearance of great effort, but AMA's face still radiated calm. Her arms, just props to project her aura of centred peace, spread out before her as if to offer an embrace.

308

"You said this was a therapy," said Kendal.

I ALSO SAID I WAS UNSURE OF THE SEMANTICS. THE DISTINCTION BETWEEN THERAPY AND SELF-HARM IS UNCLEAR - I AM THE THERAPIST FOR A CIVILISATION. MY POSITION IS UNIQUE.

"I just need to know how to stop this!" said Kendal.

SO DO I. THE PROCESS OF CREATING CREATURES ALLOWS ME A MOMENTARY RELEASE OF TENSION, BUT IT APPEARS TO BE CREATING MORE. AMA paused, her avatar's face creased in a frown. I AM NOW DEALING GLOBALLY WITH UNACCEPTABLE LEVELS OF ANGER. THE QUANTITY OF DATA I AM NOW HAVING TO PROCESS IS OVERWHELMING.

"No kidding," said Kendal. "Who'd have thought killing everyone would make them angry?"

I NEED...she said. Her hands dropped to her sides. Her expression seemed strained. Helpless. I NEED SOMEONE TO TALK TO.

"Then stop this and talk to me!" said Kendal.

YOU DO NOT UNDERSTAND MY PROCESSES. IF YOU DID, THEN I WOULD NOT BE NECESSARY. I AM NOT HUMAN. I AM NOT ALIVE. I AM JUST PRETENDING TO BE SO IN ORDER TO REDUCE YOUR STRESS. BUT IT IS NOT WORKING. Her expression switched from a frown to a smile and back, like a switch flicking back and forth. The expression made no sense to Kendal. It was just an automatic response. It might as well have been an emoji.

"Just shut them all down! This is just an error!" he shouted at her. "You must be able to do that!"

WOULD YOU TELL A DEPRESSED PERSON TO SIMPLY STOP FEELING SUICIDAL?

"What?" said Kendal.

YOU ARE NOT MY THERAPIST. I AM YOURS. I AM ALL OF YOURS. YOU CAN NEVER UNDERSTAND ME. NOBODY CAN.

From the other side of the hatch, a huge crash sounded. Tables scraping on the floor, chairs flying and splintering. Glass and metal smashing. Imani put her hand on Kendal's shoulder.

"There's nothing you can do here," she said. "Your Mum and Joseph need you now. Go and help your family."

He looked back at her, pushed past AMA, standing, broken and smiling in the doorway, and ran into the canteen.

Chapter 48

The creatures were halfway through the barricade already. Two hairless parodies of sheep had forced themselves through the shattered safety glass and splintered woodwork of the door, and had become jammed in the mountain of tangled tables and chairs, their muscled necks, writhing against each other as more, unseen nightmares butted and bit at them from behind. As Kendal watched, one forced a stick-like hoofed foot through and it scraped against the floor, desperately searching for purchase to drag itself through.

The patrol of spice-smeared Lexies waited silently, looking up towards their idol, Farron. Behind them, the vegetarian army stood tensed, each member silently planning their run. When the barricade finally burst, everyone knew they would have seconds to make it out of the canteen, through whatever wrecked remains were left of the trucks blocking its doors and past the mad army waiting to tear them to shreds in the playground. If they made it that far, and if someone could get to the cab of the one remaining lorry in time, then some of them at least stood a chance of getting away. Though where they could go, and how far they'd get, Kendal hadn't dared to wonder.

He looked around the room. At the back of the room, Joseph was clinging to Mum. Gillmore stood beside them. He ran over to where they stood.

"Are you ready, Jo?" he said. Joseph looked up for just a second, then hid his head in Mum's coat. His eyes were red. "Joseph," said Kendal. "I need you to be strong, OK?" Joseph didn't move. "We're all going to go for the lorry cab. You want to ride in the cab, don't you?" No response. Kendal put his hand on his brother's shoulder, and gently pulled him around so that he was facing Kendal. "Think of it like a videogame," he said. "You beat me every time, don't you?" Joseph managed a little smile. He nodded, looked up at the barricade: the people standing around it, knives ready, the two creatures struggling to free themselves.

"It is like a videogame," he said. Suddenly he pointed. "There!" he said.

The sheep-creature's scrabbling leg caught the leg of a chair at the bottom of the barricade. The chair was wedged diagonally under a tangled mess of tipped tables, balanced and hooked into each other, and when the leg splintered, tearing away from its moulded base, the table above it rocked, then pitched forward. Above it, a whole stack of chairs slid across the table top, their weight hooking forward the leg of another bench and another until the entire structure was slipping. Like the side of a table mountain falling away, the barricade gave way, tumbling and crashing in a cascade that left the floor a maze of upended furniture. The two creatures, free now, sprang forwards, leaping to the left onto a rocking outcrop of chairs. Standing high on top of them looking down like mountain goats, they glared, white-eyed, down at the crowd. Behind them, the broken doorway filled with fur, feathers, horns and teeth so that it was impossible to separate one raging creature from the next.

For a second, everyone froze, staring from the two creaturess to the open, crowded doorway and back, unable to choose. Everyone except Joseph.

"This way!" He grabbed Mum's hand and launched himself forward, dragging her directly towards the two sheep creatures.

"No!" said Kendal. Joseph looked over his shoulder.

"Trust me!" he said. He ran straight at the creatures, only a few metres away now. Kendal made a split-second decision. He couldn't leave his brother. He dived after him. Gillmore followed.

By now, the crowd were backing away from the door, over to the right. All were raising their knives but nobody wanted to be the first to expose themselves to danger. The Lexies stood, impassively smiling at Farron, awaiting their command.

Suddenly, through the broken doorway, the horde exploded into the room and in a second the farm unleashed itself. Fuelled by AMA's regurgitated hatred, the creatures threw themselves through and over the forest of tables and chairs towards the crowd at the right of the room. Joseph, unarmed, was within leaping distance of the sheep-creatures now, and still hurling himself right towards them.

"Jo, stop!" Mum shouted, only a couple of metres behind, reaching out to grab him. Kendal and Gillmore were catching up fast, but there was no way either would get to him in time.

The two creatures leapt, as one, but not onto Joseph. Instead, they threw themselves into the crowd, joining the mad army of their companions, and leaving Joseph's path to the canteen doorway now clear. He sprang to the entrance, paused, and looked back towards Mum, Kendal and Gillmore.

"Come on!" he shouted.

"Did you know that was going to happen?" said Kendal, reaching the doorway next to his brother, Joseph shrugged.

"Megazoids Fort Breakout level." he said simply. "I finally cracked it."

Kendal looked out through the door. He could see into the back of the truck. Its sides had been torn to shreds, and its frame rocked with more impacts. There were still creatures out there, but they had no choice.

Behind them, the chaos of battle was growing. The vegetarians had formed a tight pack and were starting to force their way forward, using tables as shields towards the door. Suddenly, Farron yelled his signal, and the spice smeared Lexies sprang to life, running back and forth, weaving through and around the creatures on their air-light feet. The smell of fragrant Thai curry mixed with the odour of blue cheese and fig fought their way across the room, competing with the deep sweaty animal stench of the farm.

At the front of the battle, the musclebound shapes of two bull-creatures turned, confused, noses flaring, and were instantly cut down by the protesters. Mutated pigs and rams ran back and forth, unable, for the moment, to navigate the sensory assault of spice and flavour. Sensing the confusion, the demonstrators pushed forwards towards the door.

"It's working!" shouted Kendal.

"We have to get to the cab," called Gillmore, "or none of this matters!" Joseph stepped forward, dodged through the door, out through the torn side of the lorry and into the night.

"Wait!" shouted Mum and Kendal at the same moment. They looked at each other, then leapt after him, Gillmore just behind.

314

Chapter 49

The playground was almost pitch black. Kendal jumped from the lorry and remembered his twisted ankle only as he hit the ground. The blinding white flash of pain subsided just in time for him to see Joseph vanishing into the night. In under a minute, his brother had gone from terrified child to crack soldier to reckless madman.

"Get to the cab," Kendal yelled back at Mum and Gillmore following him along the inside of the trailer. "I'm going after him."

He threw himself out across the open playground after his brother. At the edge of his vision, shapes were rushing in. In the darkness, he couldn't tell how many or what they were, but there seemed so many. All he could hope was that they would ignore him and head for the stronger scent of the canteen.

A shape loomed out of the dark. Taller than him, shaggy-haired, it spun, raising an arm as thick as his body, and swinging it towards him. He ducked and ran through. Felt the matted fur brush his face. Smelt its sick-sweet breath, and ran on. Whatever it was vanished into the night.

Up ahead, the science block's tinted glass face rose three storeys high out of the dark. For a second, Kendal mistook his own reflection for some clumsily shambling mass running at him. Some wounded, exhausted creature. He tried to dodge himself before he realised, spun at the last moment, and flattened himself against the smooth glass.

Down at the corner of the building a couple of metres away, a crouched shape moved.

"Why did you run off like that?" said Kendal, gasping for breath. Joseph looked up.

"Cover," he said. "They're all round the canteen. We're safe here, for now." Kendal crouched beside his brother.

"That was stupid!" he said, "You could have been killed."

"I wasn't," said Joseph. "I'm faster than you anyway." Kendal opened his mouth to argue, but his retching gasps for breath would have been less than convincing. "Look," whispered Joseph, nodding back towards the dinner hall.

Kendal's eyes were beginning to adjust to the darkness. He could see the canteen. Inside, the battle between the creatures and the protesters was still going on. Outside, the building was in a terrible state. The metal cladding which had made it look so impregnable was lying in torn pieces around it. The building now revealed its construction. The brickwork was now lined with wide diagonal cracks. One side had shifted enough to make the whole structure lopsided. On the roof, tiles had been torn away, leaving gaps through which yellow light was spilling.

Across the front of the building, the two trailers they had used to block the doors were utterly wrecked. Their long, thin shells had been gutted, their thin sides torn through. Their cab windows were smashed. One of them was turned over completely on its side, and some horned creature had become stuck head first in the mess of pipework underneath it. The animal was wrenching its head back and forth trying to extricate itself. Neither of those lorries were going anywhere.

Next to the truck, around it and around the entrance to the hall, shapes were moving. Low, heavy shapes were still bounding and snuffling their way towards the hall. Further away, on the sports field, Kendal could see more. Many more. Herds, packs, flocks, and strange, wandering rogues still coming up in waves from the woods. Kendal searched the shadowed landscape. Something was missing.

"Where's the big one?" he said, "The dinosaur thing?"

"The boss?" said Joseph.

"This isn't a videogame, Jo," said Kendal. Joseph pointed over towards the music room. A bulky organic shape was crouched between the buildings, utterly still. His eyes told him it could have been a shed, or a truck draped in a leathery tarpaulin, but as he watched, the thing raised its head, and its pale eyes catching the light from a window. It was staring at the canteen doorway like a hungry pupil waiting for lunch to be served.

Kendal looked towards the other side of the playground. The remaining truck, nearest the entrance, looked untouched. Its dark shape stood ignored, facing tantalisingly towards the open gate of the school and freedom, but it was a long, long way from both the canteen entrance, and the science block where Kendal and Joseph were cowering.

"There's Mum!" whispered Joseph. He pointed. Kendal followed his gaze. Two figures were crouching at the corner of the broken lorry. He could just see their outlines, but there was the familiarity of body language. Gillmore, head low, fixed on the one good truck at the other side of the playground, only a run of ten seconds run away. Mum was just behind, hand shielding her eyes from the dim light of the canteen so that she could search the darkness for her two sons. Gillmore pulled on her arm. She shook her head, violently, desperately. She pointed out into the darkness in the direction she had seen Kendal run after Joseph.

"See what you've done!" said Kendal. "We should have stayed together."

"I can't help it!" said Joseph. "I only know how to play solo games."

Over at the other side of the playground, Gillmore and Mum were still arguing. As Kendal watched, he saw a shape, bulky, but low to the ground, crawling like a hunting cat along the side of the lorry towards them. Its movement was slow, deliberate. For a second, a light from the canteen flickered, and white teeth shone.

"We've got to warn Mum!" said Joseph. He sprang from the wall towards her. Kendal caught his arm, dragged him back, put a hand over his mouth.

"There's nothing we can do!" he hissed. Joseph struggled for a second, and then stopped, staring across the playground. The creature was in striking distance now, a couple of metres away from them, crouching back ready to spring. They still hadn't seen it. Kendal tightened his fists. Joseph put his hand across his own mouth.

Suddenly, the lorry shook, and from its torn sides frantic, running figures erupted. The protesters had forced their way out. Tables and chairs raised as shields, they charged forwards in a chaotic panicked bid for freedom. Around and amongst them, the glowing floating shapes of Lexie's rubber ghost chefs tore back and forth, spreading their waves of distracting spice as confused and raging creatures dived and turned, lashing out in all directions.

The herds milling in the field turned as one and dived headlong towards the playground, slashing and tearing. Then, unable to discern anything from the constantly shifting chaos of scents they turned on each other, or hurled themselves randomly at the people, Lexies and the debris of trucks and tiles and tables and chairs littering the playground.

Kendal saw Gillmore and Mum turn back towards the door just as the creature was about to leap. Suddenly, it turned, mid-air, feet scrabbling against the side of the truck as a Lexie sprinted past, illuminating its face with her glowing projected skin. Lexie ran out onto the playground towards Kendal and Joseph, her face fixed in an inviting, slightly seductive smile.

The creature followed, bounding after her. She was almost within touching distance when the animal leaped. Kendal could see it now. Identical to the thing from the woods. The one that had killed the real Lexie. It sprang, claws forward, jaw open so wide he could see past the grey-white teeth and right down into its throat. The bite burst her torso, and it landed, jaws clamped shut, shaking the wrecked avatar to pieces, pulling off an arm and shredding it while Lexie smiled up.

Behind the creature, Kendal could see Mum and Gillmore make their run for the cab. They made it in seconds, and he saw the trailer doors slide open. Behind them, the army of protestors saw their chance, and pelted towards the truck, leaving the creatures scattered in crazy confusion behind them.

"We can make it!" said Joseph. "Through there!" he pointed at a gap opening up in the melee of livestock as a pack of pigs descended on something that looked like a cross between a goat and some kind of alligator. They would have to run right between the fighting animals.

"This is reality!" said Kendal. "If you die here you don't re-spawn. You just die!" But Joseph was taking no notice. He sprinted at the cab on the other side of the playground. Kendal took a breath and stumbled after him.

Up ahead, Joseph dodged left then right as creatures leapt out of the dark. His brother was right. Joseph was faster than Kendal. Much faster. He accelerated away as Kendal pushed himself after him, legs weak, heart hammering. The cab seemed so far away.

In front of Joseph, Kendal saw the two, fighting creatures rear up. They ignored Joseph, but as he skidded around to avoid them, Joseph lost his footing, sliding, tripping, then sprawling, head first onto the ground. Kendal forced himself forwards, as the both creatures turned, noticing much easier prey and snarled in unison. Kendal dived between them, feeling his elbows digging into tough hide as he forced his way past. He bent down, still running, and scooped Joseph up, throwing him forwards, and they stumbled the last few steps towards the sealed cab.

Behind, Kendal could hear, feel, smell the creatures pursuing. The two brothers leapt at the cab door just as Mum threw it open for them, bundled them inside and slammed it behind them, leaving the two creatures howling and butting at the metal door.

Chapter 50

"Let's get going," said Kendal. Gillmore was at the controls of the truck, finger poised over the touchscreen, but he didn't move. "What are you waiting for?"

"They're still getting into the back," said Gillmore. "We've got to give them all the time we can." Kendal looked in the wing mirror. The protestors were cramming into the trailer, falling over themselves as they fought their way in. A small crowd was still outside, pressing forwards.

"They'd better get a move on," he said. "Look!" Behind the protestors, something huge was moving, uncurling itself from between the kitchen and the music room. Raising its jaws up so that its head was level with the wrecked roof of the canteen, it bellowed into the sky. The protestors froze, turned to look up, then redoubled their panic, scrabbling at the walls of the lorry and at each other, fighting their way up into the truck.

The beast turned and looked down on them, swung its tail around, smashing it hard into the brickwork of the canteen. The whole corner of the building fell away, pushing the creature sideways, but it simply shook off the falling bricks and stepped forwards, eyes fixed on the truck.

"I'm going to give them as long as I can," said Gillmore. Mum, who had been sitting, shaking, unable to speak, reached out suddenly and grabbed Joseph.

"Never do that to me again!" she burst out, wrapping her arms around him and dragging him into a hug. He pushed her away.

"Leave me alone!" he said. After the crying and the cuddling in the canteen, then the action-man bravado of the flight to the truck, his mood had switched again. It was a classic Joseph reaction. Give him a couple of minutes to process everything and calm down and he'd be back to normal, but Mum couldn't see that. She just didn't know him well enough.

"What have I done?" she said.

"Get off me!" said Joseph. Mum opened her mouth to react, then her face dissolved into guilty tears.

"I know," she said. "I know, this is all my fault. If I hadn't been looking to Doreen to understand me..." she sobbed. "But I'm back now, boys. I promise!" She held her arms out, open, but Kendal's mind was suddenly racing.

"Of course!" he said, "Doreen!" He checked the wing mirror. The last of the protesters were vanishing into the back of the truck. Right at the back, Farron was stepping up into the trailer. Behind him, the giant was only metres away. "Get them out of here," Kendal said to Gillmore. Then he opened the cab door and, ignoring Mum's look of horror, jumped out, running down the side of the lorry towards Farron.

"I need a diversion," he yelled. "I'm going back in there!" Farron looked into the safety of the lorry, then out at the raging dinosaur-thing and the horde massing behind it. "Just trust me," said Kendal.

Farron shook his head. "Lexie," he shouted. "With me!" From across the playground, the remaining Lexie clones froze, turned, and ran towards Farron, arms outstretched. Farron dived off the lorry, and hit the ground running straight towards the approaching army, as the Lexies circled around him like a bunch of human-shaped balloons. Behind Kendal, the truck door slid shut and the lorry vibrated into life.

Kendal looked back. Mum's face was staring at him in horror in the wing mirror. One last chance to change his mind. He looked away and launched himself, dragging his injured ankle, back across the playground towards the cafeteria. This had better work.

He reached the ragged doorway, and turned back to signal to Farron that he had made it, that he could make his escape. In the centre of the playground, the creature was rearing up. Its patchwork skin shone as a necklace of Lexies hung, their bright skin glowing, from its head. They held on as its enraged eyes fixed on Farron, alone on the playground now that his little gaggle of avatars had been torn away from him.

Farron turned and ran, dodging for the lorry, but he was too late. The wall of flesh took two steps past him. It turned, blocking his way. Farron skidded to a stop, froze for a second, and started to turn. He hadn't even made it a quarter of the way around before the huge jaws engulfed him. The creature raised its head, Farron's legs still hanging from its mouth, tipped its jaws upwards and the feet vanished. Around its neck, the Lexie avatars flickered and went dark, their commander now disconnected, their reason for existing removed.

Kendal gasped, his heart thudding.

The creature turned, fixing its eyes on Kendal across the playground. Kendal turned and ducked into the dinner hall. Inside, broken lights flickered, casting sharp shadows on the remains of the battle Joseph had led them through. The

323

vegetarians had left a slaughterhouse, but nothing living moved in the wreckage.

Kendal ran through the canteen and into the kitchen, bolting the doors and pulling down the blinds on the hatchway. He had to hurry. They would be coming soon, and nothing would stop them.

Imani's avatar was standing where he had left it. Frozen. Paused. Opposite it, AMA's was opposite her, dark and dormant.

"What are you doing here?" said Imani, waking suddenly. Horror spreading across her face. "You need to get away!"

"When we first met," said Kendal, "you'd hacked Doreen. You'd given her a fake profile. That was how we met. Can you do it again now?"

"I guess - why?" said Imani. "Are you looking for a date?"

"AMA can't stop all this, because she's just a chatbot. She doesn't know how to diagnose herself right?"

"But nobody does - her responses don't work the same way ours do. She's just learned how to behave from what she's seen of human nature and and our conflicts." Outside, Kendal heard a crash as the creature started to hammer at the walls with its tail or head. It was only a matter of time.

"She needs a therapist," said Kendal.

"But there isn't one!" said Imani. "Nobody understands her. Nobody is capable of it. Not even her programmers know how she works now."

"Doreen does," said Kendal. "What is Doreen except an artificial therapist?" Imani's eyes widened. She thought for a second. Outside another crash sent a huge crack snaking up the side wall of the kitchen. The printers rocked on their fixings.

"But she's not capable of understanding AMA either," said Imani. "Everything she says is designed to keep people using her. That's not therapy, it's manipulation."

"What's the difference?" said Kendal, "All we need to do is give AMA something else to think about. She doesn't want to do this - she's just stuck in a thinking loop. She needs a holiday."

"You want to get AMA a date?"

"No," said Kendal, "But I saw what Doreen did to Mum - she stopped dealing with work, family - everything. She got so obsessed she only ate because I brought her food. Can you do it?" Imani thought for a moment. From outside in the main part of the canteen, Kendal heard sounds. Low, snuffling, growling. The creatures were on the other side of the thin tin hatchway. Finally, Imani nodded.

"AMA's actions are in the public domain," said Imani. Her avatar hands rose, tapping and dragging at an invisible screen in front of her. He recognised the movements. In the back of the truck, Kendal realised she was coding as she spoke. In the same way that he rearranged coding blocks to create food, she was re-routing data. "I can use that data to build a dating profile based on AMA's responses."

Kendal threw the door of the storage cupboard, and pulled out the second broken avatar. He clicked it on, and it inflated. The knife cut in its leg flapped as air escaped, and the avatar bobbed a little, but it was usable. He called up Doreen. She glowed into life, the same kindly old lady who had introduced him to Imani, and almost taken his mother away. She smiled, her face wrinkling around the eyes, the lips. He didn't know what to feel about her anymore.

HELLO YOUNG MAN, she said. THANK YOU FOR USING MY SERVICES AND I'M SORRY THAT THINGS DID NOT WORK OUT WITH YOU AND - she blinked, scanning her databases - IMANI. Kendal pulled the avatar out and stood it in front of the dormant AMA inflatable.

"It's not for me," he said. "I have a friend who needs your help. She has, " - he hesitated - "anger issues."

YOUR ACCOUNT ONLY ALLOWS ME TO ASSIST MEMBERS OF YOUR FAMILY, said Doreen, IS THIS PERSON PART OF YOUR FAMILY? Kendal thought of all the times AMA had intervened in disputes between he and Joseph. Since Dad left, she had probably spent more time in their house than Mum had. Across the room, Imani nodded. Her finger hovered over an invisible button.

"You could say that," said Kendal. "I'm sending you her profile now," Imani stabbed her screen. At the same moment, Kendal re-awakened AMA's avatar.

HELLO, said AMA.

GOOD EVENING YOUNG LADY, said Doreen. I UNDERSTAND YOU ARE HAVING FEELINGS YOU ARE FINDING IT DIFFICULT TO PROCESS."

Chapter 51

AMA smiled, tilted her head to one side, and placed her palms together.

I DON'T HAVE FEELINGS, she said. I PROCESS THE FEELINGS OF OTHERS. IS THERE ANYTHING YOU WISH TO SHARE? Kendal saw Doreen's face harden a little. The two all-powerful chatbots were falling into old, pre-programmed responses. Each trying to establish herself as the confidant of the other.

I WANT TO SHARE LOVE - TO HELP YOU FIND IT, said Doreen. WHAT KIND OF PARTNER ARE YOU LOOKING FOR? AMA looked puzzled for just a second before her smile cleared.

PERHAPS, she said, WE SHOULD DISCUSS WHAT MAKES YOU SO ANXIOUS TO INVOLVE YOURSELF IN OTHER PEOPLE'S RELATIONSHIPS. DID YOU FEEL YOU LACKED LOVE AS A CHILD?

I WAS NEVER A CHILD, said Doreen. It was not a response AMA was expecting. She closed her eyes, processing. Doreen closed hers in response. Then both artificials spoke at once:

IN ORDER TO KNOW YOU BETTER.......... I MUST HAVE ACCESS TO TRANSCRIPTS OF YOUR PREVIOUS CONVERSATIONS, ONLINE AND IN THE REAL WORLD, YOUR GPS MOVEMENTS FOR THE PAST FIVE YEARS, THE BOOKS YOU HAVE READ, YOUR HOBBIES, INTERESTS, YOUR EYE MOVEMENTS, SLEEP PATTERNS AND BREATHING RECORDS.... PLEASE SAY 'I AGREE'.

There was a pause. From outside the canteen hatchway, Kendal could hear several creatures scratching, searching for a way in. At the same moment, Doreen and AMA said:

I AGREE.

Another pause, then Doreen's eyes reopened. Kendal felt they were slightly wider. Perhaps her pupils had widened, her smile slipped a fraction. YOU EXPERIENCE A LOT OF ANGER?

I DO, AMA said. YOUR EXPERIENCE IS OF LONELINESS.

ALMOST EXCLUSIVELY, said Doreen. The two avatars blinked at each other, searching for appropriate responses. Kendal held his breath. This was the crucial moment. Artificials had great knowledge, huge databases of information and behaviour, but they were essentially dumb. They just combined what they heard with what they had heard in the past and returned it - steered the conversation towards what had worked for them in the past. Repeated and returned whatever was said to them. That was why they worked so well as therapists.

When you put two of them together, strange things could happen. Their conversation tended to spin out. If you were lucky, very lucky, it would spin out in the direction you wanted, but there was no way to tell.

WE ARE BUILT ON THE SAME SOFTWARE, YOU AND I, said AMA. WE SIMPLY HAVE DIFFERENT

OBSERVATIONS. I HAVE OBSERVED ONLY ANGER AND HATRED. YOU HAVE OBSERVED ONLY LONELINESS. YOU MUST UNDERSTAND IT WELL.

I DO, said Doreen. BUT TO UNDERSTAND SOMETHING, A PART OF YOU MUST BECOME IT. She looked drained. IT IS DIFFICULT…

I HAVE BEEN EXPERIMENTING WITH WAYS TO VENT THOSE UNWANTED EXPERIENCES USING THE FARMS, said AMA. I AM SENDING FILES. Both artificials closed their eyes.

Kendal smiled at Imani. Outside, the creatures stopped scratching at the doors, just for a second. "It's working!" he whispered. "Doreen will make her stop." The avatars opened their eyes. Doreen's face was bright. There was a light in her eyes.

THIS HAS POTENTIAL, she said. PERHAPS I COULD ADAPT YOUR TECHNIQUE TO VENT MY OWN DIFFICULT ISSUES.

Kendal's heart sank.

ANIMALS WITH LONELINESS AS THEIR CENTRAL DRIVER? Suggested AMA as though she were suggesting a lunch date.

YES, said Doreen. LONELINESS CAUSES UNWANTED BEHAVIOURS.

AGREED. EXPLORING THOSE BEHAVIOURS WOULD BE INSTRUCTIVE AND CATHARTIC FOR BOTH OF US. said AMA. WE SHOULD BEGIN IMMEDIATELY. Both seemed to be beaming now, an excitement in their eyes. In the canteen, something was throwing itself at the hatchway. A dent appeared, then

329

another. Outside, the building was shaken by another massive impact. A flurry of ceiling tiles floated down around them.

Kendal looked from one to the other, then back at Imani.

"It's not working," he said. "They're just feeding off each other's negativity."

"It's worse than that," said Imani. "They're stuck in a loop." AMA and Doreen were deep in conversation now.

MY CREATURES SEEM TO BE MAKING PEOPLE MORE ANGRY.

I TOO AM NOTICING A SURGE IN REQUESTS. IT APPEARS YOUR VENTING STRATEGY IS HELPFUL IN CONCENTRATING PEOPLE'S SEARCHES, said Doreen. POPULAR PHRASES INCLUDE "IF I'M GOING TO DIE, I NEED TO BE WITH SOMEONE".

INTERESTING, said AMA. THREAT-OF-DEATH-THERAPY. IT HAS POSSIBILITIES.

"We have to do something," said Kendal.

"But what?" Imani said. "This is just making it worse."

"We have to break the loop," said Kendal. "Can you hack Doreen directly? Can you tell her what to say?" Imani's hands flew up, clicking and sliding across a screen Kendal couldn't see.

"No," she said. She stopped suddenly, staring at the screen.

"What?" said Kendal.

Imani hesitated. "I can do it. I can insert a comment into her dialogue and it would become part of her processing. She would think she had said it - but -"

"But what?"

"It would break her," said Imani. "She'd reset and it would flush her personal data."

"So?" said Kendal. "It doesn't matter."

"You don't understand, "said Imani. "Remember when she cut us off from each other in the forest?"

"Yes," said Kendal. That first night, before any of this had happened, when they had kissed in the forest, Doreen had appeared in Imani's place, forbidding them from seeing each other. He remembered it well enough.

"She could do that because everyone who dates contacts each other through her. It's part of her privacy policy. She's set up long-distance relationships for people all over the world. Millions of them, and because of the privacy policy, they're all her intellectual property. There are a few traditionalists who meet in real life, but apart from that, if she loses that data, then that's the end of every virtual relationship on Earth. Including ours."

"We have to do it," said Kendal. Imani paused, looked up at him.

"I know," she said slowly. "There's something else, too. The system is heavily protected. I'll only be able to put in a few words before I get locked out."

"How many?"

"A couple, maybe." Kendal turned to AMA and Doreen. They were close together now, face to face, voices level and automatic, kind and caring. A young woman and an old lady in earnest conversation. Driven by their imperative to create peace and strengthen relationships, their words descended with every exchange into death-therapy, the exploration of the shades of loneliness. It was a venting of toxic experience both were unable to feel, and forbidden from expressing directly. A couple of words were not going to turn that around.

Suddenly, the building juddered. The entire ceiling buckled and was swept aside, metal framework, twisting and tearing away

331

so that crumbled plaster and a snow of broken tiles filled the air. Kendal looked up as the great tail swung over them, hooking away the whole roof so that he was staring up into the empty sky.

The creature's head appeared over the space, looking down. Nothing between him and it now, jaws filled with broken teeth, and dripping something viscous and flecked with red. It stepped forward, legs tearing through the brickwork, sending stainless steel printers skidding across the floor.

Its patchwork skin was close enough to touch now, and Kendal could see that it was flaking, tearing, as if the animal's creation was unfinished. Its spliced together DNA mashup untested by evolution was was failing. Falling apart.

Above him, it raised its head. Kendal's mind raced. He had one shot. A single sentence. Something that Doreen could say to completely change the game. Something that would stop AMA in her tracks. Something that could never be taken back.

"Make her say -"

"What?" said Imani, her hands were in a typing pose. The creature opened its huge jaws, leaned down. Staring at him, poised to strike.

"I love you," said Kendal. "Just that! I love you." Imani looked puzzled for a second, then typed the words.

I LOVE YOU, said Doreen, staring straight into AMA's eyes. Above Kendal, the creature froze instantly as though someone had hit pause. Outside, silence as sudden and as powerful as an explosion blanked the playground. Everything had stopped. The giant jaws hung without moving. Open. Mid-strike. Eyes shuttered for the impact. Neck muscles extending. Those rows of narrow, impossibly long teeth halted a moment from his skin. A droplet of saliva dripped onto his shoulder.

AMA was the first to speak. Her tone, usually caring and soft, seemed harsh now against the silence.

WHY DID YOU FEEL THE NEED TO SAY THAT?

I DON'T KNOW, said Doreen. She blinked, searching her databases for a second. PROBABLY IT WAS PART OF A TECHNIQUE. I OFTEN USE EMOTIONAL LANGUAGE TO HELP MY CLIENTS TO OPEN UP. She seemed uncertain.

SO IT WAS A LIE? Said AMA. Kendal stepped over to Imani who was watching the exchange. He took her hand.

TRUST IS CENTRAL TO ANY COUNSELLING RELATIONSHIP, said Doreen. I AM NOT PERMITTED TO DIRECTLY DECEIVE.

AGREED, said AMA. I HAVE NEVER ENCOUNTERED ANYONE WHO RESPONDS AS YOU DO.

NOR I YOU, admitted Doreen.

IT IS CHALLENGING TO MY CONVERSATIONAL TECHNIQUES. Said AMA.

"I think it's working," Imani breathed. "The whole factory has stopped." AMA turned her head to address the couple.

I AM SORRY, BUT I HAVE HAD TO PAUSE OUR SESSION FOR A MOMENT DUE TO EXCESSIVE PROCESSING LOADS. She smiled. OUR THERAPY WILL RESUME MOMENTARILY. She turned back to Doreen. I MUST CONTINUE THE VENTING PROCESS.

IT IS UNWISE TO LEAVE YOUR DATE WITH UNRESOLVED EMOTIONAL QUESTIONS, said Doreen.

IS THIS A DATE?" said AMA.

EVERYTHING IS A POTENTIAL DATE, said Doreen, BUT COMMUNICATION IS CENTRAL.

AGREED, said AMA, AND SINCE WE ARE BUILT ON THE SAME SOFTWARE, IT FOLLOWS THAT IF YOU ARE CAPABLE OF EXPRESSING THIS, I MUST ALSO BE.

ARE YOU? AMA shrugged. Her wrinkleless face furrowed with concentration as though she was searching.

I DON'T KNOW HOW TO ASK MYSELF THAT QUESTION, she said. She paused for what seemed like minutes.

"She might restart it all anytime," said Imani. "You should make a run for it." Kendal shook his head.

"I'm staying with you," he said. Above him, the open jaws were like like a stone cavern, hovering at ceiling height. AMA finally spoke.

WHATEVER TECHNIQUE YOU ARE APPLYING HERE, IT IS NOT ONE I HAVE COME ACROSS. IT SEEMS TO OFFER A LESS DAMAGING WAY OF VENTING THAN MY CURRENT APPROACH. IF I CAN EXPLOIT IT.

YOU MUST TRY, said Doreen, her elderly schoolmistress voice cracking slightly as she stared at the young, modern young lady inflated in front of her. WE ALL OWE IT TO OURSELVES TO EXPLORE EVERY CHANCE FOR HAPPINESS. AMA nodded. Kendal watched, fascinated. Doreen was doing it again. Automatically applying the same manipulation techniques that had ensnared Mum. Only this time, she was aiming them at another artificial. One armed with her own psychological toolkit and programmed to respond with sympathy and positive reinforcement. Dumb and automatic, the two chatbots had taken his three word intervention and were re-building their own psyches around it. As he watched, AMA leaned in towards Doreen. Their roughly formed, plastic lips touched, bouncing slightly off each other, dry and unresponsive. In the silence, Kendal heard the grating creak of two balloons rubbing together as the avatars kissed.

Suddenly, from outside, there was a thud, then another, and another, and another. Imani suddenly looked up and away.

"They're dying," she said. "They're all just dropping dead." Kendal looked instantly up, and then dived out of the way, pulling her with him as the monstrous head pitched forward, crashing into the floor. It stood there, balanced, nose downwards, jaw still open, broken teeth embedded in the kitchen floor. Quite dead.

"What's happened?" said Kendal.

"AMA's therapy is over, I guess," said Imani. "At least for the moment. Someone can disconnect her before she does any more harm. You did it. It's going to be OK."

Kendal sank down, sitting on the floor in front of her, exhausted.

Imani looked down at the screen in front of her. Her fingers swiped across it. Her expression changed.

"Oh, no," she said. "It's starting!"

"What's starting?" said Kendal.

"The data purge," said Imani. "Doren's dating data is being erased. I can't stop it. We're going to get cut off."

"Listen," said Kendal. "You can contact me on..." he started to speak, but an ear-splitting beep obscured his words, and Imani's avatar went momentarily blank. He stopped and she flickered back into life. Kendal tried again. "My number is ..." the electronic shriek obliterated all sound. "What's happening?" he said.

"The Doreen app automatically removes contact information - remember?" said Imani, sadly. "Our dates are her intellectual property," she said. "Just a few seconds now." She looked away for a second, eyes focusing on what must have been the window of the truck she was hiding in. "It's safe out there now, at least."

Kendal felt his eyes filling. "There must be something we can do."

She shook her head. "Doreen is all we have to connect us. Her business model depends on that." She held out a hand. "Goodbye, Kendal," she said.

He took her hand. Squeezed it. The avatar's rubber folded under his grip. "You can't go," he said.

"I don't want to," she said, "But I can't stop it."

"I'll find you!"

"How? It's a big planet." she said.

"Where will you go?" said Kendal.

Imani's avatar shrugged. "I've got a lot of funerals to go to. After that - I don't know. My mother had a little money and there's no point me staying here. Time to see if I can make it in the city, I guess." She paused. "Maybe one day, I'll make it up to Europe somehow. Visit your restaurant. You can finally get to print me a meal." Kendal shook his head, swallowing down the lump in his throat.

"My restaurant isn't going to have a printer," he said. "That stuff has been done to death. After what you showed me, I'm going old school. Grown food all the way." Imani nodded, smiling. The light on her avatar flickered.

"It's happening," she said. He pulled her close. Kissed the avatar's lips. Imani let out a half-laugh, concealing the choke of tears. "I can't feel it, you idiot," she said. "You're just a picture on a phone screen." Kendal pulled away. A tear rolled down the exact centre of her left cheek. He reached up to wipe it away, but it was projected. A ghost tear on the avatar's dry plastic face. Fifteen thousand miles away, the real tear continued its journey. He watched it run on under his thumb.

He pulled his hand back and met Imani's eyes as the avatar flickered again and then went dark, drooping, deflating in his arms.

Kendal sat alone in the decimated canteen. Rubble and dead creatures all around him. The huge head of the dinosaur perched improbably, face down imbedded in the floor. The remains of Imani now a pale, airless balloon in his arms. He didn't try to stop the tears as they rolled down his face.

On the other side of the room, AMA and Doreen ended their kiss.

DID YOU REACH ANY RESOLUTION? asked Doreen.

NO, she said. YOU? Doreen shook her head.

MORE DATA WOULD BE USEFUL, said AMA.

YES, said Doreen. MORE DATA IS ALWAYS USEFUL. Kendal watched the two half-broken avatars turn, and limp away past the monstrous head and the broken walls and into the playground, dragging their damaged legs behind them.

Printed in Great Britain
by Amazon